MURDER AT A PALE HORSE

JO YOUNG

Copyright © Jo Young 2024

All rights reserved.

No part of this publication may be altered, reproduced, distributed, or transmitted in any form, by any means, including, but not limited to, scanning, duplicating, uploading, hosting, distributing, or reselling, without the express prior written permission of the publisher, except in the case of reasonable quotations in features such as reviews, interviews, and certain other non-commercial uses currently permitted by copyright law.

Disclaimer:
This is a work of fiction. All characters, locations, and businesses are purely products of the author's imagination and are entirely fictitious. Any resemblance to actual people, living or dead, or to businesses, places, or events is completely coincidental.

PART ONE

SHE HAD LONG AGO stopped struggling against the duct tape that held her hands and feet, she was exhausted from the effort. She was hungry, but most of all she was thirsty. She had no idea how long she had been here and could only guess how long it would be before anybody would come. She couldn't decide whether she wanted somebody to come, or whether that would be too frightening. Whoever had brought her here, surely meant her harm.

Her hands were bound behind her, around a pipe, so she could not tear the duct tape with her teeth, she had tried doubling herself over to get at the tape around her ankles, but even though she considered herself to be supple, she was unable to manage this contortion. Her back and shoulders were racked with cramps, but the overwhelming desire for water was the worst of her travails.

A tear trickled down her face. "Don't do that!" she chided herself "That will use up valuable water that your body needs." Dehydration would kill her long before starvation did. To think that she had had to force herself to drink all the glasses of water, that were required, to keep her healthy! She tried to think of something else, but the thirst was all consuming. She fought against her restraints again until exhausted, she lay still and finally fell into a troubled sleep.

She awoke unable to think where she was and why she hurt so much, then it came hurtling back to her mind. She stayed quiet for a while, then stiffened as she heard footsteps approaching.

CAFÉ ON THE HIGH STREET

I WAS HOME IN Canada for a couple of weeks, during the summer holidays of Wendover College, where I was employed in the role of Dean. I was catching up with old friends and using the time to work out what I was going to do when I finished my tenure. Retirement was looming. Life without purpose would be hard, I don't cope well with boredom.

I also had no clue where I was going to settle. Returning to Ontario was a given but deciding on an exact area was tough.

At college I was known as Dean B. My parents had wanted an unusual name for their newborn daughter. Finally, they settled on Beretta which would have been fine if their surname had not been "Browning". I had gone through elementary school being called BB Gun. High school came and BB Gun was shortened to BB, and finally in university I became B which has stuck for life.

Most of my friends were still living in Mono Township, a beautiful but expensive area. My best friend, Hetty Hallkirk, had demanded I come and stay with her. Much as I loved Hetty, I loved my independence even more. I had opted for a hotel.

Hetty and I had gone to school together. Her given name was Henrietta, but woe betide anyone who called her that! We were both in our sixties, though neither one of us wished to own up to that.

She was a tall, slim, person who gave off an air of fragility, but this hid a core of tungsten steel. She had an attractive figure and was always immaculately dressed. Her makeup and silver hair were always perfect. She would not have tolerated an unswept barn! I was envious of her ability to look so great. I, on the other hand, mostly succeeded in looking rumpled and unkempt. I did not have Hetty's ability to choose the right outfit and accessories for the occasion. I was overweight, had hair that had done its own thing since I was born, and I tended to dress for comfort, rather than style. I wore what I thought I could get away with, regardless of the situation.

Hetty and I had arranged to meet at Starbucks, on Tuesday morning. I arrived early and saw a sign in the window saying, "CLOSED DUE TO FLOOD." This seemed highly unlikely given that we were in the middle of a heatwave, and it hadn't rained for weeks. I peered through the window, and saw that there was indeed water, all over the floor, obviously a burst pipe or something. I took out my cell phone, and texted Hetty, telling her I'd go to the cafe on the corner, and meet her there.

I entered the place, to find it completely empty, I chose a booth and sat down. I could hear people talking out the back, but nobody came to serve me. I waited a bit and then got up and walked over to the counter and called out "Anybody there?" A voice called out "I'll be right with you!"

I returned to my seat and was joined by a small untidy child carrying a bedraggled stuffed toy. She was about five, scruffy looking, with wild untamed red hair. Her knees were dirty and had scabs on them. Her socks had sunk down round her ankles and her shoes were on the wrong feet. Despite all this I sensed a keen intelligence in her bright blue eyes.

"Iris is out back cleaning, she'll be here when she's washed, she's nice, but Eileen isn't, you're lucky it's Iris today." She informed me.

"Thank goodness for Iris!" I replied, "What is your name?"

"I'm Maisie, and this is Henry" she said, holding up a bedraggled toy "He's a horse" she continued.

I thought the ancestry of the toy appeared more canine than equine. Maisie bounced the sad thing on her knee for a moment, and then came out with, "I like horses, I'm going to ride 'em, when I get bigger."

"Really?" I replied.

"Yup, 'n I'm going to jump 'em over big jumps, like my Mum did!" she exclaimed. I smiled at this and asked her why she wasn't in school.

"I don't go, Dad doesn't mind."

"What about Mummy?" I asked

"Dead" she replied, unconcerned. She continued bouncing Henry.

A middle aged, waitress appeared from the back room. She ruffled the child's hair.

"Oh Maisie, I hope you're not being a nuisance."

"She's fine" I said, smiling, "You must be Iris."

"I see Maisie has been filling you in. Can I get you something?" she asked,

"I'd like a regular coffee with just milk" I replied.

"Would you like something to eat?"

"I'm waiting for a friend, once she's here, we'll order."

With Iris gone, Maisie started up our conversation again,

"See, I told you Iris is nice. What's your name?"

"Baretta, but you can call me B" I replied, Maisie giggled "Like Bumble Bee!" she exclaimed "That's a cool name! You're nice, even if you are old."

"Well, thank you Maisie." I replied.

"Do you like horses?" she enquired; I nodded in the affirmative.

"Do you have any?"

"Not of my own, but I have friends who have some."

"Can I ride 'em?" came the immediate response.

"First, you need to take lessons" I said, "We'd have to ask your father."

"He won't mind." Maisie replied quickly.

"Nevertheless, you would need to ask him, lessons cost money." I glanced over as the door opened.

"Hello!" said Hetty, "Sorry I'm late, have you been waiting long?" I was about to answer, when Maisie butted in,

"Are you one of the friends with horses?" she demanded. Hetty looked askance.

"I beg your pardon?" she said. Maisie sighed, frustrated at adults' inability to follow a conversation. Before she could launch into more demands, I quickly gave Hetty a synopsis of my conversation with Maisie. Hetty rolled her eyes at me, and said, "I don't know how you always manage to get yourself involved like this!"

"B's my friend, she's gonna get me riding lessons, so I can ride her friends' horses." Maisie explained, ignoring my version of things.

Iris returned with my coffee, asked Hetty if she would like one, and enquired whether we were ready to order food.

We gave our order and before Maisie could start again, Iris dispatched her on an errand.

"I am sorry about her, she craves attention, and with her mother dead, her father is totally unable to cope. I do what I can, but it is hard." Iris gazed fondly after Maisie's retreating back. "I'll try to keep her out back so that she doesn't disturb you." Ignoring Hetty's furious gaze, I said, "Oh, she's fine."

"You are kind, but we shouldn't encourage her." Iris

replied, while Hetty was telegraphing her agreement. I turned to Hetty and enquired how she was doing.

"I've taken up water colour painting. I find it therapeutic." Announced Hetty.

"That's great!" I exclaimed. I was pleased that she had found an outlet, she needed something to distract her from all her troubles. She continued to tell me about her art, and then faltering, she frowned, and her expression changed.

"I'm worried about getting the money together for Fee's surgery." She said, Fee was one of her twin granddaughters who was going to require plastic surgery.

"How much will OHIP pay?" I asked.

"I don't know yet, but I am sure that it will not cover anywhere near the full amount." Hetty sighed.

"Well, I think we should wait until we know for sure. I told you that I would help." Hetty nodded and went on, "Fee is mad about horses, and she's helping out at the Riding for the Disabled Farm, I think that she feels at home there. Barry used to volunteer there as well." Hetty continued wistfully. She gazed off into the distance. I felt the pain that she was still suffering over the death of her son. Barry had been killed in Afghanistan.

There was an awkward silence as I tried frantically to think of something to say, but Hetty brought herself back to the moment and asked, "Do you remember that friend of Barry's, Adam, he practically lived in my kitchen when they were in high school. They used to ride together?"

"Vaguely." I said, "Was he the one with blond hair who wanted to go into film?"

"That's him! Since Barry died, Adam has kept in touch with Alice, and visits her often. He was also good with the twins, taking them out now and again, and now Felicity is gone he still sees Fee. I'm not sure where he is now, he may have gone back to California for a couple of months. What is newsworthy is that he's had a date or two with Paloma."

"Paloma, who?" I asked

"Oh B. sometimes I wonder what planet you live on. Paloma is only the top female singer these days!"

"Well, aren't you the trendy one!" I retorted testily.

"At least I am still a part of the modern world." Hetty replied tartly. I laughed at her, and decided I should show interest, and follow up on this gossip.

"I don't know if it is really a romance, or whether Paloma thinks he can get her into films, I gather he has been working with one of the big studios in L.A. The film industry is very big in Toronto, and he goes backwards and forwards, between LA and Toronto."

"And if you haven't seen him lately, how do you come by this knowledge?" I queried.

"Adam's neighbour is friends with him. She works for my doctor, and when I was in getting my flu shot, she was telling me all about it." I burst out laughing "The local gossip mill is still alive and well, I see!"

Hetty snorted, even though she would not admit it, she was a terrible gossip monger, and even though I wouldn't admit it, I enjoyed hearing all the latest goings on in our little town.

"I'll be able to ask him in person, when he comes back" added Hetty.

Iris returned with our food, trailed by Maisie. Iris put the food in front of us, and before she could sit down Maisie was told that she could not join us while we were eating. I gathered that this must be an established rule, because the child sighed and followed Iris back behind the counter.

When we had finished, and Iris had brought us coffee to finish up, I asked Hetty how Alice, her daughter-in-law, was doing.

"Not good. She is on more and more drugs. It has been a downhill spiral" Before she had time to enlarge on this, Iris hurried back over, and said the traffic cop was making his way down the street, and were we parked outside. Hetty jumped up, saying "Damn, I will not get another parking ticket, I must fly. Let's have dinner later this week." she blew me a kiss and hurried out the door.

As if on queue, Maisie appeared, back at my side. She sat herself down with Henry on her lap and looked expectantly at me.

"How old are you, Maisie?" I asked

"I'm five and a quarter" she said.

"Well, you have to be six before you can start riding lessons." I said having no clue, whether there were age restrictions on lessons at the local riding school. "So, you will have time to persuade your father to pay for lessons." Maisie looked crestfallen, and I started to feel bad about fobbing her off this way. I was rescued by Iris, who reappeared and called Maisie, "Your Dad's here, he wants you to come"

If Maisie had looked upset before, it was nothing to the way she looked on hearing this. She turned desperately to me, and said "Can I stay with you?"

"No Maisie, you must go with your Daddy." She got up slowly, picked up Henry, and looking back at me, she headed for the door behind the counter. Before she could reach it, a heavy man came through the door, and grabbed her shoulder. She dropped Henry, and tried to push off his grip, so she could pick up her toy, but he shook her violently, and pushed her through the door. I leapt to my feet to express my horror at this behaviour, but Iris came from the other door, and shook her head at me, mouthing "Don't." I sat back down, and Iris hurried over to my booth. She sat down beside me.

"He can't treat a child like that." I exclaimed.

Iris shook her head, and said "He's drunk again, and he is such a belligerent drunk that if you go after him, he will get really nasty, and could hurt Maisie, plus he might go after you."

"Are you serious? Why hasn't something been done about it?" Iris stared at me for a while.

I sat quietly and listened to the story that Iris had to tell.

I was sitting in the car, watching buzzards soaring effortlessly on the wind currents high above the pines, it was hard to reconcile them with the ungainly creatures that they were, when not in flight. Scavenging, vultures with red heads, black feathers and a strange two-legged canter that was their preferred gait.

A lot of successful people were like that, I thought. Beautiful when observed in action from afar, but with hidden ugliness in their day to day lives.

I couldn't get the picture of Maisie being dragged out of the cafe, without her beloved Henry, or that of Iris crying bitterly over the situation. I decided that I would change my flight, extend my stay, and try and do something to help. I justified this; by telling myself I could have a look at properties for sale during this additional time, research for when I returned.

I made my way back to the hotel where I made the necessary arrangements to extend my stay. I then made some phone calls, and had an early supper, before retiring to my room, to think.

An old associate of mine worked in Social Services. She told me that if Maisie was being abused or neglected, they would step in, and remove her from her father, and place her in care. This meant a children's home, and later, possibly, a foster home. This seemed to me to be even worse than the situation that she was currently in. There did not appear to be any way that Iris could take custody, business partners had no rights, when it came to their partner's children.

I had looked up the local private schools, but they all required that the children be driven to school and picked up. With Brian's attitude towards Maisie, I didn't think he would do this. Maisie was too young to be a boarder. She could be bused to the State schools, but she would be dropped off long before Brian would be home, so he would have to employ a housekeeper. I thought perhaps she could be dropped off at the cafe, and made a note to myself, to follow up on this idea.

There was a flat above the café, I wondered whether Iris could move in there. This would save her the commute. I realised I had no idea where Iris lived, and whether she owned or rented, she might have many reasons why this wouldn't work. I could only ask.

HOUSE HUNTING

I AWOKE TO DREARY weather. Mid summer and it felt like October, dark clouds, wind and rain. Having lived in England for the last five years I was accustomed to miserable weather so, undeterred, I headed out to visit the local real estate agents.

I chose the companies that specialised in rural properties and tried to pick the brains of the sales agents. The first two offices I visited were only out for a quick sale. They had an abundance of modern houses, situated in subdivisions "Bordering rural areas". I was not interested in any of these, and so I moved on to the third agency, where I met a very chatty young man who was willing to give me his "extensive knowledge of the rural real estate market." I had my doubts about how extensive this could be, as he looked as if he had left high school yesterday. Looks could be deceiving.

I had consulted some websites and had a rough idea of prices and the sort of property I would be able to afford. I wondered whether it would be better to buy now or wait until I returned in two years. The property market seemed to be quite hot at the moment, and I wondered whether that trend would continue, and I would find myself unable to afford much when I finally retired.

A young man, who introduced himself as Clive, told me that prices would continue to rise for the next eighteen months at least. He wrote down a list of websites, I could visit to read about the financial gurus' projections for this. I am no money wizard myself, so I made a note to follow through on this. He advised me to purchase now and consider renting the property out until my return. I told him I did not want the hassle of dealing with tenants, while I was in England. He assured me that, part of his services, were devoted to administering rental properties. This was all beginning to sound too good to be true, and suspicious that I was being cunningly manipulated, I thanked him for his time.

"No trouble" he said, "I have a few properties that might be of interest, shall I give you the details?" I agreed reluctantly, and waited while he gathered several sheets of paper, containing particulars of properties.

"If anything strikes your fancy, give me a call, here is my card." I went back out to my rental car, shaking my head.

Hetty told me that her current painting was not going well, and she would relish a break. We agreed to meet at a little restaurant close by. Hetty was waiting when I arrived.

"I thought you were headed back across the pond today."

"Some things came up, and I decided to change plans, and stay another week" I replied vaguely.

"What sort of things?" she pounced upon my prevarication.

"Well, I am worried about Maisie and Iris."

"Who is Iris?" Hetty demanded

"The waitress at the cafe, you remember."

"I did not get on first name basis with her, and how on earth have you got so involved, that you change your travel plans for a snotty nosed child and a waitress? Really B you are impossible, always picking up waifs and strays" snorted my friend. Despite her abrupt ways, I knew that Hetty really had a heart of gold, but was not one to rush in to help strangers. However, she would fight to the death for family and friends. She volunteered all over the place, and had received several awards, from the province, for her services to local charities.

Over lunch I related Iris's long story, and told her about Maisie's cruel treatment, by her father.

Brian McVicker, Maisie's father had become infatuated with a croupier at his casino. She was independent, with many and various interests. She collected art. She was a brilliant cook. She loved to travel, she read widely, and she had a passion for horses. Her name was Rebecca Charles."

"Well would you believe that!" interjected Hetty.

I nodded "Rebecca was brilliant. She would have gone right to the top if she had not given up." Hetty nodded.

I continued with Iris's story.

Brian romanced her with his wallet and Rebecca finally agreed to marry him. After the first year she began to realise how controlling he was. He said that he did not want his new wife working, which left Rebecca beholden to him for money. Brian refused to finance her horse activities. He slowly tried to cut her off from her friends and became insanely jealous if he caught her talking to anyone. Iris didn't think Rebecca always towed the line. Finally, she became pregnant, and then Brian would only allow her out if escorted by Brian or one of his bodyguards. Rebecca became very depressed at this point but could not see a way out. She finally gave birth, not to the boy that Brian wanted, but to Maisie, a frowsy little thing with reddish hair. Brian became obsessed with the idea, that Maisie was not his child as neither he nor Rebecca had red hair. Rebecca tired of telling him that her maternal grandmother had flaming red hair. He would have none of it, and he started becoming abusive. Rebecca became more and more withdrawn.

Her only supporter was her mother-in-law, Francesca. She was divorced from Brian's father and understood how controlling the McVicker men could be. She owned the building we were in. The top floor was an apartment in which she lived, and she ran the coffee shop and bakery on the ground floor. Seeing a need to snap Rebecca out of her depression and wanting to get Rebecca and Maisie away from Brian as much as possible, she insisted that she needed help. Brian did not like this idea, but as with most men, he was used to obeying his mother. Rebecca reluctantly came to the cafe every morning, bringing the tiny Maisie with her. This was where she met Iris, who was working as a waitress for Brian's mother. They immediately bonded, and Rebecca finding that she now had two allies, started to shake off her depression.

Rebecca's cooking skills were put to good use in the bakery, and with the new novelties that she created, custom increased. The trio were happy working together, but there was always the constant shadow of Brian and his brother.

It came to their attention that a franchisee was trying to get permission to open a Starbucks, three doors down. Francesca was enraged and could not help but think that somehow the McVicker family were behind it. She wrote that she would be attending the hearing at the council planning meeting.

On the evening of the meeting, she donned her coat and hat, and got out her little car to drive to the other side of town, to the Township offices. She never made it. A drunk driver caused her to swerve off the road and into a tree. She died on impact. The driver of the other car was never found.

Brian assumed that as Francesca's next of kin, he was now the owner of the cafe and apartment. Little did he know that Francesca had changed her will, to leave the property and business to Maisie, with Rebecca and Iris as trustees, until Maisie came of age.

Brian was beside himself with fury. He ordered Rebecca to abandon the cafe, and to stop work. Rebecca, refused, and started divorce proceedings. She moved Maisie and herself into the apartment above the cafe, and she and Iris continued business as usual.

The McVickers were not people to be crossed. This became apparent to Rebecca, when the lawyer she had hired for the divorce proceedings dropped her like a hot potato with no explanation. Following this, Rebecca could find nobody in town who would take her case. She went further afield, and found an older woman in her own practise, who agreed to take her on as a client.

This woman was not fazed by intimidation and had taken on the McVicker family before. She calmly went ahead filing briefs and claims, despite being followed around by Brian's bully boys. She was not stupid and made the police aware of what was going on, and always had somebody with her at night. Twice she and Rebecca went to discovery, with Brian and his lawyer, and twice she caught Brian out in lies, thereby getting the information on record. Rebecca and her lawyer were due to go to trial, and the two of them had a meeting scheduled with the court clerk, to go over the evidence that they planned to present. They were never seen again. The lawyer's car was finally found by amateur divers, in one of the many abandoned gravel pits, in Mono Township. It appeared to have gone off the road around a bend and plunged down into the water below. It was assumed that the two women were together. There was a massive hunt, and eventually the body of the lawyer was found, but nobody could find Rebecca. Brian filed a request, to have Rebecca declared dead after four years.

"So, what happened to Maisie?" Hetty asked.

Iris looked after her, but then Brian's grandmother, felt that it would look bad if Brian did not take the child, and that might affect the brothers' legitimate businesses. He hired a Nanny and Maisie was fine with her, for a while. Then Brian started making demands on the Nanny that were not in her job description, if you get my meaning, and so she left. There were a series of housekeepers after that, but none of them worked out.

Iris continued running the cafe, as best she could. Then Brian decided he would sell the apartment and cafe, on the grounds that it was held in trust to Maisie, and as he was now her sole parent, he would be her executor. He filed with the courts for permission to do this, but unfortunately for him the same judge who had been scheduled to preside over Rebecca's divorce case, received the filing. Having read the pleadings from the divorce, he was aware of all the facts that Brian would have liked to keep secret. He ruled that the cafe should remain with Rebecca's partner, Iris, and continue to run as a viable business, until Maisie was of age.

Brian was incensed! Iris feared what he might do. She suggested that he might like to drop Maisie off at the cafe, and she would mind her for him, during the day. As the latest housekeeper had just left, he begrudgingly agreed to this, and Maisie had been with Iris ever since. Iris explained that it was fine when she was little, but she needs to be in school now. Iris keeps telling Brian this, but he won't make the arrangements, and it requires a parent or guardian to register a child.

Iris must stay late all the time, because she never knows when Brian will show up to pick Maisie up. She must hire staff to look after the place, when she goes banking, shopping or any other things necessary for running the business. She doesn't always trust them with Maisie and the business suffers, as a result.

Hetty was silent for quite a while, and finally said "I know the McVickers, they are bad news, they have fingers in every local pie, where there is money to be made, legally or illegally.

They are not all bad though, in fact, they give to some of my charities, but I'm sure it is for some nefarious reason!" Hetty shrugged, "I have no idea what it could be, but I certainly don't trust them." She paused a while, obviously contemplating the devious ways of the McVicker family, then she continued, "Fancy Rebecca Charles marrying into that family! Of course, she always was a wild thing, we all wondered what had happened to her."

"And we still don't know." I said.

"But you said she was killed with her lawyer, drowned in the lawyer's car"

"Her body was never found." I replied.

"Don't make a mystery out of it, B, her body will eventually be found by some walleye fisherman" Hetty retorted. She was silent, and ate quietly for a while, then, abruptly she said "Caledon Hills RDA"

"What are you talking about?" I asked

"My Riding for the Disabled centre has a school for some of its students, perhaps Maisie could go there?"

"But she's not disabled!" I protested.

"Nor are lots of the kids, they take children from broken homes, children from parents who require respite from caring for other disabled family members. Then there are the children with disabilities. Riding is part of the curriculum. They find that the horses help to heal some of the trauma that these kids have suffered."

"I doubt that Brian would let his daughter go there." I said.

"Why not? He is one of the centres benefactors"

"I don't believe it!" I exclaimed.

"Yes, he is, and his cousin as well,"

"Who is his cousin?" I asked

"Why, Daniel Brady, that man that you took an instant dislike to at the Hunt Ball years ago!" Hetty said triumphantly.

Her local knowledge was amazing! All those years serving on charity boards, and listening to local gossip, I thought.

"I could send out a letter to both Brian and Daniel, under the guise of sending it to all of our sponsors, saying we are looking for new students, and see if Brian bites"

"You're brilliant!" I said joyfully.

"Well, he hasn't read the letter yet, never mind agreed to anything."

"I'll call Iris and tell her to keep at Brian about Maisie having to go to school, perhaps that will kick him in the right direction."

We finished up our meal, hugged, and promised to keep one another updated on the plan. I drove back to my hotel feeling hopeful. I went up to my room and settled down for a lengthy nap.

I awoke an hour later, and called Iris, I got no reply at the home number she had given me. I tried the cafe. Iris answered and explained that, as usual, she was waiting for Brian, to pick up Maisie. I explained the plan, for trying to get Brian to agree to Maisie going to the RDA school. Iris was sceptical, not only about Brian, but also about Maisie, wanting to go. I told her about the fact that riding was on the curriculum. She laughed and said that might well tip the scales where Maisie was concerned. She agreed to keep after Brian to arrange schooling.

We went on to discuss Iris's living arrangements, she was currently renting, and lived a half hour commute from the cafe, she told me she thought my idea of moving into the apartment would only antagonise Brian. I suggested we contact the judge and ask him.

"Can you do that?" she said

"The apartment is part of the cafe's building. Anyway, we can always ask, nothing ventured, nothing gained" I answered firmly.

I was, at least, working on solving everyone's problems. I really should solve some of mine, and therefore, phoned my secretary in England.

In a bad mood, after learning of problems at Wendover College, I went down to the dining room. I took Clive's papers and house particulars with me.

I ordered a glass of Pinot Grigio and the evening's special. Clive's assessment was probably correct, that it would be in my financial interest to buy a property now. There was an ubiquitous little box on an estate, but it did at least back directly on to open farmland, therefore meeting, in part, my requirement of a rural location. This I immediately discarded and perused the remaining four. I had told Clive my budget, but the next two were about fifty thousand more than I could afford, wishful thinking, on his behalf I thought. The next one was far too large for my needs, and although it was within budget, it's looks did little for me, so it joined the rejected heap. The final sheet had a note from Clive on it saying "This is a diamond in the rough"

I looked at the picture, it was a small cottage type farmhouse that had obviously seen better days. It had two bedrooms, one rudimentary bathroom, a galley type kitchen, and a living room with a fireplace. I liked the look of it and read over the particulars carefully. It was set back a little from a quiet road and had nearly a half acre of yard at the rear, there was also what appeared to be an old barn, at the back of the property, which Clive had said in his description, "Could be easily converted to a garage" A bulldozer might be more appropriate, I thought. I vowed to call Clive tomorrow.

Hetty was in a state, Fee had called her, to say that her mother was not doing well.

"Trouble?" I enquired

"Fee thinks she's lost track of reality all together. She's been slipping more and more. The doctor prescribes more and more drugs, but she won't stop drinking, and the combination appears to have sent her over the top. I'm on my way over there now."

"How about her parents?" I asked

"They are away on holiday."

"Oh Hetty! Do you want me to come?"

"No. There's nothing you can do. I'll call an ambulance and see if I can get her admitted on a psychiatric hold. You get on with your waifs and strays! I sent that letter last night, by the way."

We hung up, what Hetty had to contend with seemed so unfair, I wondered whether my contact at social services could help. I thought I would give her a call later that day.

Hetty's life had not been easy. Hetty's son Barry married Alice Fordham, a gorgeous looking, but highly strung girl. Alice was an only child, much indulged by her parents. Her mother suffered from "Nerves" as it was then called. Her husband doted on her and though Alice lacked for nothing that money could buy, she got little or no attention from her parents. Hetty was not well pleased with Barry's choice, but she refrained from saying so to Barry. A few months after their wedding, he was deployed to Khandahar province in Afghanistan.

Alice discovered that she was pregnant two months after Barry left. She appeared totally unable to cope. Her parents sent her a large cheque and did very little else to help. Hetty took charge, and took her to the prenatal clinic, where they discovered that she was carrying twins. Upon hearing this, Alice lost it with the doctor, and demanded an abortion. Hetty calmed her down, took her home, and made arrangements for a phone call to Barry. Barry was delighted with the news of twins. Alice pleaded with him to come home, appearing unaware that he had no say over his deployment. Listening to his distraught wife, he promised her that he would try to get leave in a month or two.

This was not to happen. Six weeks later, Alice received a knock on the door, an Army chaplain explained that Barry had been killed by an IUD, during an attack by insurgents. The chaplain told her that officer's widows receive a good pension from the army, so she should not worry about money, also Barry had a life insurance policy which would pay off the house and car.

Alice was devastated. She returned to the doctor, to request a termination, sure that under the circumstances he would agree to perform one. She was now well into her second trimester, and the doctor refused. He recommended that she go to counselling. The twins would bring her so much joy, that she would be better able to deal with widowhood.

Hetty was herself paralyzed by a mother's grief. Alice sank into a deep depression. She did not eat properly; she did not receive suitable prenatal care. The already cramped womb space was made even more crowded by a giant cyst, which had gone undetected. Fiona had lain with her face on the cyst in the womb and when she was born the right side of her face was caved in and deformed. Her twin, Felicity, was unaffected. They would have been identical twins, two little blond girls, but only half of Fiona's face resembled Felicity's.

Alice did not deal well with Fiona's deformity. Plastic surgery was not an option, until Fiona was fully grown. Alice proceeded to ignore her. She doted on Felicity who grew into a stunning little girl. Felicity was devoted to her twin, and constantly tried to get her mother to treat Fiona in a kindlier manner. By this time Alice was drinking a lot and was dependent on anti depressants and tranquillisers.

When the twins started school Fiona was the recipient of awful teasing and bullying because of her appearance. Felicity constantly defended her, furiously taking on anyone who was unkind to her sister, fighting not only with words, but fists as well. She would often be in trouble with the teachers and would go home covered in bruises. Alice blamed Fiona for this, and so Fiona withdrew from everyone except her sister.

Hetty, seeing what was happening to her granddaughter stepped in and asked Fee if she would like riding lessons. There started the outlet and purpose to Fee's life. She loved the horses, and she took to riding like a duck to water. The horses recognised the empathy that she had for them, and they responded to her. Fee took to spending all her free time at the stables.

Felicity could not understand the attraction. She had little interest in horses. She was pleased that Fee had an interest. She started to enjoy the freedom of not having Fee constantly at her side. She started to make new friends, she had grown into such a good-looking girl, and Alice, who had never acted like a proper parent, allowed her to do pretty much whatever she wanted. She was partying and running with a wild crowd. She started drinking, and taking drugs, whilst still a young teenager. Alice was too self involved to notice that her daughter was headed for trouble.

Fee although happy to spend time at the riding school missed Felicity and tried to get her to stay home with her in the evenings. For the first time the twins started to fall out with one another. Felicity told Fee that she was not going to stay at home, and why did Fee not come out with her to party? Despite self consciousness about her looks, she did go with her sister to a party, but when she got there Felicity abandoned her, and went off with friends. A group of boys surrounded Fee and started making fun of her looks, spinning her around, and calling her names. She called for her sister, but Felicity either ignored her or did not hear. Fee was mortified, and she blamed her sister. She refused to accompany Felicity anywhere else, and the twins barely talked.

Felicity continued to socialise with her new friends, and later she met a modelling scout. This woman told Felicity that she had the bone structure, and body to become a top model. She suggested Felicity should go to a professional photographer, and get a portfolio put together. She gave her a list of suitable people, and Felicity headed off to the first name on the list, one Marcus Naismith.

Felicity was totally taken up with the whole modelling idea and dreamed of it leading to a career in films. Marcus worked with her, directing all the shots. She was highly photogenic, and Marcus became excited by her possibilities. He took her out of his studio to get shots of her in urban and natural settings. Together they put a terrific portfolio together. They went back to the woman who had "discovered" Felicity. Seeing the portfolio, she put Felicity in touch with an agency.

Fiona came back late from the barn. She asked her mother where her sister was. Alice was in her usual tranquillised state and said vaguely that Felicity had taken her portfolio to a modelling agency. Fiona told her mother that Felicity was not home from this errand, and she was worried. She asked Alice the name and address of this agency. Alice had no clue. Finally becoming worried with Fiona's entreaties, she decided that there was some concern, and she waited impatiently for Felicity to return. An hour later there was still no sign of her. Alice used her usual coping mechanism, and started drinking, until she passed out on the couch. Fiona called Hetty. Hetty immediately called the police. They informed her that they could do nothing as Felicity had not been gone for enough time to start an investigation.

When twenty-four hours had passed, the police took more notice, and commenced a fairly in depth search for Felicity. They interviewed Marcus Naismith, who gave them the address of the modelling agency that had been recommended to Felicity. They went to the agency and found that Felicity had indeed dropped off her portfolio. The agency said that they had signed her up. She had stayed talking to some of the other models. One secretary thought she had seen her leave with a man, and possibly a woman, but could not say who they were. The police tried to follow up but had no success.

The police were sympathetic, they kept up the search, but felt that it was probably a case of another runaway with stars in her eyes, and the investigation became a cold case. Hetty was beside herself. She tried every way she could think of to find Felicity. She even used her limited savings to hire a private detective, to no avail. Fee appeared devastated, the person who she had loved most had abandoned her, she felt terrible guilt over having distanced herself from her sister. She pined silently, losing weight, and suffering terrible nightmares about her sister. Time went by and there was still no news of what had happened to Felicity.

I called Clive and was pleased to find that he was already at work. I made an appointment to view the little farmhouse later that day. I then picked up the rental car and drove out to the cafe.

Iris was busy with the early morning rush; Starbucks was still closed. She brought me a coffee, and then returned to serving her customers. This took a lot longer than I had anticipated. I finished my coffee and decided to take a stroll down the High Street, while I was waiting for her. I mouthed that I would be back shortly and headed out. I picked up a local paper at the newsagents and strolled down the road.

"B?" someone called, behind me. I spun around and found a tall grey-haired man looking at me.

"Alistair!" I exclaimed, pleased that I remembered his name, I was starting to have trouble with names.

"What are you doing back in Canada?" he asked. "Are you back permanently?"

"No such luck! I'm just on holiday from college." I replied, "I've got another couple of years to go."

"Do you have time to catch up?"

"Not now, I'm afraid my day is fully booked." I replied.

"How about tomorrow? We could do lunch"

"That would be lovely" I replied, "Where and when?" We set a time and agreed to meet at the Italian restaurant further down the High Street. I was feeling quite good about this chance encounter, but then remembered I should really be spending the next day with Hetty. I decided to call her later and see how she was doing. If I was worried about her, I would cancel the lunch date. I then turned around and walked back to the cafe.

Iris offered me another cup of coffee; I shook my head laughing "If I drink any more the whites of my eyes will turn yellow!" I said, "Let's call the Court House, and see if we can find the judge." Iris was still unsure about this, "He's a judge, surely you can't just phone him up?"

"Why not?" I said, "He's a public servant. See what you can find online." She opened her computer and looked up the Brampton Court House. There were various numbers listed, so I started at the beginning. It was a frustrating task, mostly I just got machines, but on the odd time I got a real person, they told me to call another number, which inevitably ended up being a machine.

My astrological sign is Taurus, I gritted my teeth, and kept going. An hour later I talked to the judge's clerk's assistant. I explained the situation, and he said he would get back to me. I was not going to leave it at that, and I demanded his name and the number of his direct line, so that I could call him back should it "slip his mind." With this information safely stowed away, I hung up and smiled at Iris.

"Wow!" she said, "you are good!!"

"Just determined" I responded, "Must go now, I'm going to look at a bulldozer job"

The house looked shabbier than in the photos, the garden was overgrown, and I fought my way through brambles to the front door. Clive greeted me, opened the door, and waxed poetic about the property. I looked sternly at him and said that I wished to first look at the house by myself, and that if I had questions, I would ask him, when I had finished. This was not Clive's usual routine, and he looked crestfallen that his prepared sales patter was not to be used.

I walked through the house, making note of all the cracks in the walls, damp patches and sagging doors. Despite this, I thought that it had good bones. I slowed down, and walked carefully through it all again, taking out a writing pad, and making notes. The house was devoid of furniture, which made it easier to see the problems. Clive was sitting glumly on the front step, he looked up when I approached, and started to say "I know it doesn't look..." I stopped him with a wave of my finger and asked why the property was being sold.

"It is an estate sale, the old lady who owns it, has been moved to a home, and her children, who have power of attorney, are selling it."

I enquired whether there was a survey, and whether Clive knew if the property was sound. "There are a lot of cracks." I added.

"There is indeed a survey. I think that the cracks are only superficial but if you are interested, you should get a structural engineer to look at it."

"How much would it cost to renovate?" I enquired

"That's like asking, how long, is a piece of string." Said Clive, happy to get a dig at me, "It all depends on what you want to do, and whether it is all internal, or whether you want to build on. If it is all internal and you are not enlarging the footprint, you can probably get away without planning permission, which will save quite a bit."

"Speaking of planning permission, what about the surrounding land, can it be developed?" I asked

"That's what is wrong with this house. It is all owned by a consortium. They want to build a big equestrian centre, on the other road behind this one. They own the whole concession. It would only be good if you like manure and horse flies!"

A lot better than a subdivision made up of little boxes made from ticky tacky! I thought.

"Well perhaps they will develop it." I suggested.

"No, there is some strange deal whereby they are going to give the land in perpetuity to the Township, to remain as designated green space, which would be fine, but a horse centre…" went on Clive, clearly not a horse fancier.

"Really, why would they do that?" I enquired.

"It's some sort of tax savings measure, they get the income from the property, and if we get the Olympic Games that could be substantial, and then they would let the Township have it. I think it is a giant money laundering scheme!

I had to admit that the site was perfect, minutes to town, an equestrian centre literally on my doorstep, and room to have a dog. I felt excitement creeping in. I counselled myself to not be stupid, and rush into anything. I asked Clive if he knew of a structural engineer, of course he did, and was only too happy to arrange to have the house inspected. He promised to call when this had been set up. I stressed the urgency: I could not put off my departure a second time.

I shook hands with him, took my notebook, and climbed back in my rental car, and went for a drive around to the next concession. There were big signs announcing the construction of the new equestrian centre. The land was park like, with many big trees and some rolling terrain. Satisfied that what Clive had said was indeed correct, I drove back and parked in front of what I now thought of as my little house. I looked at it for a while, planning what needed to be done to bring it up to date. I wondered about the elderly woman who had lived here. Had she been happy? I thought so, the house had a good feel, and I hoped that that feel would continue during my stewardship. I chided myself that I was getting far too far ahead of myself, I needed to wait for the report from the engineer. Reluctant to leave, I turned the key in the car, and drove back to the hotel.

There were messages for me from both Hetty and Iris. I called Hetty back first, on her mobile. She was still at the hospital; cell phones not being allowed she said she would call me right back. Five minutes later my phone chirped.

"It's not good." Hetty said immediately, "She is practically catatonic. The doctors have admitted her but think that she would be better on a complete psych hold, at Beeton Hall, however she has to be committed by next of kin, Fee is too young, and her parents are away for another week."

"Surely the doctors can commit her?" I suggested

"Not if she is not a threat, to herself or society." Hetty sighed.

"That's ridiculous!" I snorted "Well, we'd better get hold of her parents"

"I hate to interrupt their holiday."

"For God's sake, Hetty! They have never done a thing to help their daughter, and her family, you have done it all. It's time for them to step up!" I practically shouted down the phone, "Does Fee know where they are?"

"I think so," sighed Hetty "I'll ask her, she's still here with me."

"I'll drive right over" I said, "which side of the hospital are you?"

Having been given this information, I found the pair of them, with only a few mis directions.

Fee did indeed know where her grandparents were, and with the help of International Directory Assistance, Hetty was able to get the phone number in France.

"I'll call!" I said, despite Hetty's protests. I had only rudimentary French, but it was sufficient for me to navigate through various operators, and eventually get connected to Alice's Father. I did not beat about the bush, and told him exactly the state of his daughter, and the need for him to return immediately. At once he tried to weasel out of having to do anything, but I was having none of it.

When he argued the cost of having to get another flight, I told him his insurance would cover it. When he argued stress to his wife, I retorted that the stress to Hetty and Fee was greater. His final salvo was to say that Alice had always been "highly strung", and would be just fine, I told him that I was fetching her doctor to talk to him, and I added in a low tone that his reputation around town could be seriously damaged, if somehow it got out that he had ignored his daughter, when she was seriously ill. "Is that a threat?" he gasped, suitably surprised that someone would speak to him this way. "Yes!" I answered "Don't tempt me! Here is the doctor." I handed my phone to the doctor, who reiterated what I had already said. I gathered that he received reluctant agreement to the pair flying home, the next day. I thanked him, and turned back to Hetty and Fee,

"Obnoxious, little man!" I exclaimed, "I apologise, Fee, I know he is your grandfather, but his selfishness is beyond the pale." Fee nodded her head in agreement. She hugged Hetty, and thanked me for stepping in. We left the hospital, promising to return the next day, and went out for a quick dinner at a fast-food outlet. I told them all about my house. It was now firmly stuck in my head as "my house". They were excited for me, and I must have bored them to tears by going on and on about it!

I excused myself from the table and went outside to give Iris a quick call. She was at home and answered right away. I apologised for not calling before.

"No problem," she said, "I just wanted to let you know that Brian seems to be coming around to the idea of Maisie going to school, but he's looking at trying to get her into Toronto Junior Collegiate."

"But that's miles away!" I protested, "Who is going to drive her back and forth?"

"He thinks she can go as a weekly boarder." Iris was obviously close to tears, about this.

"She's far too young! I'm sure the authorities wouldn't stand for that" I replied. "We'll just have to hope that Hetty's letter will do the trick."

I told her I would come by in the morning and told her not to stress. I hung up and went back to the table in the restaurant. I told Hetty what Iris had said. Fee agreed that the school at the RDA would be perfect. They have great teachers there, she said, used to dealing with kids with problems, and they are very patient, she added.

"That will be highly necessary with Maisie!" Hetty laughed

"She's not that bad!" I exclaimed but Hetty went on "Maybe not, if she would ever let anybody else get a word in edgewise!"

"That's because you're used to demur little me" Fee rejoined. I burst out laughing. I was secretly pleased that Fee seemed to be coming out of her shell, she was growing up, and despite all the hardships that she had endured, was turning into a wonderful person. We finished up dinner by ordering a decadent, Death by Chocolate, dessert that we shared, and then we paid and headed home. Fee was going to stay with Hetty for the night.

The next morning, I headed straight to the Cafe. Iris was there, with Maisie in tow.

"Hi Bumble Bee!" she said excitedly

"Hi yourself!" I returned "Maisie Maggot."

"What!" she exclaimed, "You can't call me that!"

"Well, if you call me Bumble Bee, I shall call you Maisie Maggot!"

"But Bumble Bees are nice, Maggots are Icky!"

"But some turn into beautiful butterflies!" I replied, somewhat inaccurately. "Wouldn't you like to turn into a butterfly?"

"We...ll maybe."

"There we are then, Maisie Maggot it is!"

Once seated, with my coffee in hand, I ignored all of Maisie's conversational gambits, and focused on Iris. She had had no further conversations with Brian, he had just shoved Maisie through the cafe door, just as Iris was arriving, nor had there been a follow up from the judge's office. I phoned the direct line to the clerk's assistant, but there was no reply. I left a message. I then brought her up to speed on Hetty's problems with Alice.

"That poor woman, having to cope with all that!" she said.

"You don't know the half of it!" I replied, "When I have time, I will tell you the whole sorry story, now I must head to the hospital to see what is happening."

Ignoring Maisie's cries for me to stay, I waved goodbye, and headed off to the hospital.

I hurried through the hospital towards the psychiatric ward, and found Hetty, Fee and a tall good looking young man, deep in conversation, in the hallway outside Alice's room.

"Oh B." said Hetty, spotting me, "You remember Adam? He's home from California, and called me last night, I told him about Alice, and here he is." Fee looked at Adam gratefully, and he put his arm round her shoulder then he turned and shook my hand. "Alice wasn't doing well when I left, but I did not expect it to get this bad."

"Nor, did any of us." I replied, "she is very fragile, and the drink and all the drugs she has been taking, have just made it worse!"

Hetty started crying. "I should have realised" she said.

"Not your fault" Both Adam and I said, at the same time. I turned and smiled at him. He went on, "She'll be in the best place, when we get her moved to Beeton Hall. Then the doctors can sort out her meds, and God willing, she'll be back to normal"

"Have you heard when her parents will arrive?" I asked.

"Their flight gets in this evening, and I have volunteered to go and meet them," said Adam.

"You shouldn't have to do that, I will go" snuffled Hetty

"You are in no shape to go anywhere" I said firmly, "You need to take Adam up on his offer, and you should head home, and get some rest. I am sure that Fee is also exhausted, she held it together so well yesterday."

"She's a fighter." Said Adam, giving Fee a hug that was a little inappropriate, I thought.

"I suppose you are right, Adam, thank you so much, and B, I feel so bad we are ruining your nice holiday!"

"A change is as good as a rest!!" I replied, following Hetty and Fee out to the car park, with Adam following solicitously behind. He lent down and whispered something to Fee, and she turned and smiled back at him.

I ordered a San Pellegrino water and sat down to wait for Allistair. We had served on Riding Club, Pony club and various horse show committees, together. He had been a very good dressage rider, along with his wife. She had died many years ago of a brain tumour, and I did not think that he had remarried. They had been a good couple, I remembered. They had no children.

Alistair pulled up a chair, and sat down, giving me a quick peck on the cheek as he did so. He was a good looking man, and one of those lucky people, whose looks improved with age. Why did he have to wear that Old Spice Cologne? I thought.

"B, so good to see you! How is it going, overseeing two and a half thousand students? And in a foreign country to boot!"

I laughed, "Hardly a foreign country, I was born there, you know. On the whole, the job is great! Some of the students are a little difficult, you would not believe the dramas! But I really wouldn't have missed this part of my life. I only have just over a couple of years to go."

"Time flies." Alistair said, "When did you leave? It must be eight years ago now?"

"Yes, about that," I said, "I started as head of equestrian studies and then got promoted to Dean."

Alistair nodded, "Yes it must have been a year after Cynthia died." By the pinched look on his face, he was nowhere near over the loss. I remembered them being a fun couple, not very romantic, more best friends than husband and wife. This had obviously worked well for them. I often thought it was better to like a person rather than to love them. Love could turn very quickly. I decided to change the subject.

"Are you still working?" I enquired. He shook his head.

"No, I took early retirement, five years ago. I was just not up for all the tragedies, anymore. Being a homicide detective requires a younger man's stamina."

I had no idea he was a detective, it really surprised me. He saw the look on my face and smiled.

"I did not broadcast it, back then, I kept my professional life separate from my home, and riding life."

"You certainly did!" I replied, "Had you already retired, when Hetty's granddaughter went missing?" I asked.

"Yes, but I had worked in a different division, than the one investigating that. Terrible thing, still no news?"

"No, none, I don't think the police took it seriously, they thought she was just a runaway."

"I doubt that B, runaways often come from broken homes, parents having drug addictions. It becomes unbearable for the kids and life on the streets seems preferable."

I shuddered at this, but Alistair went on "We normally find them dead of an overdose, or they are picked up in a raid of street walkers."

"When kids go missing from good families, we think perhaps kidnap for ransom or..." His voice trailed off. "Or kidnap for rape, human trafficking and possibly murder." I finished for him. He nodded miserably. I went on, "Of course Alice is an addict, I think, she's dependent on prescription drugs, she's Felicity and Fiona's mother. I think that she also has mental health issues. It seems to run in her family."

"That's what I mean by tragedies! We had a young girl disappear from our division just before I left. We never solved the case."

"Well," I said, "This is not the fun lunch, with an old friend, that I was expecting. Tell me what you are doing now. How is the horse world?" I tried brightly, hoping to steer the conversation in a different direction.

Alistair told me that he had had a series of jobs in security, none of which had he found particularly interesting. He was out of work, at the present.

He had bought a nice young horse from Germany and had

been quietly producing it. "I am looking for a good young person to compete him, do you know of anybody?"

"I have plenty in England, but I'm out of touch over here. Why don't you compete him yourself? I asked.

"Too old" Alistair laughed, "And he's too good to be wasted."

"Are you going to get another job? Can you afford to retire?" I asked.

"Oh yes, I've got quite a bit squirreled away. I was vaguely thinking that if this equestrian centre, that everybody is talking about, gets off the ground, I might apply there." I nodded my approval.

I went on to tell him all about my little house. "It needs a lot of work and I'm not sure whether it is a good idea to buy now or wait until I return for good." Alistair said he thought that it was a good idea to buy now.

"I have lots of time to read the papers and the financial people think that the economy is strong and that real estate prices were going to increase exponentially over the next two or three years. I think it is an ideal time to buy."

I explained my dilemma of returning to England and being unable to oversee the remodelling of the house.

"Why not let me do it!" Alistair exclaimed "I used to be a dab hand at DIY, and I still have all my old contacts with contractors. I have a good friend, who can help me, if I get in over my head. Cynthia and I did up three houses. We lived in them for a while, and then sold them on, that way we paid no capital gains. I used to really enjoy doing it, but without Cyn, I've not thought of doing it again. It would give me a whole new interest."

"Well, I don't have a big budget" I began.

"Oh, I wouldn't charge you anything, it would give me something with which to occupy myself, to be honest I have been bored silly since I quit my last job, and taking a similar one just doesn't appeal to me"

"I couldn't let you do it for nothing." I protested.

"Well how about, if I get it done to your liking and under budget, I keep the balance?"

"You're on! "I said "But first it must pass the scrutiny of the structural engineer. I have a list of things that concern me."

"Give those to me." Allistair said, "If he can't do the inspection before you leave, I will go in your place, and you Skype us, so we can tick off your concerns one at a time."

We both raised our glasses. I couldn't have been happier. I knew that if the purchase went through, that the house could not be in better hands.

Alice was signed into Beeton Hall by her father, who then promptly went back to his wife. Hetty told me Adam had taken Fee out for a drive to see some horses that had recently been imported, and Fee was in much better spirits.

The structural engineer agreed to look at the house the following week. I was so relieved to have Alistair to deal with this. I put the two in touch with one another.

I had a moment of panic, when Clive called me to say that there was a builder interested in buying the house. I rushed over to his office and put in a formal offer, conditional on the results of the inspection, fortunately I was a cash purchaser, with no need to apply for financing, and Clive assured me that my offer would be accepted. I had had to offer more than I wanted but with another buyer waiting in the wings, I thought it was sensible. It left my renovation budget a little tight, but I discussed it with Alistair, and he thought we would be just fine. I worried that there would be no money left over for Alistair, but he did not seem worried, and I thought I could put enough aside over the next two years to give him a decent bonus.

I continued to hound the poor man at the courthouse. I had taken to calling on different phones, because he would no longer pick up when he saw my cell phone number. Tenacity paid off, and the day before I left, Iris received a call, from the judge himself. He agreed that she could move into the apartment, as long as she was running the cafe for Maisie. Iris was ecstatic. He said he would send her a copy of his ruling, in case there were any complaints.

Hetty and I discussed the issue of Maisie's schooling. Hetty said she would try ringing Brian, and Daniel as a "follow up" from her letter. She really didn't have the authority to do this and did not have much success. The men brushed her off complaining of her bothering them over something that they had no interest in, after all, they had donated to the RDA, and were certainly not responsible for how the centre was run. Two days later Brian called Hetty back, to ask whether Maisie could attend the school.

Hetty bent over backwards to comply with all Brian's demands. She agreed that Maisie could be picked up by the school bus, and dropped off at the cafe, in the afternoon. That Maisie might be able to remain at school, for odd weekends, and something could be done for the school holidays as well. She hung up terrified, how was she ever going to get the school to agree to all this? I suggested that she call Brian back and ask him for a substantial donation which would sweeten the pie for the school. Hetty said she couldn't possibly do this and so I found myself posing as the admissions officer, on a call to Brian. He eventually agreed to giving money, for which he would receive a tax credit, I assured him. The deal was done.

I went to see Maisie at the cafe. She was delighted to see me, but her pleasure vanished when I told her that she would be attending school, from now on. Before her temper could fire up, I explained to her that it was a very special school, and that she would be learning to ride as well as her schoolwork. The scowl on her face disappeared, replaced by a big toothless grin.

"Can I jump 'em?" she asked

"Yes, Maisie you can jump them, as soon as you have learnt to walk, trot and canter them."

I turned to Iris and tried to have a conversation with her. Maisie made it nigh on impossible with her many interruptions about the horses.

I invited Iris to my going away dinner, patted Maisie on the head and wished her good luck at school. As I left, I glanced back, and saw her in earnest conversation with Henry, who had obviously been rescued.

We gathered together at the restaurant, Iris, Hetty, Alistair, Fee, Adam and me. Fee had come, which surprised me, she was usually self conscious about her looks in public. We sat down, and Adam insisted on saying grace, Fee smiled at him fondly, Hetty and I exchanged looks. I decided that Fee must have a crush on Adam. I shrugged, proposed a toast "To good friends" everyone raised their glasses, and we had a great evening, and I was very sad to say goodbye to all of them, I had grown very close to them, in a very short space of time.

I had returned the rental car, and a taxi took me to the airport the following day, each one of my friends had offered to take me, but I am not good at prolonged goodbyes, and so I declined. I hurried through customs and security, and eventually got into my seat, for the long flight to England, and back to my life.

WENDOVER COLLEGE

A CAR AND DRIVER met me at Heathrow, it was about two and a half hours to the college. I sat back and watched the countryside. It is amazing, how in an island as small as England, that there is so much open space. The green fields and hedges with little copses in their midst would give way to huge fields of bright yellow rape, and ripening barley. I was glad to be back in England and looking forward to my final time as Dean of the college. We pulled in through the massive gates and drove onto the campus. The driver dropped me at my quarters, and I entered, unpacked my things, and sat and looked around my space. It comprised of a reception room, bedroom, bathroom and kitchenette. It felt strange after my stay in Canada, everything looked very small, after the spacious rooms of the hotel. I was hungry, and made my way to the staff dining area, where I ate most of my meals. I did not cook very often in the tiny kitchenette.

The college catered to approximately 2,400 students studying all things that had to do with country industries. Nearly half of these came to study different areas of equestrianism. These would lead to varied careers with horses. There were students who wanted to go into racing, ones who wanted to become riding instructors, grooms, stable managers, there were ones devoted to each Olympic discipline, some, studied equine breeding. We offered the whole gamut at Wendover. There would be students who excelled, students who muddled through, and those that did not stand the course. Like the horses, we had seen them all. Some would bite, some would kick, some would gallop to Hell but return an angel.

There were another two weeks to go, until the start of the fall semester, which was also the start of the school year. We would have a huge influx of new students. They would be arriving, and settling into residences, many of the equestrian students would be bringing their own horses. The agricultural and veterinary students were housed on the far side of campus across the love bridge, where it was said that couples love would last if they kissed on it.

Eleanor, my best friend, here at college, would be arriving back from her holidays shortly. She was head of security for the campus, a huge job. It included all the same things that required policing, in the general population.

Some of the senior students had stayed on at college with their horses, during the summer, to continue their competition season. I was saddened to hear that Jessica McIntyre, our star dressage rider, who was hopeful for a berth on the English team, had lost her horse to colic the week before. I sought her out to express my condolences. She was heartbroken, she had bought the horse when he was just a yearling and had trained him up to Grand Prix. She had little money, she taught lessons at the college to cover her competition fees, and she was from a single parent family. There was no hope of purchasing another horse. We discussed what she wanted to do, but I could see that she was not in any state to make good decisions. I told her to stay on, as an assistant instructor. I could offer her a small wage until she could make up her mind about her future.

Two days later, I skyped with Alistair and the engineer, and was delighted to discover that my little house was structurally sound. The barn merely needed a new roof. The engineer signed off and I continued to talk to Alistair about the logistics of renovating the house. First, I had to close the sale with Clive, then wire Alistair funds to pay the various contractors that he would hire. He promised to call me before every important phase and asked me to decide on fittings and fixtures. These I could access online. We went on to talk about the reconfiguring of the ground floor, and what to do about the staircase. Alistair was obviously nearly as excited as I was. I hung up feeling a little overwhelmed, but in a good way.

I kept up with the news from Mono Township, through Alistair, Hetty and Iris. Maisie settled in at school, after a few rocky days. The cafe flourished, the health department shut down the Starbucks, two doors down, permanently due to sewage leaking from a main drain underneath the building. The cost for repairing it to sanitary standards for a restaurant was so great that the Starbucks franchisee decided to move to another location. The Equestrian centre was going ahead, and construction was underway. The Grand Opening was set for six months before I was scheduled to finish my contract at the college.

Two years went by both unbelievably quickly and intolerably slowly, depending on my state of mind. I was unable to return to Canada during the next summer as we were running international competitions at the college. I insisted on giving students an opportunity to witness firsthand the complexity of the tasks involved. They were included in all meetings and encouraged to make suggestions. I believed this would help with their problem-solving skills.

With the passing of Brexit we had lost many Eastern European workers. These hard working people had filled the menial posts that the Brits were unwilling to undertake. Brexit precluded them from working in the UK without a visa or work permit. I therefore had many vacancies for housekeepers for the dormitories and field workers for the agricultural courses. My assistant and I spent many hours at the job centres. Our overheads increased exponentially as we had to offer higher wages to attract British workers.

Sadly, we had one suicide, Harry Payne, a student in the veterinary sciences program who had tried to deal with anxiety and depression by himself. Following this, I implemented a mandatory mental health program, in addition to our guidance councillors. I felt guilty that this was too little too late. Trying to comfort Harry's parents, was one of my life's lowest points.

We had two students get pregnant both of whom I had sobbing in my office. I was suspicious that Elizabeth Jennings had got pregnant on purpose to trap her young beau. There followed her wedding, a large affair attended by many of the students. I felt the chance of the marriage lasting to be small.

The second pregnancy was the result of date rape. Eleanor, my Security Officer, had to deal with the whole sorry mess. Stella Brown had been going out with Chris Hampton for a few months. They attended a party off campus and Stella had too much to drink. She had been dancing with Chris and agreed to go with him to a side room. That was where things got confusing, Chris said that it was consensual sex, Stella said that she said "Stop!"

Eleanor had to call in the police. We tried to support both students. Chris was charged with rape, but later Stella withdrew her claim. She went for a termination. Both of them left the college, their lives spoiled.

Students came and went, and I felt that on the whole, we had equipped them fairly well for life.

Going into the second year I had an epiphany regarding Jessica McIntyre. She had stayed on as an assistant instructor but seemed to be lacking purpose. I remembered Alistair had wanted someone to compete his horse, and I thought that a change of countries, and a new horse and goals, would kick start her back into a productive life. Alistair was delighted by my proposal, having failed to find anybody in Canada, and so I pitched the idea to Jessica. She was doubtful to start with, worried about leaving her mother, and overwhelmed by the prospect of leaving the college and England.

After a couple of weeks, she warmed to the idea, and she was surprised that her mother heartily endorsed the plan. I helped her to apply for a student athlete visa that would allow her to stay for a year, with the possibility of extending it after that. She worried about where she would live, and so I offered her my house now that Alistair had completed the work. I let her live rent free, until she could get on her feet.

A month later, her mother and I, saw her off at the airport. I suddenly realised what a gorgeous looking girl she was, she would turn heads in Canada. She embraced us both. Then she turned and hurried to the departure gate, moving up to a good medium trot.

I had little time for a social life outside the College, but occasionally Eleanor and I would go out. We sampled the local restaurants and attended the occasional concert.

During one of these outings Eleanor introduced me to a friend of hers, Thomas Evans. He was a pleasant unassuming man, a retired school teacher. We chatted through the intermission and then returned to our seats.

I was surprised when a few days later, he called me up, and asked if I would like to go with him to watch a play. It was being put on by a small company in a boutique theatre in Gloucester. I really did not want to go but despite my reservations I agreed.

It was an enjoyable evening, the acting was somewhat amateurish, but there were some funny moments, and it was nice to be away from work. We stopped in at a pub on the way home. I learned more about Thomas and his life. He was a widower. He enjoyed travelling, gardening and refinishing old cars. He lived on a nearby subdivision. Eleanor and his wife had been at university together.

Last orders were called, and we finished our drinks and headed home.

The next day Eleanor barged into my office.

"So?" she demanded

"So, what?" I replied

"Don't be infuriating, how did you get on with Thomas last night?"

Laughing I replied that we had had a pleasant evening

"That's all? Are you going out again?"

"Perhaps. If he invites me."

"You are maddening, I introduce you to a perfectly eligible man and you make no effort."

"Unlike you, I am not seeking an eligible man, if you think he's that good why are you not going out with him yourself?"

"It would seem odd going out with Marjorie's husband" I nodded, I could understand that.

We chatted for a bit and then I shooed Eleanor out of my office.

Over the months, Thomas and I went out with one another periodically. It was fairly obvious that he was keen to have a more committed relationship. I enjoyed our outings but had no interest in taking the friendship to another level. Thomas hinted at coming to Canada with me and settling in my little house and looking after one another in our declining years!

I decided that I had to put an end to the relationship. Our final date ended with me telling him that I was not interested in becoming a nurse or a purse and that we should stop seeing one another so that he could move on. He was not happy, but he accepted the situation.

Three months before I was scheduled to leave, the Board of Directors called me to a meeting. They were having trouble finding the right replacement for me. The person they wanted would not be available for another three months. They wondered if I would stay on for an extra six months. Three months of which I would be assisting the new person to settle in and take over. Having pumped so many years of my life into getting the college up and running, I did not want to hand it over to somebody who was unprepared. Somewhat reluctantly, I agreed to this. Therefore, I did not return to Canada until fall of 2018, by this time Alistair had been hired on as head of security for the Equestrian Centre. Jessica had extended her visa and was enjoying life in Canada and had moved out of my house, into an apartment near the farm where Alistair kept his horse.

The one thing of note that happened shortly before I left for Canada was a big headline in my daily English paper saying, "Paloma Missing!" No sooner had I read this than Hetty called me, to see if I had seen the news. She said that Adam had told her he was totally unprepared for the news, he had not seen her for about ten days, he understood that she had been recording, but this was not correct. She was missing all this time.

I asked, "Why didn't anyone report her missing before?"

"Apparently everybody thought she was somewhere else. She had a reputation for being totally private, almost reclusive, so when people hadn't seen her, they did not think anything about it, they don't even know if she was in California or Toronto." Hetty replied. We chatted a bit longer, and then said our goodbyes, and I forgot all about Paloma, despite the newspapers keeping the story going for weeks.

PART TWO

EQUESTRIAN CENTRE

I HAD GOOD INTENTIONS to make a start on my "to do" list. I had put the coffee on to brew and let Alfie out for a pee. Alfie was a splendid mutt, a rescue dog from the local shelter. I had adopted him a month after I returned from my post in England. His ancestry was unknown, but he was large, hairy and adorable He trundled around the yard checking things out, nose to the ground. Satisfied that there had been no overnight visitors he did his business and came back into the house.

I poured my coffee, looked through the mail that I had retrieved from the mailbox the night before. Tucked in amongst bills was a handwritten letter, a true rarity. I opened it and was surprised and delighted to find that it was from Eleanor. She planned a trip to Canada and was hoping to come and spend some time with me, now that I was retired.

I am very bad at keeping in touch with people, and obviously Eleanor was unaware that my retirement had come to an abrupt halt. I was now busier than ever. My new job would not prevent me from enjoying Eleanor's company, so I scribbled a reply to her letter stating that I couldn't wait for her to arrive, but that I would be putting her to work when she got here, and as long as she was OK with that she was welcome to stay as long as she liked.

I rummaged around until I found an envelope and stamps.

I put in my reply, addressed it, and called up Alfie so we could walk down to the post box to post it. That done we took a circuitous route home through a small portion of the Mono hills of Ontario. This was much to Alfie's delight, there being the most interesting collection of feral aromas along this route.

I was feeling virtuous, having walked further than I originally intended. I poured myself another cup of coffee, and flopped on the couch with Alfie joining me, his head on my lap. I looked happily around my little house, it had turned out just perfectly, thanks to Alistair. I still needed to improve on the furniture, which had been got together hastily, so that Jenny McIntyre could move into the house for the year, before I returned. I had now been home for nearly three years, and I had not bothered to replace much of it.

I picked up a book. It was mere mind candy, and after a while I lost interest, and started thinking again about things that I had to do. I was disgusted at myself for my lack of motivation. I thought vaguely about cleaning the house, paying my bills and annual memberships, or returning phone calls and emails. None sparked any desire to get off the couch. My New Year's resolution to become more active, and to stop procrastinating seemed to have wilted before it ever flowered.

The phone rang, and Jenny, my tireless assistant proceeded to apologise for disturbing me at home, but she thought that she should remind me of the meeting with the other heads of disciplines at 11.00 am this morning.

"Damn!" I said "I had completely forgotten! Thanks Jenny, I'll be right over."

I checked my watch, twenty to eleven. No time to change. I grabbed my coat, briefcase and bag, and headed to the door. Archie followed me hopefully. "No not this time Alfie. You stay and guard the house!" I ignored his pitiful look and got in my car and drove the three miles over to the equestrian centre.

I was holding the position of Chair for the Three Day Event, an Olympic equestrian sport, for the new multi discipline equestrian facility, which had been built over the last five years.

The other Chairs were Pru Carling, Chair of Dressage, Tom Clark, Chair of Show Jumping, Richard Talbot Chair of Driving and finally Randy Wainwright for Vaulting. I had a great deal of time for Randy, he was a quiet sensible man who listened, and tended to look at the overall picture rather than his sport alone.

Today all the Chairs, with the exception of Randy, who was away at a vaulting competition, would be present, along with the accountants, PR people and of course Daniel Brady, the overall CEO. Things had not changed. I still could not stand the man. My mood was not improving, as I anticipated the next two hours. Happily, for me, Alistair had joined the staff for the Centre, as head of security, and he would also be there. At least I would have one ally.

I pulled my car up in front of the courtyard leading to the main entrance of the equestrian centre. I could not help but marvel at the building. The consortium, who had decided that there would be big money returns if the city won the bid for the Olympic Games, had spared no expense in putting in this complex. It housed stabling for 500 horses, a coliseum large enough that it could host any discipline, groom's dormitories, canteens and restaurants, offices and conference rooms. With such an enormous edifice, it could have been made functional, but instead the architect had created a masterpiece. Somehow, he had managed to make it look like a giant barn that had been there for decades if not centuries, instead of its' scant three years of existence. I parked and sat in the car taking a few deep breaths.

A car horn sounded loudly, Samantha Wells had pulled up in her blond convertible, and parked in the VIP area. Rather than exiting her car and coming over to see me she sat, obviously expecting me to make the walk over to her. I sighed, and climbed out of my Subaru, and took my aged body over to her car.

"Hi Ms B. great hairdo!" I couldn't even remember whether I had pulled a brush through my hair when I got up. It is strange that in one's youth one spends an inordinate amount of time looking in the mirror, but having reached my advanced years, I could go a whole day without looking at myself. I ignored her comment.

"You can't park there, Samantha," I said, "move your car to the General Parking area." She made no effort to do as she was told. "I won't be long I just need to ask you a question." She replied.

I sighed, "I am late for a meeting, what can I do for you Sam?"

"I just want to confirm that I can have a second place in the showcase event, your secretary wasn't being very helpful."

"She was just following my instructions, one horse per rider, no exceptions."

"But Ms B. I've got to have a run on Filibuster to get to know him, before the qualifier at the end of next month." I was far from sympathetic to this argument. Sam had wheedled the ride on Filibuster, out of Roger Brandon his owner. Filibuster had been Maggie Sandler's great mount for four years, and now the poor girl was broken hearted, at the loss of her horse. Roger was such an idiot to have his head turned by this girl, I thought, and goodness knows what Helen, his wife, must be thinking.

"I would just be taking Maggie's spot." Sam had the nerve to say.

"Maggie is riding Media Circus in Filibuster's place."

"What, that old thing? He's hardly up to the calibre of the horses you are trying to attract."

"Maybe not, but Maggie is talented enough for both of

them." I snapped "Now if you will excuse me, I have work to do. If you want to enter Filibuster, you will have to withdraw your other horse."

"What if somebody withdraws? Can I have their spot?"

Without thinking I failed to negate this plan but merely said "That is not very likely at this point." And with that I turned, and marched back to my car, now in a thoroughly bad mood. I reached in, snatched up my briefcase and bag, and headed to the meeting

I entered the building and consulted the bulletin board to see where we were meeting. It was on the third floor, I argued with myself as to whether I would take the stairs or the elevator. Guiltily I rode the elevator up the three floors.

I entered the boardroom, to be greeted by Pru, exclaiming "B Darling! Your hair, what fun, it really suits you" I glared at her, and looked frantically round for a mirror. None was available. I made a mental note to go to the loo and see what the hell was up with my hair. I ignored her remark, and greeted the room as a whole, and plonked myself down in a seat around the huge table. I picked up my copy of the agenda, and quickly scanned it. Tom joined me, and the others slowly took their places, Daniel Brady made a point of waiting to seat himself at the head of the table, after we had all been seated for some time. He then gave his usual prayer that our meeting would be productive and requested that God help us all in our endeavours. This was one of the main things I disliked about him. I have nothing against religion, but I do not like having it foisted on me. I felt that if there was a God, he had better things to do than watch over our committee meetings. I also felt that this behaviour of Daniel's, was somehow fake. But let's face it, I really disliked Daniel, so anything he did would rub me up the wrong way, even if he contributed to the Riding for The Disabled.

After the prayer, where all but me, added their amens, Daniel opened the meeting, with the usual requirements of Roberts Rules of Order. When he got to the Chairman's report, he launched into a lengthy complaint about the expense reports that we all had submitted, and the necessity of keeping to the timeframe that he had outlined.

This was a familiar theme, and as usual Richard and I were in the hot seat having the disciplines that required the most finances, and many times the infrastructure of the other disciplines.

Both of our sports involved a cross country portion. This meant that the competitors in the three day event galloped over several kilometres of terrain, jumping natural fences as opposed to the coloured poles that show jumpers jumped. These jumps consisted of logs, banks, ditches and water. None of the fences knocked down, and for the average spectator, looked unjumpable. It was very exciting and was known as the extreme sport of equestrianism. The driving was similar, teams of horses were driven across country and on the way, they had to negotiate complicated hazards, passing between posts, and then doubling back on themselves several times. They went up and down slopes and through water, requiring huge skill from the drivers of the teams.

I was not in the mood to kowtow to Daniel, and so spoke abruptly once he had finished his remarks.

"You knew full well that the major expenses for the cross country course would come in this quarter, we have been on budget up until now. I cannot build water jumps, banks and feature complexes, that you want for your TV coverage, on a shoestring. I have been telling you all along that your figures were unrealistic." Daniel was not happy to be challenged before he had scored some points.

"Eventing has to meet expectations financially, and you

need to be aware that covering the cross country will require many cameras at a huge expense, which will inflate the overall budget."

"First you will have to overcome the legal problems with the FEI, they have the rights to all TV coverage as you would know, if you had read the contract. Anyway, Driving will require the same amount, and so that dilutes the cost of TV coverage for Eventing. The entire competition is only slightly over budget for the media coverage" I retorted. I was tired of being the whipping boy for finances.

"Well, Driving could probably use fewer cameras" Interjected Richard Talbot

"For God's sake Richard! Grow some and stop trying to ingratiate yourself" I snapped "you are such a kiss ass" I was starting to lose it and thought it might be time to back peddle. However, at this moment, Daniel chose to remind me that, blasphemous comments would not be tolerated. I so wanted to tell him to "Fuck Off" but managed to contain myself enough to change it to "Belt up Daniel!"

Alistair raised his eyebrows at me, shaking his head.

"That is enough, you are incorrigible. Do not think that I will not replace you...."

"Excellent" I replied, "Once you have appointed the new person, have them contact me for the files." With that I got up and stalked out of the room. Unfortunately, I lost some credibility, I had forgotten my briefcase and purse with my car keys, so I had to turn around, and go back to collect them. They all stared at me as I snatched up the articles, and I ignored Pru's "Oh B., Don't do this, we are such a great team!" and exited a second time.

As I made my way back down to the ground level, using the stairs this time, in order to give myself time to fume, I encountered Xen one of the working students of the centre, who was rushing up the stairs. He was a cute kid of about 17, with spiked hair and wild tattoos. One of which was of a dragon that curled around his neck. He had one of the best set of hands, when riding a horse, that I had seen in a long time. If he stuck to it, he would be a real talent.

"Oh, Ms B, John has asked me to come and get you, he needs you out at the sunken road complex."

"Well, he'd better get Daniel to apprise my replacement of that!" I snapped.

Xen looked totally bewildered and awkward. I started to feel bad for him, so I replied "Oh, don't worry I'll head out there."

Smiling now, he said "Sic hairdo Ms B.!"

I gave him a withering look and said with attempted dignity "We will not discuss my hair." Xen looked suitably rebuked, for all of a minute.

We headed down the rest of the stairs, Xen chattering on about the breed show that was taking place in the coliseum. As we had arrived at my car, I reached in the back, grabbed a rain hat, and jammed it on my head, with a furious look at Xen, which dared him to make any further comment about my "sic" hair.

"You had better get back to the stables" I said, as I climbed into my car. I drove to the golf cart parking, where I picked up my golf cart, and headed out on course.

As I manoeuvred the golf cart through the cross country course, I could not help but feel a frisson of excitement about this new venue, and the competitions that it would hold. This was the reason I had agreed to become involved with this huge endeavour. I forgot for a moment my infuriation with Daniel Brady. I drove through the trails, admiring the countryside. The snow had almost gone, just patches left in shaded areas. The trees showed a tinge of green, in anticipation of the long-awaited spring. We were lucky that construction could be underway, so early in the year.

I approached the area where John Rementer was working with his backhoe. John was the cross country course builder. He was a genius with a chainsaw, and unusually, with an axe. Many of his carvings were works of art. He was dressed, as usual, in plaid shirt, jeans covered with chain saw chaps, battered work boots and a cowboy hat. I smiled as I approached, John was one of my favourite people, he was quiet, introspective, and highly intelligent. I pulled up alongside, and was greeted with his wide smile, I had never seen John looking anything but happy to greet people.

"Oh, B. Am I glad to see you! I have been trying to dig out the sunken road according to the specs that Michael gave me, but this side appears to be the edge of the Canadian shield. It is solid rock, short of dynamiting, there is no way I can make it wide enough."

A sunken road is a series of jumps, whereby the horse jumps down into a space the width of a road and back out again on the other side. Course designers often added a jump before and after the road itself.

"What did Michael want as distance?" I asked.

"Two strides" replied John.

"So, he wanted what 30 or 31 feet? What have we got here?"

"The max I can get is 29 feet but I've got to rivet the sides so it would be down to 28 feet"

"Can we go deeper so the horses will jump in on a steeper angle?" I queried.

"I don't think so, because of the jump back out, it is pretty much max given the one stride to the vertical that Michael wants to follow the sunken road. I really wish I could talk to him."

Michael Frost was the course designer. He was probably the best in the world, and consequently much in demand. Currently he was designing in South Africa, in an area where there was little to no cell phone service.

"I've got to get this done if we are to be anywhere near ready for Daniel Brady's deadline."

I knew that John had no use for the CEO, but unlike most people he would never say so. I thought that this situation was yet another reason for me to throw in the towel, but I felt for John. I looked glumly at the hole in the ground, that John had dug.

"Can we turn it a bit and have the step out, by the maple tree over there?" I suggested

"Michael had said he wanted this on a straight approach, but I think under the circumstances, he would go for a bending line. However, it will mean we'll have to take out the tree, and that was a complete No No according to Daniel".

For once I tended to agree with Daniel. The tree was lovely, and I had a great aversion to killing anything as beautiful as this. "Would we be able to squeeze the step out beside the tree?" I asked.

"This place was where the dirt that was dug out for the parking lot was dumped, I'm not sure how deep it is, and how firmly it has settled, at least it would be easy digging!"

"Well, why don't we give it a try?" I said, "I vote we go ahead, and see if you can get the distance that way, without hitting more rock. See what you can get, and call me when you're done, and we'll brainstorm where to go from there" John nodded resignedly and went back to his machine.

I turned to my golf cart, climbed in, and headed back to the equestrian centre, stopping once to pick up a horseshoe that had been lost on course. I had to bring Jenny up to speed about what had taken place earlier in the meeting. She listened quietly while I paced up and down, explaining what had happened and then venting about Daniel, the Consortium, Richard Talbot, the other discipline chairs and life in general. When I finally finished and flopped into the chair opposite her, she said in a firm voice "B go home, get a good night's sleep, and see how you feel in the morning. Don't resign without giving it enough thought."

"I do love you Jenny" I said. I knew she was right. You could rely on Jenny to give sensible advice, so I dragged myself back to my feet, bade her farewell, and headed home.

I was driving around the back of the Equestrian Centre, when Samantha pulled up alongside me in her little sports car, bent on overtaking. She turned to give me a cheerful wave. My car which looked like a typical old lady's sedan was actually a Subaru WRX. A wolf in sheep's clothing. I floored it and left Samantha smelling my exhaust fumes. I chastised myself for being so childish but had a big grin on my face whilst I did that.

I spent a quiet evening at home with Alfie. I cooked myself a decent meal with fresh ingredients instead of my usual frozen dinner. I enjoyed a glass of wine, and then made it two. I pondered whether I should officially resign. I knew that I was not indispensable, but there were very few people with the experience to manage the three day eventing and everything that went along with it. There were the invitations to all the national federations, liasing with our Federation, dealing with the FEI, working out quarantine facilities for overseas horses. The list went on and on. I had done all this before, and I knew how daunting it would be for an inexperienced person. I really wanted the site to succeed, and, who knew, we might get the nod for the Olympic Games.

My cell phone rang, interrupting my musings. It was Jenny "Sorry to bother you, but I've just had Samantha Wells in here, yet again. She's insisting that she be given another spot in the invitational. I told her that they all had been allocated, but she told me you had said she could have a second horse if somebody dropped out, she says that Fiona is going to withdraw."

When Fiona was suffering following the disappearance of her sister I had returned briefly from England. Hetty enlisted my help to do something about Fee. I had considerable savings, and offered Hetty a loan, which I did not expect to be paid back. We used this to buy Fee a horse, and so Phantom Killer entered our lives. He was officially a warmblood thoroughbred cross, but I was sure that back in his ancestry there was something unusual. He was a most striking colour. White horses, known as grey, in horse circles, are normally born dark and turn lighter with age. Killer was born white and turned to a cream colour as he got older. I thought that a recessive gene had shown up some Cremello in his colouring. These horses are cream in colour, but they have blue eyes. Killer had beautiful dark eyes. He was a unicorn. He took over Fee's heart and gave her a new purpose in life.

"I don't believe that, about Fee, and I did not say that she could ride two if somebody dropped out, I just didn't contradict her, when she suggested it. That girl is totally infuriating."

"I didn't know what to say, I knew that you wouldn't want her to ride two, I told her that I couldn't help her, she would have to talk to you. I'm sorry."

"Not to worry Jenny, I'm sure that you did your best." I sighed inwardly, picturing Jenny's earnest face. She would not have been a match for Sam Wells.

"I did tell her a fib and said that you were away visiting your sister tonight, so that there was no point in trying you at home" I laughed, picturing Jenny telling this lie, Sam must have really pissed her off!

"Jenny you are an angel!"

"I'm not sure God would think so." Said Jenny, giggling. "Will you be in tomorrow?"

"Yes, I have to sort things out with Daniel." I said positively "Any way what are you doing still in the office at this hour?"

"I had so much that I had to catch up on "

"Go home Jenny! I'll see you bright and early tomorrow"

Having hung up I poured myself another glass of wine and sat back down. I could not believe that Fiona would consider withdrawing, unless Sam had done something to precipitate that decision. I made a mental note to go and see Fee, as I called her, the following day.

Jenny was in the office early the following morning and judging by the piles of papers in her out box, she had been there for some time. Jenny was a pretty girl, who did not do much with her looks, she wore horn rimmed glasses that were always falling down her nose, no makeup and fairly shapeless clothes. Her personality made up for all this, and she had a wicked, quiet, sense of humour. She dug in one of the drawers of her desk, and produced a dog biscuit for Alfie, he smiled, wagged his tail and accepted the gift politely. "He really can smile!" said Jenny.

"I know, it was that smile which made me adopt him" I replied.

"Did the night bring you council?" Jenny asked

"Yes, a saner mind this morning, I'm going to try and stick with it. Also, I forgot to tell you yesterday my friend Eleanor is coming over from England, and she can help keep me on the straight and narrow."

"I'm so glad B. I don't think I could work for anybody else."

"Well, I couldn't do it without you" I replied with feeling.

The phone interrupted our mutual admiration society. It was Fiona, "B. I think that I should withdraw from the

Invitational. Samantha says that the judges from my last competition were on the verge of eliminating me from the dressage phase for lameness."

"Fee, how do you think Samantha could possibly know what the judges were thinking?" I replied, "Did they comment on irregularity on your dressage sheet?"

"I forgot to pick up my sheet before I left, I know that was stupid" Fiona mumbled. During the dressage phase of the three day event the rider puts the horse through a series of movements similar to a figure skater or ballroom dancer. The judges mark them on each movement and give them a comment and a score that are written down by their scribe. At the end of the competition the test sheets are given back to the riders. Any sign of lameness would be commented on, and the movement marked down accordingly. If the judge thought that the horse was really lame, they would eliminate the rider from competition.

"Well how does Killer look now?" I asked

"I'm not sure, I keep watching him, and the more I watch, the more I can't decide. I don't want to risk running him if there is something wrong"

"Well why don't I come over and watch you ride him, and we can make a decision together" I suggested.

"Oh, would you B? That would be amazing. I'm at work now, but I can be at the yard in an hour, I've got one private lesson to give." Fiona sounded more positive which was a good sign. She was working at the Riding for the Disabled Stables, which was not far from the yard where she kept Killer.

"I'll see you then" I said hanging up. "That wretched Sam Wells has tried to persuade Fee that Killer is lame, and she should withdraw." I told Jenny, "I'm going over there, I'm sure there is nothing wrong with the horse, but I will have to give Fee a real pep talk, to make sure she doesn't withdraw and keeps her head together."

"I just don't believe that girl, Samantha. She is the epitome of selfishness." Jenny replied indignantly, "Go do your thing B., and put Fiona's mind to rest." The she added,

"Oh, by the way, we got approval for the provincial grant, so that will be an extra $50,000 in the kitty!"

That's amazing Jenny! Pru was telling me that they got a grant as well, the government purse strings must be loosening! Well done, I know you put a lot of work into that application."

I made for the door, nearly being tripped up by Alfie who, in his enthusiasm to leave, had got right under my feet. I opened the door letting Alfie out, and turned to Jenny, "I shouldn't be too long, hold the fort."

I hurried after Alfie who was leaving paw and claw marks on the side of my car. "Down!" I yelled ineffectually, and puffing from exertion, got to the car and opened the door so Alfie could get in. He leapt over the driver's seat and took up his "motoring position" sitting in the middle of the passenger seat eyes straight ahead.

Alfie and I arrived at the stables, and only had a short wait until Fee arrived. "Thanks so much for coming B. I am worried sick about him."

"No worries," I said, "Let's just see how he goes."

She tacked up Killer, but was having problems with the bridle, "B can you help me? I have to switch the bit round, and my fingernails are too short to deal with the billet and keepers."

I went to help, and observed Fee's hands, typical horse person, nails broken short, dirt under the nails no matter how hard they tried to clean them. As I no longer worked in the stables, my nails were clean and occasionally manicured. I had no problem undoing the billets.

"Do you only have the one bridle?" I asked, helping her with the leather.

"Yes, I am trying to save money."

"That's ridiculous," I said, "I will give you the money for a separate dressage bridle."

"You don't need to do that B."

"Don't worry, I will get your grandmother to contribute."

She gave me a smile, finished tacking up, and then hopped on board. As I had anticipated there was absolutely nothing the matter with Killer. I let Fee ride for a good length of time while I watched her. Killer had grown since we bought him as a youngster. He was now really powerful, and I imagined very strong on the cross country. Fee had done a wonderful job of training him. He had gone from a complete Novice to being Advanced, and ready to move up to international competition. Fee herself was tall, but with long legs and a short body which was the perfect shape for a rider, because her centre of gravity was low on the horse, making balance so much easier. I also noted how strong she was. This was just as well, horses on cross country, can pull really hard. If Killer took a hold to a fence, without enough strength, Fee might not be able to stop him.

Fee had no idea that I had put up the money to buy him, and I wanted to keep it that way.

The horse was fine.

"He is perfectly sound. Samantha is trying to get you to withdraw so that she can have a second ride." I informed her.

"Oh, surely not." Said Fee "She's my friend, she wouldn't be that devious"

"Don't you believe it! She would sell out her own Mother if she thought it would benefit her. Now, Fee, forget everything she said, and keep working Killer so he'll be ready and fit enough for the Showcase."

"Thanks B. I'm sorry to have dragged you over here."

"No Problem!" I responded, "Just ride and do your best!"

MYSTERY AT THE SUNKEN ROAD

ALFIE AND I ARRIVED back at Jenny's office half an hour later. I brought Jenny up to speed on Fiona and her horse. Jenny shook her head at the nerve of Samantha.

"She won't be getting any more favours from me!" Jenny muttered, then she said, "Oh by the way John Rementer has been calling he is in a bit of a tizz."

"I can't picture John in "a tizz"!" I said laughing, "He's much too laid back."

"Not this time" Replied Jenny "He..." Jenny was interrupted by the phone. "I bet that is him"

It was John calling for me. "B. I've found something terrible, and I need you to come right away."

"What have you…."

"Just come B! Oh, and don't bring Alfie" he interrupted.

"Why on …" I began but he had hung up.

I shrugged at Jenny, "He wants me to leave Alfie here with you." Jenny nodded her assent, and I headed out to the sunken road, where I assumed John wanted me to go.

As I approached, I could see John pacing up and down. He saw me coming and practically ran to meet me.

"Oh, B thank heavens you are here, I thought I should tell you first." he began "Come and look at what I've dug up" He moved over towards the side of the sunken road jump, near to the maple tree. "I dug alongside the edge of the shield, as we discussed, and then I found that there was a large rock that was not attached to it but wedged in with some hefty branches. It took a lot of work, but I finally got it out, and found that there was a sort of opening behind it, a kind of mini cave, and look what was inside it!" John pointed down into the hole. I walked over and gazed down at a collection of bones.

"What is it, John?" I asked frowning

"I think that it is a skeleton, a human skeleton." He replied

"Surely not, it must be an animal of some kind." I said peering closer at the remains.

"I don't think so B, I think I can see a scull back there, and it looks very human. Have a look."

I climbed down and craned my neck to see better, John was right, it did look like there was a skull in further.

"What should we do?" he asked, not being at all sure, I said,

"Well, I need to get hold of Alistair, and I suppose I had better call the police. Do you think that this is some kind of Chinguacousy Indian burial ground?" I continued staring down at the bones.

"I've never heard of one around here, do you think the bones are very old then?"

"I have no clue, it would take a forensic anthropologist to determine that, I think." John was standing there wringing his hands, I had thought that that was just a saying, but obviously given enough stress people actually do it!

"What is Daniel going to say B? He's on my case all the time to get this finished."

"We can't be concerned about Daniel." I took out my cell phone to make the call to the police. "Damn there's no service here"

"I know, I had to walk to the top of the hill to get any," said John.

"I'll go back to the Centre and call from there, I can fill Jenny in on what's happened, and make sure none of the Working Students ride out this way. I'm afraid you'd better stay here John" he nodded, and I hurried back to my golf cart, thoughts whirling around in my head. How could someone put a body in that hole and close it off with the giant rock that John had removed? It must be an ancient burial, but surely there would be more than one person if that were the case. How had this person died?

I arrived back at the Centre and rushed into Jenny's office.

"You won't believe it. John has unearthed a skeleton" I announced.

"A skeleton! Do you mean human?" she asked.

"Yes, we think so, I'm calling Alistair and the police"

"Alistair is at that job fair trying to hire two new security guards. I can try and get hold of him."

"Yes, do that, please Jenny."

"What and where is..."

"Not now Jenny! I must make this call, then I'll tell you everything I know." My call went through, "Yes can I speak to Inspector Thomas please?" I knew this policeman, I had had dealing with him years ago, over a theft at a riding school where I had worked, he had also been the lead on Felicity's missing person case, I remembered Hetty telling me. He had not shown himself to be brilliant in either case, and I was not sure that he was still working.

"Inspector Thomas." said a vaguely familiar voice.

"Beretta Browning here" I introduced myself and proceeded to tell him the whole story.

"Well," he replied, "I am sure that this will just be a collection of animal bones, however, it is an offense to bury large animals without a permit. I'll send a constable around tomorrow."

I ground my teeth and tried hard not to scream at the man.

"This "animal" has a human skull attached to it! Why don't you come and look for yourself?"

He sighed loudly. "Oh, very well, I have to talk to Daniel Brady about traffic control, for this competition that the equestrian centre is running, so I could spare a minute to put your mind at rest." He said.

I was fantasising about putting my hands fondly around his throat and squeezing harder and harder.

"How kind" I managed to choke out.

"Not at all. We must take our senior citizens' concerns seriously." He replied full of bonhomie. "I will see you in about half an hour."

I replaced the telephone, none to gently. "That went well, I assume?" said Jenny, with a smirk.

"You can be quiet!" I said with dignity "Jenny, we must prevent any of the students going out there, but we don't want anyone to know what is going on at the moment"

"OK, on it!" said Jenny, lifting the phone "I'll start a fire drill! Nobody can leave until they are all accounted for." I shook my head in amazement at my assistant's ingenuity.

I paced anxiously around Jenny's office. Alfie was feeding off my worry. Jenny continued to try to get hold of Alistair. Eventually heavy footsteps outside the office heralded Inspector Thomas's arrival. He entered, the picture of indignation.

"Daniel Brady is not in his office, and I gather has gone to a job fair." He pronounced "You did not inform me of this." I contemplated offering total surprise at this revelation but then thought better of it.

"Yes, I knew, but felt that the find of a skeleton on the cross country course should hold precedence over traffic control!"

"Oh, very well." He said rolling his eyes, "Let's get this over with, and then maybe I can get on with my job."

Jenny noting that I was about to do bodily harm to a police inspector, stepped in rapidly, and said, "Follow me I'll show you to the golf carts." I took a deep breath and tried to calm myself. I scribbled a note to Jenny saying, "GET ALISTAIR NOW!" and followed the two of them out to the golf cart parking. Jenny had wisely chosen Daniel Brady's luxury model. I could hear the tail end of their conversation, the inspector saying, "I'll calm her down, and perhaps you can call a doctor to give her something when we get back, if need be." I chose to ignore this and sat in the golf cart, taking the steering wheel, much to the Inspector's chagrin, and headed out to the sunken road.

I refused to engage in his conversation, that he obviously considered to be soothing and appropriate for a septuagenarian, who had lost her few remaining marbles. I drove up to John, for whom my departure earlier had entailed an endless wait. I introduced him to the Inspector and stood back while John showed him the tiny cave and it's contents. I was pleased to note that the inspector's visage changed considerably once he had seen what was below his feet. He stepped down into the hollow and produced a flashlight. He took his time looking, and then said, "It appears human."

"Really," I said sarcastically "We would never have known. We thought we were in big trouble, for burying a large animal without a permit!"

"All right Mrs Browning..."

"That's Ms"

"Ms Browning then, I apologise for those remarks, I just did not think that these bones would be human."

"Well, now that you do know that they are, what are you going to do?" I enquired.

"I will have to get them removed and checked by our medical examiner; he will likely bring in a forensic anthropologist to determine how old they are."

"Once they are removed, can we carry on with the course construction?" asked John.

"No, the area will be cordoned off, until we know more. In fact, I will want to cordon off an area from the parking lot all the way out to here to prevent "Lookie Loos" from accessing the area."

Just then I looked up to see the welcome sight of Alistair bumping up the trail at high speed in his golf cart.

"Here comes our head of security," I said "Alistair McKinnon, perhaps you know him, he used to be on the police force." Inspector Thomas looked up and broke into a wide smile.

"Why Alistair, I had no idea you were working here."

"For my sins, Bill. Well, I see we have quite a dilemma?"

"Indeed, come and take a look."

I suggested that John and I leave them to it. They both nodded vaguely, deep in conversation. John and I made our departure, in Daniel's golf cart. When we reached the Centre, we went to Jenny's office and wondered what we should do now. We needed advice from Alistair. Jenny told us that when she had been able to contact him, he had managed to leave Daniel at the job fair, telling him that "There was a small matter he had to attend to back at the centre"!

"He's going to go ape shit when he hears about this." said John miserably. I nodded,

"Well, a body is not our fault, he's just going to have to deal with it." I said pragmatically.

A series of police cars pulled into the parking lot, followed by a large black van, presumably to be used for transporting the bones. John sighed and got up.

"I'll show them where to go, I guess it doesn't matter that we have vehicles driving on the cross country course now."

"No, I don't suppose so, John." I said, "Can you ask Alistair, when he has finished, to come and talk to us?"

John headed out. I looked over at Jenny, who was on her computer.

"I'm looking up Canadian Indian burial rituals. How old are the bones B?" I told her that I didn't have a clue, we would just have to wait for the results of the medical examination.

"Whereabouts were they?"

"Out by the tree near the sunken road complex" I replied

"You mean that big maple? The one that Daniel goes on about, all the time?" went on Jenny

"Does he?" I asked.

"Yes, he didn't want the course to go anywhere near it, but Michael insisted that it would be the ideal place for the sunken road and that loop of the course. Daniel said it was a rare species of maple, and was susceptible to blight from the regular maples, and he did not want the spores of the blight being carried out there by people."

"That's strange," I said, "he allowed the soil from the car park to be dumped there."

Jenny shrugged, and we were silent for a few minutes and then Jenny spoke the words I did not want to hear.

"Do you think it could be Felicity?" I shook my head refusing to go there.

The door burst open, and an infuriated Daniel entered and practically screamed at me. Alfie lowered his ears and let out a low growl. I scratched his head and shushed him.

"What the hell is going on? There was apparently an unscheduled fire drill, and vehicles are driving all over the cross country course! Alistair left me at the job fair." I felt like screaming back at him, but thought better of it, so I tried to speak in a calming voice. "Daniel, we have a situation out on the course, John has dug up what appears to be a human skeleton. I have called the police, and Alistair is now out at the sunken road with the Inspector"

Daniel's face, that had been bright red with fury, slowly drained of all colour, his mouth opened and closed like a fish. "A skeleton, by the sunken road, by the maple tree?" he managed to get out.

"Yes." I said briskly. He continued to gape at me, and then said, "Why was he digging there?"

"Because I told him to." I snapped, "We were unable to get the width for the sunken road in the designated area, so we had to turn it and have the jump out, come by the maple tree."

"But I had specifically forbidden it!" Daniel was starting to get bright red in the face again, and was having trouble breathing, so fearing he might suffer a coronary, I quickly replied,

"No, you had forbidden cutting down the tree, we did nothing to harm it and it was fortunate that John dug there, or nobody would ever have found the skeleton."

"I don't consider that to be a good thing!" he said, and with that he spun on his heel and left the office. I was pleased that I had returned his golf cart to it's parking space, I did not want another round with him if he had found it missing.

Jenny got up and put the kettle on for a cup of coffee, apologising for the fact that it was only instant. "Any port in a storm!" I replied, accepting my cup. We sipped in silence, both jumping when the phone rang. It was Alistair calling, Jenny put the call on speaker phone.

"We're going to be here for a long time, the medical examiner is sick, and he's being so slow." He said "I would have phoned before, but I couldn't get a signal, I had to climb to the top of the hill, but at least it got me away from Daniel, he is totally stressed, he thinks I am phoning to get some flood lights out here and a heater. I think that you should both go home. There's nothing for you to do, and I'll call you at home, B, when we've finished."

We hung up the call, gathered up our things. Alfie couldn't

wait to leave, and was standing impatiently at the door, while we said our goodbyes. I promised to call Jenny when I heard from Alistair. Alfie and I drove home, he to do a quick inspection of the back yard, before collapsing on the couch, and me to pour myself a welcome glass of wine, before joining Alfie. My mind would not let me relax, a few minutes passed before I realised that I had picked up his bone in lieu of a piece of cheese and was on the point of chewing it. I apologised, gave it to him, Alfie took it back graciously.

Alistair called me later that night. The bones had been removed, and a crime scene unit had come and collected soil from around the bones. Everything was being taken to the medical examiner's building. We would not know anything for a week or more.

"First, they have to ascertain how old the bones are, and that will take a while, once that is done, if they are recent, then the police will compare dental records with missing people, and if necessary, DNA. The results from that may take weeks." Said Alistair, "I know you are stressing about whether or not it is Felicity, but we don't even know if the bones are male or female."

"This is going to get out, and Hetty and Fee are going to be beside themselves." I replied.

"You're right B. Let's keep it from them for as long as possible, but once they find out they are going to have to wait the same as all of us." I realised how tired Alistair sounded, so I told him to go home and get some rest.

I called Jenny, "I'll be in first thing in the morning, Jenny, we'll have lots to do working out where we go from here. I don't know whether we can run the showcase. If we do, we'll obviously have to reroute the cross country course, and I have to pick Eleanor up at the airport in the evening. What a time for her to arrive! Oh well sleep tight, Jenny."

"As if..." replied Jenny.

Alfie, Jenny and I spent the morning working in the office, I called Inspector Thomas to enquire whether we could go ahead with the showcase event. He told me that it was too early to tell how long the whole area would have to remain cordoned off but thought that it would just be the immediate area where the bones were found that would remain out of bounds, by the time the showcase was to take place.

John come to the office, so we could work out an alternate route for the cross country. We went on Google Maps, and drew up the property on the satellite pictures, and working with that, we put in the original design. We then came up with two alternate routes, bypassing the sunken road complex and the loop out to it. We discussed what jumps could be used to replace the ones that would be removed. We agreed that we could use some of the portables that John had already built, but that we would need at least five more. I promised John that I would measure the proposed routes with the wheel, to make sure that we were coming up with the correct distance, to meet the FEI rules.

I called up Richard Talbot, to tell him what had happened, and that he would have to lose part of his driving course while the investigation was going on. Richard can be very long winded, and it took me a while to answer all his questions, and to finally get him to hang up. Jenny was having a great deal of amusement at my expense, while the conversation was going on. I glared at her, and after I had hung up, I said, "I should have made you do that!"

Daniel appeared at the office door. Alfie's hackles went up on his back, and he emitted a low growl. Daniel looked at him and muttered something about "Dogs should not be allowed in the office." I chose to ignore this, as it had been one of my stipulations, that if I took the job Alfie would accompany me.

Daniel then berated us for not having called him, as soon as John had found the bones. He informed us that he would be taking charge of everything from now on. I couldn't resist saying "But we thought you always were in charge." He stalked out of the office, obviously on his way to annoy somebody else, I thought.

Alfie and I spent the afternoon wheeling the two different loops that John and I had worked out. The one was a better fit for the rules, and I thought the terrain would lend itself well to the obstacles that we had discussed. I found another couple of horseshoes to add to my collection. I returned to the office and got Jenny to draw up a new map showing the rerouted course, and to type a letter to Michael, explaining briefly that we had to change the course due to matters out of our control, and would he be agreeable to use what we proposed. I did not want to mention exactly what had happened until the police gave us permission. This done we closed up the office, and I headed to the airport.

Eleanor's flight had been delayed. Annoyed that I hadn't bothered to check before heading down to Pearson International, I went in search of somewhere to sit. I found a little coffee place, and ordered my ordinary coffee, and proceeded to entertain myself by people watching. I was trying to guess from where people were landing by the clothes that they were wearing. The first group had to be from the Caribbean, wearing floral shirts, shorts and flip flops. They were going to get a shock, I thought, when they went outside, the temperature was hovering at the freezing mark. The next group wore business suits and had very little luggage. I thought they must be returning from somewhere in the States, where they would have been working, perhaps New York. The next few were indistinguishable from one another, maybe Europe but no clue as to the exact country.

Boring of this pastime I called Jessica McIntyre, I had promised to come and watch her ride Alistair's horse last week, and I had not yet confirmed a time. There was no answer at her landline, secretly pleased that she was out enjoying herself, I hung up and called Alistair. He answered wearily, the day had not gone well for him. The two security guards, that he currently had working for him, were being run ragged trying to keep people away from the cordoned off area as well as their usual duties and were threatening to quit. The two extra guards, that he and Daniel had hired from the job fair, would not start until the following month, in time for the showcase, if it ran. I listened sympathetically to this litany of problems and suggested that Xen and a couple of friends might be able to help out with security. Alistair was not sure whether people would take them seriously but agreed that it might be a stop gap measure. I told him that I had tried to get hold of Jessica, to set up a time to watch her ride, but that there was no reply. Alistair said he would get hold of her tomorrow and get back to me with a time. We then hung up, and I checked to see whether Eleanor's flight had landed. The screen said that it had, and after a while, the first passengers started to trickle through. I could tell they were English, Marks and Spencer's clothes were easy to spot, and the English just had a look, a bit pasty faced I thought, with a smile, having lived over there with the endless rain. Soon enough Eleanor appeared. She was quite short, slim, her greying hair cut short, and she was wearing her usual blazer and khaki pants. She rolled her suitcase efficiently down the slope to where I was waiting.

We greeted one another enthusiastically and headed straight for the car. I paid the parking at the machine on the way out, and we headed north out of the airport towards home. During the trip Eleanor brought me up to speed with all the happenings in England, including the fact that Thomas

Harding, my former squire about town, was now engaged to somebody else!

Arriving at my house I said "Welcome to Holmeshurst Cottage! My humble abode."

DETECTIVE CLUB

I LEFT ELEANOR AT home to sleep off her jet lag and took Alfie over to the equestrian centre. Jenny and I caught up on some paperwork, I made a few phone calls to the officials who had been hired for the Showcase, to give them a heads up that we might have to postpone, I was vague about the reason for this, and left them feeling a little puzzled. When Jenny and I had completed our tasks Alfie and I headed back to pick up Eleanor. We had a bite of lunch, and then the three of us headed back to the Centre. Alfie was quite put out by having to relinquish his front seat and kept giving Eleanor accusing looks.

"Perhaps I should sit in the back?" she laughed

"Oh, he'll get over it." I replied, "Besides we are almost there." I pulled in through the big gates and Eleanor let out a big "Wow!"

"Yes," I said, "It's quite something isn't it?" We drove on past the fountain with the bronze statue of a rearing horse, and up to the main building. I noted that a student had put polo wraps on the statue's legs overnight.

I spent the afternoon showing her round, introducing her to everybody, and later we took Alfie for a walk around the course, avoiding the cordoned off area. Eleanor was impressed by it all and said that she understood why I had decided to come out of retirement to work at the Centre.

"It's only short term to get it up and running," I explained "And only if I can put up with Daniel!" I had told her about my dislike for the man, and she had already witnessed firsthand his rudeness, when I introduced Eleanor to him. He had shaken her hand, and then said to me "I trust having your friend here will not take you away from your duties."

"On the contrary Eleanor will be a big help." I retorted, and he left with no further acknowledgement.

"What an odious little twerp!" exclaimed Eleanor.

"Yes, he's a real charmer!" I replied.

We popped back into the office to see if Jenny had anything she needed me to do. Alistair had called to say he hadn't been able to get hold of Jessica, but he would go to her apartment when he went to see his horse. Other than that, all was quiet. I invited Jenny to come to dinner the next Saturday and told her I would get the "Gang" together to meet Eleanor. Jenny thought it was a splendid idea and asked what she could bring.

"Don't worry about that, I shall order in from the local restaurant!" I said.

"OK. I'll bring some wine." replied Jenny. We made a plan for the next day, and then we packed up our things, locked the office, and headed out to the car park.

"Oh no!" I said as I walked over to the car, standing there was Samantha Wells.

"What's going on here?" she demanded, "What's with all the caution tape up on the course, there's all sorts of talk in town?"

"That is none of your business Samantha, and what were you doing on the course anyway?"

"Oh B, don't be so grumpy! I was just taking a quick look at how the course was coming."

"Do that again, and you will be disqualified from the

Showcase." Seeing that I was really annoyed she made a token effort at apologising and then went on "I had not heard back from you about whether I can ride the two horses in the Showcase, I thought I would pop around, and speak to you in person."

"The answer is no, Samantha, and how dare you tell Fiona that her horse was lame." I practically screamed at the girl. She was silent for a bit, and then said.

"You must have had a bad day B, I'll talk to you another time when you are in a better mood, actually I'm taking Fee out for dinner to apologise for the misunderstanding." She turned and got in her car and drove off. Eleanor gazed after her, and then turned to me and said,

"It's like, home from home! Wendover students have nothing on her, what a sense of entitlement! Are you sure you want to cope with this stuff all over again?"

"Fortunately, she is a one off. I'm thinking of banning her from the whole competition, but her owner is one of our board of directors. I'm surprised Fee is going to dinner with her."

I noticed that Alfie was scratching at the car door, so we hastened over to the car, I opened the door, and Alfie jumped straight into the passenger seat giving Eleanor a triumphant look. She laughed and climbed in the back. "You win this time Alfie!" she said.

Hetty, Alistair, Iris, Jenny, Eleanor and myself gathered at Holmeshurst Cottage for the dinner that I had ordered in. Alistair arrived first, he had been to see his horse, and Jessica was back at the barn. She had been under the weather with a flu bug, but was better now, and would be back to riding Alistair's horse. I told Alistair that I would get hold of her and go and see the two of them working.

My guests had brought wine, and we poured liberally while we ate. Eleanor and Alistair got on very well together. The fact that both had been on the police force, and then acting as heads of security, albeit on different continents, meant that they had a lot in common. Hetty, Iris and Jenny were old friends, so conversation flowed pleasantly along through the evening. Hetty and Iris knew nothing about the skeleton, the rest of us were trying to avoid making reference to it.

Iris complemented me on my cooking, whereupon all the rest of them broke out laughing, Iris looked bewildered until Hetty explained.

"B doesn't cook food! She just opens the packages!!"

"I ordered in from the local restaurant that specialises in home cooked meals." I confessed to Iris.

"Well, you could have got away with it if it weren't for this lot." she said looking around the table at the laughing faces.

The party broke up at around midnight, and Eleanor and I cleared up after everyone had gone. I let Alfie out for a pee, He trotted back to the barn and started barking, I had to call him back in and then we all turned in to bed.

I was just getting out of bed when the phone rang, "Is it Felicity? Why didn't you tell me?" Hetty cried.

I was taken entirely by surprise, "Is what?..."

"You know full well what, the skeleton" Hetty cut in.

"Oh." I said,

"Yes Oh! When did you plan to tell me?"

"We didn't want to worry you until we knew more."

"Why not? I needed to know." Hetty was now sobbing, and I tried to calm her down. "We do not know how old the bones are, they could be those of a native American buried there for centuries, and I did not want you worrying for nothing. I thought that I would wait, until we got news from the medical examiner."

"Well, you must know by now, it is all over the local

paper!" Hetty announced "I was with you all last night, and nobody said a thing and now this…"

Eleanor had arrived downstairs, and I mouthed for her to get the local paper from out by the road, she frowned at me, not understanding, I pantomimed paper, and then nodding, she hurried to comply.

"Hetty," I said, "Are you OK to drive?"

"What, of course." She snuffled.

"Well, get in your car come over to my place, and I'll tell you everything I know. You don't want to be alone, at this time." Hetty mumbled agreement to this.

Eleanor came back in accompanied by Alistair, who had just arrived, both carrying copies of the local paper. They placed one down on the coffee table, and the front page headline read "Skeleton found on Equestrian Centre grounds" It went on to say that the skeleton had been unearthed on the cross country course, and had been sent to the medical examiner's office, where it was determined that the bones were between eight and fifteen years old, and that of a female.

"How did they find out?" I asked, and then answered myself, by saying "I suppose it was bound to get out, but where did they get a report from the Medical Examiner?"

"Heads will roll for that. Bill will be livid." Said Alistair sighing "and I'm not looking forward to the conversation with an upset Daniel!"

"Who is Bill?" enquired Eleanor

"That would be the pompous Inspector Thomas" I replied.

"He's not that bad," rejoined Alistair, "he's actually a pretty good detective, albeit a plodder." I harrumphed in reply.

"Hetty is on her way over," I said, "She thinks that the remains are Felicity."

"We can't assume anything, can we Alistair?" Eleanor said,

"They will have to get dental records first, and if there is no match then DNA."

"Yes, and they will be trying to determine manner of death."

"I'm going to give Bill a call and see what he knows." Alistair took out his phone and went through to the next room.

Eleanor and I made a big pot of coffee and put out some bagels and muffins on the kitchen table. The phone rang again, it was Iris who had just seen the local paper. She was worrying that the remains might prove to be those of Rebecca. I told her she should come on round and join the rest of us. She said that Maisie had stayed the night with her. Brian was away in the States for a couple of weeks. Maisie was having a play date with a friend of hers so Iris would come as soon as Maisie had been picked up.

I then called Jenny at the office, she answered, very flustered, "Oh B, its going crazy here with phone calls about the article in the paper, what should I tell them?"

"Tell them, no comment, at the moment, but that we will release a statement later today. I have Hetty and Iris coming round, they're in a terrible state. Alistair is here. We'll be in later this morning"

"Thanks B, do you know I bet it was that bloody girl Samantha who leaked it to the press!"

"That thought had crossed my mind, but I don't know how they got the information from the medical examiner's office before we did." We said our goodbyes, and I went back into the kitchen, Alistair had returned.

"Bill is absolutely furious, he has been in touch with the paper, and torn a strip off them. The Medical examiner's office claims they have no idea how the information was leaked, but it is indeed true. I have to go over to the Centre and meet with Daniel now. Can you see if Fee can go and ride my horse for me? Jessica has had a bit of a relapse." I nodded in reply.

Iris pulled up and she had Hetty in her car. Hetty had not felt up to driving over after all, and so had called Iris. This was a sensible plan I thought, I could see that Hetty was shaking. Eleanor sat them both down, gave them coffee, and offered them some breakfast. Hetty shook her head, but Iris tucked in.

I told them what had happened, from the finding of the skeleton, up until the present. I explained that the police did not want it made public knowledge, and why we had tried to keep it under wraps, until we knew whether the bones were historic or not. I think they both understood but were a little hurt that I hadn't confided in them. I was feeling pretty miserable about having kept them in the dark, when Eleanor spoke up.

"You should be grateful that you have not been worrying about your loved ones, all last week. B was only thinking of you. She has been stressing enough for the two of you!" I smiled gratefully at her, and the other two nodded slowly in agreement. I asked them whether the police had Felicity and Rebeccas' dental records. They both nodded miserably.

"Then there is nothing else that you can do, go home, and I promise I will call you the minute I hear anything. Alistair will be on top of it."

When they left, I thanked Eleanor for her help. I called Fee and asked her if she would go and ride Alistair's horse, she said of course she would. I then asked her how the dinner had gone with Samantha.

"It was fine," she said, "Unfortunately Samantha seemed to get food poisoning, and was taken really ill, I had to drive her to the Emergency." After I had hung up, I realised that Fee had sounded quite gleeful about Samantha's misfortune. I suffered a moment of concern that maybe Fee had had something to do with the food poisoning. I shrugged to myself and secretly thought that Samantha probably deserved it! I dismissed it from my mind and called to Eleanor that we had better go.

We went out to the car, Alfie and Eleanor, vying for the front seat. Alfie won, for a second time, and Eleanor sat in the back. When we got to the centre, I went to my office to relieve Jenny. I gave Eleanor a radio, so she could contact Alistair, and she hurried off to help him, in any way she could. I smiled at her alacrity in following my suggestion, she had definitely taken a shine to him.

I sat with Jenny, and between us we drafted a statement, and then we fielded phone calls and tried to do a little work in between. We were very happy that Alistair had kept Daniel away from us, and by the end of the day we were quite happy with what we had achieved. I sent Jenny home, and radioed Eleanor to find out where she was. She radioed back, that she and Alistair were on their way back, and that she had invited Alistair for supper! Fortunately, there were enough leftovers from the dinner party, so I did not panic about feeding the three of us.

Eleanor opted for travelling with Alistair, so Alfie was very pleased with himself, having the front seat, and having got rid of Eleanor. I reprimanded him, "Do not gloat, it is not a nice trait!" He turned and smiled at me.

I opened a bottle of wine, one cannot debate important matters without a vinous libation! With dinner on the table, we sat down, and Alistair opened the conversation with "Bill says the medical examiner has not compared the dental records. He was feeling dreadful, and now he's off sick, his associate called Bill to tell him that, and says that he can't do any more until his boss is back at work"

I groaned, "I don't believe it! Hetty and Iris can't wait any longer for news."

"I don't think Iris should be worried, if Rebecca were to be found dead, it would be at the gravel pit with her lawyer. If it was murder, why leave the bodies in two different places? It doesn't make sense. Better to leave them together, so people would think it was an accident."

"You're right Eleanor, so that just leaves Felicity and the girl from my division who are missing locally. I will follow up on that cold case and see whether it ever got resolved." said Alistair.

"But, what about Paloma?" I asked "She went missing when I was in England. Did she go missing up here or down in LA? She certainly has a connection up here, considering she was going out with Adam."

"I'm sure it was in LA. There was a huge fuss in the press up here, but I'm quite sure Bill would have mentioned it if he had been involved."

"Hetty would know, she's in contact with Adam all the time." I added.

"Well, you two should find out, in the meantime I think we need to consider who would know about the mini cave, because it would take a lot of local knowledge to think of dumping a body there." Eleanor interjected. "Who owns the land now, and who owned it before?"

"The consortium owns it now." I said.

"And who are they? Do you know who makes up the consortium? asked Eleanor. I thought for a bit.

"Well, I only know the board of directors. Do you know Alistair?" Alistair shook his head, so Eleanor continued. "We need to go to the town offices and look up who they are."

"But I think they are all businessmen, they may own the land, but I don't think they've ever walked round it." I said.

"Well, we don't know that for sure, so we'll make a list of the board members, and the names we get from the records. Who did they buy it from?"

"I know that." said Alistair "It was an estate sale. The elderly couple who had farmed the land died intestate, there were no relatives, so it passed to the province who auctioned it off. I'm sure many people must have walked over the land, before the auction."

"Damn!" said Eleanor "that widens the field." I had grave misgivings about getting involved. "Shouldn't we leave this for the police?" Alistair laughed.

"You weren't very complimentary about Inspector Thomas. Do you think he has suddenly become super sleuth?"

"No, but even you said he was a pretty good detective, and isn't he going to be pissed if we start looking into it?"

"Actually, I don't think he'll mind, he's extremely understaffed, and if we keep him up to date on everything we do, I think he might be quite happy to have Eleanor and me follow up on some things, after all, we were both police officers." I nodded.

Alfie and I drove Eleanor to the township offices. I agreed to meet her at lunchtime, when she thought she would be done. I smiled as she marched purposefully through the double doors.

I drove to the office; Jenny too thought it best left to the police. "Your friend, Eleanor, is a very determined lady!"

"She and Alistair get on very well, he's quiet and unassuming and she is like a fire cracker, but they are both smart and intelligent, two different things."

"Well, I just hope that it isn't anybody we know. Does it have to be a murder?"

"I hardly think somebody is going to bury themselves in that mini cave, and then pull a filthy great rock over the entrance!" I snorted.

"It could have been an accident, and then somebody panicked and hid the body?"

Jenny and I spent the morning working on sponsorship packages. Depending on the amount of money given by a sponsor, they would receive differing numbers of tickets, parking passes, VIP passes and invitations to gala dinners. This was an onerous task as we had to keep double checking what we had promised to whom. I then had to head back to the township offices to pick up Eleanor. I left Jenny ordering banners and planning the layout of the program.

Eleanor was sitting outside on a bench waiting for us. She climbed in the back. I enquired as to whether it had been a constructive morning.

"I have a list of people," she said, "but there are a lot of companies that are included in the ownership, and they are shell companies for other companies. I will have to contact Company House to find out who actually owns the companies. I'll show you the list of the people that I have found."

We drove over to the cafe and Iris greeted us enthusiastically, calling out to Maisie to come and say hello. She appeared from behind the counter with a scowl on her face.

"What's up Maisie Maggot?" I enquired

"You lied to me Bumble Bee, we are studying chrysalis and maggots in biology. Maggots do NOT turn into butterflies, they turn into flies."

"Flies, butterflies, what does it matter?"

"Because, I don't want to be a maggot, and turn into a fly!"

"Oh, but you are such a perfect Maggot! Say hello to my friend Eleanor."

"Hello Eleanor, does she lie to you to?" Eleanor burst out laughing.

"All the time. Maisie!!"

Iris and Maisie sat down with us, and we ate lunch. Maisie kept us entertained with nonstop chatter about school, her friends, Susan and Molly and her favourite pony, Pop Tart, who she rode at school. Iris looked on fondly, and I could see that

Eleanor was enchanted by the child. When lunch was done, I said we had to go, but Maisie begged us to come back.

"Dad's away, so I have a whole week with Iris, BLISS! So please come and see me again."

"Have you forgiven me then?" I enquired, whereupon she threw her arms around my neck, and gave me a big hug.

"Yes, I forgive you, but I shall think up a new name for you that will be just as icky as Maisie Maggot!"

"OK, you're on." I said, "bye for now"

We left the cafe, and Iris followed us out we told her that there would be no more answers any time soon. Eleanor told Iris her theory about why it couldn't be Rebecca, and Iris brightened up.

We headed back to the Centre.

Alistair took a while to get back, as he had been busy with Daniel and the other security guards. When he arrived, he told us that he had checked with his old division, and the girl that went missing when he was working there had been found. He had let Bill know about this, but Bill already knew. He had contacted all the local precincts to check for other missing girls, but there were none other than the one that Alistair knew about, who had now been accounted for.

The four of us sat around the large desk that Jenny and I shared. It was an antique, but was not in the best of shape, it was called a partner's desk because it was wide enough that two people could work from either side. It worked well for Jenny and me, as we spent much of our time working together.

"The list of members of the consortium is quite long," Began Eleanor, "We have Major Jennings, Roderick Smallwood, Angela Hall, Mary Parks and Roger and Helen Brandon." At this point I interrupted,

"Those are the board of directors and Roger Brandon is

Samantha's owner and Helen is his wife." Alistair nodded in agreement.

"Next we have two shell companies, Q.D.Enterprises and Holy Port Entertainment, I will have to try to find out what companies come under their auspices, and who are the owners and directors of those companies. I have written off to Company House to find out. And finally, we have the man himself, Daniel Brady!"

"So, he's a member of the consortium, that explains how he got the job!" I exclaimed, "Well apart from him, I can't see any of the others committing murder, they are all well into their sixties, and dragging a body, and hiding it in that little space, and pulling the rock over to cover the entrance would be beyond their capabilities! Besides I don't think they have ever walked over the grounds."

"B's right" said Alistair, "these don't seem like likely candidates for murderers, and I am sure that Daniel isn't, we'll have to wait to see who is on the list, when the names come back from Company House."

Jenny spoke up, "Daniel behaved very strangely when he found out that John had dug up the skeleton by the maple tree, didn't he B?"

"You're right Jenny. He seemed totally panicked, and then got furious."

"I'm sure he had a reason for this" said Alistair, causing us to look at him, Jenny went on,

"He had been very odd all along about that tree, he didn't want the course to go anywhere near it, and he told me some strange story about it being a rare species of maple, and so was subject to getting a blight from regular maples."

"He must have walked the grounds, if he knew about the tree." said Eleanor.

"Oh, he knows it like the back of his hand." I replied, "We

have walked it together many times, with Michael Frost and John Rementer."

"So, I suppose we have one person we can put on the suspect list." Eleanor said, "But until we know who the victim is, we have no motive."

Alistair went out in the hall to answer his phone. Looking out the window, I saw that it had started to rain.

Alistair returned a few minutes later, looking perplexed. "That was Bill, he has just got a call from the medical examiner's assistant. He says that the forensic anthropologist that they had first called in, and who was unavailable, has turned up at the office and has examined the bones, he concurs that the bones are not ancient, and on close examination of the damaged side of the skull, he is sure that he can see a bullet hole. This would most likely be cause of death."

"That blows my theory, about Rebecca not being the victim, if she was shot, whoever did it, could not leave the body to be found in the quarry, because the police would know that it wasn't a car accident."

"You're right Eleanor." Alistair went on, "Bill is sending the crime scene examiners back out to look further for the bullet, if they can find it, it will be a big help in the case, I will have to go now and tell Daniel about this"

"But, he's a suspect!" cried Jenny.

"No, He's a potential suspect in your minds, not those of the police. He is our boss, and he must be told that there will be more people on the centre's land. We must believe he is innocent, until proven guilty! Also, he is leaving for a ten day holiday, before the Showcase competitions." Alistair said reasonably. I rather agreed with Jenny, but realised Alistair was right, we would have to inform the horrid man!

"I wonder where he is going?" I pondered "Iris said Brian was away, do you think Daniel is going to join him, they are cousins, you know?" Nobody answered, and so my surmise remained in the air.

Outside, the clouds had cleared. Alfie was annoyed, because he hadn't had his usual walk, so Eleanor and I strolled out onto the course, while he cavorted round in circles searching for any smells, that would herald a rabbit. He got on the scent of a squirrel which ran straight up the closest tree and proceeded to shout abuse at him. Eleanor and I laughed at his antics, as he kept leaping up the trunk of the tree to try and get a toe hold that would hoist him up to where the squirrel sat.

"Oh look" said Eleanor "there's your house over there"

"Yes, it backs onto the centre's land, did you not realise that?" I said surprised.

"No. We drive round the block to get here, and I hadn't made the connection." Said Eleanor "If you like, I'll walk Alfie over to the house, and you can take the car back round." I agreed to this plan, and walked back to the parking lot, and got my Subaru, while Eleanor and Alfie enjoyed the long hike back to the house. I arrived first, and unlocked the front door of the house, and went inside. I put coffee on the go and checked the messages on my answering machine. Surprised at the length of time it was taking Eleanor, I went back outside to find her coming out of my barn, waving at me.

CANINE RESCUE

"Come and see what Alfie has found in here!" She said.

I hurried out the back thinking "Not another skeleton please." I reached the barn door where Alfie was standing wagging his tail and smiling. I peered into the gloom of the barn and heard a low growl. In the corner was a very bedraggled looking dog with tiny puppies at her side.

"She's not in good shape, and I think at least a couple of the puppies are dead," Said Eleanor "she looks half starved." I took a deep breath, this was an extra problem, that I did not need. I went in and surveyed the situation, I thought for a moment, and then said. "We'd better get her something to eat and drink. Then we'd better see if we can get close enough to remove the dead puppies and check her over for injuries."

"Right." said Eleanor leaving the barn, and marching back to the house. "What do you think we should feed her?"

"Something bland, perhaps some rice mixed with a little canned dog food. Not too much, or her stomach will reject it. I wonder whether milk is a good idea, or would it be better to just offer her water?"

"I'll put some rice on to cook." said Eleanor and started bustling around in the kitchen. I found a couple of spare bowls of Alfie's, and soon we had a small quantity of food ready for the dog. I decided water would be best, and we carried our offerings out to the barn. The dog gave us a warning growl but when I offered her the water she drank deeply, I had to stop her, worried that her gut would twist. Eleanor then placed the rice mixture down in front of her. She sniffed at it and then slowly tried to get to her feet. She let out a whimper, and we saw that she had a horrible injury on her side, and one leg looked as if it was broken.

"Oh, my God!" I exclaimed "she must have been hit by a car. I will have to try and find a vet who will come out here."

"You go. I'll stay here with her." said Eleanor. I hurried back to the house and looked up the number of the vet who did most of the work at the equestrian centre. He was not there, but he's secretary gave me the number of a new vet who was working with small animals. I called there and spoke to the receptionist. She asked me if I could bring the dog into the clinic, but when I explained the situation, she agreed that it would be better for the vet to come out. I gave directions to my house. The vet would be out within the hour.

Eleanor had managed to get the dog to eat a little of the food we had prepared and was now stroking her. She had also removed three dead puppies and placed them to one side, the remaining three puppies looked healthy and were vying with one another for a nipple. I looked at the dog critically, she was unusual, she was white with a black patch over one eye and a roman nose and little triangular eyes.

We waited nervously for the vet to arrive; I kept walking back up to the house to see if we had missed her arrival. After what seemed like a lot longer than an hour, a young woman drove up. She did not look old enough to have graduated from vet school. She introduced herself as Amelia Weston, and then she walked briskly down the path to the barn, carrying a medical bag and with a stethoscope hung round her neck. She entered the barn and exclaimed "Why she's an English bull terrier! They are quite rare. I wonder how she ended up in this state?"

She knelt down beside the group, ignoring the warning growl, and quietly murmured to the dog who gradually responded to her. She felt the injured leg and said that she thought it was broken. She returned to her car and came back with a portable Xray machine and a computer and lead aprons which she insisted we wear. Eleanor and I turned out to be poor veterinary technicians, but finally the vet was satisfied with the Xrays, that she had taken. "It's a clean break, I don't think it needs pinning. I'll splint it and hopefully it will heal well by itself" She then turned her attention to the horrendous injury on the dog's side, "This will all need thoroughly debriding, and stitching, I think a couple of ribs are broken but my main concern is internal injuries. She will need to be on intravenous fluids, so I think I should give her some pain meds, tranquillise her, and take her and the puppies back to the clinic." Eleanor and I rapidly agreed to this plan, and Amelia efficiently administered the drugs. I found an old table top at the back of the barn and between us we lifted the dog onto our makeshift gurney and carried her to the car. She was unbelievably heavy, even in her emaciated state. The puppies were squeaking wildly at being moved, and Alfie was getting quite worried by this, and was running round and round in circles. Eventually, we had all of the patients safely stowed in the back of Amelia's car. She promised to call later when she had a better idea of the extent of the dog's injury, she then got in her car and drove away.

Eleanor and I stared at one another, and then Eleanor said "She's a suspect! Everybody is a suspect!"

"Don't be ridiculous!" I snorted.

We dug a hole and then placed the dead puppies in a box and lowered them into the hole. We filled it in, and turned sadly, to head to the house. "I doubt she could rear them all in her state." I muttered. "Do you think she'll survive, Eleanor?" Eleanor shook her head "The vet did say they are unbelievably tough dogs, they were bred for bear and bull bating."

Eleanor and I planned a quiet evening in, after the excitement of finding the dog. Eleanor went up to take a bath, all English people, it seemed, preferred baths over showers. I took the opportunity to phone Hetty. She was fascinated to hear that Daniel was one of the members of the consortium, and agreed with me, that that was how he had got the job as CEO. I then told her about the latest news from the medical examiner. She went very quiet then, and I was kicking myself for telling her, but I then realised that she needed to know. I had kept her in the dark before, and then she had been even more upset. I hastened to change the subject and told her all about the dog in the barn.

"The vet says she's an English Bull Terrier." I concluded.

"Really!" said Hetty, "My father had one when I was a kid, he was called Montmorency, he was a wonderful dog. I just loved him. Oh, I hope she makes it, I'd love to see her."

After I hung up with Hetty the phone rang again, I frowned, not wishing to talk to anybody else, but thinking that it might be the vet, I finally answered it. It was a wrong number I replaced the receiver and in a couple of minutes the phone rang again. I picked it up and sure enough it was the same person, I do not suffer fools gladly, and so I gave them an earful, and slammed the phone down. It rang again. Totally exasperated I snatched it up and shouted down the phone, "Do not call this number again!" just as I was going to hang up, Alistair's laughing voice said, "OK B, what number would you like me to call you on?"

"Sorry." I mumbled, somewhat covered in confusion, "What do you want?"

"Panic is nigh! We have just heard that Conquistador has

qualified for the Showcase, it appears that the horse that beat him at the last show, tested positive for a performance enhancing drug, and has therefore been disqualified, so we are in. It isn't the way I would have liked to do it, but we have got the end result!"

"Alistair, that is great news! Congratulations! Is Jessica happy?"

"Thrilled, she said to remind you, about coming out to watch her."

"I'll do that. Well done, Alistair!" I hung up and gave Eleanor the good news. She smiled and said,

"I'll put the kettle on for tea." I went to remonstrate, and Eleanor immediately said "Oh, OK, coffee, who ever heard of an English woman not drinking tea?" I had never liked the drink and did not understand the endless cups of the beverage, that were consumed in the UK.

Eleanor brought two steaming cups back to the living room, and placed them on the coffee table, she sat herself down opposite me, and we were silent for a while. "How's Hetty?" she asked.

"She seems fine." I said.

"I was just thinking about what a terrible life she has had. She lost her husband, and then her son. Her daughter in law is a waste of space, and her one granddaughter is born deformed, and her other granddaughter has disappeared. How much misery can one person stand? I do wish we could solve the mystery of what happened to Felicity."

"Greater minds than ours have tried to do that!"

"What was Felicity like B?"

"She was beautiful, and as a child she was wonderfully caring, she defended Fee all the time. Fee was subject to so much bullying, because of her looks." Eleanor nodded her head "Children can be so cruel."

"I left to go to England, and did not see a lot of the twins, though Hetty wrote to me frequently about them. I think there was a problem with Alice, she spoilt Felicity, and was embarrassed by Fiona's looks, and consequently she ignored her. Hetty got Fee into riding, and then Felicity was free to do whatever she wanted. The twins grew apart, and then something happened at a party that they both went to, and Fee ignored her sister after that. Felicity then somehow got hooked up with a photographer and wanted to be a model or a film star."

"I presume the police followed up on all this?"

"Oh, yes they did, it was an exhaustive search, but it seems that she just walked away from a modelling agency and was never seen again."

"Did she have a boyfriend?"

"Not anybody in particular, the only male in her life was Adam, who used to take both girls out from time to time."

No sooner had I said this than the phone rang again, I snatched it up and barked "Hello"

"Oh" replied a startled voice, "It's Dr Weston here, I promised to let you know about the dog!"

"Sorry," I said, "I didn't mean to be so abrupt, how is she doing?"

"Well, I've ultrasounded her belly, and she does, indeed, have some serious injuries, but I've repaired what I can, I've put drains in, and stitched her back up, it's now up to her whether she makes it or not. She is unbelievably tough, she must have been hit by a car, and then crawled to your barn to give birth. I have checked her for a microchip, but she does not have one, I also called the local pounds, and none of them have had a bull terrier reported missing. I think she was probably dumped, because she was expecting mongrel pups. Speaking of which the puppies are doing fine, I will bottle feed them until she is over her anaesthetic."

"Thank you so much Dr Weston, I'll call tomorrow to see how they are all doing" I had had enough for one day and was going to head to bed. Eleanor obviously wanted to continue discussing the missing girls, but I just couldn't face it, so I climbed slowly up the stairs to my bedroom. Eleanor was a long time coming to bed, I heard her opening the spare room door, and glanced at the clock, it was 2.00 am. We both slept late the following day.

A cold wet nose poked me in my face, Alfie wanted out. I put on a robe and slippers and went down to let him out. He raced to the barn, and checked to see if his new friends were back, disappointed he did the rounds of the garden, and then came back in. I, meanwhile, had made coffee, and taken a cup up to Eleanor. She appeared shortly, also in dressing gown and slippers, and the pair of us sat at the kitchen table and upped our caffeine count. I asked Eleanor what she had been doing until so late last night. She told me that she had been reading through all the notes that she had made when she was with Alistair, and he had also given her copies of files that he had received from Bill, aka Inspector Thomas, and she had reread all of those. She had then made notes on all the conversations that we had had with Hetty, Jenny and Iris. I asked her if she was any further forward.

"No, but I have everything clearly in my head now, and not just a jumble of facts. I always had to do that when I was on the police force, and on a case in England. I found that it really helped."

"But Eleanor, you are on holiday here, you shouldn't be considering it a "case." You are supposed to be having a relaxing time, and enjoying visiting Canada. We haven't even been to Niagara Falls, or up to cottage country, I have been negligent in my duties as hostess, I can easily get someone to take you to see the sights."

"B, don't be ridiculous, this has been the most fun I've had, since I left the force!" This statement really annoyed me, and though Eleanor was my good friend, I let her have it.

"This is not a game! These are my friends, who are missing and their relatives and loved ones are all suffering. How can you say that you are having fun?" My expletive obviously stunned her, because she paused and then looked very sheepish. "I apologise B, I got caught up in the excitement of having a mystery to solve, and lost sight of the fact that this involves, real people, who are friends of yours. We were always taught, when we joined the homicide division, never to get personally involved with any of the families or friends of the victims and to keep a distance from all involved. I realise now that this is not the place to behave like this. You will have to rein me in if I step over these lines again." I was still very annoyed with her, but took a couple of deep breaths, and counted to ten, before I replied, knowing that my temper could get me in trouble, when I spoke before my brain had time to consider the ramifications of screaming at someone. Finally, I responded to Eleanor's apology.

"I'm sure you have lots of experience in these matters, and that can probably help with this enquiry, but I think that it is best left to the police. Now, I must go to the centre to do some work." I had had endless experience in chastising the students of Wendover College, and I am quite sure that Eleanor felt that she had been hauled over the coals, by the Dean. She looked suitably subdued, and said that if it was OK with me, she'd spend the morning in town, and perhaps we could meet at the cafe for lunch. Alistair was going to go back to see his horse.

I dropped Eleanor off in town, I did feel a little bad about what I had said. I left her in the town centre and said that I would meet her for lunch at around 1.00 pm. at the cafe. I went home briefly and did some chores. I drove to the equestrian centre. "Good morning, grumpy face?" Jenny said.

I confessed to Jenny about how I had lost it on Eleanor.

She pronounced that I was not in the wrong, and that Eleanor had got carried away, and lost sight of the fact that all people involved were more than witnesses or victims in this case. I immediately began to feel better. Jenny reminded me that Daniel was leaving on holiday the following day, which lifted my spirits even more. Alistair was also taking some time off in the not too distant future.

We sat down on either side of our partners' desk. The new maps had been produced, and we had to name the new jumps, and hook them up with sponsors. Then it could all go back to the printers to be finalised. We looked at the pictures of jumps, provided by John.

"This looks like a bridge that's melting!" said Jenny

"OK Melting Bridge it will be." I said, "What about this one? It's a bit boring." I pointed to a rather ordinary coop like jump.

"How about Plain Jane?"

"I suppose that will do, I'm not sure who will want to sponsor Plain Jane." I replied.

Finally, we had a Trakehner, which was a massive log over a deep, water ditch. We pondered for a while and finally came up with "Bridge over Troubled Waters" ignoring the fact that we had two bridges.

Jenny had received a reply from Michael OKing the new route on the course, but full of questions as to why it had been changed. He was going to be returning to England the following week, and so I gave Jenny instructions, to write to him giving the bare basics of what had happened. I was sure the news would be spreading far and wide and would reach South Africa soon enough. I realised that Michael was another person who had known the property for many years. He had been consulted by the consortium about the suitability of the property for the proposed usage several years earlier. I stored this knowledge away to tell the "squad", when we next got together.

I was a little nervous about meeting Eleanor, after our recent exchange. She was seated with Iris and Maisie, who was regaling Eleanor with a story, of how Fee had given her class a lesson and had made them all trot to the bottom of the ring, halt and do a half round the world, (she explained to Eleanor that this involved them lifting one leg over the horses neck and then the next leg over the hind quarters until they were sitting backwards) and then they were supposed to walk back down the ring facing backwards. At this point Maisie broke out laughing and said that half of the class had fallen off. Eleanor and Iris broke out laughing at this point, but I made a mental note to speak severely to Fee, about Health and Safety. I was happy that the bad feeling between Eleanor and me had been dissipated. We all had a good lunch, and when we went to say our goodbyes Maisie, with a wicked grin on her face, said,

"Bye Bye, Bat Bug B! That's good alliteration, isn't it? We learned about that in school. Do you know what a bat bug is B?"

"No, I confess ignorance!"

"It's just like a bed bug, but it has a hairy chest!"

"Well, I definitely can't be one, because last time I looked, I didn't have a hairy chest!"

"Yes, you are, you're Bat Bug B!" giggled Maisie.

"All right, Maisie Maggot!"

Once back at the car I asked Eleanor what she would like to do. She thought for a moment, and then said she'd like to go back to the house, she was hoping that she would get the results from Company House, in the mail.

"You must be joking!" I exclaimed, "With Canada snail mail you probably won't get them until next week."

"Well maybe I can try calling?" Eleanor asked

"Have at it!" I replied and started the car and headed home. We got there, and Alfie piled out of the car. He had been stuck in it while we had lunch and appeared to be in urgent need of an exit.

"If you like B, you can leave him with me, and we'll go for a long walk. I'd like to see more of the centre's grounds."

"That would be great if you don't mind, I'm sure Alfie would appreciate it. I'm just going to call Dr Weston and see how our girl is doing." I rang the surgery, but Amelia was out, according to her secretary. I enquired how the dog was doing, but the secretary said she was not allowed to give out information about patients but suffice to say all was well. I thanked her and asked her to have Dr Weston give me a call, when convenient. I then left Alfie with Eleanor and headed back over to the centre, to have a chat with John.

I found him in his workshop, hard at work carving a beaver. "For one of the water jumps I presume?" I said.

"Yes, pretty ironic to be carving an animal that lives to carve! It's for the second one, I'm going to make a mound of sticks to look like a beaver dam, and have him sitting on it, in the middle of the water."

I told him about the work Jenny, and I had done matching jumps up with sponsors, for the new loop, but we had failed to come up with a jump for the road construction company, that had been sponsoring the sunken road. They had not liked any of my suggestions, and so I asked John if he could come up with something suitable. He asked what their logo looked like, I had no answer for this, but said I would go and find out. With that I left him happily whistling, as he whittled away at the beaver.

I walked back to the office, and asked Jenny if she knew what the logo was, but she had no idea. The wifi was down on her computer, so she was unable to look it up. "Bloody thing," she said, talking about the computer "I have already had the IT people out twice this week. Oh well maybe third time will be the charm!" she said, as she reached for the phone to call the computer maintenance people. I told her I would drive into town and go to the road company's office. Jenny nodded and started berating the man on the end of the phone about her computer. I left her to it.

I drove downtown, and then realised I had no clue where I was going. "Bugger! I've left my GPS at home" I thought, and then decided to call Hetty, she would know where the office was. I got out my mobile, and she answered on the first ring. "Bored, are you?" I asked, "just sitting there waiting for it to ring?" Hetty laughed.

"No," she said, "I'd just hung up from another call, what can I do for you?" I told her what I needed, and as usual, Hetty's knowledge of the local area was flawless.

"It's quite complicated, if you come and pick me up, I can come with you and direct you." I accepted gratefully, and ten minutes later we were en route for the road company. I was very happy to have Hetty showing me the way. We arrived there and I popped into the office and requested a copy of their logo, a helpful secretary got me what I needed, and went on to say how excited she was to come to the showcase, she rode horses a little, and her bosses had offered her a ticket from their sponsorship package. I told her to come and find me on the day, and I would get her a good seat. I went back to the car looking at the logo, it was a picture of a backhoe and a bulldozer with the company's initials interwoven. Thinking this would give John something to think about, I climbed back in the car, with Hetty.

"Your phone just rang; I didn't think I should answer it." said Hetty. I picked it up and saw that it was Dr Weston calling back. I pressed redial and was soon connected with the good doctor.

"Your dog is amazing! So tough! You would never think

that she has been through everything that she has. She's ready for visitors, and all being well, she can go home in a couple of days." This last comment brought me up short. I had not considered the fate of the dog long term. My only concern had been getting her the medical help, that she needed. I could not take on another four dogs. Thinking that I would have to discuss this with the vet, I said that I'd be over right away, as I was already in town.

"Well, Hetty, you're going to see my rescue dog, she is up for visitors." I went to drive off, and yet again realised I had no clue where I was going, Hetty came to the rescue a second time, and we arrived at the surgery in no time.

Amelia met us in the waiting room and took us through to the back. There were a bank of cages with various furry faces looking out from them, but on the floor in a box that was about six feet by six feet and about a foot high lay my rescue and her brood. Hetty was ecstatic "Oh she is absolutely gorgeous!" she exclaimed. I actually thought the dog was pretty ugly, but I guess beauty is in the eye of the beholder, and as far as Hetty was concerned, this was beauty! Hetty plonked herself down on the floor outside the box and proceeded to stroke the dog who seemed to take a liking to her.

I went to talk to Amelia. I told her that I was happy to pay all the bills for the dog, but that I could not take on four more dogs. Amelia was a bit taken aback but said that she would call the Humane Society in the morning and see if they would take her. I thanked her profusely thinking that I had dodged a bullet. I went to return to Hetty, when Amelia asked, "Have you heard from Jessica? I haven't seen her for a while.

"Do you know her then?" I asked.

"Yes, we are good friends. We met when she was dog sitting her neighbour's dog, and it got sick, I went out to treat it, and we found that we had a lot in common. We go out now and again."

"Do you know Alistair as well?"

"Oh, I know Alistair, he owns Conquistador, the horse that Jessie rides."

"That's right, I arranged for Jessie to come over from England to ride Quisty for Alistair."

"I know she is very grateful to you both. I think she's getting on very well with the horse, but wants someone to watch her other than Alistair, because she says he always tells her that she's doing great!"

"That's probably because she is." I said laughing. Amelia smiled,

"Well then some things are going well." She said, but then reverting to earlier conversations she said, "I can't believe the find of a skeleton took place in Caledon township, it's normally such a quiet place." I shook my head and agreed with her, then not wishing to enter into a long conversation about the findings at the Equestrian Centre, I thanked her, and asked her to make up the bill, and returned to the back room. Hetty was now sitting in the box! I told her that Amelia was going to call the Humane Society, about taking the dog and her puppies, and that I was just going to pay for her veterinary care.

I went back to the front room and pulled out my cheque book. I picked up the bill, and I'm sure I must have blanched, when I read the amount on the bottom line. Holidays and treats would definitely be off for a while, I thought. I wrote out the cheque, handed it to Amelia, and called to Hetty, who came slowly through from the back room.

"I will take them." She announced, "Dr Weston do you think you would be able to help me find homes for the puppies when they are ready to be weaned?"

"Hetty are you sure?" I had never known Hetty to have a pet.

"Yes, I am quite sure. She needs a loving home, and

sometimes the Humane Societies put down dogs, that they can't find homes for. She and I will get along just fine."

Amelia said that she would be happy to help rehome the puppies but warned that the dog would need ongoing medical care for her injuries.

"I realise that." said Hetty, with dignity, "I am more than capable of taking care of all her needs."

As we drove off Hetty immediately started to make plans. She wondered whether John would make her a whelping box, like the one that the family had been in at the clinic. I promised to ask him, and said that if he made one, he would have to deliver it in his truck as it would not fit in Hetty's car.

"Tell him I'll pay him." said Hetty, after she had seen the truth in my statement.

"I doubt that he will want anything but offer it anyway." I said, "I'm going to see him now, why don't you come, and you can ask him yourself?"

"That would be great, if you don't mind dropping me at home later."

I remembered to ask Hetty if she knew where Paloma had gone missing. She thought about it for a bit and then replied,

"I'm not sure it was ever confirmed, the police tried to track her through credit card transactions, but none were made, there were no airline tickets in her name, she just disappeared into thin air. I'm sure that they are still looking in both jurisdictions." I made a mental note to get Alistair to ask Inspector Thomas if there was an active file on the singer's disappearance.

We drove in silence to John's workshop, where I gave him the logo, and laughing said "I hope that you like a challenge!" He stared at it for a while and said, "I'll have to think about it for a bit."

"Fine." I replied, "I can leave it with you" John nodded,

obviously pondering the matter. Hetty then spoke up about the dog and asked him about the whelping box.

"No problem, if B doesn't mind me using some of the old chestnut flooring that we have. I can cobble it together in about five minutes, and I can deliver it for you." Hetty offered to pay but John shook his head. "You can cook me a nice dinner, it would make a change from my normal fast-food burgers"

"You're on!" said Hetty, and they agreed on the following evening for delivery and dinner. We drove around to the front of the equestrian centre, and found Eleanor and Alfie walking along with Alistair, I smiled, obviously there had been an ulterior motive behind taking Alfie for a walk.

"Look who we bumped into on our walk." Said Eleanor, Alistair looked a little uncomfortable at this statement. I said nothing, but Hetty launched into the story of how she had become the owner of four dogs and continued to wax poetic about how beautiful they were. Eleanor, obviously pleased to have escaped an interrogation, congratulated Hetty, and said she was delighted that they had found a good home, especially as she had been the one to find them. The two of them continued their conversation, and I turned to Alistair and told him about Amelia being friends with Jessica.

"That's great, she was a bit lost when she first got here, I'm glad she's making friends." I went on to tell him about her complaining, that he was always telling her that she was doing great with Quisty.

"There I was thinking she needed to be praised! I guess she needs you to come and tell her how it is! Perhaps you can do that when I am away. Remember I told you I'd be gone for three or four days this month?" I nodded even though it had slipped my mind and said I would be up to the job of whipping the pair into shape.

"Any news on anything else?" I enquired. Alistair shook his

head, but Eleanor said, "Company House was unhelpful, they say they only mail out information, so we'll have to wait." Alistair turned to Eleanor and said, "We'd better end our walk, I have to go and ride Conquistador, Jessie is helping Fee teaching at the RDA tonight."

I drove Hetty back home and left her making lists of everything she would need for her new arrivals. I promised to help her when she went to pick up the family, it would not be easy to drive and cope with them all.

At home I made a few phone calls and realising the qualifier for the Showcase was next Saturday, I altered things around, so that I would be free to go and watch.

SOME ANSWERS AND MORE QUESTIONS

"Why do you have all these horseshoes?" Eleanor enquired.

"Oh, I have some projects in mind." I replied vaguely. I had always collected horseshoes, I had no idea why I kept them. It had started when my horse trod on one that another horse had lost. The nails were still in it, and they had run up into the sole of my horse's foot causing a lot of damage. From then on, I automatically picked up any horseshoe that I found. Instead of throwing them away, I kept them all.

Eleanor and I were enjoying our breakfast. Hetty called inviting Eleanor and me to dinner with John that evening. I turned to Eleanor and relayed the message. She smiled but said vaguely that she had plans for the evening if I didn't mind. I was fairly sure that the plans included Alistair, so I told Hetty that I would love to come but that Eleanor was already booked. I asked if I should bring anything. Hetty said everything was in hand, and I hung up, and turned to Eleanor ready to grill her. The phone rang again. It was Alistair.

"The results are back from the dental comparisons. The skeleton is Rebecca." I was shocked, we had known that it was a strong possibility, but I had been hanging on to the hope that it was nobody that we knew. "Is it definitely murder?" I asked

"There is a bullet hole in the skull. The crime scene people have found fragments of a bullet." Eleanor jumped up, I handed the receiver to her and sat back down feeling lightheaded. I thought of Iris and Maisie, and worried about how they would take it. At least Hetty would be relieved to hear that the skeleton was not Felicity, but she would now go back to her living hell, of not knowing what had become of her granddaughter. I was vaguely aware of the conversation going on behind me, Eleanor was talking ballistics and goodness knows what else. I tried to block it all out, and eventually she hung up, and said that Alistair was coming to pick her up, and that they were going to the police station to have a meeting with Inspector Thomas. I nodded at her, still stunned by the news.

"Eleanor, do you think I should go and tell Iris" I asked, dreading the answer, which of course came.

"Yes, the police will not inform her, as she is not next of kin. Rebecca was still married to Brian, and so they will be informing him."

"I don't think he needs much informing! I am sure that he is well aware that she is dead and where she was buried. He must have been the one to kill her!"

"I think that you should definitely go and talk to Iris. Give her my love."

I got up and climbed the stairs to my bedroom, and got dressed, trying to put together the words that I would use to tell Iris this news. Shaking my head, and admonishing myself for putting off the evil moment, I grabbed my bag, and marched downstairs. Eleanor was still waiting for Alistair, so I said my goodbyes and went out to the car. Alfie was not happy to be left behind, but I did not think I should take him, as I had no idea how long I would be. I drove to the cafe, and nearly ran through a stop sign in my distracted mood. I was pulled up abruptly, by a horn sounding and an angry driver, giving me the finger. I realised that it was Samantha Wells, I did not bother to look apologetic.

Iris was busy with the morning rush, but had one of her girls helping her, so I was able to pull her to one side. "Is Maisie here?" I asked. Iris shook her head,

"No, she's back at school."

"Well, there's no way to break it to you easily. The skeleton is Rebecca, they have matched her dental records. She was shot in the head, there is no doubt she was murdered." I blurted it all out, so much for tact! Iris was quiet for a while, but then she shouted,

"Bastard! Bloody Bastard! I knew he had killed her!" All the customers turned and looked at us in amazement. I hastened to take her behind the counter, and into the back room. Hazel, the young girl who was working for Iris, came running in. I shooed her back telling her she would have to look after things for the morning, as Iris was not feeling well. Reluctantly she went back to her duties. I made Iris a cup of sweet tea supposed to be good for shock, I thought, but made myself a cup of coffee. I sat down beside Iris and waited for her to say something.

Eventually she took a deep breath and said, "I don't really feel that bad. I've known in my heart that one way or another, she was dead. It's really the horror that she was shoved into a sort of cave and hidden where nobody should have found her. That bloody McVicker family, I know they did this."

"They will be the first suspects, but I'm afraid it will be hard to prove, after all this time. The police will want to interview you." She nodded.

"What do you think we should do about Maisie?" I asked.

"Well, she has been told all along that her mother is dead, so it should not be a great shock to her, but to think that her father killed her mother, that will not be good, if it gets proved.

We can't tell her anything about that until the police arrest Brian, if they do." I nodded but worried about not telling Maisie everything. She was such a bright kid. Iris went on to say that we couldn't let Maisie go and stay with the family, if she thought they were murderers. That would be a recipe for disaster. I could just picture her stamping her foot and saying, "You killed my Mummy!" to her father.

"This could become dangerous for her, she shouldn't go back to her father's house, I know he's not there, but his brother is and he's just as bad from what I hear. I don't think she should stay here either, I'm afraid that the Mcvickers may try to put pressure on you to say nothing about his relationship with Rebecca. Perhaps you shouldn't stay here either."

"I'm not afraid of him!" said Iris, her chin jutting out.

"I think you should be. I'm going to talk to Inspector Thomas about this, you may need police protection. Come with me now to see the Inspector"

"Nothing will happen to me with the crowd of people out front. I need to stay and help Hazel. You can go to the police if you like and see what they say." I could see that she was still processing the information. She wanted everything to go back to normal, and in her mind, working in the cafe was normal. I left her to her work and drove straight to the police station.

Alistair's car was parked outside. I parked beside it, and went in through the large front doors, and walked into a large reception area with a tall counter at the back of the room. There were people everywhere, some sitting on benches against the walls, some milling around in the centre of the room. I walked forward to the counter where a heavy-set woman in police uniform stood. I told her that I wanted to see Inspector Thomas.

"He's busy." she told me with finality. "If you want to wait, take a seat." She said gesturing to the benches. I wondered what I should do now, wait or exert more pressure on the policewoman behind the counter, she looked like she could handle a lot of pressure. Before I made up my mind Alistair and Eleanor appeared through a side door. They came over, looking questioningly at me. I told them that I had been to see Iris and told them about my concerns for her and Maisie, after Inspector Thomas interviewed Brian.

"You are right," said Alistair, "we should have thought of that before, the McVicker family is renowned for intimidating witnesses, come on, we'd better go back and tell Bill, and see if he can get some protection for them." Eleanor and I followed Alistair back the way they had come, through the side door. Inspector Thomas was standing in the hallway. Alistair told him he should listen to what I had to say, and I proceeded to tell him the lengthy story of how Iris got the cafe, her relationship with Rebecca and about Maisie. I finished by telling him that I myself had witnessed Brian being rough with Maisie, and that I feared for both of their safeties. He asked me the name of the judge who had made the ruling that Iris should live in the building. I could not remember it off the top of my head but assured him that I could look it up.

"Well, thank you Ms Browning, I think you are correct, and we need to make sure that both parties remain safe while the enquiry into the murder is being conducted." I noticed that I was no longer being treated like some elderly simple-minded person, and actually managed to smile at him and thank him in return.

Inspector Thomas accompanied us down the hallway and back into the reception area, where he met with two uniformed officers and gave them instructions to head to the café and wait there for him. We left through the front doors. I was happy with what I had achieved, and left Alistair and Eleanor in the parking lot. They were heading back to the equestrian centre, and I went to collect Alfie, before I to went to the centre.

Alfie greeted me enthusiastically, leaping up at me, and nearly knocking me sideways. "Down!" I commanded firmly, he took absolutely no notice, and continued to stand on his hind legs, his head almost level with mine. "There is dog training in your future!" I threatened him, and he smiled joyfully at me, having heard this many times before. He leapt into the front seat of the car and prepared himself to motor. I took up my position as his chauffeur and drove him round the concession to the centre.

We had been given permission to run the Showcase on its original date, and so there was a lot to get done in a short amount of time.

Jenny and I made up a list of sponsor boards, that would be placed on every cross country jump. We also listed banners, that would be attached to the fencing around the dressage rings and the show jumping ring. Jenny was going to go to the sign company with the list and order them all.

I called all the officials back to let them know that we were running on the original date. They had all heard the news of the find of the skeleton by then, and of course wanted to get as much information out of me as possible. Consequently, this task took me a lot longer than it should have, and soon it was time for me to leave and get ready for Hetty's dinner party. Alfie and I said farewell to Jenny and headed back to the car. I gave Alfie a short run before installing him in the car, he would have to stay home alone tonight, and I knew there would be drama and sulking from him before I left.

Once home I gave Alfie his tea, which he wolfed down, not tasting anything I thought. He then went and climbed on the couch in his favourite position. I went upstairs to choose a suitable outfit for dinner at Hetty's, this accomplished I came back down to face the music, of leaving Alfie at home, when I suddenly remembered that I had a marrow bone in the fridge.

Bribery worked well, and I was able to leave with Alfie, happily gnawing on his treat.

Hetty's normally immaculate house was vastly changed. There was a large whelping box in her kitchen, dog beds lying in the living and dining room, and dog paraphernalia all around the house. I went through the kitchen to the living room, where I heard voices. John was sitting comfortably on the settee, with a whiskey in his hand and sitting next to him, I was surprised to see Amelia. Hetty was bustling around getting Amelia a glass of wine, and seeing me coming in, she held up the bottle to me with a questioning look.

"Yes please, I could murder a glass!"

"I thought it would be nice to have Amelia see where Poppy and pups are going."

"Poppy?" I questioned; Amelia laughed "Apparently that's what your rescue dog is to be called!"

"I would have thought Brunhilda would be more appropriate!"

"B, don't be so horrid, I think Poppy is a perfect name for her, and guess what? John says he would love to have one of the puppies" John nodded enthusiastically "What is a course builder without a dog?"

"I have to agree with you there, you are about the only one I know without one." I replied. "It's a great life for a dog!"

"And what are you going to call it? Rosebud?" chipped in Amelia, I sensed a keen sense of humour behind her professional demeanor. John replied with dignity "No I was thinking of Pansy"

We all laughed, and John added that he thought he would prefer to have a boy. Amelia immediately told him "In that case you must get him neutered, as soon as he is old enough." John looked uncomfortable hearing this and seemed to squirm in his seat.

"Just look at you! All men are like that when you talk about castrating an animal! They are such babies! We have far too many unwanted puppies." John did not look convinced.

We continued talking about the dogs, Hetty went to the kitchen, and proceeded to dish up the main course, I was thinking it would have been a lot easier without the whelping box, but then thought she would have to get used to it for a while. She called through for us to come and pick up our plates and take them through to the dining room. We followed her instructions and sat down in the lovely room. Hetty lived in a Victorian town house, it had beautiful high ceilings with bay windows looking out on a pretty garden. The dining room was painted a pearl grey, there were hunting prints hanging on the walls, and all the molding was brilliant white. The furniture consisted of beautiful antique pieces polished to a perfect sheen. There was an intricately constructed medallion in the centre of the ceiling, out of which hung a magnificent chandelier, all original to the house, John observed this with great admiration. "Look at the craftsmanship in this room, you couldn't find a plasterer nowadays who could fashion a medallion like that! And the carpentry for the crown molding, wainscotting and door trims is exceptional."

"It is beautiful Hetty, how long have you lived here?" asked Amelia.

"Ever since I married, George and I bought it for a song back then! George passed away here, and I brought up my son here, and now he's gone as well." There was an awkward silence and I tried to fill the void by asking Amelia if she had seen Jessica.

"No, I called her and left a message, I haven't heard back yet but I've been so busy in the surgery that she may have tried, and not been able to get through. Or perhaps she's out with her blond mystery man. I haven't met him yet, but I've seen him out with her sometimes, and sometimes with your granddaughter, Hetty." Hetty looked up at this, "Oh really?" she said.

Amelia nodded and said "It's so nice to have an evening off. I have another vet covering for me, it doesn't happen very often, a guilt free evening! What are you looking so pensive about B?"

I was not sure whether I should tell them the news of the skeleton but figured that it would be common knowledge in no time, so I told them that it had been identified as Rebecca. Hetty exclaimed "Oh poor Iris and Maisie! How are they?" I could see that there was relief for Hetty in the knowledge that it was not Felicity found in that cave, but she was genuinely appalled for Iris and Maisie.

"Iris knew for a long time that it was unlikely that Rebecca would be found alive, I think it is giving her a little closure."

Amelia and John were looking a little lost through all this and so while we ate the perfectly prepared sea bass, I told them the long history of Iris and the McVicker family. I finished up by saying that I had worried for the safety of Iris and Maisie, and that the police had agreed with me, and were providing them with protection.

Hetty, wishing to change the subject, asked whether John had come up with any idea for the road construction company's jump from the logo that we had procured for him. He answered that he had, and he pulled out a drawing of a toy digger and bulldozer with intertwined letters similar to the logo. "I can make them as toys more easily than trying to copy the real thing, what do you think?" before I could answer Amelia butted in and said,

"You can actually make that? That's amazing"

"You should see his carvings, they are just incredible" I told her, John was blushing, and looking embarrassed at the praise, but I could see that he was happy to have impressed Amelia.

"I would love to see them." said Amelia. John continued blushing and said that she could come any time. I then suggested that she come to the Showcase, and she said she would love to do that.

We had polished off the main course by this time, so I cleared up the dishes, and took them back out to the kitchen.

Hetty brought out a sponge cake with all manner of fruit with a sauce drizzled over it. She dished it out to each of us, and sinners that we were, we all polished it off and then followed up with seconds. She offered us coffee, but Amelia stood up, thanked Hetty, and said she had early office hours tomorrow, so she should head home. John also got up and said he would walk Amelia to her car. I stayed to help Hetty clean up.

"Well, what do you think?" she asked. I drew a blank. "About what?"

"Amelia and John, of course," Finally the penny dropped, Hetty had been up to her old match making again!

I then remembered to tell Hetty about the terrible Samantha Wells, and how she had tried to get Fee to withdraw from the showcase and having been caught out she had taken Fee out for dinner to apologise, and then had got food poisoning for her sins! I told her that Fee had been secretly pleased about this, and I did not blame her! I went on to tell them that I had inadvertently run a stop sign and Samantha had given me the finger!

Hetty looked pensive for a moment and then shaking her head said, "I wonder if I should insist that Fee stay with me now Alice is no longer there."

"Well Fee is an adult now. I doubt that she would appreciate being told she had to live with her grandmother."

"No, I don't suppose she would, in some ways she seems

very immature, but maybe that's what I want her to be. I will just have to get over myself! Are you still on for Tuesday afternoon?"

THE QUALIFIER

We drove up Highway 400, early on Saturday morning. I had Eleanor and Hetty in the back seat with Alfie happy in front. He was not going to be so thrilled, when he realised that he would have to be on a leash all day. We reached the junction north of Barrie and turned off the Highway onto 11 and carried on up to Oro, where we turned off, and headed to the event site. On arrival we found a place to park near Fee's horse trailer.

I looked around, Maggie Sandler was there on her old faithful, Media Circus, I was pleased to see that he looked fit and well. Roger Brandon was trying to ignore her and was hurrying off to the dressage warm up ring. I was glad to see Helen Brandon go over and talk to her, taking Filibuster away from Maggie had obviously not had anything to do with Helen.

Xen was there, to ride in lower level classes, his wild hair was restrained under his helmet, and in traditional riding clothes he looked positively polished. He trotted over to see me, I complemented him on his turn out, and wished him luck. He went off with a smile as big as a skateboard.

Horses were behaving very badly, it being the first major event of the year. Most of them had spent all winter working in indoor arenas, so to be out in the open at a horse "party" was enough to tip them over the edge. A horse came past me on the way to warm up, and another came in the opposite direction, the first spooked at the other, and then stuck it's head between it's knees and broncoed. The second horse did a spin through 180 degrees and took off back in the direction from which it had come, thereby setting off two other horses. The one rider landed with a thud at my feet, and let out some very racy expletives, and then jumped up and left in pursuit of her recalcitrant equine. I was immediately at home in this environment.

When I got to the warmup Fee was busy working Killer, who was extremely full of himself, she had her hands full and was intent on what she was doing so I did not interrupt her. I looked round and recognised most of the local entries for the Showcase. Samantha Wells was riding Filibuster, and I was pleased to note that she was not producing the same smooth connected work with the horse, that Maggie had achieved in the past. There were several horses to go before Fee, so I wandered over to the bleachers at the side of the ring. Eleanor and Hetty joined me there, we sat and watched a couple of tests, and chatted to some of the spectators.

Samantha entered the ring, and Roger and Helen Brandon sat down on the lower steps of the bleachers. Sam did a creditable test, but without the harmony and expression that Maggie would have produced, a fact that was loudly commented on by Helen. Roger stood up and walked away from the bleachers scowling. Helen then moved up to sit beside us.

"I am so furious with that man I could spit!" she said to us. We nodded sympathetically, and talked to her for a while, she was obviously very unhappy in her marriage. I invited her to sit with us at the Showcase, saying I would organise tickets. She was grateful and said she would appreciate that. We turned to watch, as Fee came round the ring, waiting for the signal from the judge to enter. The bell sounded and there was a moment of tension from Killer, but Fee worked another circle, got him back in control and cantered down the centre line to a lovely square halt. She rode an excellent test with just a couple of mistakes, one of the flying changes was late behind, and at the final halt Killer stepped sideways. There had been some tension in the horse throughout, but this would improve with experience. He was the youngest horse in the class.

"That was great!" said Helen, "She is really going to be difficult to beat when the horse is not quite so green." Hetty smiled at her and thanked her. We were thinking of leaving, but next to come into the ring was Maggie Sandler on Media Circus. She cantered round the ring relaxed and smiling, waiting for her signal. Once the bell rang she proceeded to ride a wonderful test, although the old horse did not have the movement or flamboyance of the younger horses he more than made up for it in his obedience and accuracy. We all clapped at the end of her performance, and I said "As far as I'm concerned that was a winning test! Well done! Maggie."

We left the bleachers and went back to the Trailer parking. We met a couple of board members who had come up to spectate and who were anxious to congratulate Fee on her test. She thanked them and then turned to me to ask if he looked sound. I told her that he certainly did. She smiled, and off subject said, "It's a good thing the food poisoning wasn't too bad for Samantha wasn't it?" Hetty frowned and nudged her.

I asked about the cross country course.

"It's pretty nice B, fairly easy which is good for the start of the year, the water is quite tricky though."

"OK, that's where we'll go to watch." I said, and we left her changing her tack and putting studs in Killer's shoes, so that he would not slip on the cross country.

Eleanor said she was hungry and could do with a breakfast sandwich at the food booth. We walked over there, and ordered coffee and bacon, egg and cheese muffins. Hetty and Eleanor bagged a table, and I walked over to the score sheet that was posted outside the secretary's office. Eventing is a penalty based competition, so the lowest score is the best. I was not surprised to see Maggie and her Media Circus in the lead, Fee was standing fifth, and Samantha with Filibuster was seventh. I went back, picked up our food, carried it to the table, and let Eleanor and Hetty know the results so far. We enjoyed our artery blocking breakfast. Eleanor had picked up a program, so we worked out when we should leave to head over to the water jump to see the riders that we wanted to watch. There was a map showing us the route, Hetty and I waited for Eleanor to show us the way, orienteering not being our forte. We walked past many of the fences on the course, I was pleased to see that they were challenging enough without being too difficult. The cross country is the heart of the sport, for this competition the horses would gallop approximately 3 and a half kilometres, jumping up to 30 fences some of which would comprise several elements. It was not for the faint hearted, the fences did not knock down and if you hit one going at 570 metres per minute it normally resulted in a fall, unless the new frangible technology was being used.

We made it out to the water jump as the lower level was finishing up, I was delighted to see that Xen was one of the last to go, and he had a great ride through the formidable water jump. I cheered as he negotiated the final element, and Hetty and Eleanor joined in. We waited for the next class. The jump judges came over and moved the red and white flags over to the advanced division fences. I pointed out the route to my two companions, and they were suitably awed by the size and complexity of the combination. This consisted of a very skinny brush fence to another brush with a huge drop into the water with four strides to a carving of a giant Canada goose, followed by another skinny brush on the shore of the water.

We waited quietly until the first horse came to our fence. The rider made it through. The horse jumped in big over the drop into the water. The rider was left behind the movement and was unable to get their seat and reins back before they met the fence in the water, the horse took them over it, but then with no direction from the rider the horse drifted to the right, and the rider had to circle in order to get back under control to jump the final element of the obstacle. This circle resulted in 20 penalties. Regardless of this, they got a big cheer, and they galloped on to the next fence. The next horse refused at the jump into the water, the rider represented, but the horse would have none of it. The rider raised his hand and retired from the course. We watched several more horse and rider combinations attempt the water complex. Three went through well, one boy fell off after the drop into the water and left the course dripping and disillusioned. The next made it through on a wing and a prayer, only to fall at the next fence.

Samantha came next, and Filibuster clearly did not feel confidence in his new rider, she was hoping he would take her to the fence, instead of encouraging him with her legs and seat, consequently he stopped at the first element. Sam got her act together after that, and kicked the horse hard, and he then jumped through the complex well, but now carrying 20 penalties.

A couple of riders later Fee and Killer came round the corner to the water, a frisson of excitement went through the three of us as we watched, Fee was struggling to keep him steady and balanced, but he was not responding well to her aids, he gave an enormous jump into the water which meant that the distance to the jump in the water was too short. The horse saw this and left out a stride, jumped huge leaving Fee in the back of the tack with no reins, she did her best to point him at the fence out of the water, and he went for it, leaving long, but still managing to clear it. A huge cheer went up from the spectators, but I thought that the Ground Jury might have a good case for dangerous riding. Hetty had been hiding her eyes, and I patted her shoulder saying, "She's OK, but I think we will have to get better brakes for Killer." This meant that we might have to go to a more effective bit in his mouth. Hetty nodded emphatically.

Next came Maggie, and she made it look like nothing, just a run of the mill gymnastic exercise, so that one wondered why all the other riders had struggled, the spectators were impressed, and gave her a big cheer.

Back in trailer parking, Fee was exhilarated by her ride, but sensible enough to know that she had a lot of work to do to get Killer to be more mannerly and listening to her. "He just sees the flags, sights on the fence and goes, he is so strong, I can't hold him at times." she said. I nodded and told her she must discuss it with her coach. I asked whether he was better in the show jumping.

"Yes, he is, but he's still strong and not always very careful after cross country, and he can roll poles."

She continued to look after Killer, cooling him out and getting him ready for the final phase of the competition, the show jumping.

Eleanor and Hetty thought a coffee, and maybe a burger, were in order before we went up to the show jumping ring. Fee's round without jumping penalties would put her in good standing, as long as she did not have too many time penalties. Often when you rode a strong horse like Killer, you had to take a lot more time to balance them and set them up for a jump, this would then result in taking longer than the optimum time that was set for the course. If you rode a steady horse, that just kept galloping quietly in rhythm, and did not need much setting up for the jumps, you would be a lot quicker.

We ate our lunch at a picnic bench, and people kept stopping by to ask about the Showcase and the happenings at the Equestrian Centre. Tiring of this, I suggested we go and find a quiet spot where we could watch the show jumping. We unloaded the collapsible chairs that we had brought with us from the car and walked up to the stadium ring. I absently picked up a horseshoe that was lying on the ground and put it in my bag. Eleanor raised her eyebrows at this but did not comment.

The show jumping arena was a pretty sight, the gaily painted jumps had little flags fluttering out of the standards, on either side of them. The standards were in all shapes, some like giant butterflies, others made to look like trees or toy trains. Each jump was decorated with trees and shrubs. The show jumps in Eventing are not as big as in straight show jumping but given that our horses had just galloped round the cross country course, it was a feat of stamina and conditioning, that they were still able to come out and jump round the show jump course, and hopefully still leave the poles up.

The Intermediate class was still running, and I was pleased to see that we were in time to watch Xen. He came into the ring, totally focused on the task at hand. He jumped an immaculate clear round, and the three of us cheered. He galloped past us, fist pumping the air obviously thrilled with his performance. I went to congratulate him, while the course was raised for the advanced division.

"Thanks B, I had the greatest day! Maverick was wonderful in all three phases. I hope Fee does well, I'll go and wish her good luck." He trotted off towards the trailer parking, and I thought for the hundredth time that I loved this sport, the riders encouraged one another, and were generous offering advice on how to ride the courses, unlike the other disciplines, where any advice was kept strictly to themselves.

I returned to my seat, and we waited while the riders walked the course, counting the strides between fences. For every four human strides a horse would take one. The rider then had to work out what line they would take between fences and how many strides. It was a complex task, and you could see the concentration on the riders faces as they walked the entire course.

The judge sounded the horn to clear the course, and the first rider entered the ring. There were a mixed bag of rounds from the first ten competitors in the ring. We watched two clear rounds, one rather wild one, and the other by the Braille method, as we called it, the horse hitting each fence but not hard enough to knock it down. Two riders had cricket scores, taking down many fences to leave the ring having added 24 and 28 penalties respectively to their scores. For each fence knocked down the competitor received four penalties. And if they exceeded the time allowed, they were given point four of a penalty for each second over the time. The next six riders had one or two rails each.

Samantha entered the ring on Filibuster, and she jumped a very nice clear round, riding confidently and accurately. Begrudgingly we clapped her. Roger was beaming and hurrying over to congratulate her. We did not see Helen. Two more riders came into the ring posting good scores.

Fee entered, and Killer looked strong and powerful, they cantered a circle waiting for the horn to sound. The announcer then introduced her and said that she was lying in second place. She went between the electronic timer's eye and started on course. Killer took hold and raced at the first jump, knocking it down, this upset their rhythm, and Fee became flustered, she did not ride well and had another two rails down. She came out of the ring looking grim. Hetty stressed, but I told her that it was a learning curve, that Fee and the horse were both young, and things would improve. I said to leave her alone for a while. We stayed where we were, and watched Maggie jump a beautiful clear round to win the class deservedly. We walked slowly back to the trailer park and found Fee untacking and getting Killer ready for his trip home. Just as we arrived the announcer called out the placings for the class. Maggie had won, Samantha had come third and Fee had ended up fifth. Samantha came over and said congratulations to Fee, far from responding in kind, Fee gave her a look that would have withered most people. Sam being Sam shrugged and walked away. Hetty was very upset by Fee's behaviour, and I rethought my idea of how generous all eventers were. Somewhat deflated after a great day's competition, we got back in the car, and drove back home. We had little conversation for a while, and then Hetty said, "Fee can get very jealous, but I thought she was growing out of it. Her behaviour today was disappointing"

"I think she was just so anxious to do well, and to have three rails in the show jumping was humiliating for her." I replied, "And I did think that Sam was rather rubbing her nose in it."

"Nevertheless, that behaviour was awful." sniffed Hetty.

Thinking about it, I realised there was a gritty side to Fee.

SETTLING IN

Tuesday morning Eleanor, Alfie and I had breakfast together, apparently Alistair was going to be working on his duties for the Centre, these he had been neglecting of late due to working with Eleanor and Inspector Thomas. He was due to take time off, so he was anxious to have everything in hand before that happened. Security wise, there was a lot to do to prepare for the Showcase.

I told Eleanor what Amelia had to say about Jessica, Fee and the blond man. She and I tossed around the idea, that this man was Adam.

"Didn't Hetty tell us that Adam sometimes took the twins out?" asked Eleanor.

"Yes, but I thought that was before Felicity went missing. On the other hand, I did think that Adam was overly affectionate towards Fee the other night." I replied.

"Well why shouldn't he be? He was best friends with Fee's father, and he stays in touch with Alice, even in her current state, he probably considers himself a surrogate uncle." Eleanor was right, I thought, and it was really for the best, Fee needed friends.

Alfie started barking furiously, it could only be his arch enemy, the postman.

I watched the postal van disappear down the road, before I

opened the front door and went out down the path to the post box. Alfie was careening ahead, barking like mad, he jumped up and put his front feet on the fence, and hurled abuse after the van. I retrieved the mail, shouted at Alfie to get down, and as honour was satisfied, with the postman having been terrified and leaving, Alfie got down, and we made our way back to the house. I sorted through the mail, as usual there was nothing exciting, but there was an official looking large brown envelope addressed to Eleanor. Entering the house, I passed this to her.

"Oh, this is from Company House." She said, "Well let's see who owns those corporations." She tore the envelope open, and pulled out the contents, placing the pages on the table. Eleanor proceeded to scan them, and much to my irritation, she kept reading and muttering odd "Um hmms" and a couple of "Well Wells" Unable to contain my curiosity any longer, I practically screamed at Eleanor, "What does it say?"

"Keep your hat on! I am just working my way through the information, you have to understand there are corporations within corporations, but ultimately QD Enterprises belongs to the McVicker family, and two names that I recognise as being in your government!"

"Who?" I asked,

"Paul Hazeltine and Ingmar Singh, aren't they both ministers?"

"Yes, Hazeltine is Minister for Sport and Recreation, and Singh, I'm not sure what portfolio he now has, but he definitely has the Prime Minister's ear. That must be how the consortium were able to get all the grants, and have the nod as the equestrian site, should the Olympic Games come here."

"And I bet they have had something to do with this strange deal people are talking about, whereby they give the land to the Township in perpetuity, I'm sure it isn't out of the goodness of their hearts!"

"Well, I guess that ties the McVickers even more closely to Rebecca's body. What about the other one, something Entertainment, wasn't it?"

"Yes, Holy Port Entertainment." Said Eleanor.

"Are you going to work today?" I nodded in the affirmative.

"In that case do you mind if I use your computer? I thought I would stay here and look up all these people online, see what I can find out about them."

"Is it really necessary?" I asked, "Now we know that it is Rebecca buried there, isn't it sure to be the McVickers, who did it?"

"The more information that we gather means we can exclude everybody else; it will make it easier to prove that it was Brian McVicker."

"OK, if you think so, fine, I'll take Alfie with me, we'll see you later. I'll have to drop Alfie back here before I go to Hetty's to pick up the dogs. Will you be all right until then?" Eleanor said she'd be fine, and I quickly got dressed, and headed over to the Centre.

Jenny and I worked steadily, I got hold of our chief jump judge, and asked for a list of all the volunteers that she had managed to find, and her assessment of their expertise. She said that she would email it over right away. The volunteers' names had to be printed in the program, along with a big thank you to them. Each jump had to have its own judge, who would mark down whether the rider was clear or had faults at the obstacle. Some jumps were made up of several different elements, which made correctly judging the route taken complicated, and therefore we needed more experienced judges, and sometimes two or three at one of these types of fences. Jenny set about listing all the jumps, so we could decide how many judges we would need, and once the list came through, who we would put at each fence.

I contacted our head of Dressage and instructed her to liase with Pru about when the dressage rings would be set up, and how many volunteers they would need to accomplish this. The Dressage Showcase was running the week after my Eventing one, and we would share rings, it being redundant to take them down and put them up again.

I fielded some phone calls from sponsors wanting to know about timing and access, and quite a few from would be spectators who had seen our advertisement in the local paper and wanted to know how to get tickets. Who needed an advertisement? The discovery in the grounds had piqued their interest, and several asked for seats near the murder!

Looking at my watch, I told Jenny it was dog time! We left the office and took Alfie for a quick stretch of his legs. I bumped into Alistair, who was working out parking areas for the Showcase. I let him know that I thought there would be a lot of spectators, judging by the interest being shown. We chatted about numbers of cars for a bit, and then I told him about the letter from Company House, Eleanor had already called him with the information, Alistair said. Of course, she had, I thought! Alfie was bored with waiting for me, and started barking, so I said goodbye, and finished up our walk.

Hetty was anxiously waiting when I arrived at her house, even though I was five minutes early.

"What do you think we should take to put the puppies in? And do you think Poppy will be all right on the back seat, with her broken leg?"

"Have you got a large cardboard box for the puppies? We could put an old towel in that, they could go in the front, with the seat belt around the box, and you could sit in the back with Poppy and help her keep her balance" I replied. Hetty hustled around finding a suitable box, and I'm sure that it was one of her good towels that went in it, smiling to myself, I didn't say anything. Thus equipped we headed off to Amelia's surgery. Amelia and her technician carried Poppy out to the car, where Hetty received her on the back seat. I brought up the rear with the puppies. Poppy was upset that the puppies weren't with her, but eventually settled down, when she could hear them squeaking.

Amelia gave Hetty a piece of paper with instructions on how to care for Poppy's injuries, and then proceeded to tell her,

"Don't forget to clean out the drains in her side, twice a day, she should come back to have them removed in a week, and if she goes off her food or spikes a fever bring her back right away Hetty"

"Oh, and by the way B, would it be alright if I came by the Equestrian Centre to see John's carvings?"

"Of course!" I replied, thinking John would be thrilled.

I stayed with Hetty for a while. We settled the family into the whelping box, Poppy was delighted to be reunited with her puppies, who immediately started to tuck in for a good long feeding of milk. This accomplished, they all fell sound asleep one on top of the other. Between us we carried Poppy outside for a pee, and then back into the house. We let her down outside the whelping box, and she stomped round the house with her splinted leg, which did not seem to impede her at all. Having taken stock of her surroundings we helped her back in the box, and she lay down to have a sleep herself.

I left Hetty with instructions to call if she had problems, but she said that Fee was coming over to see the new arrivals, and was going to spend the night, so she didn't foresee any problems.

When I got home, Eleanor was preparing supper, her culinary skills were just north of railcar diner. But compared to mine, they were positively brilliant. I laid the table, and helped Eleanor bring the food from the kitchen. I confessed that I had failed to ask Hetty about the names on the list. "Really B," Eleanor said, "you must have a mind like a sieve!" I nodded ashamedly.

"Holy Port is a front for a film studio that specialises in religious productions. It is fairly well known in those circles and has produced some works that have received nominations for awards. In turn the film studio is a front for a group of people that have their own church. The leader is quite an evangelist, and had occasional slots on television, but it appears that there was some sort of scandal, and he has fallen from grace, his name is Reverend Wiseacre"

"Scandal?" I thought.

"What about the other company, the one owned by the McVickers, did you find out anything else about them?"

"There is one other person involved, who is named as John Smith, the name is so common I cannot find anything about him, but what is interesting is there is a John Smith listed as a member of the church, behind the film studio, behind Holy Port Entertainment."

We finished up the pasta that Eleanor had prepared, cleared up, and then sat down and watched a vaguely entertaining show on television about a woman who raised dragons from old eggs, before retiring to bed to have strange dreams of winged monsters!

The following morning Eleanor decided she wanted to go to the public library to look up their newspaper archives and see if she could find out any more about the consortium.

"Won't it all be online?" I asked,

"Not necessarily, I think I might as well take a look, and see if there is anything to find."

"Well, if you feel it is worth it."

The Orangeville library, consisted of three stories of unattractive brick with small windows and a heavy roof. Eleanor got out, and I said for her to call me when she wanted picking up. Alfie and I continued to the Equestrian Centre.

Jenny had completed the pairing of jump judges with fences and handed it over for my approval. As usual she had done a good job, and I told her she could start making up the clipboards with the jump judge sheets, ready to add maps and orders of go nearer the time. It was my preference to have this done ahead of time, otherwise there was a mad scramble the night before Cross Country. I then instructed her to draw up a schedule for assigning trucks to get the jump judges out to their jumps. We would use several pickup trucks, the jump judges sitting in the backs of them, and we would drive them to their respective jumps. In order to accomplish this seamlessly, we would put all judges that were judging fences close together on the course in one truck, so that the truck would make only one loop, and we didn't have numerous trucks driving all over the course. The devil was in the details.

I then spent a long time arguing with the various caterers, as to the percentage that they would be paying us for the right to park their catering trucks on the property, during the event. I also had to check that their health and safety inspections were up to date, and that they all had insurance that would cover the Equestrian Centre in the event that they poisoned somebody. Eleanor called she needed to go down to Toronto to the main library, she said she was catching the GO train down, and would call me when she was on the way back. Annoyed that I had no excuse for leaving my current task I eventually completed it.

The skies had cleared. I suggested to Jenny that we take a break, and take Alfie for a walk, so that we could check that the routes Jenny had chosen for the pickup judge delivery trucks would work. She agreed immediately, and we got out from behind our desk, and headed to the storage area, where we kept our wellington boots, these donned we headed out, Alfie scenting the way.

We only found one route that would be better for the jump judges, who were judging the second water, so we changed their assigned pickup truck, and then happy that our system was the best that it could be, we walked over to John's workshop to see what he was up to. We opened the man door.

John had carved out the two toys, a bulldozer and a digger and married them together facing one another with the initials of the company, so that the competitors would jump over the letters.

"I hope that Michael likes it." John said.

"What's not to like! Michael will be back any day now, and I'm sure he will be thrilled, he can help you place it out on the new loop. Can you take a photo of it, so that I can show the sponsors?"

"You bet B." We left him working on the best angle for this and headed back to the main building. We went back to the office, and I remembered the list of names. I didn't feel like driving downtown again, and so I pulled it out and emailed Hetty with it, asking her if she knew of any of the people, would she let us know.

I drove home via the Mandarin restaurant and bought curried prawns. I took this into the house and put it in the bottom oven of my Aga. The English stove had been one of my few extravagances, when Alistair remodelled the house. I had fallen in love with the one I had in England and bit the bullet and paid the exorbitant amount of money it took to have one installed in my kitchen. It served the purpose of heating the house and the water, as well as the rare times that I cooked. I looked at it fondly, hoping that Eleanor would be home before the meal dried out.

I did a few chores, washed the kitchen floor, which was covered in muddy paw prints, from the morning rain, I then put on a load of laundry, and was just deciding to give Eleanor a call, when she walked through the front door. Alfie greeted her ecstatically, since she no longer tried to steal his front seat, he had become very attached to her. She was manfully fighting off his slobbery kisses, and eventually made it into the living room.

"You really should teach your dog some manners B!"

"He's just pleased to see you, Eleanor. How did you get on?"

"Well, if you pour me a glass of wine, I'll tell you." I dished up the Chinese. We both sat down at the table, Eleanor took a large swig of her wine.

"The Holy Port Entertainment companies are based in California, we should have guessed that, from the information I gathered yesterday. The church is rumoured to be a kind of cult, and a lot of the money comes from people that join, and I suppose, get embroiled in all the religious fervour, and hand over their savings. Some young people got involved, and their parents tried to get them out, but they were told that their children did not want to see them. The children were all over eighteen, so when the police were called, there was nothing the church was doing that was against the law. I read all this in an article by a Colin Fray, who was an investigative reporter for a small newspaper from Orange County near LA, he had been looking into the disappearance of a girl who he had traced to the church. I found this all very interesting but couldn't find any follow up articles from this reporter."

"I then telephoned the newspaper, and was told that Colin Fray had left, the girl I spoke to was new at the paper and did not know anything about him. I went back to the archives but found nothing else about him.

The timing of the reporter's departure from the paper, being right after his article had come out. I asked the girl whether there was anything about the Reverend Wiseacre's troubles, she said that she had found nothing apart from one line in an article, which spoke of him having been hospitalised for exhaustion.

"Isn't that a polite way of saying he'd had a mental breakdown?" I asked. Eleanor shrugged, "You could be right but who knows? This Chinese is very good by the way, is there any more wine?"

We polished off both the Chinese and the wine, decided we would forego the TV and went up to bed.

I was up early; Daniel was due home from his holiday that day. The following day we would have a meeting of all the committee chairs. Complete reports would have to be given, and Jenny and I had an enormous amount to do. We had to create an agenda, get the reports proofread and then slotted into the correct order, to be prepared for this meeting. In addition to this we had to meet with the tent people, to discuss positioning of all the marquees for the Showcase.

I had brewed coffee, and was eating a piece of toast, whilst making notes. Eleanor came downstairs. I told her to help herself to breakfast. She asked me if I needed any help, which was a bad thing for her to offer, there appeared to be so many things that I still needed to do.

"Would you be able to meet with the man who is supposed to be organising the Trade Fair? I think that he is not on top of everything that has to be done. All the vendors, who have signed up, need to be contacted. They must be separated into the ones supplying their own tents, and those who want to go in the Marquee, that we are providing. We need to know how much square footage each one needs"

"OK, I can do that. What is the man's name and phone number?"

"Oh God! Names and nouns! Can you call Jenny? She'll know for sure."

Just then the phone rang, and I snatched it up uttering an unfriendly "Hello".

"B it's me, you sound grumpy." Said Hetty's voice, "Sorry," I replied.

"I'm just calling you back about that list of names you emailed me, I'm not familiar with most of them, but Wiseacre is Paul and Adam's surname, there was a Templeton, who lived out near Orangeville, I think his name was Richard, Catrin, Adam's mother, knew him. The only other one is John Smith. and the one I knew was friends with Alistair and Cynthia, perhaps you remember him B? I am sure that there must be thousands of John Smiths, so it probably isn't the same one."

"Well, that is interesting, whether or not the people on the church's list of directors are these people we will have to find out, Thanks so much Hetty, how are the dogs?" Asking this question was a big mistake, given that I was in a hurry, but I listened dutifully while Hetty described in minute detail the antics of the puppies and the perfect behaviour of Poppy. Finally, she ran out of steam, and I was able to say goodbye.

I repeated the message to Eleanor, who said "Well Adam is too young to be Reverend Wiseacre."

"But his father would be the right age, and he lives in California." I said, "I wonder whether the Richard Templeton that Hetty remembers, was friends with Adam's father as well as his mother? Perhaps he moved to California with him?"

"It's a long shot, but I'll try and follow up, after I meet with your mystery man about the Trade Fair!!"

"Anyway, don't we know that it was the McVickers who killed Rebecca?"

"We suspect they did, but whoever buried her had to know about the cave, and we do not know whether the McVickers did know that it was there."

We travelled together to the Centre, with Eleanor dutifully in the backseat. On the way over Jenny called me on my cell, to say that the tent man had arrived way ahead of schedule and was waiting for me in the parking lot.

"Bugger!" I said "We'll have to pull together all the stuff for the meeting, after I've finished with him, can you make a start on that? Eleanor is going to try and deal with the trade fair person, can you give her his phone number, and get out everything that he has sent us?" Jenny was typically unflappable and said "Of course" on all counts.

I dropped Eleanor outside the doors to the centre and drove over to meet the tent man who's name I had, of course, forgotten. This aside we got on fairly well, we drove out to where the marquees would be positioned, around the dressage and show jumping rings, talked numbers, sizes, costs and delivery times. He was knowledgeable, sensible and bright, we reached agreement on everything. I drove him back to the car park, shook his hand, and he drove off, with me none the wiser about his name. I hoped Jenny had a record of it somewhere.

I hurried through to the office, to be greeted by Jenny, "That was quick, I thought you'd be out there for ages."

"No, he was good, had all the answers, I've made notes, can you type them up, and we'll send it to him confirming that this was what we agreed to? Oh, and by the way, I have no clue what his name was."

"I've got his name on file, don't worry, I'll type that up right away, and it can go out in today's post. I got Eleanor connected with Alan Harper about the trade fair, he's picked her up, and they're working on it now. I've also pulled out all the figures that you will need for your financial report."

"Jenny pass those figures over, and I'll work on them while you deal with that letter."

Gradually the figures came together, and the bottom line wasn't too bad. I had yet to deal with the television people, but I needed to hear back from Daniel, whether he had done anything about the coverage being able to be mainstreamed, or whether the FEI were going to demand the rites. I had emailed him all the relevant information, along with a copy of the contract that he had signed and asked him to sort this out before he went on holiday, I had not heard back from him. I was secretly glad; it would be one thing I could hold over him at tomorrow's meeting. I asked Jenny when he was supposed to be in.

"He should have landed last night and was supposed to be back at the Centre this morning."

"Tut tut." I said, "He's late on his first day back!"

Eleanor returned to the office, with multiple diagrams on a clip board. She had names and contact numbers of all the vendors, along with descriptions of what they would be selling. She and Alan Harper had worked out positioning of the various stalls, so that a good variety was offered in each area. I could not have done it any better. I thanked her profusely and proceeded to add to my report that the trade fair was organised. As our discipline was the first to run, we had a lot more logistics than the rest of them, who would use the same marquees, trade fair and parking. This was a fact that I would stress the following day.

"It was really strange, that Daniel did not show up today." I told Eleanor,

"Is he like that?" she asked, I shook my head, and told her that he never missed a working day," More's the pity!" I added

"Well maybe his flight was delayed"

"Yes, you could be right. Well, I'm sure he will be back, full of himself, tomorrow."

I asked Eleanor if she was going out with Alistair, but she shook her head. I realised that the two of them had not been together as much lately. True love never runs smoothly! I thought but did not comment.

LOST & FOUND

WE GATHERED IN THE boardroom, where the planning meeting was to take place. All the Chairs of committee, the P.R. people, and the financiers were present. Alistair was there to report on security for the Showcases but was looking distracted. Jenny had come to act as secretary and take the minutes of the meeting. Everyone appeared nervous, these meetings were not normally happy affairs. We all sat around the conference table in awkward silence and waited for Daniel to appear. When this had not happened ten minutes later, I suggested that Jenny go and call his cell phone and his home. I suggested we have some coffee sent up. This duly arrived from the cafeteria, along with Jenny, who announced there was no answer at either Daniel's house or his mobile. Daniel was a bachelor, so there was no spouse to contact for news. We stood around in small groups, sipping coffee, and chatting in low voices. Sensing that somebody had to take charge, I suggested that we all sit back down, and make our reports and discuss any important issues that came up. I said that way, all our time would not be wasted, and we could reconvene when Daniel showed up. Only a few dissented.

We waded our way through the reports. The financial wizards seemed somewhat happy with the figures. They asked several shrewd questions relating to upcoming expenses, that were not included in our reports, we were not going to be allowed to get anything by them.

The P.R. people then went through all the advertising, that had been done, and what was still to come. The local radio and TV stations who were airing our ads would have pressure put on them to come out and do features. They would need somebody from each discipline to interview, so we went over our various options. Knowing that once Daniel returned, he would be the one who would crave the limelight. I suggested that we table this until he was back. The group could see the sense in this, and so we moved on. Richard Talbot from Driving had issues about the rerouting of his course, but everyone felt he had had enough time to deal with this and were unsympathetic.

Pru was happy that Eventing and dressage would work together to erect the rings, and we had a brief discussion about the banners, some were only to be used for the Eventing and were to be taken down once our dressage phase was concluded, to be replaced by those that were dressage specific. We agreed that volunteers were needed to oversee this.

Tom Clark and I held a similar conversation regarding banners and the actual show jumps that were being used. He was going to need many more jumps for his competition than we would in Eventing. We agreed to share some, but Tom would order more to be brought in after our show jumping was completed.

We reached an end to all we could accomplish without our Chairman. Jenny would have the minutes typed up and distributed by the end of day. Alistair would follow up on Daniel's absence and see if he could find the reason for it.

We all went home. I had left Eleanor and Alfie together this morning, as I was going to be tied up with the meeting. I drove back home slowly. I wondered if the police had interviewed Brian yet and whether Iris and Maisie were both OK.

I arrived home to effusive canine greetings, I managed to prevent this from continuing too long by shoving Alfie out into the garden. Eleanor suggested coffee, and I told her that Daniel was a no show.

She asked me if I remembered whether Daniel had left before or after we found out that the bones were those of Rebecca.

"Before, I think." I replied.

"If he was guilty, he'd know that the dental records would confirm that it was Rebecca." I replied, "Why would he kill Rebecca, anyway?"

"Perhaps for his cousin?" suggested Eleanor.

"He had a thing about the maple tree, and he acted strangely when he found out about the skeleton. Perhaps he was just in shock. I think that it is far more likely that Brian, or one of his henchmen, killed Rebecca and her lawyer." I paused for a bit, and then went on, "Do we know whether the police have tracked Brian down?" Eleanor shook her head and said,

"Maybe you should call Alistair and ask."

"Me?" I said surprised "You are the one that is tight with Alistair!"

"I made a mistake there," said Eleanor, "I thought that we might have something, but it appears that I am not "man" enough for him!"

"It shouldn't make any difference to your friendship."

"No, it's just that I feel awkward, since he told me."

"Well get over yourself, good friends are hard to find, and I know that he admires you. Go on give him a call, you can ask him if he has any news of Daniel."

Eleanor went to the phone and dialled, she waited a while and then left a message for him to call her back.

I had had enough for the day. Jenny called,

"I am thinking I might adopt one of the puppies" she said, I asked her how Hetty was doing, and she said she was doing fine. She, Fee and Adam were going to see Alice that evening. She was finally doing much better and being allowed visitors.

"That's good news!" I said, "I am sure that they are relieved, so Adam must be back in the country now, that's good, I want to talk to him." I did not enlighten Jenny on my ulterior motive. I told Jenny to go home, she had done enough for one day.

Alfie was now pounding on the door, so I let him in, and the three of us had a quiet afternoon watching the very old movie, Gigi with Maurice Chevalier on the television.

Alistair called first thing in the morning. He had been to Daniel's house, and there was nobody there, two weeks of newspapers were in the driveway, and the mailbox was overflowing. His car was not there either. Alistair had called the airlines to see if Daniel had missed a flight, but with no idea of when Daniel had been due to travel, they could not help him. Alistair seemed distraught; he wondered what we should do. I said maybe we should give it one more day. If we had to report him missing, then we should inform the Board of Directors.

The police had interviewed Brian's brother, Ellis, who had given them Brian's contact information in California. They were going to get the local authorities down there to go and talk to him. As far as Alistair knew Iris and Maisie were doing fine. He asked to talk to Eleanor, I handed the phone over to her, and let them get on with it.

Once Eleanor was off the phone, she said that Alistair was picking her up shortly. I finished off the breakfast things, got dressed, and tripping over Alfie, made my way to the car. We drove to the Centre and met Jenny coming in through the doors. She had tried Daniel on all his phones and had left him an email saying that we were worried about him, and would he contact us asap.

We got settled in the office. I called the District Commissioner of the local Pony Club and offered her the use of the Centre for their Rally, if they could guarantee us twenty volunteers for the showcase. She was pleased with the offer and promised to get back to me by the end of day. I also called the President of the local riding club offering them a similar deal but did not meet with a similar outcome. "Oh well" I thought "you can't win them all!" I then called my overworked Jump Judge coordinator and asked her if there was any way she could come up with more bodies. Sighing, she said she would see what she could do.

We took a break to go down to the canteen. Alfie had to remain shut in the office, as he was not allowed in the canteen. We ate the meal without enthusiasm. The vegetables were over cooked and the meat was of a species not usually consumed by people. We returned to the office, and I told Jenny to try Daniel again on all his numbers while I took Alfie down for a pee. He was enthusiastic about this idea and raced down the stairs and out onto the landscaped area in front of the centre. Mission accomplished, but receiving glaring looks from one of the gardeners as Alfie's favourite peeing spot was in the middle of one of the flower beds, I smiled broadly, and waived at the man as I hustled my dog back inside.

There had been no reply from any of Daniel's phones, so Jenny and I continued to work through our list. Mid afternoon Jenny said that she had to go and pick up the sponsor boards and banners, she would have to take one of the Equestrian Centre's pickup trucks, as all the stuff wouldn't fit in her car.

I went to the show jumping storage area to make an inventory of the poles and standards, to share with Tom Clark so we would know if we needed to order more jumps. Alfie and

I walked, and to Alfie's delight, it was quite a distance and not one of our usual routes, as it was away from the cross country course, and on the back side of the Centre's main building past John's workshop. This route offered a whole range of new smells, each one of which had to be carefully analysed. I took out my key and unlocked the door to the coverall that housed the show jumps. As I did this, I was vaguely aware of something shining through the hedge that hid the jump graveyard, where John dumped all the fences that were beyond repair. Ignoring this, I entered and spent the best part of an hour cataloging all the jumps. Alfie amused himself by hunting mice, around the perimeter of the building. When I had finished, I relocked the door, and curious, I went round the hedge to see what had caught my eye. Surprised, I found that what I had noticed was sunlight reflecting off a car. I walked over to it. It was a charcoal grey BMW, the license plate looked vaguely familiar. I couldn't place where I had seen it. I cupped my eyes with my hands and peered through the window. On the seat was a piece of paper and looking closer I realised that it was the email that I had sent to Daniel before he left on holiday. This must be Daniel's new car; he had traded in the old one just a couple of weeks before he left and had obviously swapped the number plates onto the new car. This was why the plates seemed familiar, but I hadn't recognised the car.

I pulled out my mobile, and called Alistair, there was no reply. I hung up and tried Eleanor's phone, after a few rings she answered.

"What's up B?"

"I've found Daniel's car, it's round the back of the Centre, by the show jump graveyard area." I heard muffled voices, Eleanor was relaying to Alistair what I had said.

"We'll be right there, we're almost back at the centre."

I plonked myself down on a cross country schooling fence,

these were stored here, in between clinics. They were too big to fit inside the coverall, and so were left outside in the elements, a fact that really annoyed John. On several occasions he had complained to me that we could prolong their life, if we built a building for them. Observing the state of them, I realised how right he was, and made a mental note to bring it up at the next Board meeting. I remained seated watching the clouds, the wind had got up, and changed direction. I smelt something unpleasant in the air. Archie smelt it as well, and nose to the sky he let out a yelp and ran off around the collection of schooling jumps. He stopped beside a large coop and proceeded to bark excitedly. I presumed there was a dead racoon under the coop, the poor thing had probably crawled in under it, to die. Knowing that I was going to have to haul him off his smelly find, I cursed myself, for not bringing a leash. I hunted round and found a piece of baler twine lying on the ground, I picked it up, and was making my way over to Alfie, when I heard a car, Alistair and Eleanor had arrived.

They got out of their automobile and walked over to Daniel's car. Alistair walked round it, and peered inside, much as I had done. I informed him about the email lying on the front seat, Alistair nodded, and pulled out a pair of latex gloves, he opened the car door, which was unlocked, and proceeded to search the inside of the car thoroughly.

"What in hell is the matter with your dog B? Can't you shut him up?" I had managed to block out the barking, from long practise, and was brought back to conscious realisation, that Alfie was continuing to caterwaul loudly by the coop.

"He's found a dead racoon, Eleanor, can you help me get him away from it. I'm afraid that it is a two man job." Eleanor sighed, "You really must take him to dog training B, he is out of control."

She marched ahead of me, I followed with my piece of baler

twine, as we got closer the smell increased, to almost intolerable levels, I thought I might throw up, but kept going knowing that Eleanor would not tolerate such weakness. When we reached the coop, Alfie was running around and around it, barking furiously. I made an inept attempt to catch him, failed dismally, whereupon Eleanor grasped him by the collar, planted both her feet, and hung tight. I hurried over and attached the twine to his collar. Between the two of us, we pulled him away. He jerked back to his wondrous find, and spun me around, so I was facing the coop again. I felt faint, "Eleanor…" I started,

"Shut up B, just get him back, this twine is cutting into my hand." she replied.

"But those are fingers sticking out from under the coop!" Eleanor whirled back round, letting Alfie go, he promptly tore back to the coop, and took up his circuitous route around it, barking insanely.

"Alistair!" we both wailed at once. Alistair extricated himself from the car and looked expectantly at us.

"Come here!" yelled Eleanor. Alistair started walking slowly over to us. Infuriated by his lack of speed she yelled "Hurry up!"

When Alistair arrived at the coop, pulling his scarf over his nose to block the smell, we pointed to the fingers. Alistair squatted down, as Alfie was making one of his whirlwind trips around the coop. The absurdity of what was happening started to get to me, and I tried to stifle a giggle, shock I thought.

"Can you please do something about the dog?" Alistair said coldly. This brought me back to my senses, Eleanor and I redoubled our efforts, and caught Alfie for a second time, we managed to pull him back to Alistair's car, and shoved him in the back. I hated to think of the cost of repairing the car, after Alfie had finished taking out his frustration on it. I hopped in the front, and yelling to the others, I drove the car and Alfie back to the centre. He had settled down a bit while I drove, and I switched him over to my car without too much trouble. I then drove back, and on the way, I shouted to John, who was working in his shop to come with me. He hopped in the passenger seat, and asked me, what was the matter, I shook my head, and drove back to Alistair and Eleanor. John jumped out of the car, but reeled back as the odour reached his nostrils, "What the hell?" he asked, Alistair looked up with relief,

"John, thank heavens! Come and give us a hand!" John looked far from enthusiastic at this command, but nobly walked over.

"Help us turn this coop over, it is too heavy for the two of us" I was standing well away! Between them Eleanor, John and Alistair turned over the coop, and underneath, decomposing, was the body of Daniel Brady. The smell now became totally unbearable, all three stepped back several feet, and the four of us gazed in amazement at the body. Alistair seemed beyond shocked, but was the first to recover himself, and pulled out his cell phone, and called the police.

Having completed his phone call Alistair turned to John, and said unsteadily, "John, can you take the ladies back to the Centre, I will wait here for the police." Eleanor frowned at his words and said she would wait with him. He did not seem to be happy with this, and the two exchanged words. Eleanor sat down on another one of the schooling jumps, and it was apparent that she did not intend to leave. Alistair looked upset, but I assumed that he wanted to spare Eleanor the stress of the situation. John and I turned and walked back towards the car park and entrance to the Centre. John was appalled. "What on earth is going on here? We have two murders on the grounds." I had not really clued into the fact that this was a second murder, but I told myself not to be an idiot, Daniel had hardly died of natural causes, under a cross country jump, that took three people to lift!

We walked on engrossed in our own thoughts, when suddenly, off topic, John said,

"Do you know Michael is back? He called me last night, apparently, he has been back in England for ten days."

"Why on earth did he not come straight here?" I demanded.

We made our way to Jenny's office, picking up Alfie on the way, I was pleased to note that my car had suffered minimal damage. On entering the room, I said,

"We have just found Daniel. He was murdered and hidden under one of the cross country schooling fences."

"OK, pull the other leg," said Jenny, "That's not funny even if it is April 1st." I was confused to start with, by her reaction, but then realised that it was indeed April Fool's day. It took us a while to get her to take us seriously, but finally the sound of sirens, and the sight of police cars roaring round the back of the Centre made the difference. She fell back into her chair, and just sat there saying nothing a totally blank look on her face. John and I looked at one another, unsure as to what we should do. I cleared my throat and said, "Jenny, are you all right?" She turned a furious face towards me and spat out the words,

"Of course, I'm not all right. There are two dead bodies on the grounds, both murdered, and one young girl missing with no trace, what is the matter with you people? Do you think that this is normal?" With this she ran out of the room, in floods of tears. I felt awful, I had pushed my reliable, unflappable assistant and friend over the edge. I looked at John, he too looked beyond reason. "I can't get that smell out of my nose." He suddenly said. I was glad Jenny had left, before he said this. I told him to go home and hurried out after Jenny.

I found her in the ladies' cloakroom, I put my arm around her, and guided her down the stairs, and out to my car and put her in the back, I had little tolerance for Alfie, who was trying to jump all over his Aunty Jenny. He was most surprised, when I swotted him one, and ears drooping and tail between his legs he climbed into the front and sat in mortified silence. I drove Jenny to her mother's house and went and fetched her mother to come out. She was a wonderful woman, wide in the girth, grey haired, sensibly dressed and kind to all manner of people and animals. I adored her as much as I did her daughter. I gave her a brief explanation of what had happened, and she rose to the occasion, as I had expected she would. Duly horrified, she took Jenny into the house. I told her to keep Jenny with her for the next couple of days. She nodded her agreement, and I left Jenny in her capable hands.

I returned to the Centre, Alfie was sulking, so I left him in the car. I went up to the office, and called all members of the board of directors, and told them we had to have an emergency meeting the following day. I then called all the Committee Chairs, and told them the same thing, scheduling it for two hours after the first. I had not told any of them what had happened, only that it was a complete emergency. I then locked the office and went back downstairs to my car. Alfie's mood had improved, and sensing that I was not pleased with him he tried to ingratiate himself by smiling and giving me pokes with his nose. I ignored him and drove back to find Eleanor and Alistair. I parked a long way back from the action, and got out of the car, and walked towards the gathering.

A young police officer who looked as if he hadn't even started shaving, barred my path and said,

"I'm sorry Madam, nobody is allowed through." I started to remonstrate, but Alistair saw me, and nudged Inspector Thomas who looking round called to the policeman to let me through. I tried, without success, to avoid giving a smug look in the young man's direction, and after that I walked over to join the grim-faced group.

"I understand that you were the first to discover the body, Ms Browning." said Inspector Thomas.

"Yes, that's right, well actually it was my dog." I replied.

"How did you come to find it?"

"Well, I came to do an inventory of the show jumps, and then something caught my attention, and I went behind the hedge to see what it was and found the car. I was looking at it and then realised that it was Daniel's car. He had not shown up for work for two days after his holiday was supposed to end. We had been worried about him, and so I called Alistair and Eleanor. I was waiting for them, and Alfie, my dog, started barking and carrying on around this jump. Eleanor and I went to get him, and then I saw the fingers sticking out from under the jump."

"Most distressing, I am sure." He said reverting to his "poor old lady, we must look after her." mode.

"Not so much distressing, as infuriating, that we now have another murder that you will fail to solve!" I threw at him. He was totally taken aback by my assault on his competence, and became quite bristly under attack. Seeing that this was not going to end well, Eleanor said,

"B is very upset that there has been no arrest following the confirmation that the bones found were those of Rebecca"

"This will all take time." The inspector told me, "It is complicated, by the suspect being out of the country."

"Well, I am quite sure that this was his accomplice!" I stated emphatically. I was surprised that Alistair immediately contradicted me,

"You do not know that B, we cannot make statements like that without proof!" I was surprised by this outburst, and even more surprised by the look on his face, it was almost as if he was crying. I decided that we had all had too much for this one day and suggested that we leave it to the professionals.

Inspector Thomas agreed with me, and obviously glad to be rid of me, suggested that all non police should leave the scene.

Alistair would obviously have preferred to stay, but he got in his car, and drove off. Eleanor and I got in my car, which now had the overpowering smell of dog, and drove home to my house.

When we got there, I thought about all the people that I should call, I turned to Eleanor and said,

"I don't know Daniel's next of kin, I suppose it would be in his HR file, at the main office."

"Don't worry about that, the police will look after letting them know."

I told Eleanor about Jenny's breakdown, and that I had called the meetings for the next day. I asked her if she could sit in on the meetings, as Jenny's surrogate.

"Of course, I'll give it a try, but I don't guarantee to be up to Jenny's standard!"

"No worries, just get down the gist of the meetings, and it will have to do," I was silent for a bit, and then sighing, I said, "I did not like the man one bit, but I wouldn't have wished this on him. Do they know how, or when he was killed?"

"Again, we have to wait for the medical examiner, but he was shot in the back of the head, and they think at the start of his holiday. He's been dead for some time" replied Eleanor.

"I thought Alistair was behaving strangely today." I said and Eleanor looked sharply at me, and then she said "Well I don't know if it was anything, but when he was going through Daniel's car, I saw him pocketing some papers from out of the glove box, that's why I refused to leave him. He never gave the papers to Inspector Thomas, when he arrived, and he told him that there was nothing in the car other than your email."

"That's very odd, and I thought he seemed very upset, which is most peculiar because he's always Mister Cool, under fire."

"Do you think we should be up front, and ask him?"

"I think that that is definitely the right thing to do. We cannot be making up all different scenarios for his behaviour, when he may have a perfectly reasonable answer for doing what he did."

We drove in sombre silence to the Centre early. Alfie seemed to sense our feelings of disquiet and refrained from his usual antics. When we arrived, I was surprised to note that we were not the first ones to get there, parked at the front was a large SUV. I got out and went over to unlock the main door. Alfie and Eleanor followed me, but halfway to the door Alfie whirled around, and started barking, he ran back and round the side of the building only to reappear wagging his tail, and accompanying a very tanned Michael Frost, our course designer.

"B, good to see you!" he exclaimed.

"John told me you were back," I answered, "We were surprised that you didn't come sooner, given that you were back in the country."

"Sorry, I had things to get done, so I could be free to work uninterrupted on the Showcase." He said, "How is it going? Is all going to be ready for the big day? Is our trusty CEO satisfied?" I was thoroughly irritated by this questioning, but then reasoned with myself, that he had no knowledge of yesterday's happenings, as far as I knew.

"Michael, we found Daniel Brady's body yesterday, he was murdered. We have no idea if the Showcase will go ahead!" I spilled it out bluntly, and it was obvious that he was flabbergasted.

"B, You've got to be joking!"

"We are here to hold an extraordinary meeting of the Board of Directors, to decide what to do."

"I'm so sorry, I had no idea, I was not being flippant." Michael's voice tailed off, and he stood there stunned, and then asked "Who, why? It makes no sense."

"I'm Eleanor, a friend of B's from England, At this moment we have no idea. The police have started their enquiry, but we have been told nothing. B found the body, and is naturally upset, so can you save your questions for later?"

"Of course." said Michael "I'll go and find John." With that he turned, and got into his SUV, and drove off in the direction of John's workshop.

I mumbled my thanks to Eleanor, and then turned the key in the lock, and we entered the building and went up to Jenny's office, I unlocked this door as well, and we went in. I set about preparing things for the meeting. "What should I do for an agenda" I asked Eleanor.

"There's only one item for discussion, so I don't think that you need one, let's just put out paper and pens, water and glasses, and I'll go and brew some coffee, it is an extraordinary meeting after all." I unlocked the boardroom door, and put out the papers and pens, went to the storage room, and got the water jugs and glasses. I wiped off the glasses that looked a bit dusty and put them around the conference table. I rinsed the jugs out and filled them with water, and that completed, I carried a paper folder and easel down to the ground floor and wrote on it where the meeting was to be held.

As I stood there I was joined by Xen, entering from the coliseum.

"Is it true?" he asked,

"Unfortunately, yes, we found him yesterday, it is not yet supposed to be common knowledge." I replied.

"I won't tell anybody, but the gossip is spreading like a wildfire."

I sighed, "I'm not surprised, just try and keep a lid on it for the time being." Xen nodded and returned the way he had come.

Eleanor had returned with the coffee urn and a tray of cups and saucers. I went back to the office, and got milk and sugar, and brought them back to the board room.

"Do you think that you could call Inspector Thomas, and see if they have any more information that I should be giving the Board?" I asked Eleanor. "Oh, and I should have told Alistair about the meeting"

"Don't worry, I did that last night, Alistair is going to come. I'll call Thomas now." I thanked heaven for my tough friend. She picked up the phone and dialled, she went into the adjacent room, and I could hear her muffled voice talking to the inspector. She came back into the office shaking her head.

"Nothing new to report. He will be coming over to talk to everybody this afternoon."

We went and sat in the board room and waited for everyone to arrive. First was a very subdued Alistair. He was followed by a stream of curious board members, all asking what was going on, some were less than happy to be called in at such short notice. When all of them were there, I suggested we all sit down, I introduced Eleanor and said she was filling in for Jenny who was away sick.

Where is Daniel?" Major Jennings demanded.

"That is why we are here," I replied, "Yesterday, we found Daniel's body in the grounds. He had been murdered. We are here to decide what you want to do now."

"That's total rubbish, I've never heard anything so ridiculous!" said Major Jennings.

"Ms Browning is not being ridiculous! Kindly hear her out!" Alistair spoke with conviction and simmering anger. Because this was so out of character for him, the board members all paid him attention. The major was spluttering.

Roger Brandon said, "We cannot be associated with this sort of thing! Our good names are at risk!" I thought briefly of his involvement with Samantha Wells, and wondered what Helen, his wife, thought of his good name.

"That is exactly why I called you all here." I said, "I thought you would want to consider your positions. We also need to know what to do about the Showcase competitions, which start the beginning of next month. If you want to cancel, we must do it right away. If that is the case, it will be an enormous financial loss. If you wish to go ahead with the competitions, you will need to appoint a new CEO. I think the best thing is for Eleanor, Alistair and myself, leave you to discuss your options."

I rose, and Eleanor and Alistair followed suit. We filed out of the room, leaving raised voices all talking on top of one another. I felt totally exhausted and could not face the walk down to the office, and so I collapsed into one of the chairs in the lobby, the others joined me, we were in a little alcove with a window, through which we gazed out over the grounds. There was a good view from here I realised, you could almost see the sunken road complex, now abandoned. I turned and picked up a magazine off the table, suddenly Alistair said, "Who is that?" I looked back out of the window and saw a figure walking over to the maple tree.

"I think it's Michael, our course designer," I said, "he arrived back here this morning, I wonder what he is doing, we aren't using that loop any more for the cross country."

"He wasn't here when we found Rebecca's remains was, he? Perhaps he has a ghoulish interest, some people are like that." said Alistair.

"That doesn't sound like Michael." I said.

Roger Brandon came out and called us back to the board room. He seemed to have appointed himself Chair, even though I was sure it was one of the other directors who held that position.

"We have decided that we will consult the police and the Centre's lawyers. We realise that we have a fiduciary responsibility to the Equestrian Centre, and so we feel that the Showcase competitions should run. We will address the situation again, after they have finished. We will have to advertise for a new CEO, but for the time being we feel that Ms Browning should be acting CEO." He looked at me as if this was a fait accompli. I immediately said that I was not prepared to take on the task of CEO.

"It will only be for a month or two, until the Showcase has run." went on Richard Talbot, as if I had not spoken.

"No!" I said firmly, "I will not take on the duties of CEO, on top of my own, I will however oversee all the disciplines through the Showcase." Richard Talbot went to argue, but thankfully Alistair stepped in,

"Ms Browning has made her decision quite clear. She will not be forced to do something that she does not wish to do. I personally feel that she is being generous by offering to oversee all the disciplines. As a board you should be able to perform the tasks of the CEO."

I was so happy with Alistair I could have kissed him there and then, instead I turned to the board and said,

"The results of the meeting will be typed up and forwarded to you tonight, Will you please inform me what the lawyers and police have to say. I now have to meet with all the discipline chairs. You will be copied on the minutes from that meeting." I then left the room followed by Eleanor and Alistair.

I returned gratefully to the office and sank down on my

side of the partner's desk. I missed Jenny and made a quick phone call to her mother to see how she was doing. Jenny had taken some sleeping tablets and was still in bed, her mother promised to call when she was up and about.

Eleanor was doing a frantic two finger pick on the computer, "This is going to take me forever to get these minutes done!" she exclaimed. I told her to hand over the notes for the second meeting, and I would do them. I was hardly any faster than Eleanor, but between us we completed the task, and emailed out copies to everybody. By the time we'd finished Alfie was whining to go out.

We grabbed our coats. He bounded ahead of us on a trail that took us round through a small grove of trees and out by the sunken road complex, the caution tape had been removed. Not wishing to go too close to the area we were turning to head back, when a voice called out to us. Michael was sitting on the edge of the sunken road.

"What is the matter, Michael? What are you doing here?" I asked. He sniffed loudly, and rummaged in his pockets, Eleanor passed him a tissue, he muttered his thanks.

"Sorry," he said "I was very close to Rebecca years back, we rode together, competed together, did a lot of crazy things together. I wanted to marry her so much. She was wild, funny and amazing to be around. I had no money, and she had very expensive tastes, instead she married that jerk!" He was practically shaking. I was very surprised, I did vaguely remember Michael competing, but did not realise he and Rebecca Charles, as she was then, had been an item. Michael went on "We used to ride over this land, back then, the old couple that owned it never minded. The three of us used to plan cross country courses on it! I guess we had a premonition that this Centre would be built!"

"You said three of you, who was the third?" enquired Eleanor.

"Why, Daniel, of course! That's why this is so awful, both of them, murdered, and on the place where we used to have such fun, I can't believe it!"

"I didn't know that Daniel rode, he never said anything about it." I said, feeling very puzzled.

"Oh, he was a good rider, he had a great affinity with horses, if he hadn't been gay, Rebecca said she would have married him!"

"Gay?" Both Eleanor and I said at practically the same time.

"Didn't you realise?" asked Michael, we shook our heads.

"Coming from the McVicker family, it was not a good thing to admit. Rebecca and I knew, we were his closest friends. In fact, it was through Daniel that Rebecca met Brian." Michael's face started to implode, I could see that the tears were not far away.

"Why don't we head back? It's starting to get cold. You can't stay sitting here Michael." I said firmly.

"I just wanted to be close to her." He muttered. He looked so bereft, that I said, "Very well, we'll stay with you." Eleanor and I sat down beside him, Alfie was a bit put out that his walk had come to a standstill, and he looked at us all, before deciding to join us. He sat himself down next to Michael who started to stroke him absently. Eleanor broke the silence after a while, "Who would know about the little cave that she was found in? We were suspicious of Daniel, because he always made a big fuss about the maple tree, and never wanted anybody to go anywhere near, and he was practically apoplectic when John dug up the bones."

"We all knew about it." said Michael.

"Who are< we>?" asked Eleanor

"All the crowd, that were competing at that time and their significant others, we had picnics out here, and I think a barbeque."

"Would Brian have known?" went on Eleanor,

"I think so, he used to hang out with us occasionally, none of us liked him, but we tolerated him for Daniel's sake." Eleanor and I exchanged looks. We did not continue quizzing Michael, and after a while he sighed, and got to his feet saying "You're right B, we should go back in."

I asked Michael if he would mind coming to my house that evening, because I wanted him to talk to Alistair. He said he would, not very enthusiastically, but I felt that it was important that we put our heads together about the murders. Eleanor got her phone out and called Alistair who agreed to meet us, he too seemed unenthused.

Eleanor, Alfie and I swung by the Chinese restaurant, and picked up dinner for four, we went back to the house, cleaned up, and laid the table. The Chinese went in the bottom of the Aga. We then opened a bottle of wine and sat down to wait for the men.

Frantic barking heralded their arrival, fortunately for our ear drums they both arrived at the same time. We put the supper on the table, and supplied wine for everyone, Eleanor and I taking a second glass. I started the conversation, telling Alistair that Michael had told us some very interesting things that we thought were pertinent to the case, I then let Michael explain, first about how he, Rebecca and Daniel had ridden over the farm years ago, and how many people, even Brian, knew about the mini cave. Michael stopped at this point, and so I then told Alistair that Daniel was homosexual. Alistair was quiet for a while, obviously considering his next words.

"I know," he said, "Daniel and I were together."

"What do you mean together?" I asked.

"We were a couple" said Alistair crossly,

"Daniel did not want his family to know that he was gay, and I did not want there to be any talk about my marriage to

Cyn. She was my best friend, she knew about my proclivities from the beginning, and it did not bother her. I didn't want her memory to be sullied. Daniel and I therefore lived apart, and met up in private,"

"I'm so sorry Alistair, I can only imagine how awful yesterday must have been, and how hard for you not to be able to react." I said.

"Yes, it was one of the worst days of my life, I cared for him very much. I know Eleanor saw me take something out of the glove compartment and hide it. I found our two plane tickets that were in there. We were going to spend three days together, during his holiday. I know that I shouldn't have touched them, but I could not help myself. The worst thing is that just before his holiday Daniel told me that he was pretty sure that Brian had either killed Rebecca or had her killed. Brian had told Daniel that he was not to let anyone go anywhere near the maple tree and the cave. Brian had told him, to have the soil from the parking lot dumped over the cave, he thought it would be hidden permanently. Once the skeleton was found Daniel was debating telling the police. He was tired of being under the McVicker's thumb. He was also sure that Brian would blame him, and there would be serious repercussions. I told him that Brian was still in California, and that we had nothing to worry about. And he should wait until after our holiday. Oh my God, why did I do that?" Alistair put his head in his hands. Eleanor walked over, and put her arm around him, it was a comforting gesture, and it helped to pull Alistair back together.

"The question is what do we do now? Obviously, the police have got to be told." I said. Alistair nodded, and replied, "I will go and see Bill first thing tomorrow. Eleanor, do you want to come with me?" This was an obvious way of saying that he would not try to hide any of the truth. I was grateful for this, and Eleanor said. "Of course, I will Alistair."

It had not been a comfortable evening, all the wine had been drunk, but little of the Chinese consumed. None of us had much appetite. The men both got up to leave, and we said our Goodbyes.

Absently I opened one of the fortune cookies. "You shall live in strange times!"

Alistair had defended Daniel, when we all had been critical of him. There was no telling when it came to love and attraction, I thought. On my way up to the office I tried to drag my mind back to the jobs in hand. I needed to order bleachers, and I did not know who to contact for this. I suddenly panicked wondering whether we had ordered rosettes and trophies. I so needed Jenny, I thought! Her mother had left me a message that she was doing better, but not ready to return to work.

I entered the office, and after looking through all the files that appeared relevant, I found no mention of bleachers, nor could I find a contact for rosettes and trophies. When requiring local information, the obvious person to call was Hetty. I let her carry on about Poppy. I was not in a hurry to impart my news. Having finished with all she could tell me about the dogs, she went on to say that Alice was doing so much better, and that her doctors thought that if she continued to improve, she should be able to return home.

I told her about Michael, and what he had been able to tell us, and the fact that Alistair and Daniel were a couple. I then broke off and asked her if she could help me for a couple of hours in the office. Hearing the desperation in my voice, she said she'd be right over but could not leave the dogs for too long. I hung up gratefully and realising I hadn't given Alfie his usual walk outside before I took him up to the office, I went back down and gave a careful check for the gardener, before I let Alfie go for his pee in the flower bed.

Hetty arrived shortly after we had returned to the office. Hetty immediately knew who to contact for rosettes and trophies, a friend of hers ran a store, dealing in these items. She offered to go round, and pick out what we needed, she said she would have her friend send me pictures. I agreed immediately, and we set to, and worked out exactly how many we would need of everything for all the disciplines of the Showcase. It was going to be a significant order. Hetty knew her friend would be delighted, and I suggested that she try and negotiate a good price for us. This finalised, Hetty admitted that she had no clue where to find bleachers. She thought for a moment and then suggested I try my tent man. Brilliant! I thought but then was of course unable to remember his name.

Eleanor called, "We need to meet!" I said that I would meet them in the canteen, after I had taken Alfie out.

Alfie and I descended the stairs, I took him out a side door to avoid the gardener, who I had seen busy at work out front. Alfie did his business, and I took him back up to the office, I gave him one of Jenny's cache of dog biscuits, and told him to behave himself.

Eleanor and Alistair were already seated in the canteen with an unappetising looking meal in front of them. Sighing, I picked up a tray, and went through the line up, my foraging skills were no better than theirs, and I ended up with a similar repast in front of me, which was slowly congealing as I answered questions from all the people in line who wanted an update on the second murder. I finally broke away and sat down at the table with my friends.

Inspector Thomas had not been well pleased with Alistair for failing to tell him the truth about his relationship with Daniel and the hiding of the plane tickets. He informed Alistair, that as he was closely involved with the victim, he could no longer assist on the case. Alistair was most upset by this, but he had to agree. Inspector Thomas was interested in the information from Michael that the Marcello family had been aware of the cave, the knowledge of which was a stumbling block in their case against Brian, as they could not see how he would have known about it. The fact that Daniel had feared his cousin, and told Alistair that he suspected Brian of killing Rebecca was also helpful, as well as the warning he received from Brian, re keeping people away from the maple tree. However, Inspector Thomas pointed out to Alistair that this was just hearsay and that a defense lawyer might argue that Alistair was the perpetrator and was obfuscating.

Eleanor then told me that the police in California had been unable to find Brian. The Ontario police had contacted the immigration department, and there was no record of him crossing back into Canada. Eleanor had pointed out that the McVicker family would probably have access to false identities. Inspector Thomas agreed, and said they were on top of this. They basically were aware that the McVickers had committed the two murders but proving it and finding Brian would be difficult. They were continuing to protect Iris and Maisie.

"So, we just wait?" I asked

"Yes," replied Eleanor "police work is all about filling in the gaps, they are going to have to search for witnesses, they are going to bring in Ellis, Brian's brother, and they will question him about Daniel's death. Rebecca was killed so long ago it will be hard to find anybody who remembers anything. They are also looking at Rebecca's lawyer's death as being a possible homicide. Until they find Brian it's going to be hard to make a case."

I said, "I have to go and meet with Pru about the dressage Showcase, and I must get over to Jessica's to watch her ride Quisty

"That would be great B, she needs a bit of help before the Showcase." Replied Alistair.

I then went off to pick up Alfie, and walk over to Pru's office, Eleanor and Alistair went in search of their car.

Pru and I had a productive meeting, all appeared to be in order. I showed her the pictures that Hetty had sent over, of the rosettes and trophies, and Pru was quite satisfied with them. She reminded me that we needed to organise the Prize Givings. This had completely slipped my mind. I could not remember who was in charge of ceremonies, nor could Pru. I told her I would have to go to Daniel's files to find this information, and so I left, promising to let her know what I had found out.

Alfie and I walked over to Daniel's office. When we got there, I found out that it was locked. And there was caution tape across the door with DO NOT CROSS posted boldly in the middle. Of course, I thought, how stupid of me. The police had cordoned off his office, and it was unlikely I would get in there any time soon. I realised that I was going to have to disturb Jenny, she was the only one who would know who was in charge of Ceremonies. Alfie and I walked slowly back to the office, where I called Jenny's mother. There was no reply.

Frustrated I decided to call John and see how he was getting on. When he answered he told me that he and Michael were in the process of sighting the road construction company's jump. Anxious to see it in situe, I said that I would come over to see them. Alfie and I made the walk out to the new loop on the course.

I was not surprised to see Xen had joined them. I knew he had a keen interest in course design and was using time with Michael to soak up knowledge. Seeing I wanted to discuss things with Michael he tactfully left.

Michael had chosen a little knoll on which to place the jump. Beyond it was the first water jump and the TV cameras from it would pick up the bulldozer/digger jump perfectly. I told them that I thought it was ideal. They both looked happy. The three of us sat looking down at the water jump. Goose wars were underway, the Canada geese had arrived from down south, and were fighting over nesting spots, Alfie immediately thought he should join in, but a particularly fierce gander sent him packing! We laughed at his predicament, and embarrassed he trotted off pretending that he was interested in something else.

It was cool out, the sun did not have the heat in it, that it would have later in the year. The picture was beautiful nevertheless, sunlight gleamed on the ripples on the water, and the pale green of early spring was captured in the first foliage of the season. We enjoyed a brief moment of tranquillity in what had become our horrific reality, of murder and missing people. After a while my aged joints started to act up and so I hauled myself to my feet. "I can't sit here any longer, I'm getting too stiff." I said.

"Do you think I could meet Rebecca's daughter?" Michael interrupted my departure.

"Of course, Michael, she's a going concern! I'll talk to Iris, and we'll set up a time." I walked on with Alfie thinking that it would be nice for Michael to meet Maisie, it might give him a feeling of connection to Rebecca.

I went briefly back to my office. There was a message on my machine from Jenny, she would be back to work tomorrow. I would have performed cartwheels of delight, but even back in my youth they had proved impossible to accomplish, so instead I did a couple of fist pumps with a loud, "YES!" Tomorrow I would no longer be adrift in a sea of inadequacy. I decided that in light of this I could afford to go home early. I then remembered Michael's request. I drove to the cafe, and left Alfie in the car, and went in to find everything quiet. Iris offered me a coffee and a piece of cake. I accepted both, the latter guiltily. She told me that she had heard that Ellis, Brian's brother, was being held at the police station. We speculated on where Brian was, had he done a runner from California, had he got himself back to Ontario, had he been the one to shoot Daniel? Having no answers to these questions, the conversation wound down. I told Iris of Michael's request to meet Maisie. Iris smiled, "I know Rebecca had had somebody in her past that she had cared a lot for, she always said how stupid she was to go for material things rather than her true feelings. I suppose that was Michael. Why don't you bring him around mid afternoon on Saturday, we won't be busy then, and Maisie will be home from school." I called Michael, and he agreed to this and so, with this arranged, I left Iris and headed home where I found Eleanor trying to pull a meal together from the meagre offerings in my fridge. A couple of eggs added to some onion, peppers and left-over ham created an edible omelette, and we fried up some potatoes and a wilted leek, and we had a feast fit for kings!

"We saw Fee today in town. She's so excited about the Showcase." Eleanor said. I mentioned that somebody had told us they had seen her with Adam, and she said that she may well have been with him, they were such GOOD friends!" Eleanor laughed, she said, "I think our young Fee is smitten!" I agreed that I thought she had a crush on him.

"Alistair and I think we should go and talk to Adam, do you know where he lives?" asked Eleanor.

"I'm not sure, but call Hetty, she will know. What do you need to talk to him about anyway?" I asked,

"We just want to see if he can tell us more about Brian in California." I nodded at this,

"Oh, by the way I'm taking Michael to the cafe on Saturday afternoon, he wants to meet Maisie."

"That will cheer him up! He will realise what a close thing it was, he could have ended up with Maisie as a daughter!!"

"Eleanor! You are so horrible about Maisie! She's just a little over the top on occasion."

"That's right Bat Bug B!!" retorted Eleanor.

SHOWCASE PLANNING

I FELT POSITIVELY EUPHORIC as I entered the office to find Jenny already installed behind our desk.

Anthea Charrington was apparently in charge of Prize Givings and Pageantry. Jenny contacted her and made an appointment for her to meet me later that afternoon.

Jenny then brought up catering for VIPs and sponsors, we had not yet confirmed numbers or menus. She and I poured over sample menus, the costs were astronomical, but apparently Daniel had chosen this catering company. I wondered whether it was a kick back to the McVicker family. I telephoned Alistair to see whether he would know, he didn't, but thought it quite likely. Jenny and I then called around to other catering companies, most were not available. On the point of going back to the original company I called Hetty, who of course knew just the person! She said she would contact the lady and get back to me with menus and costs later in the day. We couldn't face the canteen, so we called out for pizza.

There were a number of emails and phone calls of regret from people who had heard of Daniel's death. I asked Jenny if she was OK to deal with them, she said it would be no problem, so I left to meet Anthea. She turned out to be a friendly, round, jolly, person who seemed to be on top of everything. She had a pipe band consisting of bagpipers and drummers, who would herald the prize giving. There would be an honour guard of RCMP riders, who would head the parade of winners into the ring followed by Pony Clubbers carrying the flags of Township, Province and Country. She had volunteers who would steward the riders into the ring and assist the VIPs and sponsors to present the ribbons, trophies and prizes. Finally, she had a minor celebrity who would sing the National Anthem of the winner, while some other members of the RCMP would raise the flags of the countries, for the top three winners.

I was a little deflated, when Jenny informed me that we needed flag poles and flags, if the RCMP were going to be able to raise them! We then scurried around, to find availability of flag poles and flags. This achieved, despite a glitch in finding a flag for El Salvador, to satisfy the one show jumping rider from that country, we closed up shop, and headed home.

I remembered my promise to myself, and went grocery shopping, so that Eleanor and I could survive for another week. Alfie's feed was delivered to the door, which was just as well otherwise he might have gone hungry. I stopped by the liquor store and picked up some wine and feeling good about myself, I drove back to my house. The problem with grocery shopping is that you have to carry it all in, and put it away, I really disliked this part of the exercise, partly because Alfie insisted on helping, and it was hard to remain on your feet with a sixty pound hairy beast intent on tripping you up. Finally, task accomplished, I selected a frozen dinner for two and put it in my Aga, you can only be Martha Stewart for so long I thought and poured myself a glass of Pinot Grigio.

The wind had got up, and was howling around the house, I pushed the remote and the propane fire lit up in the fireplace making everything seem cozy.

Eleanor brought Alistair in with her. I got up, handed him a glass of wine, and hissed at Eleanor that we would have to do potatoes and veggies to eek out the meal. She got right on it, and I sat down with Alistair.

He had been holding it all together up until now, but I could see that the stuffing was falling out of him, so I discreetly left him alone, and joined Eleanor in the kitchen. She told me that they had got Adam's address from Hetty, but he had not been there, and so Hetty had then given them a number for the film studio where he worked. They had phoned, but nobody seemed to know anything. They had therefore driven to Toronto, and went on set, only to find that Adam was away for a couple of days, scouting different locations for filming. They were given a cell phone number for him, and finally managed to talk to him. He would be back in Caledon the next day, so they were going to see him then.

We dished up supper, Alistair pushed his around his plate, eating very little. I asked him how he met Daniel, and how long had they been together. This seemed to open him up, and soon it all came pouring out.

"We met at the stables, where I used to ride before I bought Conquistador. Daniel was a good rider, he was very sensitive, and enjoyed the precision of dressage. We rode together often, and then started going out for the odd meal. It gradually grew into a relationship, we would have loved to spend our lives together. The problem was Daniel's family. He had refused to go into the family businesses, but having grown up in the family, he knew too much to be allowed to leave the fold. They constantly kept an eye on him, threatening and bullying him. It affected his psyche. He became bitter." I commented that he had been a person that was not easy to like.

Alistair went on," I know, but that wasn't the real Daniel, he behaved that way because he felt that everyone was against him, he was terrified of you B."

"What!" I snorted.

"You made Daniel feel inferior."

Eleanor burst out laughing, "You are so right Alistair, B scared the pants off everyone in England."

"Don't be ridiculous, I am a perfectly ordinary, if a little bossy, elderly woman."

"Yes, and there's a squadron of pigs flying over the cottage!" retorted Eleanor

Alistair said that he was going to head off. He told Eleanor that he would pick her up after lunch, to go and see Adam.

After he left, Eleanor and I took Alfie out for his last property check. We agreed that we should try to keep Alistair occupied and included, so he did not have time to fall apart. The police would not release Daniel's body for a funeral, and so there would be no closure, until that was done.

QUIZ NIGHT

My team was being worn down by the horror of what had taken place. I would need everyone to be functioning up to speed for the Showcase. I had to come up with an idea of how to improve morale.

I talked it over with Jenny and told her that I had an idea to have a team bonding exercise and asked if she could think of anything that we could do.

"Do you mean something like Outward Bound or Tough Mudder?" she asked

"Really Jenny, I have no clue what Tough Mudder is, but do I look like someone involved in outward bound?"

"Hmm, maybe not. So, we're talking more cerebral and less physical?"

"That would be correct."

"I suppose a murder mystery would be in poor taste?"

If Jenny was into black humour she must be feeling better.

"How about a quiz night, dinner, drinks, two teams answering questions about eventing?"

"Not bad, but who's going to write the questions, and where should we hold it?"

"My Mum likes doing things like that, but she doesn't know very much about Eventing, do you think Fee would help her?" Jenny asked.

"OK, I'll give her a call, and if she's OK to do it, I'll give her your Mum's phone number. I could ask if Iris would host it at the cafe? She doesn't have a liquor license, but if she closed the cafe, and it was for a private party it would be OK. We could order pizza in."

The plan in place. I had to meet with Tom Clark, to ensure that all was ready, for the show jumping Showcase. As Eventing's third phase was show jumping, we had overlapping issues. After the fateful day, where I had made the inventory of show jumps, I had passed the list on to Tom. He had ordered more jumps, that would be delivered the following week.

We met at the show Jumping ring. Tom explained that he would need to hire more people for ring maintenance. The footing had to be harrowed and watered between classes, and the centre did not have enough full time workers to be able to do this. I told him to go ahead, but to give me an accounting of this as it was in addition to the approved budget. We agreed to share the ring crew who would put up the rails that got knocked down, as long as Tom's volunteer chair could persuade her people to do double duty. Tom's international course designer was scheduled to design the eventing course as well as those for all the show jumping classes. This would involve us having to arrange hotel accommodation for him for the entire competition, or alternatively we would have to fly him back and forth to Europe in between. Tom agreed to look into this.

The driving chair, Richard Talbot, did not appear to have a grasp of everything necessary, for his discipline to run. He had insufficient volunteers, his course designer had left before the course was complete, and two of his officials had cancelled out. I told him that I would give him three more days, and if things were not in order, we would have to look at cancelling the driving. He was not happy about this, as the running of the Showcase was written into all our contracts. If I pulled the plug on Driving, he would not be paid the greatest part of his stipend, which was due on completion. He left me in a huff. I worried about what the Board of Directors would say if driving was cancelled, but better cancelled than a complete debacle, I thought.

I finished my day with vaulting and Randy Wainwright, what a difference, I thought! He had everything organised and at the tip of his fingers. His discipline would run indoors in the main coliseum. He had more volunteers than he needed, banners would be moved from around the dressage ring indoors to the coliseum, as soon as dressage was completed. The positioning of the TV cameras was marked out, He had liased with Alistair, over crowd control involving spectators entering the seats around the stadium, so none of the horses would be spooked. Stewards had already been briefed on their duties. When he had finished explaining all the systems that he had put in place I asked him if he would like to take over driving. He looked puzzled and I told him, I was only joking.

I returned to the office where a grumpy Alfie was waiting for me. "Don't let him complain too much!" Jenny said, "I've had him out twice, and he ate half my sandwich at lunch."

"You're an angel." I said, "Everything is good except for driving, and I honestly don't know if we can let it run."

"That bad?" said Jenny, I nodded, "I don't really know that many people in the driving world. We need to pull in somebody good, to see if we can salvage the competition. I'll have to call round tomorrow and see if anybody has any ideas. I'm exhausted Jenny. Let's head home."

Jenny had been checking through all the entries, to ensure that they were qualified and had their national federation's permission to compete. She looked equally tired, and so we locked up and left the building.

I got home, and felt inspired to cook something, rather

than just heating it up, so I set to, to peel some potatoes, prepare some runner beans, and pull out a couple of lamb chops This done I called Eleanor to find out when she would be back. She told me she should arrive in about half an hour, which would work out perfectly for my meal. I laid the table, dug around in the back of the fridge, and found some mint sauce. I put on the potatoes and put the chops in the oven, ten minutes before Eleanor was due to arrive, I boiled the water for the beans and the whole meal was ready to be dished up as she walked through the door!

"Am I brilliant or what?" I asked Eleanor, as she washed her hands.

"Well, most people cook meals every day, so I'm not sure brilliant is the right adjective, for such a common place occurrence!" she said as she sat herself at the table. I stuck out my tongue at her.

"Such maturity!" she commented.

I dished up the meal, "What did Adam have to say?"

"Well, he told us about the Church where his father preaches. His father is Reverent Wiseacre. The Church bought out the film company that was making the religious documentaries. People go to the retreat to meditate, receive counseling and to recharge their batteries. The film company offers courses in all aspects of film, acting, directing, script writing, make up and costume. This brings in more income for the Church.

"We asked him who was involved financially. He said he wasn't sure but that there were Canadians who had been friends of his father who had invested initially. We asked about Brian McVicker but he denied knowing of any involvement by Brian. We didn't think he was being truthful about that.

"He had indeed been going out with Jessica, but lately she

seemed to be going off him. He had called her to find out why, and she said that she would like some distance.

"He seemed genuinely upset, about her breaking up with him. He feels that it was exactly the same when Paloma went missing, she didn't tell him anything. He is beginning to think that his relationships are cursed." finished Eleanor.

"He said that he tried to live up to his father's beliefs. The Church of Holy Point was highly respected."

"I guess that explains the prayers and religious mannerisms." I said, "Did you find out anything about the scandal involving the Reverend?"

"We asked, but Adam told us that it was all unsubstantiated accusations."

"He must be embarrassed by it." I said, shrugging.

We decided to do something different for the evening, and we had a game of scrabble. I won, of course but when we retired to bed Eleanor was still challenging my triple word score with the use of a blank tile.

Michael and I went to the cafe. We walked through the door, and Maisie hurled herself at me screaming, "Bat Bug B! I've missed you!"

"I've missed you to. Maisie, I want you to meet a friend of mine, this is Michael, he's a famous cross country course designer."

"Really! I'm learning to jump, but just boring show jumps at the moment. Fee, she's my teacher, says that I've got to be tighter in the tack and not go so fast, but you've got to go fast cross country, so that's rubbish!"

Michael stood looking at her, and burst out laughing, "You are your mother's daughter" he exclaimed.

"Well, that's a dumb thing to say! Of course I am my

mother's daughter, and if she's my mother, of course I'm her daughter!" said Maisie, with the irrefutable logic of youth. Iris butted in, and said, "Maisie, that's rude, do not tell people that they said dumb things."

"Michael, this wonderful person is Iris, she tries to half halt Maisie!" I explained. Michael laughed, he shook Iris's hand, and said "It looks like you've got your work cut out for you!"

We stayed for a couple of hours, and it was clear that there was a growing bond between Michael and Maisie. I chided myself, as I detected a flicker of interest from Iris, when Michael asked her if she was taking part in the quiz and perhaps, she could be on his team. We said goodbye, and Michael promised to watch Maisie ride. "Good, you can tell Fee that I need to go fast!"

The Driving competition was my constant headache. Jenny found someone who, the driving association thought, would be able to help Richard Talbot, but the two did not get on, and the man left, after the first day. I then got back to the association, it was the sport's governing body after all, and told them that if they wanted their sport to be represented at the Showcase they would have to take over the organising of the event, as Richard was incapable. They made all sorts of excuses, but I left it, that it was up to them, "Either shit or get off the muck tub!" I said finishing the conversation and hung up.

I went home, took Alfie out, fed him, and promised him a treat when I went out. He looked at me expectantly, and I quickly got dressed, got out his marrow bone, from the other night, and filled it with peanut butter. I left him happily making a mess on the kitchen floor. The liquor store was busy, and I had to wait in line to pay. "Having a party then?" the cashier asked. I nodded my assent and struggled to carry the bags out to the car. I arrived at the cafe and looked hopefully for a strong male to help carry in the alcohol, John saw me, and hurried out to help. After we had unloaded the booze he stood looking a little uncomfortable, and going slightly red in the face, he told me that he had invited Amelia to the quiz, and did I mind? I laughed and said that that meant she would have to be on the repair crew with him at the Showcase, the quiz was only for Eventing workers! John laughed and said he would tell her.

Xen and his girlfriend Susie were making up the numbers and arrived chattering like two magpies. Susie was a going concern, she had an infectious laugh and so many piercings I was surprised that she didn't leak like a sieve. I introduced her to everybody, Xen being too busy, talking to Michael and John about the placement of the bulldozer/digger jump.

We split ourselves into two groups, I was in charge of one, and Jenny the other. Instant rivalry began, and the questions, that were well thought out, caused many a scratched head. Jenny's team booed and hissed at my team, when we failed to come up with the winners of the gold medal at the Sydney Olympics, but honour was finally ours, and we won by one point.

Michael had been sitting next to Iris during the contest, and they were facing the street. Michael's eyes suddenly narrowed as he peered out towards the parked cars. He pushed Iris down to one side. There was a loud bang, and the sound of breaking glass. Michael was on his feet and out the door in a flash. People started shouting, John, Eleanor and Alistair jumped up. Iris was lying on the floor. She was bleeding from a wound on her arm. Susie knelt down beside her and Amelia came over with a tea towel and wrapped it round her arm, putting pressure on the wound. John, Eleanor and Alistair followed Michael outside. I pulled out my cell phone and called the police. Xen kept asking what he should do. I pointed to Jenny who was sitting shaking, and he went to her side, and started picking pieces of broken glass from off her sweater. The two of them waved me away and I decided to go outside to see what was happening. There was shouting coming from down the street, and I moved down towards the noise.

"Be careful, Michael!" I heard Eleanor yell "He's got a gun!" with that there was another loud bang, like the one before. As I got closer to the commotion I could see Michael wrestling with a man, hanging on like grim death to his wrist. John, Eleanor and Alistair were closing in on them from the opposite direction. There was a second gunshot, and the man broke away from Michael, and ran towards me, John was after him, yelling at me to move. Eleanor fell to one knee by Michael, who was lying, not moving, on the ground. I was terrified, but at the same time furious, with this person. I had no time to decide where I should hide, when the man was on top of me. I swung my arm back, and found to my surprise, that I had hold of my purse, with all my might I brought it over my head and down on top of the man's head. It made a satisfying clang as it connected, and I realised my horseshoes must have inflicted some damage. As well as that, the shoulder strap got caught around his neck. I hung on like grim death as his momentum pulled us both down to the pavement. I hit my head hard, and then heard a distant clatter, and hoped that it was the gun sliding away from the man's hand. He was punching at me, trying to free himself from my strap. I kicked out as hard as I could, and heard him gasp for air, and then John was on top of us, he was punching the man, with all his considerable strength, I was trapped under the pair of them, but attempted to help John inflict as much pain as possible, on the man. Alistair who had cut down the side alley to get ahead of the man, arrived at the scene, and the two, of them pulled the aggressor to his feet. My skirt had been pulled up almost to my face during the altercation, so attempting to preserve some decorum, I adjusted my clothing. Alistair leant down to help me, whilst still keeping a hold on the man. I tried to haul myself to my feet with Alistair's help, but I found that my left leg would not bare any weight, I let go of Alistair's hand, and fell back down, where I had to wait like a stranded whale, for more reinforcements to help me to my feet.

Sirens could be heard coming down the road. Two police constables jumped out of their car, when it pulled up in front of us. They surveyed the scene. They were obviously hard put, to tell who were the bad guys. Seeing people lying on the ground they called for an ambulance, and then recognising Alistair as one of the good, they took the man that he and John were holding into custody and put him into the back of the police car. Alistair pointed out the gun on the ground, and they put it into an evidence bag.

John and Alistair then hauled me to my feet, and assisted by the two of them, I hobbled anxiously down the street to where Michael was lying. Eleanor was looking worried and pressing on his chest. There was a lot of blood.

Amelia and Iris now ran down the street towards us, when Iris saw Michael on the ground, she cried out, and sped up to get to him, she was clasping her arm. Amelia caught hold of her good arm and held her back. The first responders arrived, they took over from Eleanor, applying pressure on the wound, they hooked up an IV, took vitals, and not happy they called in to the hospital. There was a lot of action, drugs were administered, Michael was loaded onto a gurney and placed in the ambulance, They told us they were taking him to Orangeville hospital, but that he might be taken by air ambulance to Sunnybrook, in Toronto, from there.

I watched the lights retreating down the street. Amelia came up alongside me and said that she thought Iris and I should both go to hospital. Eleanor appeared and agreed. She asked if Amelia could drive us, and she would deal with the police and the others who were all standing, looking lost outside the cafe. Amelia went and got her car, while I stood shakily listening to Iris say over and over, "He saved my life!"

I do not remember anything of the drive to the hospital, or what happened next. I woke up the next day to find Jenny sitting by my bed. I was lightheaded and felt very fuzzy, "Where am I?" I demanded.

"In hospital, and you're going to stay here for a while." said Jenny firmly.

'I'm fine!" I said, swinging the bed clothes off my legs and making to stand up. Immediately my head started to spin, and Jenny shouted, "Nurse!"

A fierce harridan appeared and pushed me back into bed.

"Ms Browning, you are in no state to leave, you have a concussion, a broken ankle, one broken rib and a bruised spleen. You will be here with us, for a few days."

"That cannot be." I said.

"Shut up!" cried Jenny, "You will do as you are told! I've had it with the lunacy of all the people involved in eventing." Fearing that she might suffer another breakdown, I was quiet. "Michael?" I asked.

"In Sunnybrook, last we heard he was upgraded to stable." She spat out, "Iris?" I queried.

"She had a gunshot wound to her arm, the bullet passed right through her arm, she stayed in hospital overnight, but will be going home today." I absorbed this information slowly, my brain was definitely not up to speed, I knew there was an important question that I had to ask, but I couldn't grasp it.

"It was Brian McVicker." Jenny said, her brain obviously working better than mine.

When I awoke for a second time Iris was sitting beside me. I was startled and could not work out where I was and why Iris was there with her arm in a sling.

"It was a through and through wound, I am lucky, if it wasn't for Michael, I would be dead. And just look what has happened to him?" I had a bit of trouble following this, my memory had some serious missing links.

"He'll be fine." I said having no idea if this was the truth. Suddenly I had an awful thought. "How is Maisie?" I exclaimed.

"She is fine, she knows nothing. Jenny called Hetty and she is staying with her. I have no idea how to tell her that her father tried to kill me and Michael."

"Oh, no!" I groaned, the lines on the machines, that were attached to me, started beeping and making strange shapes, a nurse appeared and pushed a needle into my arm, and I disappeared into unconsciousness yet again.

The next time I awoke, Amelia, John and Xen were sitting beside my bed. This exchange of people was alarming. Again, I felt disorientated.

"What are you doing here?" I mumbled, "What happened to Jenny and Iris?"

"They left a couple of hours ago. Iris has gone to Sunnybrook Hospital, and Jenny back home to sleep, as she will be busy tomorrow, dealing with everything at the Centre. Alistair is at police headquarters, he sends you his love." I tried to take all this in, but the synapses in my brain were firing very slowly. I could feel myself nodding off again.

I awoke a couple of hours later, John was the only one sitting next to me. "Amelia had to go back for morning surgery, Xen drove her." John explained. "We heard that Michael is doing better and will be out of the ICU later this morning." I knew that I should feel good about this, but my brain was still confusing me. John smiled at me and asked if he could get me anything. I pondered this question for awhile but came up with no answer. My blank face obviously gave him an answer, and he got up, and left the room. He had called a nurse, who came and injected something into my IV, which resulted in another trip to never never land.

When I finally awoke from this last chemically induced slumber Hetty appeared at my bedside.

"You were snoring!" she said

"And hello to you!" I replied grumpily, realising that I was finally feeling more normal, "I thought you were with Maisie?"

"I have been, she's at my house playing with the puppies. Fee is with her."

"Does she...?" I asked faintly, Hetty sighed and said "No, I haven't told her. I have no idea how to do it." I was just taking this in, when my brain went off on a tangent, and panic swept over me,

"Alfie?" I spluttered, "where?" Hetty interrupted. "He's with Jenny. She picked him up on her way home, she'll keep him, until you're out of here." Relief flooded over me,

"You are not to worry, and it will be good practise for her, for when she gets her puppy."

"She's going to take one then?"

"Yes, they'll all be gone, John's having one and Maisie wants one now."

"You'll have to clear it with Iris, I presume the child will be with her permanently now, and it won't be easy having a puppy in the cafe." I said, suddenly starting to feel very tired again. Hetty must have noticed as she got up and was saying something as she walked to the door. My eyes closed of their own volition, and I was away again.

I stayed in the hospital for two more days, I think they were glad to be rid of me. I was feeling so much better, and just wanted to get out of there. I drove Jenny around the bend phoning her every five minutes about things that I wanted done, things that I had forgotten and things that the other chairs of disciplines had to do. She listened patiently, and agreed to all my requests, causing me to be placated for a short amount of time until the next thought entered my head.

Finally, my doctors agreed to release me. I had a walking cast on, the break in my ankle being a clean one. My side was incredibly painful, but I was discharged with plenty of painkillers and severe warnings not to take them with alcohol or to get addicted to them. I wondered why they had given me the bloody things if that was the case. A nurse wheeled me out to the entrance in a wheelchair, the hospital's insurance did not want to risk my falling on the way out. Eleanor was waiting, with my car at the curb.

"You'll have to go in the back!" she said brusquely, "You know who is in the front."

I was delighted to be reunited with Alfie, even though his enthusiasm at seeing me involved him leaping on me and causing extreme agony. Eleanor dragged him off me, and reinstalled him in the front seat, and we drove back to my house, I reached for the pills.

REVELATIONS

TWO DAYS LATER I was able to drive myself to the Centre, thankful that it was my left ankle that was broken. Eleanor felt I should not be driving with a cast on, it would be illegal in England,

"Rubbish," I said, "Canada has no such rule!" thinking that probably it did. We arrived at the Centre, and Eleanor said that Jenny had a surprise for me, she had moved the office downstairs to an empty room, so that I would not have to do stairs. This was a great relief, I had been wondering how I was going to negotiate them, the lift being at the opposite end of the building. Alfie and I entered our new quarters, and Jenny handed him a biscuit to make him feel at home. He smiled at her had a sniff round the room, and finding his bed had been brought down here he got in it, made several fairly violent circular turns, to organise the bed to his liking, and then promptly lay down.

I sat down on my side of the partners' desk. The Driving Association had failed to pick up the torch, and therefore Driving was cancelled from the Showcase.

I contacted all the driving sponsors and explained what had happened, I offered to return their money or to hold it over, to when Driving would hold a competition. About half wanted their money, and so I wrote out cheques for them, and Jenny typed a form letter, and made up the envelopes.

I phoned John and asked him to come to the new office. He said that all the jumps were in place and had been pegged down. On cross country all the jumps were supposed to be immobile, therefore large metal screws, that looked like corkscrews, were pushed and turned into the ground, these then were bolted to the jump. Alternatively half rounds of lumber were dug into a depth of three feet behind the obstacle and bolted to it. This was a very big job, and I was surprised that John had already accomplished it.

"I hope, for your sake, that the Ground Jury don't want any of them moved." I said,

"I'm sure they won't, seeing as it was Michael who designed it!" replied John. I hoped he was correct. The Ground Jury, who were the judges of the whole eventing competition, had the ultimate say.

"Is the Technical Delegate happy?" I asked

"Oh, yes. He's happy with it all." I nodded.

"How about numbering and flagging?" I asked.

"Under control, I will be doing all the brushing, and then Tabitha is coming in to decorate the course. She has asked that the grounds people make sure that there are piles of mulch on either side of each jump, so that she can plant the bushes, shrubs and flowers." John continued. I turned to Jenny who wrote this down.

The brushing that John was referring to was stuffing certain fences, with cedar or pine stems to make it look as if they were growing out of the jump. Tabitha was a landscape architect, who had volunteered to decorate the jumps. We rented skid loads of flowers, trees and bushes that were delivered in a tractor trailer. Tabitha, and her team, would unload them and transport them to each jump on the course, where she would transform a boring coop type jump into a work of art. The course designer would then go round, and move any flowers or shrubs which, in his opinion, would make it hard for a horse to "read" the jump, by which we mean, work out where to take off in order to avoid hitting the jump. There was a science to all this. Experienced horses read a jump from the top of the fence, greener ones look at the bottom, I hoped we had pulled together the best team of people to make the jumps understandable for all the horses.

"I will need some help, with roping the course, and I still have to build the start box" added John.

Michael was on the phone, "They're going to let me out of here tomorrow, do you think somebody could come and pick me up?" I was thrilled to hear from him and told him so. I took down the details of when and where and told him that everybody would be fighting to have the privilege. He laughed at this, and then hung up. I told Jenny the good news, and we briefly talked about who should go to Toronto to pick him up, in the end we decided that most people really had enough to do to get ready for the Showcase, so we decided that Eleanor was the best person to go, if she didn't mind. I gave her a ring, and we arranged to meet at a nearby fast-food place, where we could all grab a bite to eat. When she arrived, I asked her if it would be a bother for her to fetch Michael the following day. She said she'd be happy to do it, as long as I had a GPS for her to follow in downtown Toronto. We ate our lunch, which was a slight improvement on canteen food, and then the three of us returned to the Centre. Jenny and Eleanor in the back and Alfie happily in his motoring position next to me.

When we got back to the office, Alistair was waiting.

He had a broad smile on his face, a twinkle in his eye, and it sounded like a laugh was trying hard not to get out. Frowning I said, "I'm fine Alistair, how are you?"

"Better for reading this." From behind his back, he drew

out a newspaper, and there on the front page was a particularly unflattering picture of me, with a headline that read,

SEVENTY YEAR OLD BARETTA BROWNING TAKES DOWN ACCUSED MURDERER WITH HER HANDBAG!

Jenny and Eleanor craned their necks to see what I was gazing at, with my mouth wide open.

"How dare they!" I spluttered,

"I think it's rather flattering! Your Handbag! Wasn't that a line from Oscar Wilde?!" replied Alistair.

Jenny grabbed the paper from Alistair, and she and Eleanor read the whole article, giggling to one another, as they read.

I stormed, "I'm going to call them! They should do a retraction!"

"B, don't be so stupid, it is all true." said Jenny. "Here read it." Ungraciously I snatched it from her. and scanned the article, unfortunately the article had it's facts correct, it was just the headline that infuriated me.

"It was Michael and John who really caught him, and you as well Alistair." I complained,

"Oh, but it was definitely your handbag that did the heavy lifting!" Alistair was still laughing. I thought this was probably a good thing, he had been far too upset since we found Daniel, so I decided to leave my complaints for now.

"Alistair, have you heard from Inspector Thomas about any charges?" I asked.

"Yes," He said, "Brian McVicker is being charged with three counts of first degree murder, for Rebecca, her lawyer and Daniel. Ellis McVicker is charged with accessory after the fact. Brian is also being charged with attempted murder and causing grievous bodily harm for the attack on Iris, Michael and you. It is going to be a very lengthy trial, the McVickers have hired the best lawyers, and it will be a long time until they will be brought to trial. There is no chance that Brian will get bail, but it is possible that Ellis will."

"What about Maisie?" I asked

"She will be made a ward of the court. Do you think that Iris would be willing to take her on full time?"

"I think so." I said.

"In that case she should petition the court for custody." Said Alistair.

Michael couldn't wait to get back to the Equestrian Centre to oversee preparations for the Showcase. His doctor at the hospital, told me that Michael needed continued bed rest for several more days, and his incisions dressed twice daily. We arranged for him to have nursing care, which he had not received well.

Jenny and I were starting on the work involved with the office of Health of Animals. They were in charge of the import of the horses from the various countries that were sending competitors to the Showcase. Quarantine restrictions were strict, and we had to comply with all demands, or the foreign horses would be turned back. The import and export papers for the horses were complicated, and we did not want the owners of the horses to make any mistakes. This meant we had to contact each one individually, and make sure that their vets had completed everything properly.

I then had a somewhat heated meeting with our stable manager over the requirements for isolation, disinfecting, separation of manure, and disposal of the same. She was unused to such strict protocols and said she could not do it alone. Sighing, as I saw my budget skyrocketing, I told Jenny we would have to get more people from the job centre. Jenny made a note.

Having spent a whole day on this subject, I left to go over to Michael's. He told me that Iris was coming over to see him and to bring him some things that he needed. He hoped that Maisie would come as well. I stayed and chatted for a while but left as soon as Iris and Maisie arrived.

I went out to my car; Alfie had started to chew on the handle of the passenger door. I admonished him for this, and we drove off to watch Jessica ride Quisty. Not wishing to have my car further destroyed, I took Alfie with me on a leash. He hated this and hung back behind me forcing me to practically drag him along, while he made choking noises in his throat. Jessica hearing this, worried that he was sickening for something. I informed her that it was his way of generating sympathy. She then laughed, got on Quisty, and rode off around the school. Alfie perked up, he liked horses, so he sat and allowed me to give Jessica some advice. She tended to let him fall behind the leg, so I suggested she ride him up and forward more into a light but confirmed contact.

The pair were lovely together, and we worked through a warm up and into the real work of a training session. His lateral work was wonderful, they floated across the school legs crossing and displaying massive suspension. Jessie sat quietly her aids almost invisible. He was laterally and longitudinal supple, able to lengthen his stride and cover a huge amount of ground, and then sit down and shorten that stride back into collection. His flying changes were good and expressive, he had trouble with the tempe changes, when he had to switch the leading leg in the canter from one side to the other. We worked on improving the quality of the canter, before asking for the changes, and they then improved. He struggled a little in his canter pirouettes, but I felt that this was a lack of strength which also showed up in the piaffe, passage sequence. This was where the horse sat down and trotted on the spot, and then went forward into a slow very elevated trot. This required a huge amount of strength, from the horse's hocks, which carried the weight of the horse in these exercises. Younger horses had to develop this strength, and older horses often suffered strains and injuries to the hocks. Quisty was very young to be working at this level, and like Killer, just needed more mileage and experience. We finished the work with stretching to allow the horses muscles to stretch and relax, much as a human athlete would go through a cool down period. Jessie was thrilled with her session and asked me if I would come back. I told her that my professional coaching days were over and having a full-time job at the Centre left me with little free time, but I would come back occasionally to give her a hand.

I asked her about going out with Adam, she said that she had not felt comfortable with him and had made excuses to break it off. She said that Adam had now moved on. I did not press the matter, I said Goodbye and Alfie and I went back to the car. Alfie was pleased to leave, having got bored with dressage. We went home for the rest of the evening.

Eleanor had gone, with Jenny, to Hetty's place to look at the puppies. Jenny was still having trouble choosing which one she wanted, and so had enlisted Eleanor to help her make up her mind. Jenny brought Eleanor home and came in for a drink.

They were both full of stories about the puppies who were now old enough to have different personalities. Eleanor had rolled each one of them on their backs. One had just lain there quietly, and Eleanor thought that that would be the best one for Jenny, as it was likely to be the quietest and the most obedient. One had fought wildly, and refused to stay down, Eleanor laughing said she thought it would be the perfect dog for Maisie, they would be two of a kind. The third puppy was a boy and he had been like a cross between the two, so Eleanor thought he should be John's.

Jenny agreed, she said she loved the wild one, but thought the quiet one would be a better fit for her, as she would have to bring her to work. "Do you think Alfie will mind?" she asked me.

"He will love her, he's great with puppies." I replied, "And we don't have to worry about Daniel objecting." I felt a little guilty saying that, but it was the truth.

It had been a long hard haul but finally, I felt that we had finally nailed down all the problems and we were ready for the Showcase.

With ten days left to go and only the finishing touches needing to be put on things, Jenny and I took some down time to recharge our batteries, before the major onslaught of the Showcase. Jenny went to stay with a friend in Toronto, and Eleanor and I did some touristy things. Eleanor would be returning to England following the Showcase, and I felt guilty that all she had done was work.

We spent a day at Niagara Falls, returning via Niagara on the Lake. I found my caste very annoying, and Eleanor was still complaining about my driving with it, but we had a good day and Eleanor could not believe the awe inspiring falls.

We spent another day with Hetty, and Iris joined us. Poppy was now fed up with her puppies who were super active. They gnawed her caste and pulled her tail and ears. She put them in their place growling at them, and sometimes picking one up by the scruff of it's neck and giving it a shake. John had been over and had built a run for them outside as they had started to wreck the house. This meant Poppy could have time for herself. She was a comical dog, obsessed with balls and all things round, she went mad when somebody road past on a bicycle.

It was warm outside, and we sat on Hetty's deck, Iris and I had petitioned the court, for her to gain custody of Maisie, and we were just waiting to hear back from the judge. Michael was almost fully recovered, and Maisie wanted him to come and watch her ride. She asked us if we would like to come. This was a no brainer, we all agreed and set a time for the next day.

The telephone rang, and Hetty got up to answer it. Obviously, a telemarketer was trying to sell Hetty something. She made short shrift of them and slammed the phone down.

Once she sat back down, Poppy started poking her with her nose, and let out an excited yip. She then tore round the garden, spinning in tight circles, and racing up to Hetty, jumping up, and giving her another poke. This went on for a good five minutes, and then she plonked herself down at Hetty's feet puffing and panting. We had just witnessed the first of her "mad five minutes" which, as we got to know her better, became one of her signature activities. Amelia later told us that most bull terriers do this, it was thought to be how they confused bears, when they were used for bear baiting. It was highly amusing, and after this first episode, we were laughing so loud the neighbours peered over their fence to see what was going on. Poppy was making her mark on all our hearts.

Eleanor, Iris and I headed home an hour later, it had been a lovely lazy afternoon, and we were ready to fix a quick meal, and go to bed. Iris was going to pick up Maisie, and try to get her to bed, as she would be so excited about us all coming to watch her ride the next day.

Back home I had to deal with a very cross dog. Alfie was not happy to have been left behind, and to add insult to injury, he discovered Poppy smells all over us. We gave him his tea, and then took him for a short walk whereupon he forgave us and settled down with us as we ate a TV dinner on our laps and watched Jeopardy.

Annoyingly the phone rang, I sighed heavily, but made the effort to get up and answer it. It was Hetty and she was very upset. She had heard from Beeton Hall that Alice was going to be released. Apparently, she had telephoned Fee to tell her that her mother was returning home, and that she was arranging to have Home Help come in each day. Fee had totally lost it on her grandmother, screaming and yelling that she should have been consulted, she could look after her mother, she had done it all along, before her mother went into hospital, and that she didn't think Alice was ready to come home.

"I don't know why this set her off, this time." Hetty said.

"What do you mean "This time"?" I asked. Hetty caught her breath and replied, "The last time was when I suggested she come and live with me."

"I suppose she just likes her independence," I suggested "But she has to accept that it is her mother's house, and that Alice will need some professional help."

"That's what I told her, but she just slammed the phone down on me." said Hetty sadly.

Fee needed a good talking to, everyone had always tip toed around her because of her deformity, but she was no longer a teenager and I, for one, would not tolerate her behaving like this to her grandmother. I told Hetty that I would talk to her, and would also come over when Alice came home, so there were no issues to cloud Alice's homecoming. Hetty thanked me, and hung up, I was furious at Fee for ruining her grandmother's day.

Eleanor and I brought Alfie with us to watch Maisie ride. Iris was picking up Michael, and Hetty was coming under her own steam. We arrived at the Riding for the Disabled stables. Maisie roared up to us shrieking in excitement. She was immediately reprimanded by one of the instructors, to be quiet around the horses. I was pleased to see that she immediately obeyed. She had been threatened with and received loss of riding privileges for bad behaviour, so now she was a lot more obedient. She went back to grooming a pony, a cute looking Section B Welsh, I thought. Maisie explained that his name was Nipper, and he did nip sometimes, he would also nap and go back the way he had come when he did not want to go somewhere. "Most kids don't like him, but I think he's funny, and he can jump!" Maisie exclaimed. All could be forgiven, as long as the horse would jump!

At that moment Iris arrived with Michael who climbed slowly out of the car, oblivious to his pain, Maisie flew at him, and gave him a hug. Michael staggered back wincing, and Iris told Maisie to remember what she had been told. Shamefaced she mumbled "Sorry." to Michael, and took him by the hand, and dragged him over to see Nipper, chattering away to him. The pony pinned it's ears, and went to bite her, unceremoniously she punched him on the nose. The pony suitably chastised put it's ears back forward and stood quietly. Maisie finished off grooming, and then disappeared into the tack room, and reappeared carrying saddle and bridle. Michael went to help her, but she gave him a withering look, and said, "I can do it myself!" Once the tacking up was completed, she scrambled into the saddle, and headed out of the yard at a fast clip. The instructor who's name was Tamsin, shouted at her "Maisie. Get back here! Where is your helmet? And how many times do we have to tell you that you must walk out of the yard and warm your pony up slowly!"

"SOORRY!" came the wail, and back she came equally fast. She jumped off, threw the reins at me, and went back into the tack room, and retrieved her helmet. She came back out into the sun, helmet swinging from it's harness.

Maisie got back on, complete with helmet she went to give the pony a big kick, but seeing Tamsin standing there, she walked sedately out of the yard instead. We all followed on slowly and went out of the driveway to a turning into a fenced area, which contained numerous jumps. As the pony reached the gate into this field it spun around stood up on its hind legs and refused to go forward. Most kids would have jumped off and been terrified, but Maisie just sat there, took the reins in one hand, smacked the pony smartly between it's ears with her other hand, and then walloped him behind the saddle with her whip. She followed up by shouting at it and giving it two huge kicks. The pony thinking better of its idea, shot forward into the field.

Iris and Hetty looked terrified. "Wow! Did you see that!" said Michael,

"I think she's just fine," I said.

Tamsin agreed with me. "She's the only kid that can ride him, he frightens all the others. We are going to send him back, we cannot have a pony like that here. But Maisie likes him and wanted to ride him for you guys."

Maisie was now travelling at speed around the field. She did not have a particularly correct seat, and at times appeared to only be attached to the pony by the reins. Tamsin yelled again for her to slow down. Maisie came over to us, coming to a sliding stop in front of us. "Maisie, you are to go and warm up your pony properly, using circles, loops and transitions, and don't you dare stick your tongue out at me!" The latter being said just as it was about to happen. Iris spoke up at this latest transgression. "If you do not behave, you will get off that pony right now, and you will be grounded for a week." Realising she had stepped over the line of what was permitted she went off, and dutifully worked her circles, loops and transitions. Finally, Tamsin called her over, and got her to shorten her stirrups to jumping length, and keeping a firm hold on the reins she gave the child instructions as to what she should jump.

"But those are only baby jumps!" Maisie protested.

"When you have jumped the baby jumps at the correct speed and focusing on your position, then I may let you jump some bigger ones." A dramatic sigh followed this command, but Maisie went off and jumped the fences that she had been instructed to jump. Her style was far from classic, legs and arms akimbo, but the pony responded well to her. At one point Nipper threatened to nap again, but the resulting smack from the whip dissuaded him of this plan. Maisie returned to us, and Tamsin corrected her position flaws, and made her go out and do the exercise again. There was a little less arm and leg flapping, but the improvement was negligible. Sighing Tamsin said, "OK, you can jump some of the bigger ones." Masie was gone in a flash, heading not for the medium sized fences but the ones that were clearly used by the instructors, when training for recognised events. Iris let out a squeak of dismay as Nipper and Maisie bore down on a large oxer. The pony patted the ground and flew the fence now galloping on to a big vertical gate which he cleared in equally immaculate fashion Maisie then hauled him through a corner, and down to a Trakehner which was a giant log over a big ditch. The pony unbalanced from the wild turn had to find a fifth leg as he took off for this, but amazingly they landed unscathed. The next fence was a large table and Maisie put the pony in at an impossible spot. The pony saved them by banking the table, which meant he put his legs down on top of the table and pushed off again. Tamsin was now running across the field yelling "STOP!!" Maisie pulled up reluctantly and stood while she received another dressing down. She was told to dismount immediately and lead her pony back to the yard. The slump of her shoulders and the dragging of the feet told the whole story.

Tamsin apologised to us. "She is fearless, but she has no idea how dangerous riding like that can be!" We nodded, looked at one another, and then I burst out laughing, joined immediately by Michael and Hetty. Only Iris remained dismayed.

"I've never seen anything like her!" exclaimed Michael and continued "That pony could do the Pony Championships, talk about jump!"

I agreed but said "Good luck getting them to do a decent

dressage test! Tamsin I am sorry you have such a difficult student."

"Well, it's normally Fee who teaches her, but she hasn't come into work today." Hetty and I exchanged looks, as we walked back towards the barn.

Maisie was brushing her pony off having untacked him, she was sniffing loudly, and turned tear filled eyes towards us, "I just wanted you to see how big we could jump. Tamsin didn't tell me I couldn't jump those ones." She made a sorry picture, and Michael totally melted and told Maisie,

"You jumped huge jumps! I couldn't believe that Nipper could jump that big."

"Oh, he can jump bigger than that!" said Maisie, and then seeing Tamsin thought that it would be better not to continue on the topic. Iris looked thoroughly perturbed by the conversation and what she had seen. Michael noticing this put his arm around her and told her not to worry.

"That's easy for you to say. Horses frighten me, and watching her going so fast at those huge jumps..."

"I'm fine Iris!" piped up Maisie, "Nipper is a great jumper!"

"Indeed, he is Maisie, but the pair of you need training." I said "Do you have any idea how long it took your Mummy to train, before she was jumping fences like the ones you jumped today? She understood that you have to improve your riding skills in order to be top class. Anybody who is brave enough can gallop at fences on a good pony, but to become the sort of rider that your Mummy was, you have to work at it. Improve your position, work on balance and technique, and teach your pony the same things. If you did all that you could go to the Pony Championships, and maybe the Young Riders Championships."

Maisie looked at me as if I had grown horns. "Do you think I could be as good as my Mummy?"

"It depends on how hard you and Nipper are prepared to

work, and how much you will listen to your instructors." I said.

"Well, it won't work, because they're sending Nipper back, because he's bad, like me."

Iris rushed forward, and embraced the child, "You are not bad, you just behave badly sometimes."

Hetty looked crestfallen, and I could feel a lump in my throat, which I tried to dispose of by coughing loudly. Michael stepped in, and said, "Maisie, if you could keep Nipper would you do what B says?"

"Yes, of course, but it's no good he's going back to the dealer, because they don't want him for the school." Maisie continued to groom the pony, and I could see her shoulders shaking.

Michael turned to Hetty and asked her who he should speak to at the Riding for the Disabled about the pony. Hetty said she could easily find out. He told her to do so and turned back to help Maisie finish up with Nipper.

We thanked Tamsin for her time, and all of us left the yard, Michael suggesting pizza for lunch. We drove downtown to Iris's favourite pizza place, which had an outside terrace, and found a large enough table for all of us. A waitress came out, and dealt with our complicated order, everybody wanting different toppings. Maisie insisted on having the same toppings as her hero, Michael, which included olives and anchovies. Iris warned her that she would not like these, but she gagged her way through them, declaring that they were her new favourites. After lunch we all dispersed in different directions. I drew Michael to one side and said I would like to ask him something important. He excused himself from Iris and Maisie and told them he'd meet them back at the cafe.

We strolled back to the table we had been sat at for lunch, the waitress reappeared puzzled by our return. I ordered two coffees, and without beating about the bush I asked Michael if he thought that he was Maisie's father. He had the decency to not prevaricate.

"I could be," he said, "Rebecca was rebelling against being controlled by Brian. He went away to California, and she managed to get away from Brian's watch guards, and we went away for a weekend. I begged her to leave him and stay with me, but she was terrified of what he would do if she did. I should have insisted."

"You need to be sure." I said, "This could end very badly if you do not know the truth, and she turns out to be Brian's child. It is not fair to her, or Iris, if you continue behaving this way, and then finding the truth is not what you want, your feelings change." Michael nodded. I pushed the point.

"Do not promise anything about ponies, or anything else, until you get a paternity test. Then you can make up your mind having all the facts.

Hetty brought the rosettes and trophies over. Poppy and Alfie raced up and down the hallway outside, Poppy not at all hampered by the cast on her leg. I wished that I could be equally adept at getting around with my hard boot.

Hetty had not heard from Fee. I promised her that I would find her and have a good talk to her later in the day. I suggested that we drive the ribbons and trophies around to Anthea Charrington's storage shed, where they would be safe, until she took them out for each prize giving. The three of us, along with the two dogs, drove round to the shed, it was positioned behind the marquees, that were already up. It was beginning to look ready for a great competition. The flag poles were erected at one corner of the stadium, and the bleachers were in place. The dogs were excited by the open area of the stadium and ran out into it. Poppy started her spinning and twisting, she ran at Alfie and nipped his leg, totally taking him by surprise, and then turned, ran away again, leapt up all four feet in the air, spun round and back at Alfie. She came at him from all directions, and he turned round and round trying to fend her off, but she was twice as quick as him even with her cast. As fast as it started, so it stopped. Poppy crashed down in a heap, panting. Alfie walked over to her not trusting that she wouldn't leap up and attack him again, but she licked his face, and then he flopped down beside her.

Alfie had just experienced his first bull terrier mad five minutes. He would have to get used to them, we thought.

I unlocked the shed, and we stowed all the trophies on the shelves, and then hooked the ribbons onto coat hangers, and hung them on the hooks, already installed in the shed. I relocked it, and we took the dogs for a stroll around the outside of the stadium.

The trade fair tents were being erected by the vendors, and the main marquee that would hold the stands for the vendors without their own tents, was already being moved into. We met Eleanor who was working with Alan Harper, on getting everybody in the correct slot. Alan looked harried, but Eleanor was completely calm, despite several people shouting at her at once. I went over, and thanked her profusely for having taken this on, she grinned, and said she was demanding a discount from all the vendors, so she could do all her shopping for her trip home in one foul swoop! This depressed me, it had been so good having her here, and I would miss her horribly. More vendors were clamouring for her attention, and she waived us away.

We walked back to the car and drove back to the office. The dogs were sufficiently tired that they crashed down on the floor. I called the Riding for the Disabled stables and asked if Fee was there. The secretary answered that she was currently giving a lesson and asked if she should get her for me. I told her not to interrupt her, I would come round to see her. Hetty wanted to come with me, but I said I thought it would be better if I went alone. I promised to call Hetty once I had spoken to Fee, and suggested that she stay with Jenny, while I was gone.

Jenny, seeing that Hetty was very stressed, asked her if she would mind organising the dressage test sheets onto clipboards for the judges. This involved putting stickers, with the riders and horse names, on to their individual sheet. It was a fairly boring task, but one that required concentration, so Hetty would be unable to fret.

I was not looking forward to this conversation, but it had to happen. I drove slowly to the RDA stables mulling over what I should say to her. Upon arrival I went in search of Fee, finding her coming out of the indoor arena with a child riding a small pony. Fee helped the child to dismount and got her into a wheelchair. The child's face was wide with wonder and the pleasure of having been able to move without restraint. Fee told her that she would see her next week, and left her waiting for her mother, while Fee put the pony away. Fee, upon seeing me, looked sullen and unwelcoming. I asked her to come and sit outside with me, as I wished to talk to her. I could see that she wanted to tell me to go to hell, but reluctantly she joined me at a picnic table outside.

I took a deep breath and said, "What is the matter, Fee? You have not been behaving normally, and you really upset your grandmother two days ago."

"I suppose she sent you?" Fee said, "I thought she would, she always relies on you to do her dirty work!" I was taken aback by this bold assault on Hetty and me, but I thought I might get better results with sugar rather than vinegar.

"We are both worried about you, we thought that you would be pleased that your mother has improved to the point of returning to normal life."

"Of course, I am pleased that she is getting better, but I just don't think she should come home." The aggression in Fee's voice faded and was replaced by something bordering on desperation.

"Why ever not Fee?" I asked, "What is upsetting you, about the idea?"

"You don't understand. I am so afraid." The girl's voice was starting to show a distinct tremor, I started to feel sorry for her, and sought a way to reassure her,

"Fee, I know it will be hard for you, but that is why the Home Helpers will be there. I know you will be scared that your mother will relapse, but we have to have faith in the doctors who have been treating her. I realise how ghastly it must have been to see her as she was, when she was hospitalised, but she has been slowly improving, and she wants to come home. You wouldn't want to deny her that, would you?"

Fee burst into floods of tears, and she jumped up, and ran off down the driveway. I considered going after her, but decided that would be fruitless, she had left her bag behind, the one with the embossed letter "F" on it. I was sure that she would return for it, I would just wait. My patience paid off, as ten minutes later she walked back up the drive and sat back down next to me. I said nothing, and just waited, I had found in my dealings with the students of Wendover College, that the desire to fill a silence often brought about confessions. Finally, Fee took a sniffling breath and said,

"I can't tell you; it is too awful."

"I don't believe that!" I said emphatically "You would not comprehend the things, that I have been told and what I have seen!"

Fee continued to cry quietly, and again I waited.

"My mother killed my sister!" she whispered. Of all the things I had been expecting, this was not one of them. My reaction was to tell her not to be so stupid but looking at her face I saw that she really believed this. I thought that if I denied the truth of this, I would lose her.

"What makes you think that, Fee?" I asked quietly.

"Lots of things, what happened the day Felicity went missing, things she said afterwards. She was so messed up, I didn't want to believe it, but I found the sweatshirt Felicity was wearing that day in Mum's laundry basket, and later her portfolio in the bookcase."

"But how do you know she is dead? Her body has not been found." I asked.

"Mum knows where she is, I am sure."

"But Fee, why didn't you tell anyone?" I said,

"She's, my Mum! She's been ill for so long. It's not her fault. Her mother is as bad, and her mother before her."

"But Fee, being mentally ill is one thing, but being homicidal is another, the authorities need to know."

"Why? Can't she just stay where she is? Everybody would be safe then." I could see the child in Fee, not far from the surface. It was by no means proven that Alice had done this terrible thing, but what Fee told me was pretty damning. It would have to be investigated.

"Fee you are going to have to talk to the police. You are accusing your mother of murder..."

"Don't you think I know that? It's all I've thought of since it happened. I kept thinking that maybe I was wrong, but then Mum would get drunk, and go rambling on about it." I put my arms around the girl, and held her until she calmed, she then said, "It was so good when she was taken away, I could pretend that it never happened, but then we heard she was getting better, and I have been SO scared about her coming out." I could just see the pressure that the girl had been under, no wonder she had been acting out. I told her to leave it to me. She should go and take Killer for a quiet hack, and I would look after things. She nodded, and took my hand, "Thank you B. Please don't tell my grandmother." She said simply and turned to go.

My heart was beating nineteen to the dozen, as I drove back to the centre. I needed to talk to Eleanor and possibly Alistair, before I talked to Hetty.

I drove round the back way so that I wouldn't bump into Hetty or be seen by Jenny. I found Eleanor right away, she was drinking a coffee with Alan Harper. I greeted them both, and asked Eleanor if I could have a quick word with her. Alan took the hint and headed back to the marquee.

Eleanor was silent for a bit, and then asked, "Do you believe her?" I said that I was sure that Fee believed what she had told me. Eleanor pulled out her cell phone and called Alistair. From what I heard of Eleanor's side of the conversation; Alistair was busy with security issues at the stabling complex. Eleanor merely told him to shut up, and come and meet us at the trade fair, she then hung up.

"I see how you make friends so easily." I said. She glared at me. We waited and, in a few moments, Alistair arrived, obviously irritated. He looked at Eleanor questioningly, and she turned to me, and I told the whole story again. As with Eleanor, he asked me what I thought of the veracity of Fee's tale, and as before I said I was sure that Fee believed it.

We talked about the various options, we could go to the police right away, and let them handle it. We could stall Alice's release, and investigate ourselves in case Fee was either mistaken, or fabricating the story. We could go and talk to Alice, but this might trigger a return of her mental problems. It was a huge dilemma. I had the shadow of the Showcase hanging over everything and I did not want to cause Hetty any more heartache. I decided to let the two professionals come up with an answer. They talked backwards and forwards, hashing ideas out discarding some and keeping some on the back burner. In the end they decided that we should find a way to prevent Alice from returning for a few days. Eleanor and Alistair would talk to Fee. Alistair would see if he could get the file of the original missing person case.

I told them that I thought Fee was very fragile, and they agreed that she should be handled very carefully. I asked whether they thought that I should tell Hetty that Fee was just too worried to have Alice home at the moment, or whether I should just tell her the truth. We hashed it around for a bit but in the end decided that, though hard, the truth was best, Hetty was going to have to know sooner or later.

Eleanor offered to come with me to talk to Hetty. We climbed in my car and drove over to Hetty's house, to be greeted by Poppy and Alfie. "As you were coming here, I thought I'd bring Alfie along with me to save Jenny having to wait for you to pick him up later." Hetty said. I thanked her for her consideration of Jenny, and then suggested we all sit down.

I went straight to the heart of it. Hetty looked at me for a few minutes, and then said, "I don't think Alice was in any shape to kill anybody, and a mother doesn't kill her child." I did not want to contradict her, but there were several cases of infanticide by mother. I was going to say more, but Hetty interrupted, "Fee has a vivid imagination, she has probably imagined things, and then convinced herself they are true. Also, she has not seemed herself lately"

"You could be right," I admitted "but she was very persuasive, and she is obviously very upset about the idea of her mother returning home. I think that it would be wise to put off Alice's return until we have been able to repudiate any of Fee's claims."

"But we have the Home Help people booked for tomorrow, we can't mess them around." complained Hetty.

"They are the least of our worries. They won't mind if we

pay them anyway. Alice's father is putting up the money, and I'm sure he would want this to be sorted out." I tried to make it sound reasonable, Eleanor then added,

"B's right, Hetty, I think the two of you should go and see Alice, find out exactly how she is, no mention of what has been said, but tell her she will have to wait a week or so to come home."

I felt really saddened that I had had to put this on my friend, I could see how hard it had hit her, she looked as if somebody had sucked all the air out of her. Nevertheless, I pressed on, and said that I thought we should call Beeton Hall, see if Alice's doctor was still there, and talk to him.

"We don't have to tell him what Fee has said, do we?" asked Hetty, in a panic.

"No Hetty, we just need to tell him that she cannot come home yet and ask him how to handle that." I replied. Hetty reluctantly agreed and went to phone the hospital. She came back looking relieved saying that the doctor had left for the day. I was infuriated with her but did not say so.

"Hetty, did you ask for a number where he could be reached?" Hetty shook her head.

"OK, I'll call back." This I did, the secretary told me that they did not give out doctor's private numbers. I explained to her that the patient was due to be released the following morning, and due to a personal problem, she would not be able to return home. We therefore needed to talk to the doctor about how best to tell her this. The secretary then said she would contact the doctor and have him call us back. We waited impatiently, and finally the phone rang. Hetty looked expectantly at me, and so I picked up the receiver. The doctor assumed I was Hetty, and I did not disabuse him of this idea. I rapidly explained that we had suffered a sewage flood in the house, and that it could not be lived in until the disaster company had dried everything out, and made sure there was no mould growing. I felt my nose growing, as I continued embellishing the facts.

The doctor was sympathetic, "I don't want Alice to go to a less than ideal situation. Stress is her enemy, and it should be avoided at all costs however she has been looking forward to tomorrow for a long time, I fear she will be sorely disappointed, and this, in itself will cause stress."

"We were thinking of coming over this evening to tell her of the problems." I said.

"I think that will be acceptable," He said, in his pedantic manner, "she has, I believe, another visitor coming this evening, so you will have to work around that, I will be in to talk to her first thing tomorrow morning."

I thanked him and hung up. Hetty said "It has to be Adam who is visiting, he is the only person who visits other than family."

We let Poppy nurse the puppies, and then left her with Alfie in the kitchen. I drove and went by my house, where I dropped off Eleanor. Hetty and I then proceeded to Beeton Hall.

I don't know what I expected, not having seen Alice since she had been committed, but the serene woman with her unlined face and extreme beauty was not it at all. She sat quietly in a wing back chair in the recreational room, where patients met their visitors. Her expression did not change, as Hetty expounded the lie that I had told to the doctor. Hetty's dialog petered out, and she looked desperately at me, as if I could salvage the situation. Alice looked at her hands, and spoke to us in a low melodious voice, saying, "Fee does not want me to come home, does she? She is afraid." Hetty and I looked anxiously at one another. Hetty took a deep breath, and said in a trembling voice,

"Err, she is worried, she is not sure how she will cope."

"I thought there would be difficulties." Alice went on quietly. "I tried to get my father to agree to me going to stay with them, but he is unwilling. I have therefore contacted Adam, and he is coming tonight to see me."

Her firm confidence weakened Hetty's resolve, "Maybe you could stay with me..."

"No, I think that that would be too close to Fee, for her to be comfortable, I shall make alternative arrangements. Thank you both so much for coming, I realise that you have my best interests at heart."

Hetty and I looked desperately at one another, she had called our bluff, and now we would leave with things possibly worse, than when we had first heard Fee's accusations.

Alice rose from the chair, and left the room, so Hetty and I were left with no option but to do the same.

"At least we know she has been under medical care for months, if they felt she was a danger to the general public, they would not let her out." I tried.

"But they don't know all the facts!" wailed Hetty.

"Nor do we, just because Fee thinks her mother killed her sister doesn't mean that it is true. The police investigated Felicity's disappearance thoroughly, don't you think they would have looked at Alice back then? I think that it is more likely to be a figment of Fee's imagination, you told me that Fee was in a terrible sate after Felicity was missing, and surely if she had suspected her mother then, she would have said something?"

"But what if Fee was afraid of her mother?" I could see that this was going to go on and on, the "What ifs" were too many to handle. I drove back to Hetty's and afraid to leave her alone, I went in for coffee. Hetty and I took the dogs out, we allowed Alfie to meet the puppies, and he was captivated by them, Poppy was not the least bit protective of them, she quite obviously thought they were capable of taking care of themselves. I was pleased to see that they all brought a smile to Hetty's face. The phone rang.

"Oh, Hello Adam." Hetty listened for a long time, and then said, "Do you think you can cope?" this was followed by another period of listening, and then she said, "Well thank you for letting me know." And she hung up. She turned to me, and said,

"Adam is going to pick Alice up tomorrow morning and take her back to his house.

"Let's wait and see what the doctor says, he may not allow her to leave with a nonfamily member."

Hetty nodded, I could see that there would be little sleep for her tonight, but I wanted to get back to Eleanor and see what, if anything, Alistair had found out. I gave Hetty a hug, and called Alfie, for once he was reluctant to come with me, but eventually with many backward glances at Poppy he came. We got in the car and drove home.

Eleanor was waiting for me, when we got there, she had put out Alfie's tea, and he ate it ravenously, and then collapsed on the couch, exhausted from his day. I poured us a drink, and I told Eleanor that Alice seemed totally in control of herself and had obviously anticipated Fee not wishing her to go home and saw through our ruse of a flood. We worried that this was proof that she was guilty in Felicity's disappearance and knew that Fee would be afraid of her.

I thought that I should phone Fee and tell her what had happened, Eleanor and Alistair wanted to talk to her, and Eleanor thought I should come as well, so I picked up my mobile and called her, she did not answer, I thought for a moment, and then called her on my landline, she picked this one up and said in a very small voice, " Hello, B" I explained to her that her mother was not coming back to their house, and so she did not need to worry. I went on to tell her that I wanted to talk to her again, along with Eleanor and Alistair. She did not want this, but I firmly told her that she could not make the accusations that she had, and not expect to be questioned. I told her that I had not informed the police, but we needed to know all the facts, so we could decide what to do. Reluctantly she agreed, and I told her we would come to her house first thing in the morning. I did not tell her that her mother was hoping to go to stay with Adam, one step at a time was best.

Despite Fee's grandparents' money, Alice had remained in the house that she and Barry had bought when they first married. It was a fairly nondescript, the outside was a mixture of brick and pebble dash, a finish that had not remained popular after 1953, when the house was built. The paint on the woodwork around the windows was peeling, and the garden needed a complete overhaul. There were two planters by the front door, luxuriant in dead foliage. I thought unhappily that Barry and Alice must have been excited when they first bought it.

We joined Fee in the kitchen, the floor was covered wall to wall with linoleum of an indeterminate colour, the pattern had worn off and holes threatened to appear. A 1950s kitchen table and chairs sat in the middle, these could, in a different setting, be considered retro modern.

We sat ourselves down at the table, and Fee poured coffee that she had already brewed. She looked defensive and wary. I thanked her for the coffee. Fee nodded, and Alistair opened the conversation.

"Fee, why is it that you think your mother killed your sister?"

"She told me she did for a start!" Fee's voice was high pitched and stressed sounding, Alistair replied calmly,

"What exactly did she say?"

"I don't remember her exact words, but she would get

drunk and say things like "I shouldn't have done it!" or "Felicity had to go" things like that."

"That doesn't necessarily mean she killed Felicity." said Alistair reasonably. Fee glared at him, and raised her voice,

"You had to be there, she said so many things that made me suspect, besides I found Felicity's sweatshirt in mum's laundry basket, and I found the portfolio that she had with her when she disappeared."

"What did you do with them Fee?"

"I burned them!"

"But, why? They were evidence surely you realised that?" Alistair continued placidly.

"She was my Mum! I didn't want to lose her as well."

This was a cry from the heart, and none of us was immune to it. Eleanor very quietly interjected,

"Of course, we understand that. You are not in any trouble; we just want to know what happened so we can ensure that you are safe and that your mother is looked after. Can you tell us what you remember of the day your sister went missing?"

"Not really, I was at the stables, and when I got home Felicity wasn't there."

"Was she normally there when you got home?"

"Not always, but she had been that week."

"What did you do?'

"Nothing, I made myself some tea, Mum was a bit out of it."

"How do you mean "out of it"?"

"Like she gets when she's had too many drugs or too much to drink, she gets sort of blank."

"OK, so what happened then?" prompted Eleanor,

"It got later, and so I asked Mum where Felicity had gone, and she said that she had taken her portfolio to a modelling agency."

"That sounds as if your Mum wasn't too blank then, if she could recall that." said Alistair. Fee looked furiously at him, and spat out, "Do you know how hard it is to remember something that happened so long ago, maybe I asked Mum before she got wasted." Eleanor frowned at Alistair and smiled at Fee,

"Alistair didn't mean to upset you, we know how hard it is to relive something as horrible as this, I'm sure things will get muddled in your mind, we just need a general picture of the day, so we can work out when things happened." Fee was only slightly placated by Eleanor's reasoning.

"Obviously Mum did whatever she did to Felicity while I was at the stables, and then she got hammered because of what she'd done!"

"Did your mother tell you where she had been during the day, did she try and give herself an alibi?" asked Eleanor.

"I don't remember, I think she said she was at home, that's where she always was, she never did anything."

"Why do you think she would kill your sister?"

"Because she's mad, that's why!" I worried that Fee was unravelling, and looked at Eleanor, trying to convey that I thought we should stop, but Eleanor was on a roll,

"Even mad people have a reason for doing what they do. It may not make sense to us, but it does to them, do you have any idea what could have made her do it?" Fee shook her head, and I stood up and said I thought we should go.

"Fee you must try to think of something else, we won't let anything happen to you. The Showcase is a week away, are you going to be up to riding in it?" I asked.

"Of course, I am!" Fee snapped, and then went on more determinedly, "I'll be fine without you lot interrogating me!" I suggested that perhaps she should go and stay with her grandmother, but she shook her head emphatically.

"I'm fine by myself." On this note we left her.

We reconvened at Holmeshurst Cottage, to Alfie's delight. None of us were up for his exuberant greetings, he went back to his bed dejectedly, and I gave him a bone. His life immediately improved, and I wished that mine could be as easily ameliorated.

Finally, Alistair said, "I don't know what to make of her. I think that she has heard some things, imagined some things and made some things up. She is not stupid nor is she a child anymore. She knows that burning evidence is wrong. But she was young at the time that that happened. I cannot imagine why she would want to implicate her mother, if she didn't think that her mother was guilty. She is acting very paranoid, do you think she is disturbed? After all it runs in her family. What do you all think?" Eleanor and I pondered the problem, then Eleanor spoke up,

"Fee has put up with a huge amount in her life, I am sure that she is not altogether what one would call normal. However, she has seemed to cope with everything, and has come out the other side. I don't know, but I just cannot imagine a mother killing their child without any obvious reason. Everyone spoken to said that Alice was devoted to Felicity and tended to ignore Fee. Why would she suddenly snap and kill Felicity. It makes no sense. Also, nobody saw Alice anywhere near where Felicity went missing. The police covered all that, I am sure." I listened to Eleanor's well thought out statements, but a thought occurred to me,

"What if she didn't disappear from the modelling agency, but returned home and then went missing? That would mean Alice could be implicated." I asked. The others looked at me absorbing what I had said.

"That's possible, but Felicity's body has not been found. I cannot imagine that Alice was strong enough or mentally capable of hiding a body." said Alistair.

We were at a stalemate, not knowing what was true and what was make believe. Alistair said that he was going in to see Inspector Thomas, who had been reluctant to give him any information about the initial investigation into Felicity's disappearance. He was not surprised about this after the incident with Daniel's car but was hopeful that he could persuade him to relent. It was however hard to come up with a good reason why he would want to see it.

Finally, Eleanor said, "Let's make a murder board!"

"But we don't know that Felicity has been murdered." I retorted.

Eleanor pressed on, "Jenny have you got a white board?" Jenny got up, rummaged around in our cupboard, and came out with one covered in dust. She cleaned it up and propped it up on a side table against the wall. "Post its?" said Eleanor, again Jenny found the required article, and without being asked brought out some thumb tacks.

Eleanor wrote "Felicity" on a post it, underneath she put "victim with a question mark" and pinned this to the middle of the board. Then on another note she wrote "Unknown perpetrator" and pinned it off to the side. She then wrote one for Alice and pinned it above Felicity. Having done this, she turned to us and asked who else knew Felicity, and who was close to her. Jenny and I first suggested Adam, Eleanor nodded, and added his name to the board. She then put Fee's name up. I suggested the photographer who Felicity had gone to, Eleanor nodded vigorously, "That's good" she said, "Who else?"

"There was the modelling scout and the agency," said Jenny.

"I think we can rule out the agency, it was the first time she had been there, but definitely the scout should go up, we need to find their names."

"What about all her party friends, there must have been lots of them?" I suggested.

"OK, we'll put party friends, do we know their names?" Jenny and I shook our heads

"I'll just put up one note for all of them," said Eleanor, "Anybody else?" I wracked my brain but came up blank. "I wasn't in Canada at the time all I know is what others have told me. Can you think of anyone Jenny?" Jenny shook her head, but said "I think we need Hetty"

"Yes," Said Eleanor, "We'll get her input later. Next, we take all these people, and see if we can come up with a motive." Jenny and I stared at the names, it seemed inconceivable that any of them had a motive to make Felicity disappear. We told Eleanor as much.

"OK, then we look at who had the opportunity." Again, we looked at the board. This time it was impossible to say, because we really didn't know exactly when she went missing nor did we know where most of the people on the board had been.

Eleanor said, "We know when the missing persons report was filed, we know that Fee and Alice said that Felicity did not come home the night before. We also know that the modelling agency saw her that afternoon, and one secretary saw her leaving with a man. Therefore, we can assume she disappeared between the time she was seen leaving the agency and when she was expected at home. That is if Fee and Alice are telling the truth. So, let's say between 2.00pm and 6.00 pm, shall we?" Jenny and I nodded; I could see why Eleanor had been good at her job. Eleanor continued,

"We now have a four-hour timeline. We need to find out where each of these people, on the board, were at that time."

"Won't the police have done the same thing?" I asked.

"I'm sure they have." Replied Eleanor, "That's what we're

hoping Alistair will find out, and then we can add their information to ours."

The phone rang and it was one of the chef d'equipes asking when the stables would be open for the Showcase. Jenny passed the phone to me and having trouble reorganising my thoughts I stumbled through the conversation, I'm sure the poor man thought I was less than capable. When I hung up, I told my co investigators that we would have to put the board away for now. We had a showcase to run.

Once everything was in place, the various committee chairs would take over. The showcase secretary would take over dealing with the competitors. The stable manager would look after all the tent stabling, and the four-legged inhabitants. The veterinary commission would ensure all equines were fit to compete and that their passports were up to date with vaccinations. The medical team would look after the human athletes and the spectators, who inevitably would be stung by a bee, suffer a heart attack, or stumble over a root. The officials would ensure the smooth running of the competition, and the army of volunteers would be marshalled and dispatched to their various duties.

I had ordered five office trailers, one for the show secretary and her staff, one for the radio and communications people, one for our accountants who would be paying all the mass of people who issued invoices and, finally, one to act as the media centre which would be open for reporters to file their articles. Jenny and I would have a small trailer, so we would be right on site, but given that we could easily drive back to our main office, I did not feel we had to move everything to temporary space. I had the trailers parked around a central tent that would be a marshalling area for all the various committees, they could pick up programs, golf cart keys, spare tee shirts, maps and sundry other essential items.

Jenny had packed up the necessary paperwork for our home from home, and between us, we ferried it out to the trailer. Jenny added a coffee maker, vital for our sanity.

Leaving Jenny to cope with final preparations, I went to the parking areas. There were tents at all entrance gates, and these would all be staffed, selling and collecting tickets, selling programs and generally helping the general public. We had four enormous parking areas that Alistair had set out. Cars would enter by one route and leave by another, to avoid bottle necks and traffic jams. We had an area set aside for people with disabilities, and a crew of golf cart drivers to take them to where the action was happening. I knew that there would be glitches and things that we would wish we had done differently, but on the whole, everything was as good as we could make it. Jenny had locked up our office trailer, so I drove back to the office in the Centre.

Jenny, Alistair and Eleanor were sitting around the murder board. The board looked slightly different, but I couldn't put my finger on what was changed.

"Inspector Thomas would not give me the file, but he did answer my questions about the investigation, albeit reluctantly. He did not understand why I wanted it, I had to come up with something, and so I said that Hetty was worried that the case was being forgotten and asked me to look into it." said Alistair.

"That was good thinking," I exclaimed, "he would believe that. Hetty calls him each week to see if there is any news." Alistair nodded and said he had found out that the photographer and the modelling scout both had rock solid alibis for that afternoon. They were at a fashion show that was filmed by a TV company, and there were shots of them both, all afternoon. Eleanor got up and removed them from the murder board. Alistair went on saying that all the known sexual predators had been brought in and questioned along with all the teenage friends of Felicity. He said that it appeared that the police had done a good job of investigating.

"How about Adam? Did the police interview him?" asked Eleanor

"Yes, he said that he had been scouting sites for his film company, but they had been unable to find anybody to corroborate this, but the film company said that that was where he had told them he was going to be that afternoon."

"What about Alice?" Eleanor tried.

"Apparently, she was at home, but nobody saw her until Fee came home. Fee told the police that she was at the stables. Bill did not know whether this had been confirmed. I don't think they considered Fee to be a suspect due to her age, and closeness to her twin." Eleanor listened to all this, and then said,

"I suppose that means that Alice is the most likely candidate, but Adam took the twins out quite often, Felicity would go with him. What do you all think?" We all nodded reluctantly.

"Adam has always been so helpful, according to Hetty. What could be the motive for either of them?" I asked. None of my friends had an answer.

"I think that we need to talk to both of them, Adam first, and Alice when she has had time to settle in." said Alistair, "I can use the same excuse, that I am working for Hetty, to see if I can find out anything that the police missed, Eleanor do you mind helping?"

"Not at all, I also think we should talk to the person at the modelling agency, who saw Felicity leave."

I went to see Hetty, and Jenny came with me, to spend some time with her puppy. Alfie was of course included in the outing, and as we got closer to Hetty's house he recognised the road and started to whine and bark in excitement. When we arrived, he jumped out of the car, and raced up the path to the front door, where he banged on the door with his paw. Hetty opened it, and he charged past her to find Poppy. "Well, do come in Alfie." Hetty said to his disappearing tail.

Hetty was clearly upset, "If that silly girl hadn't come out with these wild accusations, we could have left well alone. Now it is all being stirred up again, I wish we could go back to before."

I nodded but told her that the police had ruled out the people that we would not have the contacts to find, like all Felicity's party friends. Hetty sighed, and finally asked if there was anything she could do. "Alistair would like to know everything that you know about Adam. He does not have an alibi for the time that Felicity went missing. He is a rather strange young man, and he was very friendly with the twins and Alice." I suggested that Hetty take her time, and write down anything she could remember about Adam, no matter how inconsequential.

While I had been talking to Hetty, Jenny had been playing with her puppy, I went to find her. She was lying on her back with the puppy on top of her. She laughed when she saw me, and said, "She has the sharpest teeth ever! I hope her second ones are better, when they come through." She held out a finger that had a trickle of blood coming from a tiny puncture wound. Hetty fetched her a band aid, and then I called Alfie, who came reluctantly to the front door, and Jenny put her puppy back in the pen, and we headed off.

SHOWCASE UNDERWAY

HORSES STARTED TO ARRIVE in gooseneck, slant loads and head to head trailers. There were also some fancy English type horse boxes. The overseas horses came together in an eighteen-wheel transport trailer, which had brought them from the quarantine centre, at the airport. They went into the separate housing that we had provided for them. The grooms got busy settling their charges into their stalls. Horses did not travel light. The equipment that was required for each one of them included saddles, bridles, veterinary trunks, lunging gear, boxes of bits, martingales, rugs for every weather type.

I hoped that the grooms would be happy with their own housings, which I knew were far superior to average grooms' quarters.

The US horses arrived in vehicles that cost more than an average house. The trailers had slide outs that turned the front half, into luxury living quarters. The riders travelled round the continent, going from competition to competition but they lived well in their homes on wheels. The Canadian horses arrived in slightly more modest conveyances, but nowhere could be found a plain truck and simple two horse trailer.

The show grounds came to life. Food vendors arrived and proceeded to commence feeding the army. Coffee vans vied for custom, but all did a roaring trade.

The stewards posted times for schooling, the vets hurried around doing the arrival examinations and the show secretary and her helpers were overwhelmed with competitors.

Jenny and I greeted the officials. Jenny had prepared packages for them that held their identification badges, parking passes, invitations to the various functions, directions to their hotels and time schedules for the competition. John and Michael conducted them on course walks. Alistair marshalled his security detail to their various duties, and the whole place started to hum with anticipation and activity.

Fee arrived with Killer, and he was installed with the other Canadian horses, who were all housed down one aisle. Fee was quiet and withdrawn but appeared to be calmer than when we had talked to her.

Maggie was there with Media Circus, Samantha with Filibuster, my having refused her entry with her other horse, despite Roger's bullying tactics. The final Canadian had come from Alberta, his name was Patrick Briggs and his horse was named TNT, I had not met him before, but he seemed a very nice young man. He was chatting to Xen who was obviously in the thick of it all. I walked round the stabling and wished them all good luck before returning to our little office caboose.

It was discovered that our European show jumping course designer had not been picked up at the airport. Jenny ordered a limousine for him. Fortunately, he just laughed at his misfortune, I liked him immediately.

Pru and her team, helped ours to get the dressage rings up. The competition ring looked beautiful, with high gloss white boards. The letters topped with beautiful arrangements of geraniums and cornflowers. The judging booths had been built for the occasion. In front of them were shrubs and flowers all placed with care by Tabitha and her crew. The fence around the outside of the ring was covered in sponsors' banners, and the electronic scoreboard was up behind the judges' booths. Flags flew in abundance.

Before we could start, there had to be an inspection of the horses. This was conducted by the Ground Jury and the veterinary delegate. Each horse was presented in hand, matched to their passport, and jogged up to check their soundness. If there was any doubt about their fitness to compete, they were sent to another area where a different veterinarian would examine them more closely to see if they had any injury that would prohibit them from competing. Animal welfare was of prime concern. All the horses passed the inspection, and after Fee jogged up, I took her to one side, and asked her if she was OK. She looked at me quite angrily and said of course she was. I decided to leave well alone and walked away. She was becoming difficult, but under the current conditions I was not really surprised.

We held a riders' briefing, to welcome them, and to help orient them about the property, places where they could gallop, lunge, hack or train. We explained the rules and regulations that they had to follow. We introduced all the officials. Talked about stabling hours and then we gave them maps of the cross country course and opened the course for walking.

I called all the chairs of committees to a meeting under the tent by the office trailers. This was to ensure that all was ready, and that none of them had any queries or problems. The meeting went very smoothly, and I was satisfied that we were ready to commence competition the following day. Dinner was being served in the sponsors' tent for all competitors, officials and committee chairs, starting at 6.30 pm.

Hetty's friend produced a fantastic meal, beef wellington followed by profiteroles and homemade ice cream. There was an excitement in the air, with everyone anticipating the competition to come. I made a very brief speech in which I dedicated the event to the memory of Daniel. Everybody forgot that he was not well liked and cheered and clapped. Alistair had tears in his eyes and got up and left the marquee.

Maisie behaved herself quite well, being closely guarded by Iris. She was in awe of the famous competitors, who were seated in the same room. After the main course had been eaten Michael took her round to meet some of the riders, and to collect their autographs. She ran up to Fee and said that it was AWESOME that she was here riding with all these top riders. This brought a smile to Fee's face, which we had not seen for some time.

Over dinner, Hetty had produced notes about everyone that she could remember connected to Adam:

Adam Wiseacre, parents Catrin Wiseacre (now deceased), Paul Wiseacre (now Reverend) formerly a psychiatrist.

Sunny little boy, became friends with Barry in Elementary school, stayed friends until Barry's death.

Mother left to go back to Sweden, to look after her mother, Adam went to live with father in California.

Barry visited Adam on several occasions. He said that his father was becoming very strange. Barry suspected that Adam felt abandoned by his mother. Father went on to study religions and became ordained into an obscure Christian ministry.

Paul Wiseacre proved to be an effective evangelist and a powerful orator. He founded Holy Port Church and raised large amounts of money through preaching. Adam became a member of the church, as did several friends from Ontario.

Adam went to university in California, studying film and organic chemistry. There was a link between the church and a film company.

Adam went on to study divinity and became one of the hierarchies of the church. He started work at the film studio, which was finally bought out, by the church.

There were rumours of a scandal involving the church.

The film studio started filming in Toronto as well as California, and Adam went backwards and forwards between Ontario and California.

Adam remained friends with Barry, and whenever he was in Ontario the two would meet up. Adam knew Alice, and the three of them were good friends. When Barry was killed Adam stayed in touch with Alice and visited her frequently.

Adam became a surrogate uncle for the twins and took them out frequently.

He tried to help when Felicity went missing. He supported Alice and Fee and Hetty.

Adam's job took him back to California, and he stayed there for some time. (Hetty knew little of what happened during this time.)

Adam met Paloma and was said to be going out with her.

Adam continued to visit Alice, and to see Fee.

Paloma went missing, Adam is apparently questioned by police in California and Ontario, but nothing came of this.

Adam was now back in Ontario and continued to support Alice and Fee.

Adam started to go out with Jessica, but something seemed to happen to break them up.

Eleanor said that she would pull out her notes on Holy Port Church, that she had taken during her searches into the companies involved in the Equestrian Centre. It would all be added to the murder board.

I suggested that we focus on more urgent matters, and run the Showcase.

The Ground Jury took up their positions in their booths. They were accompanied by their scribes and their electronic scribes. The scribes would record their comments and marks on each test sheet, and the electronic scribe put the marks into the computer, that would then send the information to the electronic scoreboard, so spectators could see what mark each judge had given, for each movement.

A nervous Xen made his way to the booth of the judge at B. His hair was tied back in a neat ponytail. He had been excited, when I asked him if he wanted to scribe, and now here he was immaculate in a suit and Madison tie. Out of nowhere came a loud wolf whistle and we turned to see Susie now giving Xen a thumbs up. He scowled at her and blushed as the judge turned to look at him. He then hurried to take his place.

The first horse and rider combination entered the area around the ring, this was one of Pru's dressage riders who had volunteered to ride the test ride. The test ride ensured that everything was working perfectly, that the scribes could keep up with the judges, that the electronic scoring was working OK, and it also gave the judges a chance to discuss their scoring.

The drug testers arrived. I told Jenny to send them to the Veterinary Delegate who would deal with them. Horses were routinely tested for performance enhancing drugs, and we had a protocol in place, to deal with this. However, this time, Jenny said, they were here to test the human athletes as well. This was more unusual, but we had considered the possibility, and I had briefed our chief steward on how to handle this. It would be done randomly, pulling names out of a hat. The riders had to be accompanied to a washroom, where they had to urinate in a cup. This was then divided into two samples, and labelled, and the competitor had to sign each vial. All potential Olympic competitors were subject to this random sampling. I instructed Jenny to contact our Chief Steward, and left it up to her to cope, and we went to watch the dressage.

By lunch time we had two Germans in the lead, they were followed by a Brit, two U.S. riders and then Maggie with Media

Circus. Patrick Briggs had had rather an explosive test. With his horse, TNT, living up to it's name. He was now in last place. He seemed remarkably unfazed. "We are cross country animals not Dressage Queens!" he told me. Fee and Samantha would be riding in the afternoon. I returned to our office caboose, and took Alfie for a walk, he was feeling much maligned, as I had not been with him 100% of the time, and he had to stay on a lead. He suffered through this insult, and was delighted, when we met Poppy who was walking along sedately on her leash, taking Hetty for a stroll. Hetty told me they had come to watch Fee, and then they were going to Amelia's to get Poppy's caste taken off. I wished mine could come off, but I had another two weeks to go, the doctor having told me that when you get to a "certain age" your bones do not heal as quickly. So, Poppy and I clomped on round the ring and back to the trailer, where Hetty and I left the dogs with Jenny, and went to find a good vantage point, on the bleachers.

We watched two tests, and then Sam came into the ring with Fillibuster. I pointed out Roger to Hetty, but we could see no sign of Helen, I thought the marriage might not last that long, and felt that I did not blame Helen if she called it off. She had put up with more than enough from Roger and his philandering ways. Sam was tense, but she rode a better test than the last one that we had watched, and it put her just behind Maggie in the scores. There were about four more rides to go before Fee and Killer. Hetty and I watched the bleachers filling up, and then Hetty exclaimed,

"Oh look! There's Adam, he must have come to watch Fee." Adam climbed up the bleachers and sat near the top, just as Fee came in, and rode around the outside of the ring. She spotted Adam and her face lit up. She and Killer looked wonderful together, and as she rode proudly around the ring Fee looked truly beautiful, her disfigurement was hidden by her helmet, and her slim figure looked so elegant in her navy tailcoat and breeches. Killer's pale colouring was a perfect foil for her dark clothes.

The judge at C gave her the signal to start, and she came into the ring and rode the test of her life. When she finished and gave her final salute to the judges, the spectators let out a cheer and clapped. Killer erupted with this new noise, and bucked and spun, as he exited the ring. Fee sat firmly and had the biggest smile on her face as she sought out Adam with her eyes. I was watching her and cheering along with the rest.

Fee's groom took Killer as they left the ring. Fee was hugging Killer, and then handed the reins to her groom and jumped off the horse. Hetty and I had come down from the bleachers, and tried to talk to her but she was stopped by an officious looking woman and the chief steward, who spoke rapidly to her, and stopping to talk briefly to her groom, Fee turned and followed the two women. I looked back up the bleachers and saw that next to Adam was Alice. They then left their seats, and disappeared into the crowd, before I could say anything to them.

"Where has Fee gone, and why did Alice have to come?" asked Hetty,

I said "I think Fee was selected for drug testing. Alice came because Fee is her daughter, I'm sure she wanted to see her in the biggest competition of her life, let's go and see Killer." Hetty nodded, "I've brought him an apple." She said.

Hetty and I hurried back to the stabling, or as hurried as I could make it with my caste. I asked Fee's groom if she had seen Fee.

"No, those women took her away, she did so well, did you hear she's in 3rd place? I thanked her, told her I thought Fee would be back soon, and asked her to take good care of the horse, she nodded, I didn't have to worry, she obviously loved

Killer. Hetty gave Killer his treat, which he obviously considered his due, and we left him to be pampered by his groom.

We strolled back though the hordes of people, over several heads we caught sight of Adam and Alice. He had his arm around her and was kissing her. Hetty began to express her displeasure, but then we saw Fee coming across the grounds, she stopped when she saw Adam and Alice, and even from the distance that we were from her, we could see her fury. The crowds increased as they left the bleachers and blocked our view. When we could see clearly again all three had gone from sight. I thought that I caught a sight of Fee, but in a completely different area of the show grounds. I pointed this out to Hetty. but then we could not see her.

"You must have been mistaken." said Hetty, "She can't be in two places at once."

"You're right," I said, "But that look on her face did not look good, she looked furious." I said, "Do you think she will do something?"

"I don't know, she certainly looked as if she was about to lose it. Do you think we should try to find her? Perhaps she'll go to Adam's house?" Hetty suggested.

I thought about it but then realised that we should check the showground, before we drove there. We went back to stabling but her groom had not seen her. We walked to the food tent and went in. It was packed, I went one way and Hetty the other, but there was no sign of Fee or Adam and Alice. Eleanor came into the tent. I rapidly explained to her what had happened. She told us that she would call Alistair, and they would cover the showground. The three of us decided if we couldn't find them that somebody would have to go to Adam's house. I said that I should really stay at the Showcase, and so Eleanor and Hetty headed off to collect Hetty's car.

I walked over towards the office trailer and heard over the loudspeaker system that the top three riders were to attend the press conference at the media centre. Fee, standing third should be going. I therefore walked over to the media trailer, but there was no sign of Fee. The conference was held without her, much to my embarrassment. I returned to the office trailer to find it locked with a note on the door from Jenny, she had taken the dogs, and gone back to the Centre. I drove over and met them all in the office. I suddenly thought to call Amelia, to tell her that Hetty had been held up. Amelia said not to worry, she would bring her shears with her, when she came to help the repair crew the following day, and she could remove Poppy's caste then. I told her that I had not been serious when I told her she had to do that, but she said she had been looking forward to it.

I called Hetty, she told me that nobody was home at Adam's house. I suggested that she go home. I would drive Poppy home and had arranged it with Amelia to have the caste removed the following day. As an afterthought, I added that I would pick up Eleanor from there.

The first day of the Showcase had finished and everybody was leaving. We had no social engagements, and so I told Jenny to head home. I gathered up the dogs and loaded them into my car and headed off to Hetty's.

As I was driving down the side road, it occurred to me that Fee might have gone home to be by herself. As it was just a short detour for me, I headed over that way. While I was driving Alistair called to say he had finished at the show grounds, and had seen no sign of Fee, Adam or Alice. I told him I was going to Fee's house, and then on to Hetty's, and why didn't he join us there.

As I pulled up to the house I spotted two figures, it was very hard to see, the sky was nearly black, but one was Fee. I could not make out who the other one was, when Fee suddenly lunged forward and grabbed the other by the throat. I jumped out of the car, catching my caste in the seat belt strap, and landed on my rear end. Yelling, I struggled to get myself to my feet. The two dogs were going crazy in the car trying to get out. I slammed the door on them, turning my attention back to the two people, who were now on the ground, Fee on top. I saw that the other person was Alice. Fee was screaming unintelligible words, her hands tight around Alice's neck. Her fingernails, digging into Alice's throat. Alice was scratching frantically at Fee's hands, as she fought for air. I grabbed Fee by one arm and her collar and tried to pull her off Alice, she was still screaming, spittle spraying out of her mouth. I shouted "Fee, Stop it!" over and over. I was making very little headway, my hands were slipping on her collar, which felt greasy, I grabbed Fee's ear and pulled that, but even the considerable pain I must have been causing, had little effect on her. I could not believe how strong she was, and how fury had rendered her totally out of control. I tried slapping her, kicking her, all to no avail. It seemed that I was unable to prevent her from killing her mother. Finally, I grabbed a rock, and brought it down smartly on Fee's head. She collapsed on top of her mother and her hands fell away from Alice's throat. Alice lay still, I pushed Fee off her, and praying that I hadn't hurt Fee too badly, I checked to see if Alice was breathing, she wasn't, and I tried to remember my CPR. I started compressions, tipped Alice's head back pinched her nose and blew air into her mouth, I kept this up for what seemed like an eternity. I was almost in tears from exhaustion, when a car's headlights lit up the scenario, the car squealed to a halt, and Alistair jumped out. He took over from me, not asking any questions, and I turned my attention to Fee, she had got herself to her feet, at least I hadn't killed her, I thought. She was leaning over, hands on her knees, panting. I turned back to Alice and in that moment, Fee took off round the house.

Alice appeared to be improving with Alistair's ministrations, and finally she started coughing and breathing by herself, she remained unconscious. Alistair called 911, and requested Ambulance and police, I tried to stop him summoning the latter, but he shook his head, and said that it had become a police matter, and there was nothing we could do about it. He asked what had happened, and feeling very shaky, I told him.

"Fee was trying to kill her mother,"

"Did they say anything? Why was Fee attacking her mother?" asked Alistair. I shook my head, "Fee left, she went round the house." I seemed unable to put thoughts together.

"Fee screaming, couldn't understand." Was all I managed. Alistair sat me back in my car, and then made another phone call, I was vaguely aware of him saying,

"Bill you must get over here, to Alice and Fee's house." I could then hear sirens in the distance, and was so glad of Alistair's presence, I did not think I could cope with all this. The ambulance arrived first and attended to Alice. Alistair was looking for Fee, but there was no sign of her, and when the police car arrived, he told them to get a search going, and that when Fee was found, that the two casualties should not travel in the same vehicle. He also told them that I needed medical attention. This spurred me into action, and I said in a more normal voice, that I was fine. I continued to sit in my car while, Alistair gave a brief statement, of what he had observed. The police hearing that Fee had been unconscious, with a head wound, while I was performing CPR on Alice, immediately came over to interview me, despite Alistair entreaties to leave me alone. I answered the questions as best I could, but it was obvious that the two constables considered me to be dangerous.

My phone rang, and at the same time the second ambulance arrived. I looked at the call screen and saw that it was Hetty. I was confused, and could not decide whether to answer it, when Alistair came over and took the phone from me. He spoke briefly into the phone and hung up. The second ambulance departed, and the police walked back over to me. Fortunately, at this moment Bill Thomas drove up, and the two men went to greet him and tell him their version of events. From the way he was looking at me, they were not being very complimentary about my behaviour. He walked towards me, and Alistair intercepted his path, but Inspector Thomas told him to stand back.

"Well Ms Browning, what happened?" I told him as succinctly as I could, but even to my own ears, I sounded as if I was rambling. When I had finished, he turned back to Alistair, who told him the whole story. He went back to Fee's accusation of her mother's culpability in her sister's death, of how she had been unaware that her mother had been released from the hospital, and upon seeing her at the Showcase, the anger that Fee had displayed.

To say that Inspector Thomas was annoyed with us for not reporting Fee's accusation, was an understatement. He clearly blamed us for the afternoon's happenings, and quite frankly, I couldn't fault him. Alistair pointed out that Fee had seemed hardly credible, and that he, Inspector Thomas, must have considered Alice a suspect, and dismissed her from his enquiries. Finally, he nodded at Alistair, told the constables to bag up the rock I had used on Fee, and was about to send us all on our way, when Hetty and Eleanor arrived, flat out, in Hetty's car. Inspector Thomas looked infuriated by this and said,

"Oh, here come the rest of the detective club!"

Eleanor walked over to me and said,

"I think B should be checked at the hospital!"

"Very well, you can drive her there. I will have to come and interview Alice, when she is fit to talk."

"The dogs..." I started to say.

The doctor checked me over, despite my protestations of being fine. "Ms Browning, this is the second time in a few weeks that you have been involved in some sort of an altercation, the first time you were seriously injured. The stress on your body, at your age, is not something to be taken lightly. You are suffering from shock, your blood pressure is dangerously high, and I would like to keep you in for observation."

"Impossible!" I snorted, "The cross country is running tomorrow at the Showcase, and I am acting CEO of the Equestrian Centre." the doctor sighed, he had been told that this would be my reaction.

"I cannot discharge you without medical assistance." At that moment Jenny spoke up, I was confused, where had she come from? She hadn't been with us earlier, why was she here?

"I am a registered Health Care Support Worker, and B will be with me in the Organiser's Office at the Showcase Event, we have paramedics on site and two trauma trained doctors will be there the whole day." I was becoming more and more confused, Jenny a Health Care Worker? What was happening?

"In that case, Ms Browning, I will discharge you into this young lady's capable hands." The doctor said, beaming at Jenny. I was about to argue, when Jenny pinched me painfully, and smiling at the doctor she said she would take me home. I frowned angrily at her, as the doctor left the room.

"I didn't know that..." I started to say, but Jenny hissed at me, "For God's sake B, of course I'm not, but you've got to be at the event tomorrow. Just shut up!"

In the waiting room, we found Eleanor, Alistair and Hetty.

I sat myself down next to them, despite Jenny trying to keep me heading to the outside.

"How is Alice?" I asked, Eleanor rose, and came over beside me "Alice is still unconscious, and they have concerns about her brain having been deprived of oxygen for too long." I stared at her, and then turned to look at Hetty, but amazingly, she seemed to be coping better than I was. I turned further and saw Alistair in deep conversation with Jenny. He stood up, and took me by the hand,

"B, you must go home get some sleep, the Showcase cannot go without you. Jenny is going to go home with you and stay at your place. Hetty, Eleanor and I will stay here. The police are going to have a lot of questions." I went to stand up, but the room was spinning alarmingly, I sat back down, and put my head between my knees. When I felt a little better, I looked up to find Jenny had a wheelchair in front of me. She, Alistair and Eleanor heaved me into it, and Jenny wheeled me out, before the doctor could see my latest episode. Somehow Jenny got me in her car, drove me home and got me onto the sofa, where I collapsed. She covered me with a blanket, and I was out like a light.

I awoke the next morning with a pounding headache, and to Jenny bringing me a cup of coffee and some aspirin, "It's 6.00 am B, you'd better get up. We've got to be at the show ground by 7.00 am." I thanked her and tried to pull myself together. I stumbled up stairs and took a shower, which was no mean feat with a caste that you were not supposed to get wet. This accomplished, I put on clean clothes and descended the stairs. My head was thumping, and I felt very alone with no furry body following my every step, I hoped he was behaving at Hetty's house.

Jenny had made toast and brought me up to date. Alice was

still unconscious. Fee had been picked up at stabling. She was denying everything. She said that she had been with the drug testers, and with Killer the whole time. She had no visible injuries, but had been taken to hospital, nevertheless. She was furious, demanding to be released, but if that were to happen, it would only be to the holding cells at the police station, a policewoman was sitting with her, and Hetty was also staying with her. She was under caution and would be interviewed by Inspector Thomas later this morning. He would also be coming to speak to me. I nodded; this was to be expected.

Jenny and I drove over to the show ground. The jump judges, all wearing their orange tee shirts, had assembled, Xen and Susie amongst them. They collected their brown bag lunches, clipboards, whistles and their radios. The Technical Delegate was in the middle of briefing them, the radio guy was in the wings ready to demonstrate the correct use of radios. I was pleased to see that the trucks were lined up and numbered and would follow the routes laid out by Jenny and me, to deliver them to their assigned jumps.

The TV cameras were in situe, and the two jumbotrons were up and working, the media people appeared to be on top of everything, they were showing the current leaderboard, which still had Fee listed in third place, as I watched the screen it switched to a very good picture of Daniel, surrounded by a black border and "In Memorium" printed at the bottom. I turned to Jenny, and said "That is perfect, I am so glad they did that, what good people they are!" referring to the media group. Jenny nodded, and then broke into a big grin as she looked back at the jumbotron. I turned to look, only to see the picture of me that had appeared in the paper, along with the headline,

"I'll kill them!" I exclaimed, "Did you have anything to do with that?" I demanded.

"As if..." Jenny said adopting the most innocent air.

Furiously I stalked on ahead of her and found John and his crew lined up with all their repair tools. Amelia was sitting in the front of John's truck grinning, and John was the recipient of a lot of ribald teasing, from his coworkers, about needing a girl to help him. He seemed to be handling it all well.

'Where is Michael?" I asked,

"Out on the course helping the Technical Delegate." replied John.

They had to make sure that the jump judges, who had complicated options to their fences, understood which routes the competitors could take without penalty, and which should be penalised.

I asked Jenny if she could run back and get us a golf cart so that we could make a tour round to ensure everything was in place. I hobbled slowly back after her and past a mother and child, the little boy was tugging on his mother's arm, and saying "Look Mum! There's the handbag lady!" I went to scowl at him, but then thought better of it, and swung my bag round in a threatening way. He giggled. I continued on my way, Michael pulling up beside me, asking if I needed a lift. He had Maisie bouncing up and down in the front seat, "High Bat Bug!" she yelled, Iris who was in the back tapped her on the shoulder and made a shushing sign with her finger to her lips.

Jenny pulled up in Daniel's golf cart saying, "This is for the CEO, so I guess that means you! "We drove on in unfamiliar luxury, I asked Jenny to go by the parking lot entrances. All were very busy with spectators arriving, in their droves. The parking attendants were at their posts, and all seemed to be running smoothly. The first aid tents were up and staffed, and the ambulances were heading to their allotted positions. We found a horse ambulance unmanned with no keys in it, so a quick radio call to the man in charge, had the attendant running back to his truck. We then drove to the control centre, where the commentator was on one side and the controller and his staff on the other. The controller was in charge of everything regarding the cross country course. He knew where each horse was on the course, at any given moment. Should there be a fall of rider or horse, it was his responsibility to decide whether to hold the start, to dispatch medical or veterinary help, to pull up a horse that is on course, if they are likely to cause an accident by coming upon the fallen horse or rider. It was an extremely difficult job and one needed to have a personality that could work well under extreme pressure. Seeing Jenny and me, he gave us a thumbs up, and asked me if I had my handbag! He received a dirty look from me.

In the warm up area, the stewards were watching the competitors warm up. All appeared well, and we could see the starter in his tent, the timers were ready and the time of day clock in place. I asked Jenny if she knew where Alistair was, and she said she thought he was at stabling, I gave her the nod, and we drove over to find him. He was trying to cope with a breach in the fencing around the stabling, obviously, a corner cutting groom, had found a quick way back to their trailer to get tack, and now it was being used as the main route out to the cross country with all the equipment the grooms needed to have at the start and finish of the course. The guard, who was supposed to be preventing this very thing happening, was being hauled over the coals by Alistair. Efforts were being made to mend the fence. We did not interrupt things until Alistair was finished. He came over to us fairly fuming. I suggested that he take a break, and ride with us to watch some cross country. He nodded and climbed into the rear seat. I got Jenny to drive us to the knoll where the toy bulldozer and digger jump was, from there we could see the first water jump, and we could stay away from the crowd of spectators that would be at the water jump.

We parked. The big maples were coming into leaf, the

entire course had been mown, the jumps were works of art, and the floral decorations were a riot of colour against the wood of the fences. We were blessed with a perfect day, the sun was shining, but the temperature was in the high teens, and so the vets should not be coping with overheated horses. We had misting fans set up in the veterinary holding area, which was at the end of the course, this was where horses could cool down, and be checked by the vets before returning to the stabling.

Alistair told us that Alice was still unconscious, and the worry was that she may have brain damage. Alistair had stayed with Bill Thomas for quite some time, and Fee was still denying everything. She had been taken to the hospital. She became quite hysterical and had to be sedated. She was now more coherent but kept saying that she could not remember what had happened, but that she was sure that if it was true, she must have acted in self defence, and that Alice must have been the aggressor. I shook my head at this "I clearly saw Fee attack her mother. They were standing facing one another, and then Fee lunged at Alice and put her hands around Alice's neck and pushed her to the ground. She was like a mad woman, and so strong, nothing I did could pull her off Alice. I just don't understand why she did it. Earlier she was saying that she hadn't told anybody about the fact that she thought Alice had killed Felicity, because Alice was her mother, and presumably she cared for her." Jenny listened to what I said, and then asked,

"Do you think she is insane? Look at Alice and Alice's mother and wasn't her grandmother supposed to have killed herself? Perhaps it just runs in the distaff side?"

"It's as good an explanation as any." said Alistair, "Poor girl."

"Never mind poor Fee, what about Hetty, and for that matter Alice?" I asked, "Do we know where Adam was while all this was going on? Alice was supposed to stay with him."

"That's another weird thing, apparently, he got a phone call from somebody saying they were Jessica and needed his help. He did not want to leave Alice at his house, and so dropped her off at her house thinking she would feel better in familiar surroundings. He then went to find Jessica, but when he got there, she hadn't called him." Alistair told us.

"How did you find that out?" I asked.

"I phoned him from the hospital, when he finally picked up, he was on his way home. When he heard what had happened, he came to the hospital. He talked to me and then went and sat with Alice, he seemed totally blown away by it all."

"Look the first horse is on course!" said Jenny. We suspended our conversation. The Germans made the course look easy, I hoped our young riders were watching and learning. Patrick Briggs came soon after them and he and TNT were brilliant. Some riders were having problems at the water, some horses were clearly overfaced, by the course, but overall, if the course was ridden properly, it jumped very well. Patrick and TNT sailed through the water with total confidence.

Samantha and Filibuster were having a good round until the first water, she did not ride strongly enough at the jump in, and I thought Filibuster was going to stop, but he climbed over it and bravely took her through the other elements. I thought she would have to be a lot more positive for the bigger second water. They rode off onto the next half of the course and we watched a classic ride from a Brit, showing how the water should be done. Once over the last element, he galloped off to face the next fences amid cheers, as Samantha made her way back to the second crossing of the water. I could see that she was panicking about this jump, and was riding so strongly, that it was worrying the horse rather than encouraging him. She came too fast, and Filibuster went to take off, but at the last moment lost his confidence and stopped. Sam was halfway up his neck as this happened, and went straight over his ears and into the water. She emerged spluttering and filthy, from under the water. She climbed up the bank and threw her whip on the ground, in fury. Filibuster took one look at her and took off at a brisk trot in the opposite direction. Sam squelched after him, and I took pity and got out of the golf cart and told Jenny to take her back to the stables. Jenny and Alistair went and picked her up. Her language was far from gracious, apparently, but they took her back to the stables, where Filibuster was returned after a joyful gallop around the course, until he was captured by one of the stewards. It couldn't have happened to a nicer person I thought! I watched Roger making his way back to the stables in less than happy mood.

Maggie was the final Canadian and she looked polished and professional though rather slow round the course. I mourned the loss of Fee and Killer, but nothing could be done about that. I had sent a message to Fee's groom telling her Fee wouldn't be riding, and I had withdrawn her from the start list. Jenny came back to pick me up, and we went back to our office trailer, after dropping Alistair back at stabling. Jenny and I had little to do. The competition was in the hands of the officials, and so we left them to it, and went over to the big marquee to see whether the arrangements for the competitors' party were under way. The caterers were buzzing around, the band was setting up, and the bar tenders were stocking their shelves, so all seemed under control. As we emerged from the tent we found Eleanor struggling with a rambunctious Alfie and a sedate Poppy. She was delighted to find us, "I have been looking everywhere!" she exclaimed. Alfie leapt exuberantly onto my lap, I seemed unable to get through to him that he was beyond the size of a lap dog. He smiled in my face, and adopted a motoring position, digging his toenails into my thighs, meanwhile Poppy sat with great decorum on the back seat with Eleanor. I turned round, and glared at Eleanor and said, "Don't say it! I think he is perfect and that is all that counts!" Jenny drove off trying hard to hide the smirk on her face. We went back to the office in the Centre and called Alistair to join us.

Hetty phoned, "They have taken Fee to the police station, I decided to stay with Alice. I phoned her parents, but they wouldn't come, and so the poor girl has nobody. Fee was creating a terrible scene here, they were glad to get rid of her. This Fee is not my Granddaughter, I think that she has lost the balance of her mind." I told her that we had been discussing the very same thing.

"Do you think I should try to get her a solicitor and a psychiatrist?" Hetty asked. I thought about it and said that I thought that a lawyer was what she needed right now, and that they would arrange psychiatric help. "Hetty, I'm going to ask Alistair if he knows a lawyer who could deal with this and try to get one sent over to Fee. She should not be talking to anybody without a lawyer with her."

"I don't think it matters, she is not really coherent, nothing she says at the moment can be believed." said Hetty, sadly. I told her I would phone her back in a few minutes and hung up. I waited impatiently for Alistair to appear. He did a few minutes later, his face drawn with exhaustion, apparent round his eyes. I felt really bad, we leaned on him too much, and it was hard to remember that he was grieving the loss of the love of his life. He wiped his face with his hand, and tried to smile,

"It went well B, you should be happy." I nodded and thanked him, and then asked him if he knew of a lawyer for Fee. He furrowed his brow thinking, and then said that he did.

"John Smith, would be good, he is Cyn's cousin, he only does criminal work. He is licensed to practise in Canada and in the US. He may be too busy to take it on. He is not cheap, if he can't do it, he'll recommend somebody else."

"Thank you, Alistair" I said, and had Jenny look up the phone number, "I think you should go home, you look totally exhausted. Go, have an early night, and if you don't feel up to tomorrow, then stay home, I can appoint Eleanor as acting Security Chair." Alistair was about to argue, but he could see the sense in my suggestion. "I think you are right B, I need a decent night's sleep, I only got a couple of hours last night, and it's been a busy day."

"I can look after everything until you feel better." Eleanor spoke up. Alistair nodded and turned to go. Jenny stood up and said she was going to go to Hetty's to look after the puppies. She passed me the lawyer's phone number as she was leaving. I dialled and got a secretary, I asked to speak to Mr Smith, and was immediately quizzed on why I should want to talk to the big man. I explained briefly, and having passed scrutiny, I had to give my name, address and credit card number. This was overkill but I gave it anyway. I was then put on hold, while she relayed the information, and finally a cheerful voice answered the phone enquiring what he could do for me. I explained that we had a young girl who had tried to kill her mother, after making an accusation that the mother had killed the girl's sister. There was silence on the end of the line, which in retrospect was not surprising, the whole thing sounded so farfetched, I attempted to bring veracity to my tale by explaining that the girl was currently at the police station, and the mother was unconscious in hospital.

"Inspector Thomas is wanting to question Fiona now." I added.

"Well, that had better not happen without a lawyer present." said John Smith, "I had better get over there right away. Please call and tell them that I am coming." He abruptly hung up leaving me looking at the receiver in my hand. I told Eleanor what he had said, and she said she would call the Inspector, she picked up the land line, and I called Hetty back on my cell phone. Once again, I had to wait for her to call me back. I told her that a lawyer was on his way to Fee, as we spoke. She asked who he was, and I told her his name and said that it was somebody Alistair knew.

They say that God never gives you more than you are capable of dealing with, but I thought, that if indeed there was a God, then he had dealt out far too much for this one good person to handle. I thought if it was the case, then he was not a God that I wished to know.

Alice had been taken up for more scans. I suggested that Hetty go home, get some rest, and go back tomorrow, she said she would think about it. I let her know that Jenny had looked after the puppies, and that I had Poppy, so there was no cause to worry. I urged her to go home once again, and then said goodbye.

I turned to Eleanor, "What did Inspector Thomas say?"

"Surprisingly, he was quite happy. He thinks that Fee has severe mental health problems, and needs somebody to advocate for her, otherwise he will be held responsible. When I told him who was coming, he said "I see you've got the best." So, I guess Alistair's recommendation was a good one."

As we were finishing our conversation Jenny arrived back looking flushed,

"Those puppies are a going concern! Mine is going to Puppy School as soon as I take her home!" Eleanor and I burst out laughing. "B we'd better get over to the Competitors' Party if you want to get anything to eat!" It was a well-known fact that Eventers could consume their own weight in food.

"I hope it isn't pulled pork." I said, "I hate it, and it appears to be the standard fare at all competitors' parties."

"It isn't. I've heard you whining on about that for too long! I ordered roast chicken, baked potatoes and salad." said my amazing assistant.

"I love you!" I said.

"I know."

We took the dogs for a quick pee. Alfie relieved himself, yet again, in the flower bed, by reflex I looked round for the gardener, even though I knew he had the weekend off. Poppy took herself off into the long grass. Their business concluded, both were OK to stay in the office for a while, and the three of us took Daniel's golf cart to the competitors' party. The line up for food was already considerable, but I pulled rank, and we cut in the line. Once served, we looked round for a place to sit, and found Michal and John, with their guests, seated near the exit. We joined them and had an entertaining meal. Amelia had had a blast apparently, there were not a lot of repairs needed, and so they had been able to watch the majority of the competition. Maisie was beside herself with excitement, words spilling out of her mouth at an even faster rate than normal.

"B, why didn't Fee ride?" she asked, "I waited and waited for her to come but Michael said she withdrew."

"She wasn't very well." I said feebly, not having any other excuse, other than the truth, and I was not about to tell the whole horrible story here.

"Well! She's a bit of a wimp! I would still ride if I wasn't feeling well!" looking at Maisie's determined freckled face and her flaming red hair, I thought that this was probably true.

"Oh, look there's Gunter! Hi Gunter! Well done!" she yelled at one of our German riders, he came over and ruffled her hair. "Did you enjoy it little one?" he asked,

"It was AWESOME!" Maisie replied.

"Next time I come, you will be riding!" he said.

"Of course!" said Maisie, with no doubt in her mind. She was a good antidote to depression.

We went up for dessert, I was in line with Michael, I raised my eyebrows at him in question.

"I am on it B, I am getting a paternity test. It sounds like Iris will get temporary custody of Maisie. We are taking it one step at a time."

"Iris is a very good person, she does not warrant being treated as an extension of Maisie." I said solemnly.

"I realise that B, but Iris is a strong person, she will not allow me to treat her like that." Michael replied.

"I am glad to hear that." I felt very defensive of Iris, and I'm not sure why I felt forced to confront Michael, but I thought, rationalising, it can't do any harm.

We ate our dessert, apple pie and cream along with paternity! Delicious!

John said he had to go and help bring some of the flowers and shrubs in from the cross country course that were needed to decorate the show jumping. Amelia jumped up and said she would help. Following their lead Jenny, Eleanor and I got up to leave. We said goodbye to Michael and Iris, and of course Maisie, who was shouting at us that we should stay for the dancing, I shook my head, the band was starting to warm up and Xen and Susie were already on the floor, gyrating in a strange non rhythmic manner. That was definitely a cue for us to leave.

Jenny opted to stay at my place for the night, it being so close to the show grounds, and did not involve the commute that her own home did. The dogs were glad to see us, they had obviously been anxious about the lack of routine to their life, and one of them had ripped up a cushion. Judging by the way Alfie was looking sheepishly at me, I guessed that it was him. We let them out into the garden, while I prepared their supper. They returned from their sentry duties and ate voraciously; you would think that they hadn't been fed in weeks. Alfie, having wolfed his down went over to Poppy's hopefully, but she let out a low growl, and Alfie thought better of the idea of trying to persuade her to let him eat hers as well. They took up residence on the couch, leaving us mere humans to sit in the uncomfortable chairs. The phone rang, Alice had regained consciousness, but was still not vocalising. The doctors wanted to run tests tomorrow to check her brain activity. Hetty had gone home and was now missing Poppy. I told her that Poppy was happy with life and enjoying my couch.

"Oh B! She's not allowed on the furniture!" I told her rubbish and left her mumbling complaints.

Another ring, this time it was John Smith, he said that Fee was in a very unstable condition. He had arranged for her to leave the police station, and that she had been sent to a hospital that dealt with the criminally insane. I was horrified at this and asked why she could not go to Beeton Hall, but he explained she had been charged with attempted murder and had to go to a hospital with sufficient security precautions. He went on to say that the place was not as bad as it sounded, and that Fee would be in a wing far away from the convicted inmates. He wanted to know when it would be convenient to come and talk to me. I explained that the next day would be impossible due to the Showcase being in it's final day. I said that I could meet with him after the Prize Giving, he said in that case, he would come and watch some of the competition, and meet with me afterwards. I promised to leave him a ticket at the Will Call and explained where he could find me. I hung up. Jenny was scribbling in her notebook, "Ticket for lawyer!"

I was totally horrified by what had happened to Fee. Eleanor told me that John Smith was right to get her somewhere she could receive treatment, and have doctors make a proper diagnosis. She would need this in order to establish that she was not fit to stand trial. Jenny and I nodded at this, it made sense, but was still hard to process. We talked on for a while, and eventually I plucked up the courage to phone Hetty back. I just told her that Fee had been sent to a hospital and I was going to talk to her lawyer the following day. Hetty said she would like to meet him, and I suggested that she come and watch the show jumping with us the following day, and then she could have a word with him when it was finished. She agreed to this and said she would go back and see Alice tomorrow morning, and then come to the show grounds. I told her to park outside the Centre, and we would leave a golf cart there, for her use. Jenny made another note.

We went to bed shortly after that and got up early to watch the final Horse Inspection. The stewards had prepared the jog strip, John and Amelia had supplied the shrubs off the cross country course that formed a circle in the middle of the turn around area. The horses had to trot down, turn clockwise around the shrubs and trot back again. While we watched, the ground jury and veterinary delegate took up their positions, and the announcer called for the first horse to be presented.

This part of the competition was often the most stressful for the competitors. If the examination panel decided that their horse was not fit to continue, then it was the end of the competition for them. Most competitors knowing that their horse was not 100% would opt to withdraw. Today was cold and windy and this put even the most tired horses on their toes. Some behaved very badly, bucking and cantering sideways, and even kicking out, causing the panel to jump backwards to avoid the horse's hind feet. Most horses flew through this exam, but unfortunately the horse from El Salvador was not sound. Maggie presented Media Circus, he looked immaculate, beautifully turned out, but he was obviously very tired. The panel sent him to the holding box where he was examined by the associate veterinary delegate, he returned from there and jogged up a second time and this time was passed by the panel. A big cheer went up from the spectators, and Maggie looked relieved. She looked round, and came over to me and asked,

"Do you think he's OK to jump B?"

"I think so Maggie, but the old boy is obviously tired, it will be hard for you to keep the rails up."

"Thanks, B, I'll warm him up, and if I don't think he's up to it, I'll withdraw." Maggie was a good soul and thought more of her horse than of winning, she led him back to the stables.

There was now a break so that the competitors could walk the show jumping course. They walked around it to learn the route and work out how many strides their horse would take in between fences. The course opened with a related line of six strides, it then rolled back to a big oxer with five very forward strides to a triple bar and then riders were forced to shorten up the strides to get to a skinny vertical. There followed a combination of oxer to vertical to oxer, finishing very close to the arena boards which meant the horses could think that they were going to jump into the crowd. Then a tight turn to a massive wall followed by planks painted with the Canadian flag and a long gallop to the final line of a vertical to oxer combination and the final fence a big Swedish oxer.

They would jump in reverse order of go. The last placed competitor jumping first, and the first place jumping last. Half would jump before lunch, and then there would be a break which allowed for ring maintenance and spectators to spend money at the trade fair as well as grab a bite to eat.

We watched the first group of horses jump, they were not stellar, but being the weakest group, it was to be expected. Our European course designer had lived up to his reputation for setting stiff courses. He remained in the ring, ordering his ring crew around, and measuring each fence that was knocked down once the rails were back in place, to ensure that they always stayed at the same height. He waved to me and raised his eyebrows obviously not happy with the standard of jumping. The final horse of the morning managed to keep all the rails up, but went too slowly, and had time penalties.

We went to the sponsors' tent for lunch and Hetty joined us there. Alice was quite a lot better and was now talking. She said that the fight with Fee was entirely her own fault, and she did not wish to press charges. This was what any mother would do, we all thought, but sadly I knew the truth of what had happened. Inspector Thomas was going to talk to her, when he was back at work on Monday.

We finished up our lunch of smoked salmon with cream cheese, colossal shrimp and various cold meats and salads. It was wonderful, just missing a hot soup, on such a cold day. We moved back, over to the show jumping ring, and climbed up the covered bleachers, and took our seats. The top fifteen horses were to jump this afternoon, and the announcer was getting everybody into the spirit of things as he calculated the penalties of each rider, as they came in. He was doing impressive mental arithmetic, to predict what would happen to their scores if they had a rail or time penalties. Unlike the morning's rounds, we saw some beautiful riding, but a clean round with no time penalties was still proving elusive. Coming in standing in eighth place following a spectacular cross country round was Patrick Briggs and TNT. We held our breath as he started the course, the horse was difficult to ride, he would come in sideways to each jump, at the last minute he would straighten, fire into the air, and kick out a hind leg as he cleared the jump. This is extremely difficult to sit to, but Patrick was obviously accustomed to this behaviour, and sat quietly on his rambunctious horse. They crossed the finish line clear and in time, to the approval of the crowd, who cheered loudly.

"And that's going to put pressure on the leaders." came the announcer's comment, "All seven of them only have two rails in hand."

We sat forward in our seats. The next three rounds had jumping and time faults which meant Patrick moved up three places in the standings. Maggie came into the ring on her old partner and saluted the judges. Media Circus looked brighter than he had that morning, and he tried his best to keep all the rails in their cups, but the big oxer coming out of the triple combination was too much for him and he took the back rail down. He and Maggie crossed the finish line just two seconds over time, to give themselves 4.8 penalties, which just kept them ahead of Patrick and TNT. I could hear Maisie shouting and cheering over the other side of the ring, where she was sitting with Michael. The British rider came in, and rode a perfect round, which left the two Germans to complete the competition. Maisie's friend Gunter came in and equalled the Brit to remain in second place. There was a hush as the final rider came in and commenced his round. There is a huge amount of pressure on the rider in first place, should he have any penalties he would lose the competition, and unfortunately the pressure got to the young man, he had the first fence down, a groan went up from the crowd and he proceeded to have two more rails. Gunter had won, the British rider was second, Maggie was third and Patrick fourth. Anthea Charrington swept into the ring and orchestrated a perfect Prize Giving. A lone bagpiper headed the parade and colour guard, Pony Club members, and the winners filed in. Ribbons and trophies were presented, the Flag raising went smoothly, and the German national anthem was played. The winners went on a victory lap, and Gunter as the winner, did a second lap by himself. As they left the ring the announcer called Maggie back into the ring. She trotted back in, and Maggie dismounted, ran up her stirrups and removed her saddle. A portable microphone was passed to her. With tears in her voice, she announced that her great horse Media Circus was going to be retired. She thanked him for years of service, and then lead him, amid great applause, out of the ring. I had to admit, that I to, had tears in my eyes at this gesture from this kind girl, who would no longer have a top horse to ride.

The Eventing Showcase was over. I had done my best to make it memorable. It had proved to be memorable for some very bad reasons, as well as good. I thought of Daniel, of Alistair's grief, of poor Rebecca, her body hidden in the grounds, of Fee who did not get to ride Killer, and of Alice and Hetty and the horrors that they would have to face. Tears poured silently down my face. I stood alone and bereft at the foot of the bleachers. Jenny and Eleanor had left to collect the golf cart. Hetty stood quietly a little piece away from me, waiting for the moment to pass. When my gaze fell on her I felt pathetic, I had nothing to feel bad about compared to my dear friend. I sniffed loudly and walked over to her. She smiled sympathetically at me, and we waited for the golf cart.

Jenny drove us back to the office trailer, picked up some papers, and then took us all back to the office in the centre. She and Eleanor then took my car and went back to my place to pick up the dogs. Hetty and I waited to meet with John Smith. He drove up in an 8 series 840i Coupe, which I thought appropriate for a successful lawyer, as I saw him arrive though the office window. We walked out to greet him, and he bustled in, carrying a large briefcase. He was of medium stature, wearing a business suit and a vicuna over coat on top of it. He had a round face, small shrewd looking eyes and an oversize moustache. He looked very busy and capable. In contrast his voice was soft and melodic. He introduced himself, told us to call him John, and the three of us sat down. He thanked me for the tickets and said that he had really enjoyed the afternoon's sport. He then asked what he could do for us. Hetty explained that she was Fee's Grandmother and Alice's mother- in- law. John nodded and made a note on the legal pad, that he had brought out. He turned to me and said,

"I understand from David Thomas that you witnessed the attack Ms Browning?" I nodded, and he asked me to walk him through exactly what had happened. I told him that it was hard to know where to start. Did he just want to know about the attack itself?

"For the time being, yes." he replied. I took a deep breath, and proceeded to tell him everything that I remembered, as clearly and succinctly as possible. He took notes but did not interrupt me until I finished.

"And you are quite sure that, from your perspective, it was an unprovoked attack?"

"Yes, from what I could see, but of course I did not hear what had been said." I replied,

"But Alice did not push or hit or in any way threaten Fiona?" I shook my head, "No" I said.

"OK, now can you tell me what had happened in the lead up to this attack?"

"Fee had not seemed herself for quite some time." I started "She was very rude to Hetty and furious with her, when she was told that Alice was coming home from hospital. I went to speak to her about her behaviour and to see if I could find out what was wrong with her. She became increasingly more upset during our conversation about Alice's return from hospital, at one point she ran away. She finally returned, and then told me that she thought Alice had killed her sister." At this point I realised that John knew nothing about Felicity's disappearance, so I back tracked. "Felicity, Fiona's twin sister, disappeared nearly ten years ago, and despite all the police investigation, she has not been found."

John, who I am sure, had heard many a sorry story, looked at the pair of us in astonishment. After a moment he said, "And you had the skeleton of Brian McVicker's wife found here, and your CEO was murdered. I also heard that you were responsible for Brian's apprehension, were you not?" We nodded.

"Brian is a psychopath." said John, "I represented him on a case in California. He contacted me when he was arrested this time, but I refused his case." He shook his head, and then said, "Do continue." I told him that the arrangements were made for Alice to come home and stay with her friend, Adam. We did not tell Fee that Alice was leaving the hospital, which in hindsight was a bad error. Fee was competing in the Showcase, and then saw her mother with Adam amongst the spectators, she became extremely upset. I went on to say that we tried to find Fee, but until I saw her at her house, we had no idea where she had been.

Once I finished, I looked up, John was busy writing notes. He looked up at Hetty and asked her if she had anything to add. She said that she couldn't think of anything. John just sat there, and I became aware of how hard it was to sit with a total silence, my Wendover College method was being played back at me. John looked at us both, but we had nothing more to say. Finally, he nodded.

"Good, I have the information that I need." He said with finality and rose to leave. This was not what I wanted.

"Please tell us what we do from here?" I asked.

"You do nothing, we wait until the doctors have examined Fiona, before we do anything." The emphasis was on the "we". John left telling us that his assistant would be sending an accounting of what they had deducted from my credit card balance, as a retainer for services rendered. He then left to get into his BMW. Hetty was beside herself about his latest statement,

"How are we going to pay for this?" she demanded. I suggested that we wait until my credit card limit ran out. "This is not a joke B." she replied.

"I know Hetty, but let's see where this goes? I can cover it for a bit, why don't you find out from Alice's parents, whether Alice has any money. If not, they are well enough off that they could cover Fee's legal costs." I suggested to her. There was nothing else that we could do, and so I proposed that we should go home.

"Come back with me, and pick up Poppy to take her home," I suggested. "The puppies are all going to their new homes in a couple of days, so you need to enjoy them while you still have them." I said positively.

She nodded, and we headed back to my place. Eleanor and Jenny were there, the dogs had been looked after, and so Hetty took Poppy, and left to go home. Jenny, who was off work for the next few days, told Hetty, that she was going to pick up her puppy tomorrow.

I suggested that Jenny spend the night with Eleanor and me. We hunted out something for supper, ate it, comfortable with the silence, and then collapsed into bed. We had no firm timetable for the next day, so we all slept in. Jenny, being the youngest of us was the first up. She was sitting at the kitchen table, with a long list in front of her. As we had nothing on the agenda for two days, I asked her what she was doing. This was a list for all she had to accomplish before she picked up her puppy, she said. I tried to keep a straight face at this utterance and wished her good luck. I said I would see her, and her puppy, at the office in a couple of day's time. She scurried out of the house, definitely on a mission, and I sat and enjoyed my coffee, trying not to think about all the troubles that invaded our peace.

Half an hour later Eleanor appeared. She poured coffee, and sat for a while, then she said,

"We should go and see if Alistair is OK." I realised that he had not appeared yesterday, even though I had given him permission to do this. I nodded reluctantly realising that Eleanor was right, Alistair was not a person to take advantage of permission to not show up, unless he was feeling really bad. I hoped that he was all right, and suddenly became worried that we should go immediately to his house. We both dressed hurriedly and drove over there. We hammered on the door, but there was no reply. I was beginning to panic, when finally, a very sleepy Alistair answered the door.

"Sorry, I took a sleeping pill, had no idea the effect it would have on me," he said. We were both so relieved to see him safe, in one piece, that we both let out a great expletive, "Thank God!"

"I'm very pleased to see that you are so happy!" he said, "Give me a moment to get dressed," Looking at his checkered pyjamas, we concurred.

He appeared later looking positively sartorial. He stated that there was nothing that we could do until we had information about the state of Fee, and what they intended to charge her with. He also thought that perhaps we should go and talk to Alice, before we were shut down. I realised that yet again we were putting too much on Alistair. He looked at me and said,

"B, I need every moment of my life filled with something to do, to take this awful pain away." this was said with such sadness, that I could think of nothing to say, Eleanor looked at me and back at Alistair with compassion in her eyes, even though her next words belied that,

"OK let's get going over to the hospital, stop mooning around!" We headed out, taking Alistair's car, and drove to the hospital. We checked at the information desk to find what ward

Alice was on and were reminded to use the hand sanitiser. This accomplished we marched through the hospital to E Ward. Alice was sitting up in bed looking frail, she had dark bruises around her neck and her hair was badly in need of washing and combing. She looked a shadow of the person, that we had seen at Beeton Hall. She smiled at us weakly and thanked us for coming. I explained to her the fact that we had got Fee a good lawyer. She nodded and smiled her thanks. There was an awkward moment of silence, when I could not think of what else I should say, but Eleanor was more forthcoming,

"Alice, what happened? You were to be staying at Adam's place, how did you get to your house?" Alice's voice was very soft, almost a whisper,

"It is all a kind of blur, Adam drove us back from the Showcase, he made me some tea. Then he said he could hear the phone ringing, he answered it, and said that a friend of his was in trouble, and he had to go to help her. He said he would drop me at my house, but I can't remember why. I was in the garden outside the house, and I must have done something, because Fee was there, and she was fighting me off, it wasn't her fault, I just can't seem to remember what I did." With this she burst into tears. We waited for her to regain her composure, and finally she said, "I thought that my stay in the hospital had cured me of these lost periods."

"Lost periods? How do you mean Alice?" I asked.

"Well, I would be doing something, and then it would be an hour later, and I would have no idea of what I had done during that time."

"What did your doctors say about that?" I pressed,

"They thought it might be dissociative amnesia. In the hospital they slowly weaned me off all the drugs I was taking, they said that some were having a bad interaction with others. I had masses of therapy, it took a long time, but I was finally feeling like a normal person, but now I am right back to where I was before, I don't know that I can go on." It seemed so cruel to continue, but this might be the last chance we would have to talk to her.

"Alice, do you know that Fee thinks you killed Felicity?"

"Yes, and I am sure that she is right. I don't remember doing it, but Fee would tell me that I did kill her. She showed me a sweatshirt of Felicity's, that apparently, she was wearing when she went missing, and Felicity's portfolio. I had hidden them in the house. I wanted to tell the police, but Fee said she couldn't handle losing me as well. I should have gone to them, but I kept losing time, and I couldn't think, and finally I didn't remember any of it. My brain does not work like other peoples. Poor Fee, she is not responsible for any of this. I told the policeman, that I would not press charges." We all looked at her in disbelief. The life she described was horrible. She looked so miserable, that I thought we should tell the doctors here, that her depression was so profound that she could be suicidal. Finally, Alistair said,

"Alice, I am afraid that it won't be up to you, whether charges are laid against Fee. The police can do it themselves, Fee nearly killed you. If it wasn't for B you would have died."

"I wish I had!" said Alice in a voice so low we could hardly hear it, once again she started to sob. I looked at Alistair, and said, "Oh, what have we done?"

We walked silently back to Alistair's car, and got in. Then all our thoughts came pouring out.

"I think that she believes everything that she told us, but whether it is true or not is another story." said Alistair.

"From what I saw, she did nothing physical to provoke Fee, she might have said something, I suppose..." I replied. Eleanor then said, "She does not seem the provocative type, she is so soft spoken, and what could she have said to set Fee off like that?"

"I do not understand why this poor woman was not hospitalised, and treated for this dissociative amnesia before, she's been ill for years" I said,

"Perhaps she never complained of it, maybe she feared what she might have done. If she seriously thinks she may have killed Felicity, then that might be the case." Eleanor said thoughtfully. I suddenly had a thought, that was not very pleasant,

"Do you think Fee suffers from the same thing? Does it run in families? We were thinking that she was mentally ill to have attacked Alice like that, she did not seem to know what she was doing." The others considered this, and nodded, Alistair spoke positively,

"We have several things we must do. I think we should tell John Smith about all this. Then Alice's doctor from Beeton Hall needs to be consulted. Alice also needs a lawyer, if Fee's accusations come out. John cannot act for them both. He can probably suggest someone else. This is just one crazy mess."

"I hope Alice has enough money to pay for a lawyer." I said, there was no way I could pay a second set of legal fees, and I was not at all sure I could pay the first.

"I think we should find out if she has any savings or whether the military will do anything for her, she gets a pension from them. Or she could mortgage the house" Eleanor chipped in.

Having got a to do list in our heads, we drove back to Alistair's house, went in and divided up the tasks. I said that I would talk to John Smith and find out his thoughts on a lawyer for Alice. Eleanor said she would go and talk to Hetty about Alice's finances, and she would try to talk to the doctor at Beeton Hall. Alistair interjected, at that moment, saying that he thought we should know what the lawyer had to say about talking to the doctor, before we did something that would compromise the situation. We both accepted this as sensible. Alistair then said that he was going to follow up on the things that we were going to do, before Fee had attacked Alice.

We grabbed some lunch, it had been a long morning, and I was starving. Eleanor seemed to live on air, which was probably why she looked as good as she did. She then took my car to go over to Hetty's place. I telephoned John Smith's office. His secretary told me he was in court, but was expecting the hearing to be adjourned, so he should be back before the end of day. Thwarted in my task, I made a half-hearted effort to clean the house. As frequently happened, I became bored with this work, and so sat back down. There were a couple of things nagging at the back of my mind, but I couldn't put my finger on them. Deciding they were probably unimportant, I started flipping through a horse magazine that had arrived in the post. Eventually the phone rang, and when I picked it up it was John Smith calling back. He kindly reminded me that telephone consultations were billed at his usual rate. I thanked him for this information, and immediately launched into the happenings of the day, attempting to impart the information as quickly as possible, being all too aware of the clock ticking away with dollar signs. At least the man was quick on the uptake, and I did not need to repeat myself. He agreed that Alice needed a lawyer, and he said he would have his secretary send me a couple of names. He was having Fee examined by a psychiatrist and would mention her mother's diagnosis. I thanked him and hung up.

Eleanor returned with some welcome news. Alice had considerable savings from a trust fund left to her by an aunt, so payment of a lawyer would not be a problem. Also, Hetty thought that Alice would want to pay Fee's lawyer, and if not Hetty had the money that she had been saving up for Fee's surgery. I was glad that I would not be on the hook for this fiscal responsibility. I asked how Hetty was doing, and Eleanor said she was doing surprisingly well. She was looking forward to the puppies leaving, John was coming with Amelia the following day to pick up his "Pansy", Jenny as well. Michael was apparently doing something with the backyard at the cafe, so that Maisie's puppy would have a place to run around, despite all the protestations "I will walk her every day!" from Maisie.

CONTINUING QUESTIONS

I WAS FEELING A little lost. I glanced at my calendar hanging on the wall. I still preferred this method of keeping track, rather than using my phone. Something was scribbled in for today. I looked closer, and it said 11.00 am remove caste.

"Shit! I'm going to miss it!" I thought, hurrying to the phone I called the hospital, and told them I had been held up. I was told to come immediately, otherwise the doctor would be gone.

Eleanor was out walking Alfie, and I scribbled her a note, and then pulled on an odd selection of clothes that were the closest to hand. I hurried out to the car and drove to the hospital arriving at the fracture clinic totally out of breath. The technician removed the caste leaving a pale, skinny looking leg, exposed to the elements. I was then wheeled to Xray, to see how it had healed. The radiologist came out and said it appeared to have healed quite well, and that I should take it easy for a while. I headed out on the maiden voyage of my unsupported leg, which felt very weak and strange, but at least I was free of the beastly caste.

I drove, finally legal, having two legs to use on the pedals. Eleanor would be pleased, I thought. I went home, and picked up my two friends, one human, one canine, and went to the Centre. Jenny was off for a few days, and I worked perfunctorily getting done some report filing, and sending the results of the Showcase to the FEI. Jenny had already prepared these. I called Pru, who was chipper, and seemed on top of everything. The event horses had left the stables, and the crew had disinfected the stalls, so all was well for the arrival of the dressage horses. Thinking about this, I remembered that I had failed to go back to help Jessica and Quisty. I called her up and offered to come that afternoon.

"That would be awesome B. Can I run through my test?" I agreed, and we set a time. I turned to Eleanor who had lugged out the murder board and was staring at it. "What?" I asked, Eleanor shook her head,

"I don't know, but there is something not right." I looked at the board, Eleanor had added what Fee and Alice had said, in point form. I walked closer and read it carefully. Suddenly it came to me.

"If Felicity had gone to the modelling agency to drop off her portfolio, then why would it be back at her house?" I exclaimed,

"You're right," said Eleanor, and then thought for a moment, "But it could have been a copy."

"Yes, in that case it would have nothing to do with her disappearance, because she could have left it there herself. Both Fee and Alice thought it was proof that Alice had murdered Felicity, because it was back at the house. We must ask the modelling agency if Felicity actually left it there."

"What about the sweatshirt? Fee said she found it in her mother's laundry."

"We only have Fee's word for that. Do we know for sure that Felicity was wearing it? We have taken Fee's word for everything, and we don't have the items, because she said that she burnt them."

"Do you think Fee could be capable of framing Alice?" I shook my head; I had no idea. Before the night, when Fee attacked Alice, I would have said no, but having witnessed her behaviour then I was not so sure.

"I wonder if Alistair has been to the modelling agency yet, we should call him, and tell him about the portfolio." Eleanor reached for the phone and dialled, we waited for an answer, but the door opened and in came Alistair, phone in hand, "You summoned me?" he asked. We laughed, Eleanor hung up the phone, and we told Alistair what we had come up with.

"Well not just pretty faces! However, we have a problem, the girl who dealt with Felicity is on maternity leave, and the others were not working at the agency ten years ago. They said that if the portfolio had been kept it would be in their archives, and they had no idea where, I was going to try to visit the lady on mat. leave."

Alistair wanted to come and watch me give Jessica and Quisty a lesson, in preparation for the Dressage Showcase. Eleanor said she would tag along. We took my car, Eleanor complaining, that she and Alistair were forced to sit in the back, as Alfie had taken up his normal seat. I chose to ignore her. We got there just as Jessica was finishing tacking up the horse. He was looking amazing. He was a beautiful dark dapple grey. Unfortunately, his coat would lighten up as he got older, he had two white socks in front and a star mid centre on his face. He was a big boy, standing about 17.00 hands. Alistair was very proud of him, and Jessie adored him.

Before she got on him Alistair asked her about what had happened two nights ago. Jessie said that it was very strange, Adam had come banging on her door, Jessie had opened, and he had demanded what was the matter. She did not understand, and Adam got quite cross saying that she had called him for help, which she had not done. She grinned and said she had told him that it must be another one of his girlfriends, at which he got mad, and stormed off. She said the whole thing was crazy, she did not know what had got into Adam's head. Alistair asked her how long it had all taken, and she said that it could only have been about five minutes max.

"Don't worry Jessie, I just wondered." Said Alistair, "Now, let's see what you can show B."

We spent an enjoyable forty minutes watching while Jessie put Quisty through his paces. She had been working hard since I last saw her, she had improved the quality of the canter into the flying changes, consequently she was able to complete the tempi changes without error, the canter pirouettes were still a little weak but the piaffe and passage were better, just lack of carrying power in the transitions was causing a faltering. I left her with some exercises to improve the pirouette canter, working squares with quarter pirouettes at the corners and sitting him down in between.

I told her that she had done a great job. Alistair was positively preening, with my assessment of their work. I asked her when she was shipping in for the Showcase, and she said the next day. I wished her luck, and left Alistair giving last minute instructions.

I had to put in token appearances at the office, as I had agreed to oversee the entire Showcase. There was some housekeeping work, in the form of queries from the accountants, regarding invoices from some of the suppliers. I was having difficulty getting confirmed numbers of spectator cars, in order to match up with the monies collected. I am not a mathematician and it seemed that we were short changed, by a considerable amount. I decided to pass this on to the accountants, so they could count beans, and I would not have to. I was thinking that I had done everything I had to, when the postman appeared with a very official looking envelope that he required me to sign for.

Puzzled, I took the letter opener and ripped it open across

the top. Inside were forms in triplicate which informed me as Organiser of the Eventing Showcase, that human drug testing had been performed at my competition, and that Fiona Hallkirk had tested positive for a banned substance. It went on to describe the options, that we as the Organiser, and Fiona as the athlete, had available to appeal. A second sample would be made available for us to test should we so wish. Fiona, if found guilty, would be subject to a minimum of a year's suspension from competition, during which time she could not appear on any showgrounds as a coach, spectator or competitor. The drug in question was a mixture of psychotropic compounds.

I nudged Eleanor, who was busy making lists of something, and passed the document to her. She read it, and then in typical Eleanor manner, read it a second time more slowly. She put the papers on the table looked up, and said,

"Well, I guess we know why she attacked Alice, she must have been high." I nodded,

"I'd better give a copy of this to John Smith." Eleanor nodded, and I lifted the phone and dialed John's number. I told the secretary that I did not need to talk to him, but would she please let him know that I had papers that he should look at urgently, and that I would drop them around to his office right away. She told me that he would be in for the morning. I relayed this information to Eleanor, and we headed off for John Smith's office. Parking was a problem, and I had to drive round a couple of blocks to find a space. I did not want to leave Alfie in the car, so we took him with us.

The secretary looked astonished at having a large hairy client in the waiting area, and rapidly took the papers,

"Er... You'd better wait here in case Mr Smith wishes to ask you anything." She said looking disapprovingly at Alfie who, unaffected by her lack of courtesy, smiled at her.

We waited for ten minutes, obviously the great man read

papers as slowly and as many times as Eleanor. He then appeared from his sanctum, patted Alfie on the head, as if used to dogs in his office, and said,

"This is very interesting, it obviously gives us something to argue, to back up the diminished capacity plea. What we need to find out is where she took this drug and preferably where she got it from. Do you think she has been a regular user?" We shook our heads,

"I don't think so until recently, when she has been behaving out of character." I said, Eleanor nodding.

"Can you ask around? Any information could be useful. We should probably hire a private detective."

We actually had two people who met this description, but I told him we would indeed make some enquiries. I decided to leave before more minutes ticked by of his costly time. We thanked him and left.

The High Street café was busy, Maisie was at school, so we were not interrupted, as we would normally be. Iris came over as soon as she was free waving Hazel, her helper, away from our table. "Hi! Good to see you! Sorry we are a bit busy today, what can I get you?" We ordered the daily special, and she smiled gratefully, "That's nice and easy, I'll get it right out." She was back in no time and told us she'd come and sit with us when the rush was over.

We ate while observing the other patrons in the cafe. It was certainly a going concern, Iris must have hired a chef, and she and the other girl were kept hopping, delivering food to the tables. Most of the patrons appeared to be young professionals from local businesses, one couple came over to us, as they were leaving, and said how much they had enjoyed the showcase and thanked me for the tickets, I couldn't place them, and seeing my blank expression the girl said, "We work for the road construction company that sponsored the toy jump." Recognition flooded back, and I thanked them for coming.

"That's nice B, you must be proud of what you achieved, look it's on the front page of the newspaper." said Eleanor picking up a copy, that the people from the neighbouring table had left behind. We looked at the article and photos, they were quite good, the headline read "International Equestrians shine at Eventing Showcase." Eleanor stuffed it in her bag.

Iris eventually came and sat with us; I complemented her on how business had grown in the once quiet little cafe. Iris nodded, "Sometimes I wish we were back to those days, but the bank balance has improved, so I guess that is the important thing" I told her not to run herself ragged, and she said that she had been thinking of taking on another waitress for the lunchtime rush.

"Well, if today is anything to go by, I think you should." said Eleanor. Iris nodded and then said,

"Guess what? The hearing for Maisie's custody is set for next week. My lawyer says that all being well, it will just be a formality, because nobody in Brian's family is contesting it." I immediately said I would attend with her, and Iris smiled gratefully. Eleanor butted in at this point and asked,

"So, what is happening with Michael? Has he done a paternity test, are the two of you an item?"

"Really Eleanor!" I protested.

"What?" she said, "you want to know as much as I do. So, Iris what is the scoop?" Iris laughed.

"He has sent off the paternity test, but DNA takes quite a while, not like you see on TV. As for us, we are good friends at the moment. We have Maisie in common, but I don't know how Michael will feel if it is proven that he is not Maisie's father, and I'm not sure how I will feel either way. We will just have to wait and see. Meanwhile, it is very useful to have a man around the place, you must come and see what he has built out back." We all got up and walked behind the counter and through the back room to the rear door.

"It was all just a mess out here, we had used it to store the garbage before taking it out and the shed was full of stuff that nobody had wanted over the years, and I hadn't been bothered to throw it away." We looked in amazement, there was a little patio, and then a large newly sodded area and a smart fence around the shed, which was surrounded by cement.

"The shed has been turned into a top-notch doghouse, and we can hose down the cement from any messes that the puppy makes. I'm going to get some planters and try my hand at growing things. Also, I shall buy some lawn furniture for the patio." Iris looked very happy at the prospect of this.

"When do you get the puppy?" I asked,

"Kipper, Maisie wants to call her Kipper! Maisie and I are going after school today. I pity her teachers today! She was so excited when she headed off!" We all laughed.

Eleanor and I had to leave, as Alfie had been left in the car. We took him out so he could relieve himself in the little parkette close by, and then we drove him home. Whenever I left him in the car for too long he would give me the cold shoulder, so when we got back to the house he disappeared off. I suspected he was on the bed. I was about to sit myself down, when Eleanor said, "Come on you've been putting off house cleaning for too long. Let's get it done. You can do the living room, and I'll do the kitchen and bathroom." This did not sound like a good idea to me, and I grumbled at her energy and bossiness. Nevertheless, I got down to it, and it didn't really take us too long, and it was quite satisfying to eventually sit down in a clean house.

"We can do the upstairs tomorrow!" trilled Eleanor,

"Have I mentioned that I am looking forward to you going

home, so there will be nobody nagging, day in day out!" I retorted.

"Charming! Actually, I was thinking of inviting Alistair to come and stay with me for a while, what do you think?" I smiled at Eleanor,

"I think that would be a great idea! He'll want to be back for the trial, but if he had something to do in the meantime, I think that would be really good for him." Eleanor nodded, "That's what I thought."

I decided that having accomplished housekeeping I had done enough for one day, and so I told Eleanor I wasn't going to go back to the Centre. We therefore settled down for a quiet evening, Eleanor pulled out the newspaper that she had taken from the cafe. We carefully cut out the article and I thought I would take it to get framed.

"We should try and get all the press cuttings. I must see if there are copies of all the papers at the newsagents," I suggested, "We could put them into an album."

We settled for a bowl of soup and a sandwich for supper. Alfie came back downstairs and looked expectantly at me. I fed him and let him out while I heated the soup. Eleanor made sandwiches of what she could find in the fridge, and we sat down at the table to eat. As soon as my rear end had settled in the chair Alfie pounded on the door, and I had to get up to let him in. "Don't say a word!" I threatened Eleanor, who was going to tell me that my dog ruled my life. I sat down again, and had just picked up my soup spoon, when the phone rang. Sighing, I got to my feet. Hetty was calling to say that she and Poppy were very lonely, because all the puppies had left. I was hoping to get to my soup, but the cord on the landline would not stretch far enough. Eleanor was making appreciative slurping noises as she consumed hers. Finally, Hetty completed her tale of the three puppies leaving, and then said she hoped she wasn't interrupting my supper. Before I could reply, she went on, that she had contacted the lawyer that John Smith had recommended, and she was going to go and meet her and Alice at the hospital. I told her that this was excellent, and she finally hung up. I sat down to my now tepid soup.

Finishing up the supper we put the dishes away and watched the news on television. It had just begun, when Alfie leapt to his feet, barking, there was a knock at the door. I had had it with being disturbed and Eleanor, looking at my face, got up and opened the door. It was Alistair. He walked in and sat himself down in the chair opposite the couch. I turned the TV off, and Eleanor asked if we wanted something to drink, I was not sure what we had left in the way of alcoholic beverages, but Eleanor found a bottle of red lurking at the back of the cupboard. She opened it and poured us each a glass. Alistair explained that he'd gone to see the lady from the modelling Agency. She was very surprised to hear that Felicity was still missing. She said it was hard to remember that long ago, but she was certain that Felicity had left her portfolio with them. She remembered this, because they had just had an advertising agency in, looking for a young model to be the "face" of a makeup line, and that the boss of the agency had been very excited about Felicity's looks, and thought it would be a good fit. He had taken a picture out of the portfolio and couriered it over for the ad people to look at. I then asked her if she could remember what Felicity had been wearing. She could not remember exactly what but said that it had been very hot that day, and their air conditioning was not working, so she thought maybe a tank top. I asked about the people she had left with. The lady had said she really could not remember anything about them, but she was fairly sure that it was a man, and maybe a girl, and they had been waiting for Felicity outside.

We all looked at one another. It looked like Alistair had just removed any, so called proof, that Alice had killed Felicity. I wondered whether this meant that Fee had made it all up, and if so, why?

"So, I have done a lot today, how about you two? "

"Some things came up" I said, getting up to find a copy of the drug testing letter, "this arrived by registered mail today." Alistair took it from me and read the whole thing. "We took it over to John Smith." I continued. Alistair nodded and said,

"I wonder where she was getting the drugs from."

"That's what John Smith wanted to know, he wanted us to ask around, and see if we could find out."

"And we definitely need to talk to Adam again." said Alistair, "Too many things involve him."

The bulk of the horses were arriving for the dressage showcase. Alistair was on security duty, so Eleanor took my car and went off in search of Adam. Alfie and I hung out in the office, and then went for a walk over to stabling. Grooms were busy settling their charges into their new accommodations. On the whole, I found the dressage riders and owners more demanding than their eventing counterparts. I was glad that Pru would be interacting with them, on a day-to-day basis. I found Jessie, busy with Quisty, she preferred to look after her horse herself and only had a part time groom. Jessie seemed happy, and looking forward to the competition, she had realistic expectations. Quisty was two years off in his training to be top class, so she was just hoping to put in a creditable performance that would give the pair of them a lot of experience. I wished her luck and walked around the stabling with Alfie on his leash. I heard some whining and complaining about the schooling schedule, the footing in the warm up ring and the fact that the coffee did not come from a large corporation.

In the office, my phone started ringing. It was John Smith on the line. He told me that he had phoned the drug testing agency about Fee's positive test to ask them exactly what the drug compound was that had got her the positive result, as her lawyer, he was entitled to this. He went on to tell me that it was an extremely unusual mixture of hallucinogens, including mescaline, Lysergic acid, morning glory seeds and small quantities of nutmeg. Altogether it was a very potent combination.

John went on to say that the testing that was performed was not quantitative testing, it merely tested for the presence of a drug. As different drugs had different withdrawal times it was impossible to know when Fee had ingested the drug and in what quantities. He also said that it was extremely rare. What was very strange was that he had seen it used in another case he had handled in California.

Still pondering his comment, I arrived at the food court and was greeted by various people from the dressage community. I had been a fairly well-known judge, but because I judged mainly eventing dressage, I was not deemed to be a "Proper" dressage judge, by that community, which bothered me not a jot. A lot of the Queens were so intense, and I did not believe we would achieve world peace by a square halt at X!

Despite our having tried to keep the murders and attempted murders quiet people were aware that something had gone on between Fee and her mother, not to mention Daniel. The group here were keen to know what I had to say about it. I told them that both incidents were private, and that lawyers had advised me to say nothing. Disappointed at the lack of gossip, they changed the subject and asked about the Equestrian Centre and where was it headed. I told them that it was a matter for the board of directors, and the new CEO, when one was elected.

Anne Hagar, who was an ex-competitor, and now an

owner, asked me if I knew Richard Templeton. The name seemed very familiar to me, but I couldn't place where I had heard it before. I shook my head.

"Well, he is keen to become a sponsor. He lived in Orangeville and then moved to California and is now back here. One of his companies is behind the Centre, I think." said Anne. The penny dropped, he was the person that Hetty had said was a friend of Adam's mother, and Eleanor had found his name on the board of Holy Port Entertainment.

"Really?" I said, "We need a lot more like him, if that is the case. Is he living locally?"

"I think he's over in Newmarket, but he's going to come to the Showcase on Saturday."

"That's great!" I said, "Perhaps you can introduce me?"

"Of course." said Anne, "then perhaps you can persuade Alistair to sell his lovely horse to me!"

"Absolutely." I lied.

Back at the office, Hetty had returned my call, so I called her back.

"How did it go with Alice and the lawyer?" I asked Hetty,

"She is very nice and treated Alice perfectly normally, which I think Alice appreciated. Everyone is walking around her on eggshells. She made Alice describe her condition, and how it had affected her over the years, and in particular, on the day that Felicity disappeared." As she paused for breath, I broke in and told her what Alistair had found out from the lady at the modelling agency, and also about Fee's drug test. Hetty managed to hold herself together, yet again. I wondered how many shocking facts it would take, to rock her strength of mind. She thought about these things for a while, and then said,

"Fee was not responsible for what she was doing when she attacked Alice, but she must have been lying about finding the sweatshirt and the portfolio."

"It would seem so, but we do not know how long Fee has been on drugs, perhaps her paranoia about her mother is as a result of that."

"I suppose that could be right," Hetty sighed, "I had better call Alice's lawyer about all this."

With little else to do, I phoned Eleanor to see how she was getting on and how long it would be before she would be picking me up. She answered saying that she would only be another ten minutes, as she was on her way. She went on to say that she had a lot to tell me, and could we invite Alistair for dinner. I replied that there was nothing in the fridge, but we could shop or buy it on the way home. Eleanor laughed and said,

"And what would you prefer B?" with dignity I replied that we would have to shop sometime, but not necessarily tonight.

I packed up any papers that I would need and called Alfie. We walked out to the car park to wait for Eleanor, who was good as her word, and drove in very promptly to pick us up. I had to take the rear seat and as such, enjoyed a chauffeur driven ride. We stopped and picked up fish and chips, which Eleanor said she had a craving for. She was obviously starting to get herself back in "Brit" mode. We stopped at the Liquor Store for wine supplies and made it home just as Alistair was pulling up. Eleanor and I unloaded our bounty, and Alfie greeted Alistair enthusiastically. I opened the front door balancing the fish in one hand, and papers in the other. We went and deposited it all on the kitchen table. Deciding we would eat the feast out of the paper to save on dishes, we only needed glasses for the libation. These procured we sat down and ate.

Alistair complained about the dressage people who had run him ragged over security for their horses,

"I never realised how demanding they are!" I roared with laughter, "Well, you are one of them, so now the boot is on the other foot!"

"Don't tell me I was that bad!" he said. We chatted about the people for a while, and I told them about Richard Templeton coming to the Showcase on Saturday. They were both intrigued to meet him.

"Do you realise that we have never asked John Smith about whether he is the John Smith on the board of Holy Port Entertainment and the McVickers' company?" Eleanor said.

"He seemed to know Reverend Wiseacre, and he said he had represented Brian McVicker." I put in.

"Anyway, you guys," said Eleanor, adopting a Canadianism, "You haven't heard what I found out today!" she was obviously bursting with anticipation at her great reveal.

"I tried everywhere to find Adam and had no luck. So, I tried the film company's office that he works for. He wasn't there but I managed to find a very chatty young girl, who is obviously infatuated with him! She told me that Adam is rarely in the office, only comes in for important meetings. He acts as a scout and procurer of sets for different films. In addition to that, he finds people to be extras in some of the productions. He is working to become a director. (The young lady thinks he has wonderful talent!)" Eleanor went on, "Reading between the lines he puts himself out as being very important in the film industry, and he is quite a lady's man. Adam had told this girl that his father was a well-known evangelist, with his own TV program on television in California, and that he filled in for him sometimes. She also told me that Adam did good works helping the mentally ill."

"That puts Adam in a whole new light." I said.

"Yes but wait until you hear what else I found out!" Eleanor said, I thought she looked unwarrantedly smug, "I called back to the newspaper in California that ran Colin Fray's article, and this time I got hold of somebody who knew where he was, I got a number, and I managed to talk to him. He did not really want to say anything, but I can be quite persuasive! Apparently, he had just got married when he wrote the article, and just after it was published his wife was threatened that if anything else was printed about the church, there would be serious repercussions. His wife was terrified and begged him to get a new job, and so he is now working for his wife's father. I don't think he is very happy, but you know what they say, happy wife, happy life.

"I asked him who had threatened his wife. I asked if it was Adam or his father. Apparently, it was neither of them. I think, from what he said, that it was Brian McVicker. No wonder his wife was scared!

"I kept pushing him, but he was unwilling to tell me anything over the phone. A lot of his information came from a friend he did not wish to name. I gave him the address here and said that if he felt he could help us more, to let us know."

"Wow!" said Alistair, when Eleanor had finished, "This does not sound good. Brian must have been heavily involved with the Church and therefore with Adam and his father."

There were too many questions. It was too complicated for us to work out answers. We had to talk to Adam, if we could find him, and we also needed to find out what John Smith knew, and possibly Richard Templeton. I told the others that we should tell Inspector Thomas everything. Alistair nodded and said that he would give him a call. He did not think that he would be very pleased. "Why not?" said Eleanor, "we're helping him."

"I'm not sure he will call it that." replied Alistair.

We were spending far too much of our time thinking about murder. Alistair wanted to know if he could warm up Jessie for her dressage test, even though he was the Security Chair. I told him that there was no conflict of interest that I could see.

Eleanor was standing in for Alistair, who was with Jessica. I went to watch. Alfie was not a fan of all day dressage, he much preferred cross country as a spectator sport, sitting on bleachers as far as he was concerned, seriously sucked. We watched some of the Intermediare ll tests, and then decided to go for a wander. Alfie's day improved considerably, when we met Hetty and Poppy. I took my friend by the arm, and we walked out onto the Centre's grounds away from the horse show. Here we could let the dogs off their leashes to play. Poppy went from perfect decorum to mad five minutes instantly, running round Alfie, leaping all four feet in the air while twirling through 180 degrees, tearing off and back at him, and jumping right over the top of him. It was hilarious. Alfie, though becoming accustomed to his friend's antics, was nevertheless left totally bewildered.

Hetty and I found a log to sit on, and I told my friend all about what Alistair and Eleanor had found out about Adam. Some of it surprised her, and she shook her head,

"My friend Catrin would be so sorry that her son had turned out like that, but I am still sure there is a caring side to him, look at all the times he visited Alice even when she was at her most difficult? I think his father was the cause of his problems, the man was so bitter when Catrin left him. He was a good psychologist, you know, people went to him for all sorts of problems including addiction therapy, and he was supposed to have a very good success rate. I wonder why he decided to change his career?"

I asked Hetty where she thought Adam could be, she thought a while, and then she said that she really had no clue. He would be absent for two or three weeks, and then he would suddenly appear. He had been like that over the years, since Barry was killed, other than the years when he was living permanently in California. Hetty said that she knew Catrin had had money of her own, and when she died it would have gone to Adam, so he probably didn't have to work full time to have enough money to live. I asked her why Catrin had divorced

Paul, Hetty wasn't very sure, but thought that Paul had been becoming stranger in his ways, and difficult to live with. He was always good with Adam but paid little attention to Catrin. Hetty thought that Catrin might have had an affair.

I asked her if she had got in touch with Alice's lawyer, she said that she had told her about Fee's drug test. Apparently, Alice was doing much better, and hearing that Fee had been high when she attacked her, made Alice feel much better, and she had retracted her claim that she had provoked Fee. The lawyer was hopeful that there would be no charges laid against Alice for Felicity's death.

"Well, that is good news." I said, Hetty gave a nod in agreement, and sighed,

"I am just grateful that Barry did not live to see all this."

"I am sure you are." I replied, "But I think things would have been very different had Barry lived."

The dogs had come back to us, having cleared the grounds of marauding critters, and so we got up and wandered on. We made a plan to get together and try to find Adam, once the dressage Showcase has finished, and I told Hetty about Iris's court date over custody of Maisie.

"You know, Michael has done a paternity test?"

"I hope it works out that he is." Said Hetty,

"I know, I am really worried about what will happen if he finds out he isn't."

"Let's keep fingers crossed."

At that moment a stray dog appeared, we called our two, Poppy came dutifully, but Alfie, of course ignored me. I had to pursue him, until the other dog ran away, and then I ensnared him and reattached him to his leash. Hetty was suitably proud of her dog, and made to make some comment about mine, seeing the look on my face, she thought better of it, and we walked back to the show ground. As we went, I remembered what Anne Hagar had told me about Richard Templeton, and told Hetty that he wanted to become a sponsor and had been living in California. We tossed around the idea that he was the man on the board of Holy Port and agreed to try and meet him the following day.

When we got back to the competition, we had missed a particularly good test, a Dutch rider had scored 81.535%, to go way in the lead. Dressage competitions are judged in positive percentages, unlike three day eventing, where the lowest score wins, so anything over 80% would be phenomenal. We would have to see whether this rider could produce an equally good Grand Prix test.

Hetty and I climbed into the stands to watch. We saw a good test from the Danish girl, and then a poor US rider came round the ring, and his horse spooked at something in the bleachers, jumped sideways, and stepped on himself causing his leg to bleed. Blood on a horse is not permitted in the ring, and so the rider had to withdraw.

Unfortunately, Jessie was next in the ring. She still had time to spare but got confused when the competitor before her came back out of the arena. She hurried Quisty into the arena, and then had some trouble settling him. Her test was a little tense and lacking the harmony that the two of them usually displayed, however Quisty's superior movement kept the marks up to a reasonable standard. She left the ring scoring a 67.415% which was creditable. Anything over 65% was considered to be fairly good. I'm sure Jessie was disappointed, but she now had to set her sights on the following day's competition. Hetty and I walked back round to the stabling area and waited for Alistair to come out. He was not too upset by Jessie's test and was taking the right attitude by saying that it got them both into the ring, and that experience would stand them in good stead for tomorrow.

"I heard from Bill Thomas he wants to talk to me. I told him to let us know what it was about this evening.

My term as acting CEO would be over soon, and a new CEO would need to have things in order to take on the job. Jenny would be back the next day, so I told Alfie he was going to have to make room for another dog. He did not seem impressed and slumbered on. I realised that I really should take a look at Daniel's office, I had never moved in there, and had just had Jenny retrieve files that we needed. I left Alfie where he was and walked over to the official office of the CEO. The police had gone through it all when they were investigating his death, and I was only interested in the working files. The main filing cabinet was locked, and I wondered where the key was, I checked in the desk with no luck. I did find a lovely picture of Daniel and Alistair, in the bottom drawer. I kept it out to give to Alistair.

I finally found the keys on a hook hidden behind the door and was able to get at all the files. Daniel had been meticulous in his record keeping, far better than I was. Everything was completely up to date until his death. Jenny and I could finish this off I thought, his system had been fairly straightforward. There was one file marked correspondence, and with a quick look I realised that some of these letters should have been answered some time ago. I felt very guilty that I had failed to attend to this, so I took the file and the photo.

I sat down in my office and started to read the correspondence file. There were the usual requests for quotes for use of the facilities, in upcoming months. There was a letter from a catering company requesting an opportunity to bid for the services of the canteen. Daniel had clipped this to a sheet that itemised the cost of employing our own catering staff. I personally thought a change would be a good idea. There were a couple of resumes from people, hopeful of securing employment. Daniel had marked these to go to HR. One letter in the file really got my attention.

Eleanor and I headed home via the Chinese restaurant, to pick up a take out. We bought enough for three and called Alistair leaving him a message that we had food and would be at home. Alistair arrived ten minutes later bearing wine, so we laid out our feast and started in on it. I gave Alistair the photo I had found in Daniel's office, he was so happy to have it. He said he had very few things to remind him of Daniel, and he would treasure this.

I took out the letter that I had found in the correspondence. It was from a woman in California who had read in one of the horse magazines that a skeleton had been found in the grounds of the Equestrian Centre. Her daughter had gone missing years ago, from either a film company or from Holy Port Church. She had hired a private detective, and in her investigations, she had discovered that the church and the film company were linked to the Equestrian Centre. She wondered if the skeleton could possibly be that of her daughter.

Between mouthfuls my two private detectives gave their input on this. They wondered if the detective in California had found out any more about the girl's disappearance. We thought we should contact the lady and let her know that the body was not her daughter. The poor woman was suffering the same way that Hetty was. We should also find out what the private detective knew.

Alistair said "The police are not going to pursue a case against Alice, in the death of Felicity. They were, however, going to charge Fee with grievous bodily harm, due to the assault on her mother and on drug charges. They were very keen to find out where the drugs had come from and were trying to locate Adam. It seemed that their enquiries had followed the same lines as our own.

The next day was going to be taken up with the Grand Prix and the sound checks for the Freestyles, which were being ridden on Sunday. Eleanor was acting Security Chair for Alistair, while he helped Jessie. I was going to be a spectator and look after any disasters that might happen. Jenny was arriving back and bringing her puppy.

We checked the time difference between Ontario and California and decided that it would be a good time to call the West Coast. I dialled and put the phone on speaker, so Eleanor and Alistair could hear what she said. Once I established that I had the correct person, I told her right away that the bones had been identified and were definitely not those of her daughter. I invited her to tell us what had happened, and she seemed very pleased to be able to communicate with people who wanted to hear her story.

It was long and rather rambling. Christine and her daughter Zoe had moved from Ontario to California. Her daughter had been a patient of Dr Wiseacre, when he had lived in Ontario. When they got to California the daughter tried other therapists but did not really like them. They discovered that Dr Wiseacre had moved to the same area. He was no longer practising but suggested that her daughter might like to join his church. She did and was very happy there. She enrolled in university and settled in well. Her father had died, leaving her a trust fund, so she could afford school and a shared apartment, with a new friend, Sarah, who was also a member of Holy Port, and the girlfriend of Adam.

Christine remarried, and went on an extended honeymoon trip, around the world. Her daughter emailed and texted her telling her all about the church, university, and about the film company that was associated with the church. After a while the communications stopped, and the mother became very worried. She contacted the university who told her that her daughter had dropped out. She contacted the church but was only told that they would pass on her message to her daughter. She cut short her honeymoon, and she and her husband returned to California, and went to the church but were told that her daughter did not wish to talk to them. They went to the police, but as their daughter was over eighteen the police would do nothing. Christine and Quentin, her husband, did not know what to do. Time went by, and there was no news of Zoe.

One day Sarah knocked on their door. She told them that Zoe had started a relationship with a new boyfriend, she had decided to leave the church. She left without saying goodbye. Sarah said she thought that she should tell them as Zoe's parents, so that they wouldn't worry. The situation seemed very strange to Christine and Quentin, but they were so pleased to hear news of their daughter, they did not think it through.

Six months later another girl, named Nancy, came to see them. She to, had been a member of the church. She said it had been wonderful when she first joined, but it had become increasingly controlling and frightening. Every day they were made to drink "vitamin water", which the girl was sure was laced with drugs. Members were behaving in bizarre manners, and they were no longer allowed to leave the compound unless accompanied by a senior member of the congregation. Strangers came and bought the "vitamin water" at the gate. Adam, Reverend Wiseacre's son was running the sales with another man. More and more of the day-to-day operations were being run by Adam. Sarah was constantly at his side, and Nancy feared her.

Adam encouraged all the church members to join his film school. They were mainly girls. Zoe had joined, and one day she had gone on a film shoot and not returned.

Nancy was seriously worried about the goings on. She decided to leave the church, but it had been months before she could find a way to leave. She had had to smuggle herself out of the compound in a food truck. First, she had gone to a friend who was a journalist and told him the story. Then she came to Christine and Quentin. They had all gone to the police, and finally, they started an investigation. Drugs were found and there were criminal charges laid against the Reverend, who had a breakdown. Adam and Sarah had left and were never charged, and Christine's daughter was never found. Her disappearance was to be brought up at the trial of the Reverend, but he was unlikely to stand trial, his lawyers were pleading him unfit to stand trial.

This was an upsetting story and the three of us, hearing it for the first time, were left speechless. I told Christine that we would stay in touch.

DRESSAGE

THERE WERE A LOT more spectators in the stands today, to watch the Grand Prix dressage. Jenny was already in the office with so much equipment for the small canine person, who accompanied her. She was sitting quietly in her cage looking out with big eyes at this new place. Jenny had named her Franny after her grandmother, who was called Frances. Alfie was delighted to see a new plaything in the office and proceeded to bark and pounce at her. She was not one bit intimidated, by this big hairy thing, and barked right back at him. We took the pair of them for a short walk, staying well away from the show grounds. Franny tootled along after Alfie who appeared enchanted by her. They ran around and played together until Franny just crashed and lay down. Jenny carried her back to the office, and I moved Alfie's bed over next to her cage. I then left Jenny to update Daniel's files, and leaving Alfie with her, I went over to watch the Grand Prix.

The Dutch man put in another brilliant test to put him well into the lead, and the US rider who had had such bad luck the day before when his horse was injured, rode a great test to put himself into second place, receiving great cheers from the crowd. Jessie was following this rider, and I hoped that Quisty would not be upset by all the noise. I need not have worried, he handled it like a pro and put in a much better test than the day before. Jessie was beaming as she came to her final halt. She scored just over 70% which was excellent for their level of training and the difficulty of the test. I was so happy for her and for Alistair, who was the epitome of a proud father, as he stood at the exit waiting for the pair of them to come out. I climbed down from the stands and walked over to congratulate them. Jessie was anxious to get Quisty back to his stall to get him looked after, and she told Alistair to go with me back to watch the rest of the tests before lunch. Alistair was positively bubbling, he went over the test, movement by movement, as if I hadn't actually watched it myself. It was so good to see him this happy. We watched another four tests, the Danish girl rode beautifully, and she knocked the US rider out of second place, but the other tests were mediocre, and to my mind, Quisty had done quite a lot better than them. I was pleased to see that the judges agreed with me, and Jessie was sitting in the top third as we broke for lunch.

Alistair and I wandered over to the food court arguing about what we should eat. A hand tapped me on the shoulder, and Anne Hagar was standing behind me with a tall, good looking, grey haired, man in a beautifully tailored pin stripe suit and what looked like handmade shoes.

"B, I wanted to introduce you to Richard Templeton." I smiled, put out my hand to shake his, and then turned and introduced him to Alistair. I went on to say, "I think you two don't need any introduction, do you?" meaning Anne and Alistair. They laughed,

"Anne is constantly trying to buy Quisty." Said Alistair

"And I guess that is going to be even harder, after his test today." Said Anne "Congratulations, your girl has done such a good job with him."

We turned to Richard and asked if he and Anne would like to join us for lunch. Richard said he would love to, but Anne had to get back to the stables, to check in on her rider. So, the three of us decided on souvlaki, on a bun, with salad. We found a spare picnic table and sat down.

"So, Anne tells me you are interested in sponsoring dressage?" I asked,

"Well, not just dressage, but Anne is convinced that dressage is the way to go." I laughed,

"We all have our main loves, and Anne is 100% dressage. What interests you in sponsoring Equestrianism?"

"My late wife was an avid rider, when she was alive, I could not afford to support her love of horses, and I have always regretted that. Since then, I have made a lot of money in the dot com business, and I would like to give back in her memory."

"That is a lovely thought, I'm sorry to hear that you lost your wife, she must have been young when she died." Said Alistair.

"Yes, she was only in her twenties, we were high school sweethearts, married when we were in university and had six wonderful years. She developed MS, it was heart breaking, unlike most sufferers she did not get many remissions, and she went downhill quickly. She died here in Ontario."

"That must have been awful." Said Alistair. "I feel for you, I lost my wife to cancer." The two of them appeared to drift off into their own worlds of grief. I wondered which old love Alistair was thinking of Cyn or Daniel.

"I was introduced to a wonderful therapist at that time, Dr Wiseacre, my wife had been friends with his wife. He really helped me through the worst of it, and then he left Ontario and went to California. I was still feeling very fragile, and I decided to follow him down there." Alistair and I both felt a jolt of excitement, as he told us this. We exchanged looks, and I encouraged Richard to tell us more.

"He didn't really practise down there, although he saw a

few of us who had come from Canada. He had changed a lot since his wife Catrin, had left him. To be truthful, he had become rather bitter. He wanted to reinvent himself and studied religion. I suppose it was just an extension of his psychology. Anyway, he founded a church, and I joined, and in fact, became a board member. The Church was very successful, and Paul was an amazing orator. His son joined him when Catrin went back to Sweden. The Church's parent company put up some of the money for this Equestrian Centre, along with another Californian Company, and that made me think about sponsoring.

"Did you have much to do with his son? We have been trying to reach him and find out some more about his film and church activities." Alistair asked.

"Adam? A little, he was very friendly and outgoing, unlike his father, he seemed to like the ladies. He went to university down there, studied film and biology or some such thing. He took over a small film studio/school as a subsidiary of the church. The film studio made a couple of documentaries. Members of the church, who were interested, worked on all aspects of producing a film, from hairdressing and make up, to wardrobe, and to set production, and lighting, as well as acting and directing. There were some well-known people who came and taught courses. It could have been a great introduction to the industry but unfortunately, it seems that one of the film company's backers started experimenting in ways to get the actors more involved in the characters that they were playing. He used drugs for this.

I believe Adam was under pressure to supply them. He started growing cacti, plants, shrubs and mushrooms, I'm sure not, for horticultural reasons! There was a laboratory in the compound and sales of compounds were made at the gate.

Eventually this caused a lot of trouble, Paul was arrested

and charged. Adam managed to leave at that time, and I don't think he was ever charged, Paul took the brunt of it, and then he had a breakdown. All very sad."

"Do you happen to know anything about a girl named Zoe who went missing down there? We received a letter from her mother." I asked.

"There was a rumour going around about a girl being missing, but to tell you the truth after the drug scandal, I immediately distanced myself from the church. I have officially resigned as a director. If you want to know more, John Smith is the man to ask. He is a criminal lawyer who works both here in Ontario and in Calfornia. He represented the Church in all this mess. I can introduce you if you like."

"Actually, we know him. I will take your advice and ask him." I said and then changed the subject and asked him what he envisaged for a sponsorship. He really hadn't thought it through, but was keen to receive suggestions. To that end, I invited him to dinner the following weekend. He carefully wrote the date in his diary, I was pleased to see, not punching it into some electronic gizmo, dot com millionaire, or not! We all got up and Alistair and Richard walked back to the stands to watch the remainder of the dressage.

I returned to the Centre to rescue Jenny. There was a strong smell of disinfectant in the office. Franny had had an accident Jenny said apologetically. I laughed and told her not to worry, there would be many more! We decided to take the two dogs out for another play outside. They really enjoyed themselves, I wondered about the feasibility of getting John to build them a run but decided we would need the blessing of the new CEO. Jenny had done a great job of bringing Daniel's files up to date.

"You know," she said, "he really was good at his job." I nodded,

"I noticed that." I said, "if only he had been more pleasant in person."

As she was going out the door Jenny pointed to an envelope on the desk, "Oh, there's a courier package for Eleanor, it just arrived."

Jessie had just squeaked in to the top third of competitors. She was therefore eligible for the finals, a fact that she and Alistair were ecstatic about. Neither one had considered that they would score this well. The finals were on the Monday, Sunday being the freestyles. In Freestyle riders performed a set of movements, of their choosing, and set it to music. Many riders spent large amounts of money to have the music and choreography professionally created for them, so that the rhythm was perfect for their horse's gaits. Alistair and Jessie had put their own music together, they freely admitted that their effort was amateurish, and they had no expectation of scoring well, however they felt the routine was fun. I had declined to do anything to help them, I am not musically inclined, so it was better that I stay away from that side of things.

As we were mid way through the dressage Showcase, I turned my thoughts to Vaulting and Show Jumping. Randy Wainwright was so organised, there was very little to do for vaulting, but since it was being held in the coliseum, we had to deal with parking and spectators around the centre. Alistair had hired some new parking attendants, and we had to move the people, who manned the entrances to the show ground, to the main entrance, and the other two gateways that we were creating to handle the people entering there. It was going to be a bottle neck, and Alfie and I took a walk outside the gates, to see if the two new entrances that we had planned on using had been widened sufficiently to handle the traffic. Calling the grounds keeper to meet us, I put Alfie on a leash as we went down the road.

It was quite amazing the propensity for people to not follow instructions. The entrances were not wide enough, the grounds keeper argued that they were as wide as the culverts, that he had put in.

"Well, you clearly did not put in wide enough culverts!" I was totally frustrated by his ineptitude. "They will have to be replaced." This was obviously not what he wanted to hear, but I left him with my instructions to get it done ringing in his ear.

I was marching back to the main entrance when a car came towards me. I pulled Alfie to my side and stood while the car passed us. I was amazed to see Adam and sat beside him was Fee. I waved frantically at them, but the car just drove on. I had been sure that it was Fee sitting in the passenger seat, which was closest to me as the car went past. If that was the case, what was she doing out of hospital? She couldn't be, I thought, which made me second guess myself, and there was something that seemed odd about her appearance, perhaps it wasn't her after all? Then I wondered, where had Adam been all this time? These questions caused me considerable perplexity. I hurried back to the office, and called John Smith, there was no reply at his office, and so I left a message for him to call me urgently. I then phoned Alistair, he said he was on his way back to the office with Eleanor. I waited until they got there, before I told them what I had seen.

"Are you sure?" Eleanor asked. This was a good question, the more that I thought about it, the more I wondered whether I was wrong. Haltingly I said,

"I think so, I was looking right at the car, and I am sure that it was Adam driving and I was pretty sure it was Fee. I called John Smith to see if Fee was still at the hospital. I left a message for him to call me."

"Well, I can't imagine they've let her out." said Alistair, "Bill told me they were still holding her."

"Adam was definitely driving the car." I said, "We must be able to find him now, if he is driving in the neighbourhood, and we can ask him who he was with."

Alistair nodded, "Eleanor, fancy coming for a ride to Adam's house?"

"Hang on! I haven't opened this courier package… Well, well it's from Colin Fray." Eleanor proceeded to read it, doing her usual, read once, read again very slowly, leaving Alistair and me gazing at her impatiently. Unable to stand it any longer I spat out,

"For goodness' sake Eleanor! What does it say?"

"He says that he was approached by an old friend of his, who had been a member of the Church. She told him that she had been frightened by what was going on at the Church. There was widespread drug use. Congregants were not allowed to leave, and she had had to hide in a food truck to get out. She was worried about what had happened to a friend of hers, Zoe, who she had not seen for the last three weeks that she was in the compound.

"His friend went to talk to Zoe's parents and then they all went to the police."

"Is that it?" I said, expecting a whole lot more.

"Yes, that's all he wrote!"

"He could have given us more details, it just reiterates what we already knew from Christine and Richard." I grumbled.

"Well don't blame me!" replied Eleanor.

"Anyway, it confirms that we should talk to Adam to find out more about what was happening at the Church. Shall we go and see if we can find him Eleanor? We'll ask him who was with him in the car." Said Alistair.

"You bet! Let's see what we can find out." The two of them

got up to leave, I decided to stay a little longer, and as they went out through the door I sat and considered what I had seen. I knew it had been Adam driving, but the passenger had been less clear. Perhaps it had been Jessie, they both had the same-coloured hair, but I did not think Jessie wanted to be with Adam. I couldn't understand why my subconscious mind had immediately thought Fee, but then thought something was not right. It was also strange that they hadn't stopped, if I had been by myself, I could understand their not stopping, but I could not see how they could not have recognised me, having my big hairy dog with me made us instantly recognisable. I pondered for a while, but no obvious solution came to mind. I decided to go and check the coliseum to make sure the cleaning staff had everything ready for the vaulting. I was just getting up, when the phone rang. I picked it up. It was John Smith returning my call. I asked him if Fee was still in custody, and he assured me that she was. He went on to say that she was demanding to talk to me, but that under the circumstances, he thought it better that that not happen. I thought for a moment, and then asked him if he would have time to talk to me. He said I should make an appointment with his secretary.

"No, I was talking to Richard Templeton, I had some questions about California, and he suggested I talk to you. I wondered if we could have a drink together." There was a long hesitation, then finally he said, "I suppose I could do that, when and where?" I named a quiet place that I went to occasionally with friends and asked if he could make it that evening. Again, I was met by silence, but then finally, he agreed. I suggested six o'clock, and he said that would work. Hanging up I thought he was far from happy about my invitation. "Well, he can suck it up!" I thought, "he's getting paid enough for the work with Fee."

Alfie and I went for a quick walk round the coliseum. We

needed a lot more garbage and recycling boxes, but beside that it looked like all was ready. I liked Randy Wainwright a lot but was not a fan of his sport's use of horses. They had to be able to maintain a perfect rhythm on a circle while people performed acrobatics on their backs and hind quarters, they only ever went in one direction and to my mind this put enormous strain on the horses. I had to admit I really did not know enough about the sport to be so critical; it was just my gut feeling.

I called up the head housekeeper and asked her to ensure that the garbage and recycling bins were put out and that we had scheduled a pickup for it all. I then took Alfie to the car and headed home. I changed into an outfit that I felt appropriate for meeting a lawyer for drinks, but as usual when I looked in the mirror the effect wasn't what I really wanted. I shrugged, it was too bad, it would have to do. I fed Alfie. I did not have any treats for him, so I had to put up with the wounded look that he gave me, as I went out the door. Before I got to the car, I realised I should leave a note for Eleanor, so retraced my steps. Alfie thought I had changed my mind about taking him, and was standing, tail wagging at the door. I disillusioned him about this, scribbled a note and left.

For once I was early, but John Smith was already seated at a table. I joined him and ordered a glass of wine. I felt strangely uncomfortable, and not sure how to start the conversation, when John looked at me expectantly.

"I wondered if you know Reverend Wiseacre?" I began

"Yes, we were at university together, we did our undergrad, and then he went on to do his masters in psychology, and I went into law."

"Did you stay in touch when he moved to California?" I asked.

"In fact I moved first, my mother was American, so I have dual citizenship. Once I was called to the bar. up here, I went to California and got qualified there as well. My mother had property down there so it was fairly easy for me to live, and once I could practise, I opened an office down there. When Catrin divorced Paul he was pretty broken up, and so I suggested he come and stay for a break, and he did. He had plenty of savings, and so he bought a sect of land in wine country. He managed to get his green card, so he could work down there. He was a very good psychologist and had many of his patients from Ontario visit him for treatment. In addition, he was building up quite a practise with local patients. In California everybody has a therapist!"

I sipped my wine nodding and then enquired, "How did the Church come about?"

"I think Paul tired of being a psychiatrist. He had always been interested in different religions. He studied divinity and qualified. Next thing I knew he was Reverend Wiseacre and building a church! I was very doubtful about his career change, but he totally made a go of it."

"How did a film company become involved?" I asked.

"Paul proved to be a great orator and word got around about him. A local company that made low budget religious programs made a documentary about Paul, the Church and the retreat.

"This brought in lots of donations and Adam, Paul's son, persuaded the board to put up half the money to buy the film company. Another Ontarian put up the rest. Adam's idea being, to turn the company into a film school. This, in turn, would attract more congregants and bring more money into the church.

"Adam had studied film, science and divinity in university, so he did know what he was doing."

"How did the Church get into trouble?" I asked.

"I now believe that the Ontarian who put up half the money to buy the film company was Brian McVicker. Adam had always been a recreational drug user and used his science background to grow plants and mushrooms to manufacture drugs. Brian, having supplied the money, now had a hold over Adam. He used Adam and his girlfriend to make large quantities of these drugs, which he sold. The drugs were also given to members of the church who then became addicted and this, in turn increased sales.

I was also sure that Brian intended on having the film school producing pornographic movies.

"Brian was indicted on charges for other offences in California, but Holy Port Church and the film school were mentioned in the trial."

"Was Adam's girlfriend named Sarah?" I asked, John nodded,

"I think so." He said,

"And do you know what happened to a young girl named Zoe?"

"Her disappearance was mentioned at the trial, but there was little evidence."

"Do you think that Adam is evil or was he just corrupted by Brian?" I asked

"I think he is deficient morally. I think Brian was able to easily manipulate him, for his own uses. I think Adam is weak but uses corrupt methods to control people especially women."

"Do you think that he is involved, with what has happened here with Fiona?"

"I am sure that the drug she took was given to her by Adam. Its makeup is exactly the same as the drugs Brian was selling in California, I'm not sure how else he could be involved. Anyway, that is all I have to say. By the way, you asked me if Fee was still in hospital, why was that?"

"It's just that I thought I saw her driving with Adam."

"Well, it definitely wasn't her. She will not be released on bail."

I thanked him for taking the time to talk to me. I didn't add that I also hoped he wasn't going to charge me!

We left the bar together, and I drove home. Eleanor and Alfie were watching television. I asked her how she and Alistair had made out.

"Well," she said, "Adam was at his house, he was most surprised that we had been trying to find him. He said he had just been hanging out, working, out with friends, he couldn't understand why we were not able to reach him. He said that he knew nothing about you seeing him outside the Centre, if he had seen you, he would have stopped. He had not seen Fee, nor had he been to see Alice, but he intended to do that shortly."

"Did you ask him about California?"

"Yes, he told us that his father had had a breakdown after he had been experimenting with drugs. That he, Adam, had seen what was happening, and thought he should leave before there was big trouble."

"The lying little toad!" the expletive was out of my mouth in an instant. I told her the real story according to John Smith.

"John is sure that Adam gave Fee the drug, apparently it has exactly the same content as the ones that he was selling in California."

"So, he was linked to Brian McVicker down there?" said Eleanor, I nodded, and she continued, "I wonder what the charges were, besides drug charges, do you think they were making pornographic films?"

"That's what he thought." I said, "John Smith must be a good lawyer to have got Brian off that, relatively unscathed."

"What did he say about Zoe?" asked Eleanor.

"Zoe's disappearance came up in the court case, but John got it excluded due to lack of Evidence."

"It can't all be coincidence. That Adam was around when Felicity vanished and he was making a film with Zoe, and she has disappeared as well.

"You're right. Oh, and by the way, Alistair phoned Bill Thomas, and told him that Adam was at home so hopefully he will have been picked up and taken in for questioning about the drugs that Fiona had taken."

The freestyles were in full swing. My leg was aching, and I was feeling sorry for myself as I gimped along over to the bleachers. Alfie wasn't helping by towing me, making it obvious he was not happy to be on a leash. I spotted Hetty with a well mannered, Poppy walking quietly.

There were very few empty spaces, and we looked round in vain to find room for the four of us. I saw Pru and waived to her, and seeing our predicament, she took us into the reserved seats. We settled in and watched a couple of mediocre kurs, which the freestyles are called. The Dutchman who had scored so impressively up until now, came round the ring. He halted, held up his hand, the music started, and he entered the ring and halted and saluted. His freestyle, which I understood was new for today, was spectacular. The rhythm matched the horse perfectly in all three gaits, and the horse responded to it. It was perfect execution, and at his final halt people were on their feet cheering and applauding.

He was given a run for his money, the US rider rode a flawless test, and his music was perfectly matched to his horse, but it lacked the excitement and harmony of the Dutch pair. His marks were good but not as high as the previous pair. Jessie was next, it was such a pity that she had to follow these professional performances, I thought.

The music started and it was immediately recognisable to all who had lived during the 1960s and 1970s. She rode to a medley of classic rock tunes starting with the Who's, Substitute. It matched the pair of them perfectly through their trot work, and the crowd started to clap, Quisty played up to it, their work was far from flawless, but they were fun and enormously entertaining. They finished to an enormous cheer, and Jessie was beaming from ear to ear. Their score was higher than I thought it should be, but I was delighted for them. They had done Canada proud!

Hetty and I left our privileged seats to go and congratulate them. Alistair was so happy, which thrilled us. Jessie was beside herself. All she could do was thank Alistair and me for her chance to ride Quisty. Anne Hagar appeared and congratulated the trio. It was so rewarding to see good people having good things happening to them. We left them to enjoy themselves, and Hetty and I went for lunch. Alfie misbehaved by jumping up on the picnic table, trying to steal my burger. Before Hetty could comment on this I interrupted her and told her about my conversation with John Smith.

"Nothing surprises me anymore." she said, "I always thought Adam was a very likeable young man. Incidentally, I heard from Alice, she is coming out of hospital, and is going home to her house as Fee is not there."

"That is good, that poor woman has been through enough, and I'm glad she is not going back to Adam's"

"I'm going to do some shopping for her, so she has the staples in the house. I suppose you are here tomorrow?" Hetty enquired,

"Yes, but I have promised to go to Iris's hearing, regarding custody of Maisie."

"Has she got a lawyer?"

"Yes, but she feels that she'll be OK without one at the hearing."

"Everything is fine until it all goes pear shaped, then you need a lawyer." said Hetty prosaically.

"Well, we'll have to wait and see. Apparently, nobody in Brian's family wants custody, and Iris has been there all along, so I think that it will be OK."

We finished our lunch, Hetty headed home, and I couldn't decide what to do, whether to watch more freestyle or go and do some work in the office. Neither were appealing, so I decided to walk over to the workshop and see if John was there, and perhaps Michael. I was lucky on both counts as I rounded the coliseum I saw John's truck, and alongside it, was Michael's car. I let Alfie off the leash, and he bounded forward to greet the two men and John's puppy, who had been sleeping in the shade. The men looked up at Alfie's arrival and greeted me. They were working on producing some schooling fences that could be used for Pony Club Ralley.

"How is it going B?" asked Michael.

"Fine, Pru has it all in hand, I'm feeling a bit like a spare part now. I see we're going from Showcase to Pony Club, good stuff! Our top riders have to come from somewhere, so this is a good thing! Michael are you off on your world travels again?"

"I have to go back to South Africa for their Continental cup, and then I have a couple of gigs in the States, otherwise I will be hanging around here with my daughter!"

"You've heard, you fink, you didn't tell me. That is wonderful news!"

"I only got the letter yesterday and was too nervous to open it so I just carried it around. Iris made me open it this morning. It is so exciting! I just wish Rebecca could have known."

"Maybe she did in her heart." I suggested, "Does Maisie know?"

"We haven't told her yet; we're going to wait until after the hearing tomorrow. So far only you and John know."

"I won't tell anyone, that is your job! How is your new acquisition John, and what is his name?"

"He's called Lieka, after the first dog in space! He is perfect, he loves the truck. He hangs out with me all day and then sleeps all night. Amelia and I are very pleased with him."

"Amelia wants me to carve a dog for the outside of her surgery. I think I'll do a golden retriever, I'm not sure what my boy is going to end up looking like."

I gazed over at the puppy, he could end up looking like a Heinz 57, but I knew he would be loved. He was currently chewing Alfie's collar, Alfie stood up, and Lieka was swinging from it. Alfie gave a shake and Leika landed in a heap, he was not deterred, he jumped back up and tackled Alfie's leg. We stood laughing at the pair of them. I then asked John if Tom had been in touch with him about anything he needed for the Show Jumping. John nodded,

"I have to move the big judging gazebo into place on Monday and other than that it is all set."

I congratulated Michael again on fatherhood, and then clipped Alfie's leash on, and we walked on towards the Centre. John had to retrieve Lieka, as he was making a determined effort to come with us. I could tell that the dressage had finished, as there were cars leaving the parking area. Eleanor would be making her way back, when they were all gone, so we shouldn't have long to wait. Alfie and I sat in the office doing nothing at all. He didn't seem worried, and neither was I, we had done sufficient for one day.

The final day of dressage dawned with disappointing weather, it was drizzling and calling for increased steady rain to come. Eleanor borrowed rain pants and a goretex raincoat from me. I rummaged around and found similar garb for myself. Wellington boots were a must, but my feet were much larger than Eleanor's, so she had to go in regular leather boots, saying she would stop by the trade stands, and buy something more suitable. I had to push Alfie out of the door, and he rushed through his morning business and then ran back into the house. "OK you wimp!" I told him, "You can stay here."

Eleanor and I headed over to the showgrounds, Eleanor picked up her golf cart, which at least had a windshield and roof, and she headed off to fulfill Alistair's duties, whilst muttering under her breath. I picked up Daniel's cart and drove over to the office trailer and had conversations with Pru over actions to be taken should we experience thunderstorms. The rain, as it was, would not put the show on hold, but lightening was something to be taken seriously. Our safety officer would monitor the radar and make a call to hold the show, if a storm was imminent.

The consolation class ran first for the competitors who did not make the final. There would be a break for lunch unless the weather deteriorated, in which case we would move the afternoon tests up by an hour. Having made sure that all was under control, I took a drive round and saw that we were going to have a disappointing number of spectators. The car parks had few vehicles, and the trade fair was not going to be making a lot of money today, although the man selling raincoats and wellingtons was doing a brisk trade. Even some of the competitors were proving to be fair weather riders, and withdrew from the morning's class, preferring to pack up and head home. The safety officer suggested we not break for lunch, and so the announcer called for all the riders scheduled for the afternoon be ready to ride an hour earlier. This meant that Jessie would be going fairly soon, as they were riding in reverse order of placing. Alistair would be busy warming them up. I drove over to see

Pru. We could cancel the day, and ride tomorrow instead. The problem was that the forecast was not good for tomorrow either. The other option was to move it all into the coliseum. This would involve a lot of work to set up the ring, the competitors had not had any ring familiarisation in there, and the stewards had not got a seamless warm up to competition ring plan, in place for the coliseum.

Pru was on the verge of losing it, as more and more owners, coaches and competitors swarmed her trailer. I stood outside and ordered them all away saying that there would be an announcement in ten minutes, more if they continued to harass the organiser. Not happy, they moved back and stood around bad mouthing us. I asked Pru what she wanted to do, she was not sure, the radar showed the worst of the storm to come. I suggested we cancel the rest of the day, put the class in the coliseum tomorrow which would give the rest of the afternoon for ring familiarisation, and give the officials a chance of getting their act together. This was going to be a giant headache for Randy with Vaulting starting on Wednesday, but Pru's crew would have to help. She was stressing about sponsors and spectators who had paid to watch, and I told her rather briskly, that it came under the category of shit happens. We made a quick plan and then radioed the announcer, so he could let everybody know. This accomplished I left Pru to work out the logistics, while I went back to the Centre office to let Randy know what we were planning.

Randy took the news in his usual unflappable manner; in fact, he had been wondering if we would have to move indoors. I gave him permission to use as many Equestrian Centre workers as he needed, and pay them whatever overtime was necessary, to prepare the arena overnight Tuesday. He thought it would be fine, if we could finish the dressage by lunchtime. I thanked him profusely. I wondered what else I should be doing, and then decided I should go and stand beside Pru, to face the onslaught of complaints that would inevitably arise from the change.

The rain had increased and was now a steady stream. I took my car, whether driving on the grounds was not permitted or not, I was too old to sit in a golf cart on a day like today. At Pru's trailer, I was happy to see that the majority of complainers had been driven away by the rain, and Pru was coping just fine. Her secretary had drawn up a timetable for the following morning, and we pinned it on all the notice boards which now had their plexiglass windows pulled down. I drove on to stabling with the final schedule and posted it there. Everyone seemed resigned to riding tomorrow, and as the weather continued to deteriorate, the consensus was that we had made the right decision.

Alistair appeared at my side, Jessie had put Quisty away and was fussing over him like a mother hen,

"You would not think that horses were meant to live outside!" Alistair exclaimed, but I could see that he was secretly happy that Jessie looked after the horse this way.

"I should go and take over from Eleanor." He went on, "do you know where she is?" I shook my head,

"Can't you radio her?" he proceeded to do just that, and we drove over to where she was dealing with an owner who had drunk too much champagne and was making a nuisance of himself in the food tent. Alistair got out and went over to back her up. She had taken the car keys from the man, and he was infuriated. After a few minutes the man's wife returned, and seeing what was happening, she tongue lashed her husband, grabbed him by the arm, and dragged him out of the tent. Eleanor followed with the car keys, and that was the last we saw of them. Eleanor came back, and we saw that she was drenched.

Alistair said, "You two go home, and get dried off and changed, I'll finish off here."

Eleanor and I drove home happily, with the heat blasting full on. We ran up to the front door and opened it in a hurry, trying to avoid as much rain as possible. Alfie bounded up to us, but looking at the rain, he decided to keep his legs crossed and stay indoors.

I let Eleanor shower first, as she was frozen through. I followed suit and then wrapped in terry towel robes we sat and had a bowl of soup. I had turned on the fake fire, glad for the enth time that I had got a propane one. Crackling wood fires are only romantic if you are not the one that has to light them and clear up afterwards! All this had a soporific effect on us, and we dozed off.

I awoke, unsure of what had brought me back to consciousness. It was truly dark out now. I could still hear rain falling, but I was sure that that was not what had awoken me. I got up and walked through to the kitchen. There was a large puddle of urine against a chair, obviously Alfie should have made the trip outside earlier. I dropped a tea towel in it and mopped it up before ringing it out and starting again. I got out some Lysol and mixed it with warm water, before cleaning up the rest of the mess and tossing the towel in the washer. I then heard a scratching outside the door, I switched on the outside light and looked through the glass in the door. There was a figure crouching outside, I couldn't make out if it was male or female. Who could be out there in the pouring rain? I went back to the living room and woke Eleanor, I then called Alfie, who was hiding upstairs because of his indiscretion in the kitchen. The three of us went back through the kitchen to the back door. I opened it slowly holding Alfie's collar in one hand. Outside I saw a very wet Adam.

"What are you doing?" I asked, holding Alfie even tighter

"I thought I would come and tell you that it wasn't me you saw outside the Equestrian Centre."

"On a night like this?" I questioned. I was not at all comfortable with him being here.

"I had already told B that you had said it was not you. I think you should leave." Eleanor said.

"I realise it was a mistake, I am sorry, I just wanted to set the record straight. Would you mind if I came in for a few moments, just to talk to you?"

"Yes, I would mind. Now please go. If you want to talk to us, you can make an appointment, and come to the Centre, where my Chief of Security will be."

"Very well," said Adam, and turned to go. I slammed the door behind him.

"How creepy was that?" questioned Eleanor. "I think that we should call Alistair."

"What's he going to do? We've got rid of the man, and he knows that there are two of us here with a dog, he's hardly likely to come back." I retorted, "We can call Alistair in the morning. Let's go to bed."

We turned out the lights, but I left the outside lights on, and checked that everything was locked up. We climbed the stairs and said good night to one another. I got into bed and felt comforted by the bulk of Alfie lying beside me. I could not get to sleep. I tossed and turned wondering what Adam's motive had been. Did he plan to harm me in any way?

I tried to read, picking up a book that I was determined to finish, Churchill's biography of the Duke of Marlborough. Inevitably I could not concentrate.

Adam was clearly in a close friendship with Brian in Ontario. Did Adam travel to California as he stated for his job, or for more nefarious activities with Brian? That association would have stopped now Brian was in custody, but what about other members of his company, were they still active? What of the girlfriend Sarah, was she still in California? Eventually I must have fallen asleep because I awoke to still more rain battering my window at seven a.m.

Eleanor was up and making coffee downstairs. I hurried to get dressed, and took Alfie downstairs with me, and booted him forcefully out of the house, closing the door behind him. I did not want more accidents, that could be avoided today.

Eleanor had called Alistair about our evening visitor, and Alistair had phoned Bill Thomas, and left a message for him. Eleanor said that she thought I should keep Alfie with me today, even if it was raining, as both she and Alistair would be busy. I agreed happily enough to this. I let Alfie back in, ignoring the pained looks he was giving me, and I swear he timed his shake to inflict the most moisture on me possible. Eleanor and I drank the coffee and ate some toast in record time, so we could get over to the Centre as quickly as possible to check on the arrangements for the final of the dressage.

The championship started promptly at nine a.m. The horses were not as settled in the coliseum, spectators dribbled in, and doors were banged. Two horses had gone before Jessie, and as she rode into the big ring, I could see that she would have her hands full. Quisty's eyes were out on stalks, and he was insisting on doing passage around the ring. Alistair stood in the entrance shaking his head, however he was laughing, as Quisty launched himself down the centre line. It was a memorable test, but not in the way that we wanted! Jessie managed to harness some of the power into a few good movements, but overall, she deserved her last place finish.

I went to meet the three of them, after she came out of the ring. All we could do was laugh. Up until this moment Quisty had done an amazing job, but the atmosphere in the coliseum had sent him over the top. I promised to arrange for them to have time to work in the ring once the Showcase was over. I assured them that Quisty had achieved an amazing result, just getting into the finals. Alistair was fine with what had happened, but Jessie felt that she had let us down. I told her to get over herself, and work towards her next competition. She nodded and headed off to take care of Quisty, who would be heading back to his home barn later today.

Alistair stayed with me and told me he was worried about Adam and was going to keep an eye on me throughout the day. We hung out in the coliseum for the rest of the dressage, the tests were all substandard except for the Dutch pair, who put in an outstanding performance. Anthea Charrington did her best to give a prize giving worthy of the Competition, and the Dressage Showcase wound up. As soon as everybody left the arena the dressage ring was removed, and work started to get it ready for Vaulting. I made a note about needing more time between disciplines, to deal with inclement weather. Amazingly the coliseum was ready for the vaulting to start on time on Wednesday morning. Spectators and competitors had packed up.

Alistair grilled us on what had happened the previous night. He agreed with us that it was very strange behaviour.

"Do you think he would have knocked on the door, if you hadn't turned the light on?"

"I don't think so, he was crouched beneath the kitchen window."

"Did you check outside to see if he left anything?"

"No, we weren't going to go outside last night, and we didn't think about it this morning."

"Then I think we should go and check right now."

We went outside to find that the rain was finally tapering off, we took the two cars and drove back to my place. I let Alfie out and he hurried off and sniffed around the house. Alistair followed him and Eleanor went round the opposite way. I went in to make coffee for everyone. I was just finishing up and laying a tray with mugs, milk and sugar, when they all came back in.

"Look what Eleanor found." said Alistair. Eleanor was holding up a small electronic device.

"What is it?" I asked.

"It's a listening device that Adam fastened to the kitchen window."

"But, what for?"

"Well B, would you believe, for listening to us!" I rolled my eyes at Eleanor.

"You can stop being a smart ass." I said, "I meant, why would he want to listen to us?" Alistair replied,

"Presumably he couldn't listen in to the police, so we were the next best thing, now the question is, what do we do about it? Should we give it to the police now, or should we put it back and see what they want to do?"

"We must give it to the police." I said immediately, "I don't want him listening in, anyway he'll have heard now that we have it." I said gesturing to the thing.

"It's turned off B, and anyway it will only have a short range, he will have to be within a quarter of a mile, I imagine he thought he would come after dark, park and listen. If we put it back, we could give him misinformation."

"What good would that do? Surely it is illegal to listen to other peoples' conversations, the police could arrest him for this."

"Yes, it is an indictable crime, but he would be out on bail in no time."

As if on queue, there was a knock at the door. We all froze, Alistair pocketed the listening device, and went to answer the door. It was Inspector Thomas.

"I'm sorry I did not get back to you before, but I was away

at a conference and nobody gave me the message, until I was back at the station, so what happened here last night?"

I told him everything that happened. Alistair produced the device. Inspector Thomas took it and looked at it very carefully.

"Can you be sure that Adam put it there last night?"

"Well, no, we didn't see him do it, it was only by chance that we caught him outside, it was raining so hard, even Alfie didn't hear anything."

"I can't arrest him, unless we catch him in the act. That would mean putting it back, and watching out for him parking somewhere to listen in. Then we could charge him, and he would be subject to up to five years imprisonment. Would you be willing to let us do that? It would be really helpful, I cannot get a search warrant based on any of the stuff that you have found out about California, but if we could get him on unlawful eavesdropping, we could get one in a heartbeat."

I wasn't sure, but both Alistair and Eleanor were keen to put it back, judging by their faces, so reluctantly I agreed. Alistair pointed out that we were surrounded by parkland belonging to the Equestrian Centre and it would be quite easy for Adam to find somewhere to hide, without parking on the road. David Thomas nodded. "We can start with the road, and if we have no luck, we can think about putting officers in the park."

Alistair and David Thomas went outside to replace the listening device, they came back in and said it was in place. Inspector Thomas said they would start surveillance the following evening. He thanked us and left.

Alistair and Jenny would be back at their usual duties the next day. I asked Eleanor to fill in for me, as I had to attend the hearing with Iris in the morning. The vaulting was scheduled to start at one p.m. so there would not be a lot to do, unless something untoward happened.

I had a frozen stir fry in the freezer, and so I heated that up and we had some wine, and then called it a night. I would have to be up fairly early the next day to make the forty-minute drive down to the Brampton Courthouse, so I set my alarm and slept much better than the previous night.

LIFE CONTINUES

Traffic was heavy heading down Highway 10, and then finding a parking space at the courthouse was not easy. I had to hike across the endless parking lot to get to the entrance. Iris and Maisie were already waiting. Iris had done her best to present Maisie in a neat and tidy fashion, but she was already scuffing her polished shoes, as she kicked stones, a lock of her unruly hair had escaped the band that was supposed to restrain it, and she had a juice stain down the front of her dress.

"Hi Bat Bug B!" she said, "We have to wait here until they unlock the doors." She restarted her attack on the stones. Iris sighed,

"I'd hoped she would behave today!"

"Where's Michael?" I asked

"We decided it was better if I came by myself, the situation is complicated enough without adding the paternity into the mix." I was not sure about this. I didn't think you should hold things back from the court. I wished that they had brought the lawyer.

Before I could say anything, a security officer came, and unlocked the door. We entered the big hallway, and the security man directed us to the board showing which court room was holding which case. We made our way down there and sat down outside the room. I asked Maisie how Kipper was doing,

"She's great, she likes to chew things though, and Iris got grumpy because she chewed out the back of her new shoes. Guess what Bat Bug? Michael says he's going to buy Nipper! He says I've got to learn to ride dressage, and if I don't, he'll give Nipper to a good dressage rider, I know he won't though. I hate dressage! It sucks." Before I had a chance to remonstrate with her, our case was called, and we walked into the court room. I hoped that Maisie would be in awe of the surroundings and stay quiet, but of course, nothing fazed the girl.

"Hi!" she said to the judge who was seated at a table not as I had assumed in robes and enthroned above us. She plonked herself down at the table and said,

"Are you the one who says I can have Iris as my Mummy? My real Mummy is dead you know." Iris leant over and whispered to Maisie to be quiet. The judge however smiled, and asked Maisie if she wanted Iris as her Mummy.

"Of course, I do! Iris is awesome except when she gets grumpy, when my puppy eats her things."

"Well, I think anyone would get grumpy if their things got eaten." Replied the judge with a smile, "Maisie, would you mind going outside with this lady?" he indicated a matronly person who had been sitting away from the table, "I need to talk to Iris for a while."

"I suppose, can she get me a drink?"

"Yes, I think so." Maisie got up and followed the woman outside. The judge turned to Iris and produced a file. "This is a sad story, but the child does not seem to be emotionally scarred by all that has happened to her. You appear to have been the one constant in her life. I have read through the file to refresh myself with the details. Given that the father is incarcerated, and no other members of her family are seeking custody I am granting you temporary custody, subject to visits from social services to check on her welfare. If all is well, after a year, I will revise the order to a permanent status. Do you have any questions?" Iris shook her head, obviously relieved that it had all been this easy.

"Very well then, my clerk will mail you the paperwork, and I wish you good luck! It looks like you will have your hands full!" Iris murmured her thanks, and we left the room.

"Well done!" I said, Iris nodded, and then we looked around for Maisie who we finally found running up the hallway, and once she had gathered enough speed, sliding over the tiles, the matronly lady in pursuit. She looked relieved to see us, and relinquished care of her charge happily.

"So?" said Maisie,

"So what?" said Iris.

"You can be very irritating!" Maisie exclaimed, "Are you my new Mummy?"

"Yes, I am, poor me!" Iris replied

"What do you mean? Poor you, it's poor me more like!" The two of them hugged, it seemed to last for an hour.

I hoped to make it back to the Centre in time for the start of the vaulting, I might have, but there was an accident on highway 10, and I got detoured out and around.

Jenny was back at work. Franny was gnawing on a chair leg as I entered the office. I thought of Iris's shoes and made a mental note to shut mine away.

I told her we had better now focus on getting the Show Jumping Showcase organised. Vaulting was looking after itself, with Randy in charge. I asked Jenny to set up a meeting with Tom, to go over all his plans, and to dig out what we needed in the way of personnel and decorations. I told her that John was moving the large gazebo into the ring for the judges and sponsors, and that we would need Tabitha to decorate it. I was pretty sure that Anthea would have the prize giving planned but thought that we should check with her to see if she needed anything special. Leaving her to this I walked over to find Eleanor. She was sitting in one of the box seats, looking CEO like, presiding over the vaulting.

"Oh, good, you're back! I was feeling a bit stupid sitting here." She said.

"You look just fine, just the right amount of regality!"

We watched a little more of the competition. Thinking we had put in a long enough appearance we got up to leave.

"Do you realise it is only a couple of weeks until I will be making my way home?" I nodded sadly, I did not know how I was going to feel, when Eleanor left.

"Have you invited Alistair?"

"Yes, he's thinking about it, but I think he will come, even if it only for two or three weeks."

We strolled back to the office, and when we got there Franny was sound asleep in her cage, and Jenny was beavering away getting Show Jumping files out and calculating the number of bodies needed for ring crew and assistant stewards. Tom was away, with our nice course designer, until tomorrow, so we would have to wait for our meeting.

"Can I borrow your car to pop back to the house? I'll let Alfie out and bring him back with me." said Eleanor. I handed her the keys.

Franny was just waking up, when Eleanor and Alfie arrived. We took the two dogs outside for some exercise, and they played until Franny started to tire. Jenny picked her up protectively and put her in her car. I announced to Eleanor that we should go grocery shopping.

"Good heavens! How are the takeout places going to survive!" Eleanor said rudely. I ignored her and drove off to the supermarket. We loaded up the cart and were back in the car in no time. On the way home we discussed how to deal with our conversations with the listening device.

"I'm sure he won't listen until after dark, but don't mention anything about it at any time just in case. Once it's dark, let's talk about Adam coming and how strange we think that is." Eleanor said.

We unpacked our groceries, and put everything away, we argued for a while over what to have for supper and ended up with a steak and salad. I wanted to do some work outside, the garden had been totally neglected. While I pulled weeds, Eleanor did the dishes. She joined me outside with coffee, we went to the barn, and pulled out some lawn furniture, and sat while the sun went down, and sipped our coffee. Alfie had done a complete check of his territory and finding nothing out of order came and sat with us. I sighed and told Eleanor that I was going to have to employ somebody to do the garden. There was no way I would be able to cope with it, by myself.

It started to get cool. We put the chairs away and went indoors. We watched a news program about rebuilding slum areas for affordable housing and then, when it was fully dark, we chatted about Adam, and why he had come to the house. We came up with some ludicrous ideas. We then talked of Fee, and I said I must call her lawyer, and find out what was going to happen to her. Would she be held at the hospital, or would they release her, I had no clue. When we thought we had said enough to be interesting, we called it a night.

I could not get to sleep, Alfie grumbled, I was upsetting his sleep with my tossing and turning. I got up and went down to the kitchen and made a cup of cocoa. I turned the light out, and was taking my cup back upstairs, when I saw a car go down the road. After a while the cocoa did its job, and I fell asleep.

The next morning, we went over to the Centre. Our nice wooden chairs had been replaced with cheap plastic ones.

Franny was in her cage but let out excited yips when she saw Alfie. We took the two of them outside and took them for a walk to John's workshop. He said the gazebo was now in the show jumping ring, but that it had been a bear of a job to get it through the entrance between the towers. We chatted about that for a bit, and then he asked if it was still OK for him to take a week's holiday after the Show Jumping Showcase. Jenny told him it was on my calendar from when he'd requested the time several months ago.

"Are you going anywhere nice?" I asked

"Leika and I are taking Amelia to my cabin on the outskirts of Algonquin Park, we hope to do some hiking and canoeing."

"I hope the bugs aren't too bad up there."

"I know they can be deadly, we'll go prepared."

John pulled off a sheet that was covering a carving. Jenny and I gasped. The golden retriever looked so real you felt you could pet it.

"Do you think Amelia will like it?" John asked shyly,

"If she doesn't, she needs her head seeing to!" I said, "This is your finest work, John." He looked so pleased; he covered it back up carefully.

"Going to give it to her tonight."

Jenny and I both liked John. I told Jenny that I hoped that it worked out between him and Amelia, because I thought they made a good couple. Jenny agreed, she said she would have to get Hetty to do some match making for her. We were laughing when we arrived back at the office. Alistair was waiting.

"Have we been downgraded?" he asked indicating the chairs.

"Temporarily, until Franny's teeth are removed." I replied. Jenny was pushing the aforementioned dog into her cage, which she was not happy about.

"Oh dear! Did we have a problem?"

"Only two inches off the bottom of the chair leg." I replied then looked questioningly at Alistair "Any luck last night?"

"No sign of him, David said. They're going back out tonight."

"The vaulters all seem to be very well behaved," I agreed that it seemed very quiet.

"Do you think Eleanor and I could leave early today? We had an idea about Adam, and we wanted to check it out."

"Well, I don't want both my Security Chiefs to be the latest to disappear." I said,

"We're not going anywhere dangerous, just to the property records. Eleanor is much better than I am at looking things up." replied Alistair.

"OK then." I said, as they packed up to go.

Jenny and I were uninspired, there was nothing urgent to do until my meeting with Tom. I went to check that all was going well in the coliseum, and as far as I could tell the competitors were doing fine. They all looked like little toothpicks, all decked out in lycra, and probably the most supple group, I had ever seen. I caught Randy's eye, and he gave me a thumbs up, and I went back to the office declaring it another early day for the workers.

I locked the office and drove home to check if the listening device was still there, and under cover of walking Alfie and pulling the odd weed, I saw it hidden behind one of the climbing rose branches. I then went into the house and sat down on the sofa for a while until I had to put on the supper. I sat back and tried to think of something that we could say tonight that might make Adam act in a certain way. I remembered that I hadn't called Hetty, and so picked up the receiver and dialled her number. When she answered we chatted for a bit, and then I asked her about a gardener. In typical fashion, she knew just the person, and gave me her phone number. After hanging up with Hetty I dialed the number.

The gardener said she'd be glad of another garden to maintain. I told her that it had got out of control, and she said not to worry she would come often to start with, and once I was happy with it, she would just come often enough to maintain it. We worked out a price, and I told her she could come whenever she liked, that I was most days at work, tools were in the barn, so she could just go ahead.

I then got up to organise supper, I thought I would do a beef stroganoff which was one of the few meals that I cooked that generally turned out OK. I fixed a salad to go with it, and then Alfie announced the arrival of our guests.

I continued to work in the kitchen, while Eleanor poured drinks Alistair told me that they had gone to the registry of properties in Barrie and in Orangeville. They found that Paul Wiseacre owned a farm near Creemore, and Adam owned a house in Caledon East, in addition to the one he currently lived in. He apparently rented it out, but the last tenants had left two months ago. They had not discovered if Paul's farm had tenants or not.

I dished up the food, and we sat down to eat. We finished our meal, and all the plates were completely empty, so I took that as being a good sign that it had been edible. It would be dark soon, and so we would be having to think of topics to talk about to seem natural and at the same time be interesting to someone listening. It was strange how difficult this was to achieve. We rambled on about the Showcase, which we felt would seem normal. There was a dinner the following night for the sponsors and competitors of the vaulting, and we would all be attending. Alistair said that he thought there might be some drugs being used by a couple of the competitors in the show jumping, and he was going to keep an eye out for it. We then went on to talk about Fee's positive drug test, though we did not mention that John Smith had found out what drugs it contained.

Alistair said that he must go home, thanked me for the meal, and went to the door. I took Alfie over, and let him follow Alistair out, I stayed at the door and watched Alfie, when he came back, I closed and locked the door. Eleanor and I made our way up to bed. We had a whispered conversation, wondering whether Inspector Thomas had caught Adam tonight.

The next morning Eleanor called Alistair, he said that he was about to call Bill Thomas, to see if they had had any luck last night. I called Jenny and asked her to come in and take the minutes for the meeting with Tom Clark, and then go home until the dinner, if she wished to come.

The plan in place, I drove over to the centre. Eleanor took Alfie for a walk. Jenny had left Franny at home.

The meeting with Tom went well enough, he brought me the schedules, and I warned him to have a Plan B, in case we got more storms, he made a note of that. We had to work on how to seat the sponsors and owners in the bleachers, and Tom had done nothing about the dinner that would be held on Saturday. This took some time to talk through this, and Jenny volunteered to do a seating plan for him, as he had not thought that that was part of his job description. The actual running of the competition, he had totally down pat, so after the meeting I thought it should all go well, if Mother Nature was kind to us with the weather. We closed the meeting, and Jenny said she'd type up the minutes at home, and work on the seating plan. I told her to email both of them to me and to copy Tom. I then asked her if she was coming tonight. She said she wouldn't pass up a free meal!

Alfie and I sat and watched some of the vaulting. Alfie found it quite engaging for a while, so we stayed through a complete class. Randy came and joined us once it was over and asked if he could convert us from our eventing discipline.

"I don't think I have quite the figure for vaulting, and I really don't look good in spandex!" I replied, Randy laughed, and we chatted easily for a while, I asked about the dinner, and he said it was all in hand.

"Can I introduce you to a couple of our sponsors, they are anxious to meet "the handbag lady"!" I frowned at him but said I would like to meet our sponsors and I went and spent a pleasant half hour with them talking about the plans for the Equestrian Centre. Of course, they couldn't resist bringing up the topic of murders, but I just gave my stock answers that I was not allowed to comment as the case was ongoing. I thanked them for their contribution, and Alfie and I made our way back to the office. I had just got myself sat down, when Alistair and Eleanor came back.

Alistair got hold of Inspector Thomas, but unfortunately it had been a busy night for the police. They had had a hit and run on Airport Road, which had kept them too busy to look out for Adam. Bill Thomas said we still needed to catch him in the act. He wanted us to make sure our conversation was interesting enough, to keep him listening in for enough time for them to find him. It would have to be the following evening, as we were off to the Vaulting dinner tonight.

I hadn't been really looking forward to the evening, but it turned out to be a lot of fun, I was glad Eleanor appeared to be thoroughly enjoying herself. Randy had arranged to have a DJ, who played Beatles medleys, as well as music to appeal to the younger audience. Randy proved to be a fantastic dancer, and with a couple of his friends, kept Jenny and Eleanor on their feet for most of the evening. Xen and Susie joined in with their strange syncopations of the beat. I was glad that Xen rode with a more rhythmic fluidity. Alistair danced a couple of numbers, and offered to squire me round the floor, but I declined, sighting my leg, and lack of soundness. We all had a good evening and forgot about Adam and Fee for a while. The party rounded up at midnight.

The next morning, we all went into the coliseum to watch the final class of the Vaulting. Now we had met so many of the competitors, it was a lot more enjoyable. It all finished up by lunch time, and we had a spectacular prize giving, orchestrated by Anthea. It was very special having all the competitors, the faithful horses and the pageantry in the big amphitheatre. The sounds of the bagpipes radiated out and round the seating, so that you felt it in your bones. It was so stirring that you could imagine why people marched after the pipes and into battle. The Pony clubbers did a quick demonstration of their mounted games vaulting, to the enthusiasm of everybody. I made a mental note to try and get Anthea on salary, to do all pageantry for the Centre. With much cheering the Vaulting showcase finished up, and we only had the Show Jumping to go. I was going to be pleased when it was all over.

I invited Randy back to the office, and we opened a bottle of champagne to celebrate the Showcase. We all then packed up and headed off to our various homes. Eleanor and Alistair came back to my house, and we strategized our conversation, for that night. Alistair asked if the two of us felt we could handle it, he wanted to go out into the park land behind my house and see if Adam was there. He knew that the police would be on the roads, and he wanted to maximise the chance of catching him. We agreed that we were both good at talking and could probably manage without him! Our plans in place, Alistair went home, and Eleanor and I put our feet up for the afternoon. I took Alfie for a short walk, as evening approached, Eleanor fixed us a bowl of soup and a salad, this we consumed, and then we filled the time watching another session of Jeopardy on television.

Once it was dark, we turned the TV off, and talked about the dinner from last night. Eleanor then started on a story telling me that Alistair had been talking to the police in California, and that they were continuing to investigate Zoe's disappearance. They thought that Brian and Adam may have been involved, and that they want to talk to Brian, while he is awaiting trial in prison. They want to get the OPP to search his house again and any other properties that he might have access to. I then asked why they didn't search Adam's house, and Eleanor explained that there was not enough evidence to get a warrant, as yet.

I thought we were doing a pretty good job at this considering we were making it all up as we went along! I continued to surmise what they might have done with Zoe, and then I got onto Paloma, and the possibility that Brian and Adam were responsible for either their disappearances or their deaths. I brought up the possibility that they could have been making pornographic films as well as drug trafficking. I was running out of lurid topics, when the phone rang. Eleanor picked it up. It was Alistair who said briefly, "We've got him! I'll be with you in a minute." Eleanor hung up and said, "Mission accomplished!"

Five minutes later Alistair arrived, feeling very proud of himself. He had found Adam hidden in the barn ruins that were in the parkland behind my house. He had phoned Bill, and two constables had come over and arrested Adam. He would be held in custody for a couple of days, during which Bill would get a search warrant for all three of Adam's properties.

"Does that mean that he will be let out after the two days?" I asked.

"That depends on whether they find anything to link him to the girl's disappearances, any drug paraphernalia or any pornographic films. If they find that, then he will face a lot more charges and he will not be granted bail." explained Alistair.

I called Hetty first thing in the morning, she was grumpy as she and Poppy were having a lie in.

"She's not sleeping on your bed is she Hetty? I thought she wasn't allowed on the furniture."

"Shut up! Why are you calling at this unearthly hour?"

"Adam was arrested last night." I exaggerated our cunning somewhat, but only to make it a better story! I told her that we had to keep our fingers crossed that something implicating him in more serious crimes would be found, when they enforced the search warrant.

"Alice will be happier to come home if he is not around, I think she had not been comfortable staying with him, and it sounds as if he might have drugged her." said Hetty, who seemed to have forgiven me for waking her up. She asked if I was busy and I said, "No today is free, and then we get into the Show Jumping Showcase."

"Lunch at the café? I want to congratulate Iris on getting custody."

"No, you don't, you want to grill her on her relationship with Michael. You are incorrigible!" Hetty laughed, and we set a time to meet for lunch.

Eleanor was wandering around in her dressing gown yawning, she said that she would like to come for lunch as well. I then called Jenny, and told her to stay home, the phone calls were forwarded to her number when we were not in the office, so she could attend to anything urgent from her house. We were going to be busy enough for the rest of the week, so she might as well enjoy a quiet day, she was grateful for that, and said she and Franny would enjoy the nice weather outside. I called Alistair to say that he should stay home, but he was already on the way to the Centre. He needed to have a meeting with all his security guards about their duties for the Show Jumping. There would be many more people competing, and with good weather predicted, spectators were likely to be as numerous as for the Eventing.

It felt good to have a little down time, the Showcase was taking its toll on me, and I would have to make some changes, once it was over. I thought that as soon as it was over, I should call a Board meeting to find out whether they had come up with somebody to take over as CEO. Although I had said that I would not act as CEO, I had in fact performed many of the duties on top of my own as Chair of Eventing and overseeing the other disciplines. I was not willing to continue to do this. I chatted to Eleanor about the situation, she suggested I send a letter to each member of the board making it quite clear that the current situation could not continue and asking that they attend a meeting to present their decision. I thought that she was quite right. I would work on drafting something after lunch.

We went for a stroll around the park, and out of curiosity we walked by the barn ruins where Alistair had found Adam. Alfie immediately smelt that someone had been there, and was circling round and round, nose to the ground.

"You'd have caught him, wouldn't you boy!" I told him, he smiled up at me, and then took off after a rabbit that had appeared from behind a tree. We watched him as he chased it down the hill, and then Eleanor said, "Look someone is down there." She pointed to a grove of trees off to the right of where Alfie had run. She was right, I could see a small figure down there.

"Probably a dog walker." I said, "They are not supposed to walk in Centre grounds, but they often do."

Hetty was already at the café. Iris had a table set aside for us, and Hazel was looking after the other customers. Maisie was at school, and so we would have an uninterrupted conversation. We quickly chose the special, in order to keep Iris's life as free of complications as possible. It was a seafood lasagna and quite delicious. Iris told us how well her new chef had worked out, and custom was increasing.

"We are taking it slowly, but Michael is looking at buying a farm nearby, not too many acres, but enough to have horses and to grow hay. He wants me to move in with him with Maisie, but I am a city girl and I'm not sure how I would like to live in the country, but I do think it would be good for Maisie. Also, I must think about the cafe. It is Maisie's inheritance, and I want to see it grow and become a real money earner for her. Michael has to travel quite a lot, although he is thinking of cutting down the number of courses that he designs. I don't know, I just think that we should not rush into anything."

"I think you are being very wise." I told her, "It would be very easy to take the convenient way, but sometimes that does not work out, and it is hard to go back to the way it was before." Iris nodded,

"That's just what I think." She said.

I asked her if she had ever seen Adam with Brian. She said that she had, a few times. Iris then told us that the police and the prosecuting counsel had been to talk to her repeatedly. They were gathering more evidence against Brian. They had also talked to Maisie, but Iris thought that she had not really had very much to say.

Hetty said how upset she was that she had been such a poor judge of character, and that she had not seen through Adam. I pointed out that he had fooled many people, and that Barry had really liked him. Hetty nodded, "Barry did say that Adam was not the same after he went to California, something must have happened down there."

"Perhaps it was his father being so bitter after his divorce, or maybe it was when he met Brian? Or the girlfriend seems to have been an influence. We will never know." I said. We continued to chat, Eleanor told them that she was returning to England after the last Showcase, and that she had persuaded Alistair to come and stay with her for a while. We all thought that this was a great idea and would be good for him. We then proceeded to have a good gossip about his relationship with Daniel, and how they had managed to keep it secret for so long.

I asked Iris if she had any idea when the court case against Brian and his brother would be heard. She shook her head," I know it won't be for at least another year and maybe two."

It had been a fun lunch, and we parted promising to do it again before Eleanor left. We drove back to my house and spent a quiet afternoon and evening. I made a start on drafting my letter to the Board of Directors and felt virtuous about that. We heard nothing from Alistair, so we assumed he had heard nothing new from Bill Thomas. The next day, the majority of the show jumpers would be shipping into the stabling, and security would be ramped up. Eleanor had offered to join Alistair's team, to help ensure the safety of these horses, valued in the hundreds of thousands of dollars. Several of those competing had won over a million dollars, and we could not afford to have anything happen to any of them.

We left early, Jenny was already in the office fielding phone calls, but she said that there was nothing pressing that needed attending to. She had brought in a couple of newspapers that had written articles on the dressage and vaulting Showcases. I cut them out and put them in the file, so I could create an album. The monthly horse magazines would run pieces, once the whole showcase was completed, so I was hoping that we would get some excellent coverage. I thought I would drop in at the media tent today and ask that they put together everything that they could find.

Tom called to say that he needed a good electrician out at the jumping ring. The loudspeakers were cutting in and out, and the usual guy couldn't figure out what the problem was, and the TV people had run a live wire across the entrance to the ring and Tom was having trouble getting them to reroute it. I left the electrician to Jenny, and took Alfie over with me, to deal with the TV crew who just wanted to make things easy for themselves. I pointed out to them that horses could not take anywhere near as many volts as a human being, and if they trod on the wire with their metal shoes and studs the result would be a dead horse, and a TV company being sued for millions of dollars. Once it was put to them like that, they thought that it was wise to reroute the wiring. I went and found Tom and told him I had sorted the problem, but that I wanted him to double check where all the other wiring went. He said he would send someone. I told him I would rather he did it himself. Sighing he went off to do as I asked.

I stopped in at the media tent, but they hadn't set up properly, so I just left them a message with what I wanted. Alfie and I then stopped by stabling to observe the arrival of some of the top jumpers in the world. They were treated like film stars, some travelled with their own pony or goat to keep them company and stop them stressing. One had his own hydroponics unit growing him a daily ration of grass to help his digestive system, that had been compromised by colic surgery. Many had their own hay steamers which killed the moulds that existed in even the finest hay. Some travelled with their own treating vet. With this amount of value in horse flesh, we had to ensure that the stables had everything that could possibly be required. I asked the stable manager if the fire extinguishers had been checked and she assured me that they had and that the fire drill had been updated for the jumpers. I decided to leave, as I was becoming far too neurotic. Alfie and I returned to the office, and we took Franny out for a short walk, while Jenny was still coping with the electrician, who was telling her that the problem with the loudspeakers was with the supply from Hydro One and not with his work.

Alfie and Franny had a great time, unfortunately Alfie was introducing Franny to the joys of peeing in the flower gardens. I made a mental note to tell Jenny we would have to go further afield before we let them off their leashes. When we got back to the office Jenny had sorted the electrics out, and I gave her my draft letter, and asked her to type it up and send it out to the Board. We needed to set a date for the meeting, so we settled on the Wednesday after the Showcase finished. I took over manning the phones, while Jenny took on the task of typing the letters for me.

There were a couple of calls from sponsors who had not received their packages with their free parking passes and dinner vouchers. I told them that they would be left at Will Call. I made up the packages and put their names on them. Jenny asked if I had seen the personal letter? I opened it up, and it contained a letter and a photo. I looked at the photo of a pretty young girl in her early twenties, there was a second girl with her. This girl had her back to the camera but was looking over her shoulder at the photographer. It was windy and the girls' hair was blowing wildly. The second girl's face was partially obscured by her dark hair. The letter was from Caroline and Quentin from California. It asked me to pass the picture on to the local police.

"This is a picture of Zoe with Sarah (Sarah with her back to the camera) It is the most up to date picture of Zoe that we have. Although a lot of time has gone by, we are still hopeful of finding our darling girl. To this end would you give this photo to the officers looking into the other missing girls, perhaps there is a link." I felt the pain that this couple was suffering and wondered whether I should suggest that Hetty contact them, sometimes a pain shared is a pain halved, though in my heart I knew nothing would take away the profound grief that these people were suffering. I dropped them a line saying that I would take the photo to Inspector Thomas, and I wished them well.

I told Hetty about the letter and photo and asked if she would like to talk to the people. She said she would feel a little awkward talking to them out of the blue but would write them a letter. I then broached another topic that I had been remiss in not bringing up earlier. We had to decide what to do about Killer, with Fee in hospital for the foreseeable future. I proposed we ask Maggie Sandler to ride him, having retired Media Circus, and with Samantha riding Filibuster, she had no upper level horse. Hetty sighed, she said that she to, had known we had to do something about the horse, but was too upset about Fee that she had ignored the problem. She really liked Maggie, and thought it was a good solution, but said that she could not afford to pay Maggie to ride the horse. I told her that I was pretty sure that Maggie would do it for nothing, and that I would contact her to find out. I said that we should probably tell John Smith, and he could let Fee know what was happening. Hetty started crying,

"Poor Fee! It is all so awful; how did my family end up this way? I am so grateful that Barry did not live to see this." I let her cry for a while, and then asked her about Alice,

"She will be home in a couple of days. I should be feeling for her. Her one daughter is missing and the other in hospital for the criminally insane."

"Perhaps she's stronger than we think, after everything she has suffered, she is well enough to come home. Everyone always walks around as if on eggshells with her, maybe she needs a dose of reality."

"Really B, that's pretty mean. I'm sure her doctors wouldn't want us to do that!"

"Well, you could ask them, are you going to pick her up?"

Hetty said she was, so I went on, "Ask if she should be treated normally." Hetty agreed to do that, though I was doubtful that she really meant it.

I said why didn't she bring Alice to the gala dinner on Saturday night, for the show jumping? It would be good for both of them. Hetty was obviously hesitating, and before she could respond negatively, I told her I would have Jenny drop round the tickets on her way home. I then rapidly said goodbye.

I picked up the receiver again, and made the call to Maggie, who was thrilled to have the chance to ride Killer, she said she would arrange to pick him up the following day.

Jenny had finished the letters, and handed them to me to sign, I told her about the sponsors' packets,

"I knew we should have handled all that, Tom is no good at that side of things." said Jenny, I nodded, "We'd better put that in our final report." I said, "Also can you drop off two tickets for the gala at Hetty's house, on your way home?"

Once the dogs were looked after I helped Jenny with the boxes of files, and we set up our show caboose once again. Jenny then took the sponsor's packets to the Will Call entrance, and then got ready to leave for the day. I phoned Eleanor to see if she was ready to leave. She told me that she'd be another hour, but that Alistair would bring her home, so not to worry. I decided that take out was in order, so Alfie and I drove downtown, and picked up a variety of cooked foods from the local supermarket. I should have put the food in the trunk, because I had to fend Alfie off the packages that smelt too delicious to ignore. When I got home, I put the food in the lower oven of the Aga to keep warm and went up and took a shower. I put on sweats and came back down, fed Alfie, and let him outside. I noted, with satisfaction, that my gardening lady had made an assault on the back flower beds, and things were looking better. I wondered how long it would take her to conquer the whole garden. Alfie nosed around, aware that we had had a visitor, he smelt the flower bed, and looked up at me, I told him that it was fine, he wagged his tail, and we went back into the house, and I sat down and read the local paper. There was a short article saying that additional charges were expected to be laid against Brian McVicker following extensive investigations by the police. There was no mention of what these charges were. There were a couple of pictures from the vaulting Showcase, which I thought I would add to my album, otherwise there was little of note in the paper.

Alfie started to bark, and my security duo arrived. I got up and laid the table and put the food out while they cleaned up. Eleanor was excited to have met some of the horses. Her favourite, a son of the great Hickstead, she waxed poetic about for some time.

We ate and chatted. Apparently, the search of Adam's house had revealed some drugs but little else, however they had impounded his laptop, Ipad and cell phones. These were in the hands of the technicians, and it would be a couple of days before all the files were retrieved, as they were all password protected. I asked if Alistair had heard anything about the additional charges against Brian, but he said that he had not. I told them about my letter from California and showed them the photo.

"What a pretty girl!" said Eleanor handing the photo back to me. I looked at it again. There was something familiar about it, I wondered where it had been taken, I couldn't put my finger on why I seemed to recognise something. I hadn't been to California for years. Shrugging, I put it down. Alistair said he could drop the photo in to the police station, on his way to the Showcase. I thanked him. It would not have been easy for me to accomplish this errand. We spent a pleasant evening before clearing up the dishes. It would be an early start the following day, and we needed to be fresh.

SHOW JUMPING

THE WEATHER WAS GLORIOUS for the show jumping, and crowds of spectators flocked in to watch some truly spectacular jumping. The trade fair was as busy as it could ever want to be. The line ups at the food booths and food court were stretching back further than we had seen them before. Tom was happy, and there were few problems.

The accountants, who had investigated the anomalies between gate numbers and monies collected during the eventing, had traced it back to one gate and the person responsible had been arrested and replaced, so we hoped that there would be no more trouble on that score.

During the second night one of the horses suffered a bout of colic and was shipped off to the Ontario Veterinary College in Guelph. I was pleased to hear that it was not the horse that had already had colic surgery. Although the horse remained at the college, he recovered well and was only treated medically, so his career would continue, when he was fully recovered.

Canadian riders were doing well, much to the crowd's enthusiasm. Jenny and I had little to do, and so we were able to watch a fair amount of the jumping. Michael brought Maisie to watch, but Iris did not come, I felt that horses were not her thing. We chatted about the farm that he was hoping to buy. He had seen a couple, but they were not really what he wanted, so he said he was going to keep looking. Maisie regaled me with tales of Nipper and Kipper, her puppy, who Michael thought would benefit from having a large acreage to run off some of her energy. I gathered that the back yard was not sufficient space. I told them about Franny eating the leg of the chair.

John brought Amelia, and she showed everyone pictures of her dog that John had carved.

Yawning, I said, "It's time to go home, tomorrow is a big day." The main individual class was being held the following morning, it would be concluded by lunchtime to give everyone time to get ready for the Gala, and then the Showcase would finish up with the Nation's Cup on Sunday.

The following morning, I met with Alistair to discuss how we could better handle the crowds, when they were leaving the show grounds. I did not want any trouble. He ran his fingers through his hair as he thought about it, and then he said he would pull everyone off their duties before the class ended and get them out on crowd control. He then told me he had some news. Bill Thomas had called him and said that he had interviewed Adam about the eavesdropping. Adam had been uncooperative but had become very upset when he was told that his computers had been taken away and had demanded a lawyer.

Alistair then climbed into his golf cart and drove over to pick up Eleanor, who was gazing at her equine hero, in stabling. The morning's class would start early, at eight thirty, to ensure that it wound up by lunch time, and the two of them wanted to brief the stewards on the morning's protocol, and where the security people should be. I stopped by at Tom's office, he was looking nervous, the little tic that he sometimes had at the corner of his eye, was more pronounced today. He said that he thought everything was ready for an on-time start. Jenny was greeting the judges and escorting them to the gazebo, all the timing equipment had been double checked and was ready to go. They were just waiting for the title sponsor of the class to arrive, and then Tom would take them out to the gazebo so that they could take the salute from the competitors. I said that I would leave him to it and walked out to meet up with Jenny on the way back from her errand. Her face was full of fun as she approached, she told me that the course designer had stood behind the judges as they came into the gazebo, and mimicked the actions of the one judge, who was renowned for her fussiness. She had wiped the electronic timer down with a disinfectant wipe, flicked the dust off her chair, requested extra water and a larger map of course. He had taken on her mannerisms to perfection.

We made a quick stop at our trailer, but found nothing needed our attention, so we walked back to the arena to watch. As we went past the warmup area, I noticed that the steward who was there to ensure that all the fences in the warmup were legal and of the correct height was having trouble with one of the coaches. This man was getting right in her face and using his six-foot three height to intimidate her, into allowing an illegal schooling practise. I rapidly radioed Alistair, but it was Eleanor who appeared, and used her command presence, to stand down this man. She ordered the man out of the warmup, and he had slunk away, all bombast having left him. Jenny and I laughed; it was good to see. Eleanor gave a toss of her hair, and went back to her golf cart, driving past us she wiggled her eyebrows at us, and Jenny let out a whoop of approval. We watched the class; it had a very exciting jump off against the clock which had everyone sitting forward in their seats. A huge cheer went up when the last rider, who was Canadian, shaved points of a second off the time of the person standing in first place. I was delighted to hear the Canadian National Anthem played at the Prize Giving.

The gala was being held in the sponsors' tent, and Tabitha and her crew had decorated it to the nines using huge bunches of lilies as a backdrop and miniature orchids on every table with wooden horse heads on tapers inserted into every vase. It was a black-tie affair, and I was glad that the weather had held. Ball gowns and inches of mud weren't a good mix. I gave the caterers a quick call to check on their proposed arrival time, and when I was convinced that all was in hand, Jenny and I went home to change. Jenny wanted to be back early to put the name tags on the appropriate seats, so that it matched the seating plan.

The last cars had left the grounds, the horses were back in the secured stabling and so security was no longer needed, besides the skeleton crew that would be on duty tonight. Eleanor joined me, and we went back to shower and change. I had laid out my dress, fresh from the dry cleaners, on my bed. I added underwear and sheer tights to the mix. I couldn't remember when I had last worn this dress, it must have been back at Wendover College, so it would be several years ago.

Eleanor went first into the shower and came out with a towel turbaned around her head, and in a terry cloth robe. I waited a bit, as she had been quite a time in the shower, and I did not want the hot water to run out. I let it reheat a bit before I got in. I pampered myself with body lotion, and a new conditioner that I had bought, that had such a great smell. I got out of the shower, towelled off and clothed myself in the identical manner that Eleanor had used, and headed back to my room. Eleanor called me in to her room to ask what I thought of the jewelry, that she had selected. She wanted to know which necklace I thought went better with her outfit.

"You're asking the wrong person!" I said but walked over and stood behind her looking in the vanity mirror, as she held up the choices. I was struck by how different she looked in the mirror. The slight asymmetry of her face was reversed, and the scar she had on her forehead was on the other side.

"What's the matter?" she asked, I shook my head, "Nothing" I said, "I'm just not used to seeing you in the mirror. I think you should wear the blue necklace it accentuates your eyes."

I left her to it and went to make an effort with my makeup, this finished, I did my hair and then turning my head this way and that, I admired the effect. I then pulled on the new underwear, tights and slip that I had purchased, and then reached for my dress. I pulled off the cellophane covering and pulling down the zip I stepped into it. It felt rather tight pulling it up over my hips, but I put my arms through the sleeves and pulled it up. I reached round to grab the zip and pulled but it would only go up about an inch. I wriggled around and breathed in and tugged again. I got it about half an inch further. I called Eleanor to come and help, she walked into the room looking amazing, she had done her hair into an updated French pleat. Her shift dress hung to her ankles, and showed off her trim figure, and the necklace looked perfect. She looked at me quizzically and I told her that I needed help with my dress. I turned around, she looked at the zip and said, "You've got to be joking B, we'll never get this done up." I do not give up that easily, so I said, "At least give it a try." I commanded, try she did, by getting a pair of pliers to grab the zipper. She got it up by a further two inches at which point I had to shout at her to stop.

"I can't believe what the cleaners did to my dress!" I exclaimed.

"Good one B, when did you last wear it?"

"Well, it might have been four years ago." I said defensively "but it's a perfectly nice dress, you don't have to buy a new one every year."

"You do, if you put on two dress sizes of weight!" Eleanor exclaimed.

"You think?"

"Yes, I do, I kept telling you to take more exercise in England." I was furious and embarrassed, "What am I going to do now?" I asked. Eleanor opened my closet door and rummaged around amongst the clothes.

"I can't believe you have kept all this stuff, some of it is donkey's years old." She pulled out a pair of loose black pants and a long thigh length blouse. "Put these on." She said, I thought it would look awful, but I had no other option. Once I had them on Eleanor produced a scarf that I had long forgotten that I owned, she draped it around my neck and fixed it with a brooch. She then looked at me critically putting her head to one side, as she did so. It was as if she was looking at a dressage horse!

CELEBRATIONS

WE ENTERED THE TENT, several people crowded around the bar and Jenny was busy putting out the name tags on the tables. Tom Clark and his wife hurried in after us, Tom looked good in his dinner jacket, and his wife Penny, who I had never met, turned out to be a funny entertaining person. They immediately started mingling and breaking the ice with the sponsors. Competitors dribbled in, and pretty much stayed in a group, until Tom made them come over and talk to the sponsors. I was pleased to see how good he was at this sort of thing. Randy Wainwright arrived wearing an orange dinner Jacket over jeans, with a purple bow tie. Ignoring the looks he was getting, he waded in amongst the sponsors, and pretty soon I could hear gales of laughter coming from his group. I really liked the man. Alistair came in looking tall and distinguished, he ran his hand through his hair, a sure tell that he was either nervous or concentrating. I thought it was probably the former, because he smiled gratefully as Eleanor went over to join him, she steered him over to Randy's group.

Jenny came and joined me at the bar. The tent was filling up, I asked Jenny who was on our table. She glanced at her list, and then said, Hetty, Alice, Michael, Iris, Tom Clark and his wife, the course designer who was called James, and the main sponsor who's name she could not remember. It seemed like a good mix, and I decided to take my seat. On my way I saw Pru and her husband come in. Pru looked like she could be the fairy on top of the Christmas tree. Her dress shimmered with sequins and had a kind of bustle at the back of wonderful flowing material, her sleeves were sheer, and she wore long white gloves, and had diamonds at her throat and in her ears, she smiled and then eyed me up and said, "You look amazing B!" I was seriously pleased, I never got complemented on my looks. If Pru looked like a Christmas Barbie doll, her husband, Frank, looked more like a bulldog. His dinner jacket was in danger of popping buttons, the trousers because of the added girth appeared too short, his bow tie was crooked, and his jowels hung over the top of his collar. He had bushy eyebrows above beady eyes. He was one of my most favourite people. He was so kind, and would always be the first to volunteer, he was witty and smart and a great conversationalist. I could see why women were attracted to him, but he only had eyes for his beautiful wife.

"Hi B!" he exclaimed "How good to see you! I gather you have pulled off an enormous success with this Showcase!"

"Thanks in a large part to your wife." I said, he turned and looked at her fondly "I know, isn't she wonderful?" I told him that indeed she was. At that moment the person in question called him, to come over. Obediently he toddled over to join her posse.

I proceeded to take my seat. Jenny, who had been chatting to James the course designer, drew him over to the table, and indicated his seat. I looked over and saw Hetty entering with Alice. They both looked good, but Alice looked extraordinary, she wore a dress of the lightest filmy material I had ever seen, it changed colour as she walked. Her pale blond hair was pulled back and up in an attractive chignon, but with wisps of hair hanging down on either side of her face. Her ethereal beauty took your breath away. She walked with her eyes caste down, avoiding all those gawking at her. Hetty guided her to her seat, between Hetty and me. They sat, and we were soon joined by Tom Clark and his wife, who were escorting our main sponsor. Hurrying in came Michael and Iris, who had been waiting for the babysitter to arrive. Our table was now complete.

Conversation flowed easily, Tom and Penny helping it along, they were both funny and entertaining, and brought out the best in the more shy ones amongst us. Alice however said nothing, so I tried to include her, telling her how much I liked her dress and hairdo. She looked up at me with her large doe like eyes, and in a voice that was practically a whisper, said that Hetty had taken her shopping and had insisted they buy the dress.

"I should think so!" said Penny, "It is quite stunning. At which store did you find it?" Alice looked blank so Hetty answered, "At Mulberrys"

"Oh, I love that place! They have such unusual clothes, but unfortunately you need to have a better figure than mine to wear them!"

"Your figure is perfect." interjected Tom fondly.

The talk continued, and even Alice put in the odd word, normally to answer a question, but the group were good at drawing her out of herself. Michael and Iris regaled us with tales of Maisie's dramatic actions, to try and get herself included in the evening. The conversation then turned to children and Penny asked Alice if she had any. Alice blushed bright red, tears filled her eyes, and she looked around frantically, as if for escape. Hetty immediately said, that sadly her daughters were away, and Penny sensing a problem, changed the subject.

I turned to Alice, and said for her not to worry, nobody knew about Fee, and there was no need to talk about Felicity's disappearance.

"I knew I shouldn't have come!" Alice whispered, drawing her mouth into a small moue.

"Rubbish!" I said firmly, "you've got to face it sometime, so stop feeling sorry for yourself, and get on with life." Hetty sent a horrified look my way, and Alice looked astonished, sniffed rather loudly, and looked a bit like a scolded child, but stayed in her seat. Tom asked her if she had watched much of the Showcase, and she replied rather defensively looking at me out of the corner of her eye,

"I have been unwell."

"But you're fine now." I retorted, "so perhaps you should come and watch the Nations Cup tomorrow?"

"That's a great idea," said Penny, "you can sit with us." Alice was about to decline, so I said "Excellent, Hetty can you pick her up?" Hetty was giving me vicious looks, but I smiled innocently at her raising my eyebrows questioningly.

"I suppose so." She mumbled.

"Super!" said Tom, "We'll see you both tomorrow." He and Penny then turned their considerable social skills to the sponsor, a rather pompous man, who could not keep his eyes off Alice.

James and Jenny were in deep conversation, and judging by the flush on her cheeks, and the girlish laughter coming from her direction, she was quite smitten. I thought what a pity it was that he lived in Europe, Jenny needed a man, not a penpal.

The food had been average, but the wine was excellent, so nobody seemed to mind.

I assumed that it had been Penny who had arranged for the band, which turned out to be a string quartet, who were exceedingly good. Tom led Penny on to the dance floor, and slowly other couples joined them. Michael and Iris looked very comfortable dancing together. Jenny and James stumbled around, treading on one another's toes, and laughing hysterically. They returned to their seats, and James commented that when he was at school, they were taught ballroom dancing, and he had been very short, and had therefore always had to be the girl.

"I had no idea they taught ballroom dancing in school." commented Hetty.

"I went to a private school, for my sins," said James, "they try to equip you with all the social graces. I was a sad disappointment to them!" He went on to tell us of other schooldays happenings. As Jenny had said he was a great mimic, and soon had the table in stitches when he took on the voice and mannerisms of the school's matron. Iris was captivated by him, and shook her head when Michael asked her to dance again. He then stood up and went to ask Alice to dance. She immediately averted her eyes and shook her head. I was having none of that.

"He won't bite, don't be so boring! Get up and have some fun!" Hetty glared at me, but Michael held out his hand, and eventually Alice got to her feet. Her posture was totally rigid, but she followed Michael's lead, and finished the dance. Alistair and Eleanor had been dancing, and when Michael and Alice sat down, Alistair came over and took Alice back out onto the floor. Eleanor was left standing doing a great impression of an abandoned lover, so Michael jumped back up and danced with her.

The evening continued, everyone got on the dance floor, even myself, duty pressing me into action, when the sponsor asked me to dance. This was a prelude to asking Alice, who reluctantly followed him onto the floor, but when he tried to press her for a second dance she firmly refused. That's what I was hoping for – firmness of any kind.

FINISHING UP

THE NATIONS CUP WAS an exciting competition, the winners were impossible to predict, Hetty showed up with Alice, and they went and sat with Tom and Penny, in their box. A large amount of beer was being consumed in the beer garden. Jenny and I made the rounds of the office trailers, looking in on accounting, where I was needed to sign cheques. The media tent was a happening place, with reporters from all over, waiting to get the final results to wire their copy to their various newspapers and periodicals. I repeated my request for copies of all articles and photos. The communications people were complaining. They were missing radios. We had a sign out sheet, and so I asked them to list all the people who had failed to return their radios.

All was going well, and so we went to the sponsors' tent for lunch. Tom, Penny, Hetty and Alice were already there. I sat next to Alice who seemed to be coping quite well with being out at a sporting function, and she chatted quite happily to me. I kept the conversation light with no mention of her daughters or Adam. She was very grateful to Hetty, who had been driving her around. She said that she needed to become independent, but was nervous of driving, because it had been so long since she had driven a car. She didn't even know where her car was, because Fee had been driving it. I told her I was sure we could find it, and I suggested a couple of refresher driving lessons, to get her comfortable again behind the wheel.

"You are so good at making what I feel are enormous problems, seem manageable."

"Most things are, just break them down into small pieces, and solve them one at a time." I said giving her an encouraging smile.

"Would you mind coming and seeing me this week? It would be good to talk to you about so many things, and I don't want to keep putting all my problems on Hetty."

I told her that I would be happy to, and that I would call her to set up a time.

Lunch was interrupted by an urgent call from the media tent, the wifi had crashed. I called our IT guy and told him to get over there asap, and Jenny headed to the tent to try to nurse the reporters until the problem was sorted out. I was glad that I did not have to go. My knowledge of technology was zero. That's why I have people for that, I thought smugly. Within twenty minutes the problem was solved and jumping had started again with the second rounds. Everybody hurried back to their seats, except for a few rowdies in the beer garden.

Anthea had a fairly complicated Prize Giving to orchestrate with individual winners as well as the winners of the team competition, and I saw her martialling her troops. She had all trophies and ribbons lined up. Prizes were to hand, and long lists prepared for the announcer. It was vital that every sponsor be mentioned and be connected to the class that they had sponsored. It was very easy to make a big mistake, which would result in us losing a valuable sponsor, for next year. I was glad that Anthea was in charge and wondered what her background was. She was definitely a keeper.

James had designed a tricky course for the second round. It was huge, and the skinny to the double of water oxers, took their toll. There had been no clear rounds until the last competitor from Ireland managed to leave all the poles up, and just squeaked in within the time. A huge roar of approval went up from the crowd. Ireland had won, followed by the US and Canada had finished third. I breathed an enormous sigh of relief, the Showcase was over, and all had gone well. I was seriously glad that we had not run driving as well. I could not have coped with the pressure of one more discipline. The prize giving went off without a problem. Alistair had moved his people into place ready for the grand exit, and overall, it went quite smoothly. Unfortunately, a fight had broken out in the beer garden. One of Alistair's men had been punched and knocked to the ground, whilst trying to break it up. Alistair and one of his other guards went to the poor man's rescue, but it took all three of them to pull the wretched people apart. Alistair had called the police, who arrived promptly and took the brawling men away with them. I made a mental note that the beer garden was a nonstarter for next year, perhaps we should have a wine tasting instead.

I had a lot to do to prepare for the board meeting on Wednesday. Eleanor dropped me off at the Centre and took my car to go shopping for her trip home, she wanted to take some souvenirs and small gifts for her close friends. She headed off happily and I, somewhat morose, stomped into the office with Alfie. Jenny was already hard at it; Franny was in her cage.

I sent a memo to all the discipline chairs, thanking them, and asking for their reports to be completed in time for the meeting on Wednesday. I then contacted the chief accountant to ask if she had any figures from the first three Showcases, she told me that Eventing and Dressage were complete, and Vaulting should be done by Wednesday. Show Jumping would take a lot longer. I asked her to send over what she had, and to see if the figures for Vaulting could be ready in time for the board meeting. I contacted the head media person and asked that they get everything to me by the next day, so I could put my album together for the meeting.

I had not really been paying attention to Jenny, and when I glanced over, she was fidgeting in her chair and looking at me with worried eyes, she was pushing her reading glasses up her nose repeatedly, a sure sign that she was nervous.

"OK," I said, "What's up?" she looked even more worried, when I asked this,

"Um...m" she began, almost stuttering "Can I have the afternoon off?" the latter came out in a burst, the words all mashed together. I frowned in puzzlement, this was so unlike Jenny, she carried on blushing furiously, "I wondered if I could take James to Niagara Falls, and he leaves tomorrow?" I laughed uproariously,

"Of course, you can! Go now and have a great day!"

"Leave Franny with me. I'll take her home, and you can pick her up there." She needed no encouragement. She gathered up her purse and keys and was out the door in a flash. I sighed; it was a long time since I'd felt like that!

I wrote the report for eventing, which I achieved by lunchtime. I took a break and took the dogs for a walk around to the show grounds, which looked sad and abandoned. The work crew from the Centre were taking down the roping, collecting garbage, and clearing the way for the tent people to come and dismantle the tents. I had trouble keeping the dogs out of all the delicious garbage left around the food court, and so put them on leashes, and lead them back. Franny was not yet good on a leash, and kept rearing back against the pressure, Alfie was trying to tow me along so by the time I got back I was exhausted, I wrangled Franny into her cage, which she was not happy about.

Finally, I sat back at the desk, and tried to get my thoughts together, to write an overall report on the Showcase, with recommendations for improvement for the next one, if that were to happen. Jenny had written all my thoughts down in a little notebook, but I was unable to locate it. As usual I was not able to function properly without my assistant. I hoped she was having a good time and did not want to bother her by phoning to ask where the book was. I therefore had to write the report from memory. I was certain that I had forgotten a lot but thought I could finish it up tomorrow. I looked at my watch, it was only three o'clock, but I decided to call it a day. I called Eleanor who said she'd had a good day, and she would be right there to pick us up. I packed up my things and had to make three trips to the carpark to carry all Franny's possessions, along with mine. The three of us waited like a trio of migrants with all our worldly goods by our side, until Eleanor arrived. Alfie was pleased to have Franny join us, and for once decided to sit in the backseat with her. When we got home, I carted all my stuff in, and then returned to carry Franny, in her cage, with Alfie tagging along. I let them run loose in the garden. Eleanor brought in the remainder of the cargo.

My garden was undergoing a metamorphosis under the capable hands of my gardening lady, Fleur. A name which I thought was totally appropriate. When I addressed her by this name, she laughed and said, "Fleur is my nickname, but actually my name is George." I smiled at this and complemented her on the state of my garden.

I was not so happy about the border she had been creating using my collection of horseshoes. She had used them upside down. Any self respecting, superstitious horseperson knew that luck would run out if horseshoes were placed that way up.

I realised that if I wished the garden to remain in good order, I was going to have to curtail Alfie's wanderings in the flower beds. I was thinking about seeing whether I would be able to purchase a half acre from the Equestrian Centre as a dog run, when the two dogs tore back straight through a newly weeded and planted flower bed. I called them back into the house and went to try and undo the damage that they had caused to the plants. When I finished this task, I went back indoors and called Alice. I made arrangements to stop by her house the following evening after work. I then called Alistair, but there was no answer, without turning round I asked Eleanor if she had heard from him. There was a gruff, "No." followed by a pointed clearing of her throat. I spun around and saw what the problem was. Eleanor was feeling neglected, she had laid out all her purchases, and I had failed to comment on them. I pulled myself up short, and made suitable oohing and ahhing noises over everything, and then told her she must leave them out for Jenny to see. This pleased her and made up for my lack of initial interest.

We fixed an easy supper of pasta with pesto and a small salad, and we sat and ate it. I fed the dogs, Franny was very fierce guarding her tea, when Alfie came over, hoping to share. And then I took them for a stroll round the garden, trying to defend my new flower beds, to little avail. We went back in. and I told Eleanor about my idea of trying to buy a half acre of land for dog walking, she thought it was a great idea, but said,

"Why stop at half an acre? Why don't you buy the whole park? After all it's for Alfie, surely nothing is too much?"

"Very funny!" I said. We continued to tease one another for a while, I knew I was really going to miss this sort of fun and camaraderie. Before I could become too maudlin there was a knock on the door, and the two dogs joined their voices in unison, to protest the noise. I opened the door, and a radiant Jenny stood there. There was no need to ask if she had had a good day, she was positively glowing. I invited her in but blushing and scraping her hair back behind her ears, she said she had just come to pick up Franny, and James was in the car waiting. I could feel the corners of my mouth twitching, wanting to laugh, but I controlled the urge, and helped Jenny carry everything out to the car. I greeted James, and then returned to the house to find Eleanor on the phone. I tried to understand the conversation, but with only one half audible, the only thing I could gather was that it was Alistair with some news. The phone call went on for some time, with Eleanor mostly listening. Eleanor hung up, and turned to me,

"The technicians have managed to open the computers and have got into the files. It appears that Adam was heavily into drug manufacturing. He was experimenting with all sorts of drugs, growing a lot of the ingredients from natural sources. Also, he seems to have been using hypnosis to enhance the effects of the drugs and develop control over people this way. Brian was his partner in a lot of this, especially on the marketing side. The worst thing that they found was that the two of them had been producing, and starring in pornographic films, using girls who appeared to be so high, that they had no idea what they were doing. Bill thinks that Zoe may be one of them."

"What about Felicity? Any sign of her?" I asked,

"No, none at all. There was a dark haired, girl involved in the making of the films, she was helping to direct and film, but apparently you cannot see her face. They were calling her Sarah."

"Caroline and Quentin said that the girl who told them about Zoe having gone off with her boyfriend was her friend Sarah."

"Well, it doesn't sound like she was much of a friend, if it is the same Sarah."

"This Sarah shared an apartment with Zoe, but according to Nancy, she lied about what had happened to Zoe."

"In that case I think it is the same girl. Apparently, Bill

would like us to go and watch these films to see if we recognise anyone."

"I don't want to go and look at pornography!" I said immediately, "Who am I likely to recognise? That sounds stupid. They should get people from California to look at them."

"They are doing that, but they feel that there is a big tie to Ontario, and they want to cover all bases."

"Well, I still don't want to do it." I said firmly.

"OK, well I suppose Alistair and I can go. I can't imagine I can be much use." Eleanor replied, "We are supposed to go tomorrow morning. Oh, and Alistair said he wrote his report for your Board meeting."

"That's good," I said, "he can pick you up in the morning, give the report to me, and take you to the police station. I've got to finish off all my reports, I didn't get finished, because Jenny was away."

"I know, how about that! She seems really taken with James, what a pity he lives in Europe." We chatted on about this for a while. We seemed to have put together several new couples, Michael and Iris, John and Amelia and now Jenny and James. Eleanor started humming "Love is in the air" and then laughed, and said self deprecatingly, "Except for me who made a big mistake in who I fancied!"

I let Alfie out while we decided what time to set the alarm for the following day, and then we all went to bed. Alfie was hogging the larger half of the bed, and I woke up with a cramp in my shoulder from sleeping uncomfortably on the edge of the bed. He yawned at me and smiled as I complained.

I ate my toast in a hurry, anxious to get everything finished today, I took Alfie, and yelled Goodbye to Eleanor, hurrying to my car. Alistair's car pulled up as I pulled out. We waived to one another, and I grabbed his report and drove over to the

Centre. Jenny was already there, and obviously did not want to talk about James.

I asked her to locate her notebook, so I could correct and add to my report. She took no time to produce it, and then I requested that she create an agenda for the meeting We worked in silence for a while, and once I had finished the report, she passed the agenda to me, I made a couple of corrections, and then turned to the reports that everybody had sent in. These all had to be photocopied and collated into files, one for each board member. I tasked Jenny with this, and meanwhile I phoned the accountants for the figures from the Vaulting, and the media people for the articles and photos. I was fairly sure that neither of these groups had done as I requested, they both said they would get the files to me by the end of day.

I then left Alfie with Jenny, and drove into town to buy an album, I wanted something specific and had to go to three stores, until I found what I wanted. As I hurried out with my trophy, I bumped straight into Amelia. We both stopped, and Amelia told me she was just getting a few things together for the trip she and John were taking to Algonquin Park. She was excited, and she said she was looking forward to a time away from her practise.

By the time I was back at the office Jenny had finished preparing the files, and we just needed the last two to come in to finish the preparations for the meeting. We took out the press cuttings that we already had, and started sticking them in the album, Jenny typed up some titles for the photos, and I thought that it was looking quite professional.

The accountants emailed over the vaulting figures, and Jenny added them to the files. There was a knock on the door, and a courier dropped off a huge envelope from the media group. Sighing, and thinking," be careful what you ask for," we sorted them out, picked out the best ones, and added them to the album, there were too many, and I wasn't about to go and buy a second album, so we inserted the good ones and left it at that. The day had been highly productive. We made plans for the following morning and left. I dropped Alfie at home, called Eleanor and left her a message, that I was going to see Alice and would be home later.

I parked in the road and walked up the path where Alice had come close to losing her life, I wondered if she thought about it herself. I knocked on the door, and Alice opened it right away. She was looking more normal, in jeans and a sweatshirt, with her hair in a ponytail, and with bare feet she looked like a teenager.

"Hi B! Thank you for coming, I've made some nibbles, perhaps you would like a glass of wine? I no longer drink." She said, the words spilling out, one over the other.

"A wine would be lovely." I said, sitting in the overstuffed armchair that she indicated. She brought over a glass and a bottle of Chardonnay, and then went back to the kitchen to bring in some finger foods and an opener. She opened the bottle, and poured a glass before sitting opposite me, she then jumped up again, and went back to the kitchen this time bringing plates and napkins. I realised just how nervous she was and tried desperately to come up with a conversational opening, that would put her at her ease. I could have used some of Penny's social skills. In the end I said,

"How are you settling in?"

"I'm doing OK, I think. With all that has happened, it is very confusing. I cannot believe Adam is under arrest. He was my rock for years, but looking back now, I am thinking that he was doing me no good."

"In what way?" I asked. She took a long time answering, she pulled her mouth into her signature moue, and then said.

"I think that he was feeding me drugs, I was totally out of

it a lot of the time, and could remember very little, but I remember thinking after he had left, that I had done things that I should not have done. He would come back and talk to me, and somehow take that feeling away. He seemed to control me somehow."

"Did you know that he was a talented hypnotist?" I asked,

"Really, I had no idea, but somehow that makes sense. I think I agreed to things that I did not want to do, or permit." She faltered at this point, and tears slid down her cheek, her voice dropped to a whisper "I think that I slept with him, I don't know for sure, but flashbacks come to me, and I don't know if they are real or not, I am so ashamed."

"You don't need to be, Adam is a dangerous, manipulative man. He was in business with Brian McVicker, who is now charged with two counts of murder. I am sure he thought nothing of feeding you all sorts of drugs, and planting ideas in your mind through his hypnotic expertise. That is a despicable thing to do, given that you were suffering from mental health issues. None of this is your fault."

"B you are so forthright and sensible, it makes me feel less awful about myself."

"If you are to heal, you have to start to believe, that you were not to blame. You must forgive yourself."

"You are right, and given time maybe I can do that, about the things I did that impacted myself, but I can never forgive myself for allowing him to use my daughters."

"What do you think that he did to them?"

"I'm sure he must have given them drugs, how else would Fee have ended up with that positive drug test, and attacking me? I thought that I must have provoked it, but I'm not so sure now. I think that she was in the throes of a psychotic break, brought on by those drugs. I have told the police that I don't want to press charges, I want her treated and released."

"I don't know whether that will happen, Alice, she was clearly homicidal at that moment, and the police have a duty to protect the public, including you. Nobody is more upset about it then me, I love Fee, but I cannot forget what I saw with my own eyes."

"Can you please talk to her lawyer and see if there is anything that he can do to help her."

I felt so sorry for her, to have one's daughter locked up, must be the worst feeling. I promised to talk to John Smith, and then asked her if she thought Adam had anything to do with Felicity's disappearance.

"I am sure that he had both twins convinced that they were in love with him. I think I thought that I was in love with him as well. Perhaps Felicity went off with him, of her own accord. Oh, I wish I had been in my right mind back then, I might have seen things more clearly."

"I think you are doing just fine now, Alice! You have got to be strong, and no longer hide behind your illness. All that is behind you, stand up for your children, and have a good life. You are young, you can have a whole new life." Alice jumped up and hugged me. "When I am with you, I truly believe that."

"Good, but what is more important is that you believe in yourself and your ability to stand up for yourself. You don't have to have me there, but if you ever need me, you only have to call. Now how be we eat these yummy looking things?" We polished them off. When I say we, I mean I consumed 80% and Alice 20%. I promised myself I would forego supper. I got up to leave, and Alice pressed the remainder of the bottle of wine on me.

"I don't want the temptation." She said. I took it from her hand, smiled, and nodded at her, and we parted better friends than we had been, when I arrived.

What would her life have been like if Barry had not been killed in Afghanistan?

When I got home, I was greeted, by a somewhat sombre Eleanor.

"You were right to not go and watch that stuff, it was awful." She said. "They totally degraded those girls. We need to bring them to justice for what I saw."

"Was it definitely Zoe?" I asked,

"We all think so, but there were many other girls, I suppose the parents will have to confirm it."

"Oh no, that is not fair." I said, "Can they not do it with facial recognition?"

"Bill said they would try, but he thought he might need the parents' confirmation."

"You did not recognise Felicity or Paloma?" I asked.

"No, they weren't there, but what is bad is there were references to more files, but they were not on the computers."

"Do they think they can find them?" I asked,

"They are going to search all the properties again, but they could be anywhere, either here or in California, either in Adam's property or Brian's"

I then told Eleanor about my meeting with Alice.

"It all seems to be adding up against Adam." Eleanor said. I agreed with her and asked her what Alistair thought.

"He is convinced that there is enough to charge both Adam and Brian with unlawful drugging, and forcing the girls into sex acts, where they were recorded without their permission. He thinks that this woman Sarah is also culpable, Brian is asking the California police to find out who she is. If it's the same woman, she had lived with Zoe for some time."

Board meetings seldom bother me, but I was unusually nervous. Nobody else was to blame if the board was not satisfied, the buck stopped with me. Jenny, seeing how nervous I was, dropped an ice cube down my back. At first, I was furious then

I realised that she was remembering the story I had told her about riders, about to go in the ring, doing just that, to calm their nerves.

"You could have warned me." I grumbled.

My composure restored, I asked her what she thought about taking on a bigger role in the running of the Equestrian Centre, she thought briefly, and then said she thought she would like that. I told her to wait and see what happened in the meeting, she nodded, obviously intrigued.

She carried on laying out the cups and saucers and put the coffee on to perc. I had bought some pastries at Iris's on the way in. We put a small, raised table next to the snacks, and opened the album on it. The files were laid out on the conference table.

First to arrive was Helen Brandon. She informed us that Roger would not be attending the meeting, and that he had given her his resignation from the board, she proceeded to hand this to me.

"I have left Roger and will be having nothing more to do with him." She announced.

"Good for you! That man is a fool!" Helen beamed at me, "You don't know the half of it, for all his grand gestures, funding things, donating to charity, the money was all mine. He will only have his salary now and I don't know how long Samantha will stick with him, when she finds that out!" Jenny giggled when she heard this, and Helen turned and smiled at her,

"Anyway, enough about my troubles B, I came to support you, this could be a tricky meeting. We will have to see, but without Roger stirring things up, it may go a lot smoother." I thanked her, and turned to the door as the other board members trickled in. I greeted them all and offered them refreshments. Helen, who I felt had grown in confidence, showed them the album, and told them that they should be proud of the

Showcase. They spent some time flipping through it, and it was a good ice breaker, as I had hoped.

I started the meeting by telling the board of Roger Brandon's resignation. Then we went through the individual discipline chair's reports and ended with my overall report. Overall, the reports were well received, there was some criticism over the lack of preparedness for inclement weather, which I took on the chin. I had included it as one of the topics needing addressing, in my overall report. We discussed a few other problems that had come up, and then we turned to the next agenda item. The position of CEO had to be filled. I turned it over to the board for discussion. Apparently, little had been done since the last meeting.

Helen said that they were derelict in their duties, that an advertisement must be placed in all the equestrian magazines, as well as the national newspapers, seeking a CEO. She went on to say that they had received the letters, informing them that I was not willing to continue to act as overall head. I had done this, to see them through the Showcase, but that now it was over, this would end. She asked me what I thought should happen. I told them that the advertisement was long overdue but would be a start. The interviewing process would take some time, and it was not a job you could just walk into, any candidate would need at least a month of assistance, to get up to speed on what the job entailed. I told them that they needed to decide on a committee of three or four, task them with drafting the advertisement, and interviewing the candidates, bringing forward a slate of two or three to the board, as a whole, to make the decision of who should be offered the job. I suggested that they ask Jenny or Alistair, or both, to become assistant CEOs, and oversee the first month's tenure of the chosen candidate. I said that their salaries should be increased substantially from their current rate. I would remain in my position, for a further month, but beyond that they were on their own.

I was glad that I had laid it on the line, I had no intention of working full time any longer. I said that I was now going to leave the meeting. Jenny would continue to take the minutes for them. I then got up and tried to leave with suitable grace. I returned to the office to wait for Jenny to return and bring me up to speed.

While I was waiting, I put in a phone call to John Smith, to explain that I had been talking to Fee's mother, who was very concerned for her daughter, and wanted to know if there was any way she could be let out on bail. Alice would not press charges, and so it was the prosecuting attorney who had the say, as to whether she was charged or not. We wondered whether John could put pressure on him, to drop the charges.

John said that Fee had undergone rehab and was clean of drugs. She still refused to admit that she had attacked her mother. He said it would be better if she took responsibility for her actions. He would continue to advocate on her behalf. He was certain that the courts would not allow her to go back to her house, where her mother was living, but he might be able to get her out of the hospital, where she was currently being held. I thanked him and said I would keep in touch.

Jenny returned saying that the only sane voice in the room was Helen's. She would take charge of the three-man committee, who would handle finding a new CEO, and so hopefully it would get done. Helen had asked Jenny if she was willing to take on the role, that I had suggested, and Jenny had told her that she was. Jenny was clearly excited, but I told her not to bank on the new job, the board could easily not accept my proposal. She nodded but thanked me for putting her forward. I told her to deal with the minutes, and to then go home. We had little else to do that was pressing. I wanted to go and see Killer at his new home, with Maggie.

I drove over to her barn, which I found after a couple of mis turns. Maggie was in her manege, working a young horse. I went and watched her patiently deal with the horse's silliness over a pair of standards that were stored in the corner of the school. Her patience prevailed, and after a while, the horse was trotting happily past the corner. She had been so intent on her task, that she had not noticed me, when she did, she slowed to a walk, and came over to talk to me,

"B, how nice to see you. Have you come to see Killer?"

"More to see you, and to find out how you were getting along with him."

"He's fine, to start with he was a little unsettled and unsure about having a different rider, but now he's just great. Fee did a wonderful job with him. Here, I'm finished with this guy, let's go and look at him. She jumped off, made a fuss of the youngster, and led him back to the yard. She took care of unsaddling and rubbing him off, and then, having put him back in his stall, walked me over the corner stall. Killer looked good standing in his box. Maggie went in put on his headcollar and led him out into the yard. He was in perfect condition, his coat shining, and eyes bright.

"I've already ridden him today, but perhaps you could come back another time to see him work."

"I'd love to do that Maggie, I just promised Hetty I'd stop by, and make sure he had settled in OK. He looks perfect, what plans do you have for him?"

"I thought I'd give him an easy Intermediate outing at Hunters Glen, and then take him advanced at Saddlers."

"That sounds perfect." I replied, and happy with the situation I said goodbye.

I got back in my car and gave Alistair a call. I thanked him for his report and told him of my suggestion to the board. He said he'd think about it, I told him that Jenny had already agreed to be an assistant, if she was formally asked. I pictured him nodding slowly, and brushing his hair back, I asked him if he would like to come over and have an early supper with Eleanor and me. We made plans time wise, and I hung up. I glanced at my watch it was three thirty. I had just pulled out onto the road, when my cell phone rang, cursing under my breath, I pulled back over to answer it. It was Michael, he told me he had found a farm and wondered if I would care to come to look at it. I was somewhat surprised to be asked, but I thought it would be a huge leap for Michael to become a property owner, and a farm to boot. He probably just needed some moral support. After all, Maisie would love every place they saw, if Nipper could live there. Iris was not keen on the country life, so he probably needed somebody who would give him a more honest assessment, than the two of them. I agreed to go the next day.

Eleanor and Alfie had had a lazy day. Eleanor had been reading and watching television, and I suspected Alfie had kept her company on the couch. I suggested a brisk walk was in order, Alfie was more enthusiastic than Eleanor, so I left Eleanor reclining, and took Alfie out into the parkland behind the house. He raced around looking for rabbits and squirrels, but there were none to be found, so we made our way back to the house. I told Eleanor that Alistair was coming to supper, so we argued back and forth, about what we should prepare. We settled on chicken alfredo, and I pulled out the ingredients, after washing my hands. Eleanor went up to take a shower, and I fixed a Greek salad to go with the meal. I then sauteed the chicken and onions and followed by preparing the noodles and sauce. Alistair arrived just as I was combining the two. I put him to work laying the table and opening a bottle of wine. Eleanor came back down dressed casually in jeans and tee shirt.

"Oh good," she said, "I timed that just right, everything is done!" I snorted at her, and sat down saying,

"The least you can do is dish it up!" This accomplished, we all dug in, and the meal was consumed with much appreciation. Eleanor got up and cleared the dishes. She put coffee on, and we moved to the living room to drink it. I told them of my conversations with Alice and John Smith, and they in turn talked of the films that they had watched with Bill Thompson.

"Strictly speaking they are not illegal, if what is going on, is consented to by adults. Where it becomes a grey area is, were the girls drugged, and unable to give their consent?" said Alistair, "We all thought that the one girl was Zoe, but it would need a better identification, to be sure who it was." I got up and went over to my desk and opened a drawer where I kept important items. I took out the photo of Zoe and Sarah, and stared at it, "There is something familiar about this picture, but I can't work out what it is. I don't think the background is anywhere I recognise, but I can't be sure." I passed it to the two of them, and they looked carefully at it again, but nothing sparked recognition. I took the photo back and put it back in the drawer.

"I wish we could find the rest of the tapes." Said Alistair, Eleanor nodded.

MAISIE IN CHARGE

I SAW NO NEED to go into the Centre the next day, and consequently we had a lazy morning, ate our breakfast and read the local newspaper. There was a picture of Adam, and an article saying he was accused of drug offences and wire tapping. I wasn't sure that wire tapping was the correct term but thought that the paper would have to deal with a libel claim, if they had got it wrong. We then took Alfie out for a walk, and then left him in the house. I was going to drive to the cafe, and then Eleanor was keeping my car, while Michael drove me to the farm. We did a quick switch over of drivers, and as Eleanor took off I entered the cafe, to be greeted by a small tornado who hugged me round the hips and screamed,

"Hi Bat Bug! Isn't this exciting! We're off to look at our new farm!" I told her that it was not theirs' yet, and that we had to look at everything about it, to see if it was suitable. She wrinkled her nose at me, I sat down at a table.

"Oh, B don't be such a stick in the mud! I know it is quite perfect!"

"Well, if all the rest of us agree with you, then it will be fine." She sat down on the opposite side of the table to me, her legs swinging backwards and forwards, obviously anxious to get going. She glanced at the newspaper on the table, and turned it around,

"Oh look, that's my old Dad's friend!" she said pointing at Adam's picture.

"He and Dad used to spend all sorts of time in the secret room."

"What secret room Maisie?" I said forcing myself to remain calm, and not frighten her.

"The secret room, behind the bookcase. I was not supposed to tell anyone about it, I won't get into trouble, will I?"

"Not a bit of it. It is really good that you have told me."

"So, you'll say that the farm is perfect?" the cunning little minx! Her mind turned things quickly into her own favour! Iris and Michael appeared from behind the counter.

"Ready for off?" Michael asked,

"I've just got to make a phone call." I said, I let them head out onto the street, and then called Eleanor to tell her about the secret room. She said she'd get hold of Alistair, and then they'd go and see Bill Thomas. I hurried out to Michael's car, and we headed off on our mission. Maisie talked nonstop as we drove, until Michael offered her a dollar for every minute that she remained silent over five minutes. She didn't even make it to five minutes. I asked Iris if she had been tested for ADD, Iris nodded, and said she was borderline, but Michael thought that if she was on the farm and had to work, she will grow out of it. I nodded perhaps a more active lifestyle would be better for her, I hoped so, what could be forgiven when you are small is not so endearing, as you grow older. I asked about her schooling. Iris sighed and said, "The RDA school has been perfect for her, but she has to move on next year and frankly I am beside myself worrying about it."

"Iris do not stress so much. We will find somewhere for her." Said Michael,

"Perhaps I could be home schooled?" chipped in Maisie.

"That would not be good for any one of us." said Michael

laughing, "I would be up on charges!" Fortunately, we were nearing our destination, and Michael had to get Iris to navigate. We turned in down a maple lined lane. It led to a small, unprepossessing bungalow with an old bank barn behind it. Iris looked doubtful, and Maisie looked radiant, "Come on Bat Bug, come and see the barn." She ran ahead of me, and I followed her to the barn which had been totally restored. The stone walls had been parged and new horse stalls built in the lower portion of the barn. The top of it had had all the old barn boards replaced. Behind the barn there were five post and rail paddocks, and then there was a field that must have been at least twelve acres which was also fenced. Behind that the land rose, into some scrub area, with what appeared to be a stream meandering though the lower part of it. Out in front of the barn the previous owners had started to make a large manege, but it was not yet completed.

Michael looked at me quizzically, "What do you think?"

"Well with the school completed, it could not be better from the point of view of horses."

"That's what I thought. The people who owned it before, did up the barn, put in the fencing, started the manege, but then the husband's business took a big hit. They were going to tear down that house and build a whole new fancy one. I can't afford to do that, we could do a bit to upgrade it, but of course Iris is dead set against it."

"Well let's have a look." I said. We went into the house, and I could see why Iris was less than enthusiastic. The kitchen came out of the fifties, small and boxy with ancient appliances and few cupboards. There was an ugly dining room next door, but it led into a good size living room overlooking a pond that was totally grown in, and with hills behind that. "Clear that pond out and it would be a beautiful view, and this room has potential." I said, "Perhaps you could knock the wall out between the kitchen and the dining room and make it a farmhouse kitchen where you could have a big harvest table. What are the bedrooms like?"

"They're not too bad, a bit small but a coat of paint would improve things no end." Said Michael "However the bathroom is ghastly, even I can see that. We walked to the end of the corridor, and I peered in. Michael was right. Ghastly hardly described the room. The bathtub was stained with years of iron water, as was the toilet, they were a bilious green in colour, and there was a mismatched sink in purple. There was a hole in the floor, something had obviously been leaking, and the smell of rot was overpowering. The room was however a half decent size.

"Well, you gut the lot, fix the floor, and then spend the money, to put in some really nice fixtures. There is no other way round it. That is the first thing you do, if you can't afford it on top of the purchase price, then don't buy it. If the building is structurally sound, you can fix it as you go, you can do all the painting to keep costs down. I'm sure John would help a bit."

"I can paint!" announced Maisie. We gave no response to that, pictures leaping into our minds of what Maisie could do with a pot of paint and a brush. I turned to Iris,

"You need to watch some of the shows on TV that show you what can be done with run down properties." She looked at me doubtfully, and Michael told me not to give her ideas.

"Can we buy it? Can we?" Maisie implored Iris, who replied, "It is for Michael to decide." I felt that this was a discussion that I should not be involved with, I told them so, and we drove home ignoring the subject. I was able to distract Maisie by telling her that we would be running a one day event for children at the Centre in two months time.

"Really, that would be so awesome!" then her face fell, and she said, "Michael says I'm not allowed to compete until my dressage is better. He says I have to take lessons from somebody called Jessie, I bet she's horrible, apparently, she only rides dressage, how boring is that!"

"As it happens, Maisie, I know Jessie very well, and she is a lovely person, not a bit boring, I used to teach her in England."

"You did? Why don't you teach me then?"

"Because I am retired, and I am too old to deal with somebody like you!" I said.

When we got back to the café, I called Eleanor to come and pick me up, and I suggested to Iris that she come and look at my house, and the pictures that we had taken before the renovations took place.

"It is very hard to picture how nice things could be with very little work." I went on to tell Michael he should ask Alistair to take a look at the property and see what he thought about it.

I hardly had time to drink my coffee, before Eleanor pulled up in front of the cafe. I said my goodbyes and hurried off. I wanted to know whether the "secret room" had been found, but the answer was no. The room with the bookshelves had been searched multiple times, and though they could tell that it was possible for a small room to be hidden behind the bookshelves, they could find no way to open it.

When Iris, Maisie and I got to Brian's house, Inspector Thomas and some uniformed officers were waiting outside. They unlocked the door, and we all went in, Maisie, marching ahead of us into a room that had served as an office. It had a big bow window looking out on an overgrown lawn. I supposed nobody was paying for any upkeep on the property. A beautiful antique desk sat looking out on the view, and on the west wall were bookshelves floor to ceiling.

Maisie walked unerringly to the bookcase, pulled out a volume reached in behind it, and pressed a recessed button, that was camouflaged as part of the wood panelling. Part of the bookcase slid back silently to reveal a small room. Inspector Thomas glared at his men, "As simple as that!" he exclaimed. He then turned, and thanked Maisie who bowed theatrically.

"That's enough of that!" said Iris, and grabbing Maisie's sweater, she propelled her out of the office. Maisie skipped around the entrance hall, and said,

"I am so glad I don't live here anymore; do you know where I want to live? The FARM!" she exclaimed "B can't you persuade Iris, she's being most stubborn about it."

"That is her right." I replied, "Iris likes city life, and she doesn't want to live in an ugly house."

"But we'll make it beautiful, we can paint your room purple, and then it will look just wonderful!" I doubted that, but at the moment Maisie was going through a purple phase, all Nipper's bandages and saddle pads were purple, therefore a purple room would be the height of elegance according to Maisie.

Iris sighed, "The two of them have their hearts set on it. I'm just not sure that I want to move all the way out there."

"Well, you'll always have the apartment over the cafe, maybe you could divide your time?" I suggested, Iris shook her head, "I just don't know."

I felt that it wasn't my place to push the matter. I thought that it was perhaps more that Iris was not sure about her relationship with Michael, rather than about moving to the farm. I changed the subject, and Iris's mood lightened considerably. I invited her to dinner, to look at the before and after of the renovations.

"Your house is so lovely, I can't believe it was ugly before."

I smiled, "Just wait and see the photos!"

We drove back to the cafe laughing at our thought that Maisie could be traumatised by the visit to Brian's house. We were the ones upset to find the room and wondering what it might contain. Maisie just took it in her stride.

When we arrived, Michael was waiting with Jessie,

"Maisie, this is Jessie, and we are going to get started on your dressage lessons." Maisie wrinkled her nose. Laughing at this Jessie said,

"So, you hate dressage? I used to as well, I just wanted to jump, until I learnt how important dressage is for your jumping, and then I fell in love with dressage by itself."

"Really?" said Maisie, looking at Jessie as if she was totally insane.

"Yes really, come on let's give it a try, tell me about your pony." That sent Maisie off a mile a minute, and the three of them left to embark on a dressage learning curve.

LOOSE ENDS

I BADE FAREWELL TO Iris and drove to the Centre. Jenny was there with Franny, who was growing in leaps and bounds. I told Jenny all about finding the secret room. She wanted to know what was in it, but I told her we weren't allowed in. We chatted for a while, surmising what it could hold, but then we had to get on and do some work.

There was little to do, compared to the pre-Showcase work. We set out a schedule for the next three months with performance indicators to ensure that we were on track. We were due to host one competition per month. In addition to that, we had Pony Club Rally, various clinics and the breed show extravaganza. Bookings for the daily use of the property continued to come in and had to be dealt with.

"Oh look!" said Jenny who had just opened another letter. "These people want to run a dog show here, with dog agility, what do you think?"

"Well, I suppose if they are willing to pay the usual fee, it will be all right. Find out what they need in the way of facilities, and tell them what we charge, and we'll see if it goes anywhere." I replied.

"I wonder if Franny would enjoy agility? It would be good for working off some of her energy."

"I think it would be excellent for her." I said thinking it

would give Jenny an interest, she'd been a bit down since James went home.

As if we were on the same wavelength, Jenny said, "James is designing in Rochester, New York next month and he's going to come up and stay for a few days afterwards."

"Jenny, that's great, you must be thrilled!" she smiled, and nodded.

We decided that we would move to a half day working schedule, as things were so quiet. We packed up and I headed home. Alfie was pleased to see me, he had been with Eleanor, but she had gone out with Hetty to look at a country store in Creemore. They were going to have tea there, her note told me. I let Alfie out, and then the pair of us sat on the couch. I was just about nodding off, when the phone rang. I picked it up unenthusiastically, "Hello" I said, in a manner far from pleasant.

"Ms Browning, it's John Smith here, you told me to get hold of you if there was any news about Fee. I have petitioned the court, and they have agreed to send her to a halfway house, she will have to wear an ankle monitor and be restricted to the house, but it is at least better than being in the psychiatric hospital."

"Thank you so much, "I replied in a friendlier tone. "Will she be allowed visitors?"

"That, I'm not sure of, I would imagine not for the first week. I'll let you know." I thanked him again and hung up. Hetty would be happy, I thought, and so would Alice. I hoped that all would be well, I could not help remembering that awful night, with Fee totally out of control.

Alfie and I did then manage to have an uninterrupted nap, and when we woke up it was time for food for both of us. I fed Alfie, and heated a frozen quiche for myself, with both of us replete, we rejoined the sofa, and turned the TV on to watch the news.

I completely forgot to tell Hetty about Fee. Eleanor and I sat up until late gossiping and wondering what would be found in the secret room, and about Fee. Eleanor had some news of her own. She and Hetty had driven round and found Paul Wiseacre's farm. They had driven up the drive, and it had looked as if someone was living there. There were tyre tracks, and what looked like an oil spill, where a car was frequently parked.

They had then driven into downtown Creemore and saw the brewery and all the touristy shops. Eleanor had bought all sorts of stuff in the General Store and asked if she could borrow a suitcase to transport it all back to England.

The following morning, I went in and did my token effort at earning my salary. There was very little mail. At one point the District Commissioner of the Pony Club called about the Rally and reminded me that they had supplied members to volunteer at the Showcase. I assured her that our deal still stood, and we were happy to welcome the club to the Equestrian Centre. She wanted to know whether the neighbouring clubs could also run their rallies at the Centre. I said that they could but would have to pay.

The phone remained silent after that, so we switched it over to Jenny's cell and locked up the office, having had an unproductive morning. I stopped for some groceries on the way home and feeling virtuous carried my food into the house and unpacked it. Eleanor had done some housework while I was at the office, and I was not sure where she was now. She might be out buying up more stuff to take home, or perhaps she'd hooked up with Alistair to plan his trip. I decided to call Hetty and tell her about Fee. She was delighted to hear that Fee was leaving the hospital and hoped that she could receive visitors soon. She then told me she was heading over to Alice's house and would let her know the good news. I asked her if she had any idea where Eleanor was, but she had no clue.

It was sometime later that a very subdued pair, in the shape of Eleanor and Alistair, arrived at the house. Alfie greeted them enthusiastically, but they did not return his glee.

"We have had the worst afternoon. Bill Thomas asked us to come in. They had found the secret room to be full of files, computers and tapes. Bill wanted us to see if we could recognise any of the girls on the tape." said Alistair.

"It was the worst I have ever seen." enjoined Eleanor, "There were so many child pornography tapes. The OPP are handing it over to the child exploitation unit. We don't think that Brian or Adam made the tapes, but we are sure that they were distributing them.

"There were plenty more of the pornographic tapes that we saw before, but worse still, we think that in one tape the sex act went so far that the victim appeared to have been killed, and it may have been Zoe. They may have staged it, but it certainly looked real enough. Brian and Adam were in the film and so was that girl, Sarah."

"That is awful!" I shuddered, "what is going to happen now?"

"Well, the tapes have been sent to the California police. They are looking for the girl, Sarah. Adam has been rearrested, and this time I hope he will be denied bail. More charges will be brought against Brian."

"I can't believe all that was going on in the house, when Maisie was living there. What if she had been exploited?"

"It appears that Brian had some limits to his depravity."

"Did you recognise any body?" I asked

"No, Bill thinks it was all taped in California, and so the police down there will have to handle most of the identifications. They are going to visit Adam's father to see if he can tell them who the girls are, and they are going to see Zoe's parents

"Those poor people, I can't imagine anything worse!" I said, and both Eleanor and Alistair nodded, Alistair went on,

"There were also more fake passports in the room. Brian did a thriving business providing them for people who did not wish to travel under their own name."

FEE MISSING

ELEANOR AND ALISTAIR HAD gone out for the day, Jenny was holding the fort at the Centre, and I had planned a long lazy day. Alfie and I were sitting on the couch, and I was reading a book when my cell phone rang. As usual, I couldn't find the wretched thing, I rummaged around in my handbag which was like a black hole, it sucked everything in, but never gave it back. I finally found the phone, down the back of a cushion, but of course by then it had stopped ringing. I saw that the caller had been John Smith, and so I rang back.

"Hello Ms Browning, I have some bad news. It appears that Fiona has absconded from the halfway house and has removed her ankle monitor. There is an all points bulletin out for her. Under the circumstances, I think we should warn her mother." I was totally taken aback by this news, up until now it seemed that Fee was doing well.

"Oh, my goodness, yes," I said, "I am really shocked by this. I will contact Alice and her grandmother right away. Thank you for letting me know."

"I will get hold of you as soon as I hear anything new about the situation."

With that he hung up leaving me feeling awful. Poor Alice and Hetty, more bad news. I really didn't want to make these phone calls.

I let it ring at both numbers until the answering machine picked up. There was no reply at either Hetty's or Alice's houses. On a whim, I tried phoning the café and sure enough Iris told me they were both there. I told her to keep them there until I arrived. I then used my car's excellent horsepower to reach the café in record time.

"Why would she do that?" Hetty cried, "I don't understand. She was supposed to be improving." Alice was silent but I could see that she was distressed. I shook my head,
"I have no idea, she is clear of drugs and her mental health had improved, but I think you should both be careful in case she is having a complete relapse and breakdown."
"Alice must stay with me. We should be safe together, with Poppy to guard us." Hetty announced. Alice was reluctant but saw the sense in taking precautions.
"I wonder how she got away. Perhaps the halfway house was derelict in their duties. I think I shall go over there and see what I can find out. Do you know where it is Hetty?" I got directions from her.

I knocked on the door and was greeted by a pleasant looking lady. Lying all the way, I told her that I was Fees Grandmother and that I wanted to know what had happened, that had precipitated Fiona's departure. She said she would ask Mr Beamish, the director, if he would speak to me. I waited in the hallway noting the sophisticated alarm system mounted by the front door. Eventually a self-important man came out and announced that he could not comment on an escaped felon. I retorted that Fiona had never been convicted of a crime, so could hardly be called a felon.
"I am not going to discuss semantics with you. I suggest

you contact the police for more information." He then turned on his heel and left me standing there fuming.

The lady, who had admitted me, returned to show me out, she said in a quiet voice obviously not wanting the unpleasant Mr Beamish to hear, "My name is Wendy, I am the house mother here. Unfortunately, the day Fee went missing was my day off, but I cannot believe she just ran off, she had been doing so well. She was going to start a job outside the home in a couple of weeks, and she was looking forward to being able to receive visitors. I am so sorry."

Just then a plain mousy haired girl came up to us, and in a voice hardly above a whisper said,

"She didn't run off. I was watching out of the window. Somebody grabbed her as she got out of the library van, they put a black bag over her head and shoved her into a small van type car."

"Melanie, why on earth didn't you tell anyone?" cried Wendy incredulously.

"I told Mr Beamish, but he said I was making it up to cover for Fee, but honest I wasn't!"

"I believe you Melanie." said Wendy, "What did the man look like who grabbed her?"

"I couldn't see his face, I think he was wearing a mask, he wasn't big or fat I think his hair was dark. I'm sorry I can't remember, I'm not good at that sort of stuff."

"How about the car? Do you remember anything about that?"

"Not really, it had back doors and it was green I think."

"Never mind, Melanie. If you think of anything else, please come and tell me." Said Wendy, she and I shared a look, Wendy went on,

"What should we do? I cannot overrule the director."

"No but I can!" I replied, "I'll go to the police right away.

I'll keep in touch; do you have a number I can reach you on directly?" Wendy nodded, and scribbled something on a piece of paper, which she handed to me, and then she said, "I'll see if I can find out anything else."

I got to the police station, and was surprised to find that Bill Thomas was in. He came out, greeted me and ushered me into his office. I told him about my visit to the halfway house, and what I had found out. He was very sceptical of what I told him. He had seen Fee at her worst when she was on drugs, and the picture that Wendy had painted of her, did not ring true to him, however I was reporting a supposed kidnap, and therefore he would have to investigate. He said he would pay a visit to the halfway house and ask some questions.

Having done all that I could do I went home feeling upset and dissatisfied. If someone had taken Fee off the street, it was not for good reasons. She could be in danger, or could she have orchestrated it herself, and got Melanie to back her up? I did not think that she was that cunning, but the past months had shown that I did not know Fee at all.

I sat on the couch with Alfie and tried to think it all through. I needed to know whether Adam was back in custody, he was the only one I could think of who might have grabbed Fee. I berated myself for failing to ask Bill Thomas that question.

With nothing else to do, I decided to try and work out what I was reminded of in the photo of Sarah and Zoe. I went to my desk, and pulled it out, brought it back to the couch, and sat and looked at it. Zoe smiled back at me, a lovely looking girl, with an open sunny expression, blonde hair, and she had a light dusting of freckles on her nose. She was holding a bag out towards the other girl. Sarah had her face turned mostly away from the camera. Her dark hair was cut in a pixielike shape, she was obviously equally attractive, even though you could only see part of her face, her one hand was resting on Zoe's shoulder.

Behind them were some buildings, they were slightly out of focus, but as I stared at them, I knew I had not seen them before, so they weren't what was niggling at my mind. I wished I could see more pictures of Zoe and Sarah, to work out what it was, but there was no way I could ask Christine and Quentin. They might have just heard from the police, that Zoe could be dead. I supposed that I could ask Alistair if they could get stills off the videos, of the two girls, I had no desire to watch the tapes. I needed to talk to Eleanor and Alistair.

No sooner had I had that thought, than the two of them arrived. I hardly gave them time to come through the door, before I started pouring out the story of my day. They listened in amazement; they could not believe that Fee would have absconded. I asked if they knew whether Adam was out on bail, but neither of them had a clue.

"What do you think of the Melanie girl? Could she be covering for Fee?" Alistair asked.

"I have no idea, but the house mother seemed to think she was telling the truth." I replied, "Do you think we should check Adam's house?"

"It might be an idea; Eleanor are you up for a drive?"

"You bet! Let's go." They headed back out and left me to my thoughts.

I was surprised to receive a phone call from Wendy at the halfway house. She said that Melanie had remembered something else. The green van that had been used to abduct Fee had a written logo on the side, and she thought it said, "O.D. on the top, with a word underneath beginning with an E." I scribbled this down, and thanked Wendy, and told her I would pass it on to the police. She asked me to let her know if there was any news of Fee. I promised to do so, and hung up, pondering if this information would be in any way useful. O.D. meant nothing to me, I looked in the yellow pages to see if I could find a business with those initials, but there were none. Deciding to leave it for a while to see whether an idea would come to me, I took Alfie for a walk. It was a beautiful day, and we strolled through the Centre's property, I sat on a log and enjoyed the panorama. I looked up at the raucous sound of a raven calling. I searched the sky until I found two of them flying a complex ballet together. As I watched the male bird flipped himself upside down and flew in this manner. I hoped the female was impressed with his versatility; I certainly was. It never ceased to amaze me when I witnessed this feat of aeronautical acrobatics.

Alfie had finished chasing imaginary rabbits, and came panting back to my side, I stood up and we made our way back to the house. The garden was looking pretty now, under the care of my gardener. I stopped to admire a little tree that I had not noticed before. There was, surprisingly, still attached to the main stem, one could hardly call it a trunk, a plastic tag that must have been attached when the tree was planted. Idly, I picked it up and looked at it. The tree was an orange quince. Well, I thought, you live and learn I didn't think I had ever eaten a quince, but I was vaguely aware that you could make quince jam.

I went back into the house and filled Alfie's water bowl. I was just setting it down, when the thought came to me. The logo on the van that Melanie had seen could be Q.D. not O.D. The Q could easily be mistaken for an O. Therefore, it was Q.D. Enterprises! That was one of Brian McVickers's businesses. Presumably Adam would have had access to Brian's vehicles, which meant that Adam must be behind Fee's abduction.

I wondered whether one person could abduct Fee by themselves, she was strong, having ridden and worked around horses for so long. You had to be able to lift bales of hay, feed bags and five-gallon, water buckets. I did not imagine she would go without a fight. One person would have to drug and subdue her, until the drug took effect. Then they could put her in the van and drive off. Surely somebody other than Melanie would have seen something. I then started to think who could be Adam's accomplice, could it be Sarah? From the description of the video tapes, it seemed that Sarah and Adam had been behaving like Karla Homolka and Paul Bernado, the infamous Canadian killers. Could Sarah be in Ontario? Thoughts were whirling around in my head. I remembered Eleanor and I had seen somebody by the ruins in the Equestrian Centre Park the day after Adam had been picked up for using the listening device, but that could equally well have been a dog walker. Thinking of Eleanor, I remembered her telling me about the farm near Creemore, that she and Hetty had visited. I wondered whether Fee could have been taken there. I smiled remembering the sight of Eleanor lugging in all the bags of souvenirs, that she had bought on that trip, and suddenly I remembered what had triggered a memory for me about the photo of Zoe and Sarah.

I made a phone call to Hetty and Alice to ask them something that would confirm my recall. Once I received their confirmation, I started thinking of other discrepancies, that I had not recognised before. I pictured Fee working, looking after horses, grooming, oiling their hooves, cleaning their saddlery and riding. Fee, quiet and shy, Fee having a crush on Adam, Fee out of control, thinking her mother had killed her sister, finally attacking her mother, and Fee receiving a positive drug test. There were so many contradictions. I tried to think back to the night I had found Fee in the garden, trying to kill her mother. My memory was hazy, I had been so intent on stopping the attack it was hard to remember all the details.

Finally, Eleanor and Alistair returned. There had been no one at Adam's house, and it didn't look as if anybody had been there for a while, the post box was full of flyers and mail, and the newspaper had not been picked up. I told them of my thought that Fee might be at Paul Wiseacre's farm, if indeed she was still alive. My friends agreed it was a possibility. We considered calling Inspector Thomas but did not think he would act on a hunch that Fee had been abducted and was being held at an out of the way farm. When we thought about it that way, it did seem farfetched, but nevertheless we all got in Alistair's car and drove off to Creemore.

On the way I told them my suspicions. I wouldn't say they immediately embraced them as being the truth behind all this, but at least they didn't outright dismiss them. It took us about thirty-five minutes to reach the turn off to the farm, Eleanor was navigating. We drove up the long laneway and parked in front of the house. The house was locked, and we went all around it peering in the windows. There was no sign of life, and every door and window were shut tight. Short of smashing a window, there was no way to get in. There was a dilapidated garage off to the side, and Alistair managed to force the side door open, and there we found the green van with the logo on the side!

"Well done B! Now I am sure Bill will take us seriously." said Alistair.

"But where is Fee? Do you think they have killed her?" I asked in dismay.

"The car tracks lead further back," Said Eleanor, "let's drive out there."

We got in the car and drove back down the farm track to the remains of an old bank barn. The hay mow had collapsed in on itself, but there was a door leading into what had been the cattle housing underneath. I got out and strode to the door. I did not realise that Eleanor and Alistair had seen something and had gone to investigate and were not following me.

I pushed the door open and could hear some muffled sounds coming from the back of the cattle stantions. It was dark and smelt damp and musty, my eyes were taking a long time to adjust to the gloom, but eventually I could start to make out what was going on. Someone was lying on the floor struggling, and another figure was attempting to pull a plastic bag over their head. I screamed,

"Stop that!" I then yelled for Alistair and Eleanor to come. I hurried forward to the murderous scene, that was being acted out. The figure with the bag turned towards me in surprise, giving the person on the ground a slight advantage, but before she could get away, the other person turned back, and pulled the bag tight over her face. I could hear Alistair hurrying in followed by Eleanor, they were struggling to see, as I had been on entering the dark.

"Take that bag off her." I shrieked, "Stop it Sarah, or should I say Felicity?"

The girl stopped in astonishment, and Alistair ran across the barn floor, and grabbed her, pulling the bag out of her hands. Eleanor followed hot on his heels, and between the two of them they restrained the girl. I saw a roll of duct tape lying on the floor and passed it to Alistair who used it to bind the girl's wrists. I turned to Fee who was lying on a filthy bed of straw, "Oh B" she sobbed. I struggled to undo her taped hands and feet. "Water." She croaked, I hurried back to the car and brought her back a half bottle of water, that Alistair had in the console. She gulped it down. "More." She said, I shook my head,

"That's all we've got. I'll see if the tap works," I said, I went over, and after much effort managed to turn the rusted tap, after a minute some rusty coloured water came out. I let it run for some time, and then filled the bottle and returned to Fee. She drank greedily, I told her to slow down, or it would all come back up again.

Alistair had dialled 911, and then phoned Inspector Thomas, and was in deep conversation with him. Eventually a police car arrived, and Felicity was taken away. We helped Fee to the car and drove her to the hospital, where she was admitted right away, suffering from severe dehydration. I spent an agonising time on the phone to Hetty and Alice, telling them what had happened.

EPILOGUE

INSPECTOR THOMAS CAME TO interview me, "Well, well Nancy Drew!" he said

"That joke is getting old." I told him.

"Very well, let's be serious, can you go through all your thought processes, that led you to decide that Sarah was, in actual fact Felicity Hallkirk, and the accomplice of Adam?"

"Well, there were many different ideas that I had, but mostly it was her fingernails, the bag in the photo of Zoe and Sarah, and when I saw Eleanor's face in the mirror!" He looked at me as if I was mad. "Her fingernails?" he asked.

"Yes, Fee has worked with horses for years, her fingernails were always chipped and as with all horsey people, it is practically impossible to keep them clean. The girl who I assumed was Fee attacking her mother, had long painted fingernails.

"In the photo of Zoe with Sarah they are holding a leather bag tooled with the letter F on it. It was very distinctive. Fee has an identical bag she carries with her all the time. I checked with the twins' grandmother and mother, and they told me that Adam had had them made for them by a craftsman in California. They did not remember seeing the one that belonged to Felicity, after she went missing."

"And the mirror thing?"

"When I saw Eleanor's reflection in the mirror, I was struck by the fact that the scar she has on her face looked strange, because it was on the wrong side. Fee's deformity is on the right side of her face, but I could only see the right side of the girl's face, when she was in the car with Adam, and when she was attacking her mother, there was no deformity. My subconscious told me something wasn't right, but I didn't work it out until I saw the reflection. Obviously, Felicity had made her face up to look like Fee's when she was looking in the mirror and had put the deformity on the wrong side.

"Well, I'll be..." said Inspector Thomas.

"Also, I knew that I had hit Fee hard with a rock when I was trying to get her off her mother. It rendered her unconscious for a short while, it made no sense that when Fee was taken to hospital, she had no visible injuries. I was quite certain that it was Fee, but the girls are identical twins, and if you only see the one side of Fee's face, she looks exactly like Felicity. We heard from Richard Templeton that the film school in California, that Adam ran, had the most wonderful reputation for producing makeup artists and actors. I think Felicity learnt all about both, at the Holy Port Church, and so she could make her face up to look as if she had Fee's deformity. In the dark I would not have been able to tell the difference."

"But Sarah looked nothing like Felicity." Interjected the Inspector,

"Well, they have the same bone structure, but dying her hair dark, and wearing it in a completely different style, plus wearing coloured contact lenses, and carefully applied makeup would fool everybody."

"Why would Felicity have run away from home, why would she have done all this? What were her motives?"

"I really don't know, I think that she had no parental support, she had fallen out with her twin sister who had been the mainstay of her life, and mental illness runs in her family. I think that Adam Wiseacre is a psychopath, Felicity was young and impressionable. I think that he encouraged her to leave home, and go with him to California, with promises of modelling and starring in films. Brian McVicker had numerous false passports, so there would have been no problem with them crossing the border.

When they got to California, Adam introduced her to drugs and the film school, and I think he gradually created a situation where she became dependant on him and obsessed with him. I think she romanticised the life they were leading, like Bonnie and Clyde and Karla Homolka and Paul Bernado. I am quite sure she would never have done any of these things, without Adam's influence."

"Why did she come back to Ontario?"

"To be with Adam, but she could not handle him being with other women. Her mother came out of hospital and instead of going home, she stayed with Adam. I think Felicity saw him with her mother, maybe she saw him kissing her, and she was so incensed she felt she had to kill her. Disguising herself as Fiona would mean that her twin would be blamed for her mother's death, and sent to prison, thereby getting rid of another rival for Adam's affections, in her mind."

"I think Adam, who lives to control people, had been giving Fee drugs unbeknownst to her, and persuading her of her mother's guilt in her sister's supposed death, making her more and more paranoid. He had no idea that Fee might be drug tested at the Showcase, and that it would lead back to him through John Smith. When that happened, he felt that he had to find out what we knew about his activities, so he decided to bug my house, in order to hear what we were talking about, not thinking that this would be his downfall."

"Well thank you Ms Browning, I hope that this is the last time you get involved, in such a matter."

With that he took his leave. I was exhausted, this year had proved too much for me, and I realised that I really needed to retire, and lead a quiet life with my dog. At least for a while!

I was dreading my friends leaving. Eleanor and Alistair were flying out in three days time. I had become so accustomed to sharing my house with Eleanor, that I was not sure how I would cope without her.

We were having a big party at the cafe the next day. I had mixed feelings about this but decided that I would go and try and put everything that had happened behind me and look forward to the future. I decided to purchase a new outfit for the occasion, and took Eleanor along with me, as my fashion consultant. I regretted this decision as she made me try on endless clothes, discarding them one after the other. Finally, she pulled out a dress that I thought I wouldn't be seen dead in, but miraculously when I put it on it hid all the bulges, accentuated any positive curves that I possessed, and the colour made my eyes appear much brighter. Who knew? Wincing, I tried to ignore the purchase price, and handed over my credit card.

I then left Eleanor and went to work with Jenny at the Centre. My tenure was winding down and I wanted to finish up all the items for which I felt responsible. Jenny was coming to the party, but she said that she had some exciting news. She had been accepted as assistant CEO at the Centre, and for the time being was going to be acting CEO until the new person could take over. Helen had called her to let her know. Helen had been voted Chair of the Board of directors. I thought that Jenny would be in good hands with Helen at the helm. I asked her if a new CEO had been appointed. She told me that she was not allowed to say who had been appointed until it was officially announced. I felt that she could have told me, but she was obviously taking her responsibilities very seriously.

Alfie and I left Jenny and Franny finishing up. Franny was

becoming quite well behaved, under Jenny's tutelage, an example for me, I thought, as my dog ignored me when I called him. He finally came, we drove home, and were spending a quiet evening, when Iris arrived to look at the pictures of my house pre renovations. She was really impressed and asked me if I thought the house at the farm could turn out as well. I told her that I thought over time it could be done, but would be expensive, and it would depend on what Michael could afford. She thanked me, and said it gave her a lot to think about. She would see me again the next day.

The following evening, we gathered at the cafe. Iris had decorated in a festive manner with a banner reading "Safe travels, Eleanor and Alistair" with the help of Xen and Susie. Maisie was dressed up and was hanging on Michael's arm whilst trying frantically to engage me in conversation. Michael told her to wait until I had had a chance to greet everybody. Typically, she pouted, and equally typically, Iris told her to behave. Some things never change!

Amelia and John were back from their holiday in Algonquin Park, they were positively glowing. Jenny arrived and with her came James who was up from the States, where he had been designing in Rochester. Alistair arrived and with him, I was delighted to see Randy Wainwright. It seemed all my good friends were finding partners. Last to arrive were Hetty and Alice, accompanied by a very thin Fee, who I hurried over to give a hug.

Iris had pulled all the tables into one big oblong, so we could all sit together. I sat down, and Maisie immediately plonked herself down beside me,

"Guess what Bat Bug?"

"What Maisie Maggot?"

"Michael has bought the farm, and he and I are going to live there all the time, and Iris is coming at the weekends! I am going to have Nipper there and Kipper as well. Michael says I'm going to have to work really hard, so I am good and tired, and don't drive him round the bend!" I roared with laughter at this, and turned to Michael,

"I hope you know what you are letting yourself in for?" before he could answer, Maisie went on,

"Jessie is going to bring Quisty to our farm, she's really not bad, considering she's a dressage rider! She says I am getting better on the flat, but Michael says I have a long way to go before he will own me at a show!!" Michael smiled indulgently at her, and I asked him if Iris was OK with this solution.

"I think so, she did not want to commit to moving in full time, she loves her apartment and likes being in the town, but she can't be separated from Maisie for long. She thinks she can cope with only seeing Maisie at the weekends. We will be back and forth anyway, in between. She will be trying country life at the farm little by little, once we have done some work on the house." I was glad that Iris was keeping her independence, but I worried about them both having claims to Maisie if their relationship did not work out. They both had a lot to lose. Suddenly Maisie noticed Fee, and she flew round the table and gave her a huge hug.

"Fee, I couldn't believe that you didn't go Cross Country at the Showcase, I waited and waited to watch you!"

"I'm sorry Maisie. I was ill but I'm better now." Alice put her arm round the girl and said,

"She certainly is and so am I. We are going to become a team now, aren't we?" Maisie butted in,

"What about Killer?"

"Well Maggie has been riding him, and she's been doing a very good job, I'm taking a year off to have surgery on my face, so she's going to compete him for me." said Fee.

"I like your face! It's different." Exclaimed Maisie, Fee laughed,

"It certainly is, but I think you'll like it better when it is fixed, I know I will!" I was astonished at her composure, the resilience of youth is astounding, I thought.

Jenny perked up and said, "I think Alistair has some news for you B." Oh goodness, I thought, he and Randy are moving very fast. I learnt quickly that that was not the case.

"B, I applied for the job of CEO of the Centre, and I just heard that I have been accepted. I start as soon as I return from England, and with an assistant like Jenny, it should be great!"

"That's wonderful news, Alistair, you will be great in that role."

"Yes, I think I can do the job, and it will be a sort of tribute to Daniel. Of course, I must find a security head, and a chair for the three-day-eventing when we are running competitions. Any suggestions, Eleanor or B?"

"I don't know about Eleanor, but I need a long holiday and retirement is looking good after this year!" I replied, Eleanor laughed, and said they'd talk about it in England.

I took the moment to propose a toast to the new officers of the Equestrian Centre, and to all who had done so much the previous year. It had certainly been memorable.

THE END

Printed in Great Britain
by Amazon